Also by Anna Gill

THE DREAM LIVES ON

ANNA GILL

CORDGRASS
Publishing

ROCHESTER, NEW YORK

Published by:
Cordgrass Publishing, Rochester, New York

Paperback: 978-1-951212-04-9
Mobi: 978-1-951212-05-6
EPub: 978-1-951212-06-3

Library of Congress Data on file with the publisher.

www.CordgrassPublishing.com

Printed in the United States of America

10 9 8 7 6 5 4 3 2 1

This book is dedicated to
all farmers who give us our daily bread and so much more.

Prologue

There once was a land so fair and so grand that it is said God surveyed it himself to make sure it was perfect. When it was finished, explorers and people who traveled there from other colonies down the coast fell in love with the great waters and the extraordinary Bay, the largest anywhere around. People found an abundance of fish, crabs, and oysters—more than they could imagine—and men who farmed the land with their families found the land fertile and lovely, perfect for growing vegetables and grains and for raising livestock, including chickens. They soon found the scrappy fowl took well to the land, could be fed with their grains, and harvested in great numbers. An industry, large and proud, grew from their care and farming.

This great land became known as the Eastern Shore of Maryland, Virginia, and Delaware. Some called it Delmarva; others, Chesapeake Country.

In this land, farming and fishing families stayed to their own and married within their clans. They were respected by one another, and familiar family names were soon known by outside businessmen and travelers who also came to live here. They were a proud, resourceful people who loved life, loved what they did, and loved to have fun, when time permitted.

As the years went by, small changes occurred, but nothing too great to alter the ways of the culture. Then, something began happening. After the locals had spent hundreds of years on this land and in these waters, outsiders began to move in, and, after awhile, they found it provincial and demanded changes be made for "better living." As all things do, it got out of hand, until the inimitable Dickie Short down in Somerville, a water community, began writing letters to the big city paper, describing what was happening as "murders."

To him, they were. The developers were murdering the land he loved and changing things to such a degree that he knew, if it kept on, it would transform the area forever. Demand for crabs would help dwindle its populations; oysters and fish as well. He couldn't stand it anymore, and, after so many letters had been written, the big city paper in Baltimore sent a young cub reporter named Tug Alston down to check it out.

What happened over time to that old man and the young reporter became legend in these parts. They fought the system and made considerable progress. Tug, a Boston blue blood, fell in love not only with the land but also with Dickie's grandniece. But could their love overcome their very different backgrounds? Well, with the help of Dickie and a community grateful for what Tug had done for them, love did conquer all.

As that story was unfolding, a wonderful island woman was also trying to help her water community. She lived about thirty miles offshore of Somerville on a unique part of James Island.

James Island was really a group of four islands, three of which were connected to each other by bridges. Tuckerton—which Frances and Jimmy Evans, among others, called home—was the only one carved out eons ago in a way that made it accessible just by boat.

Miss Frances Evans was about to embark on a journey that would take her to the nation's capital and allow her to meet a young writer who would interview her and become so entwined in her story and her island that she would help her accomplish her goal: to speak before a congressional committee about her beloved crabs. Her appearance would change things dramatically for her people.

It would also change the way a young up-and-coming congressman from Virginia would look at things. He was about to take a path that would lead him to learn what was important to a culture as old as any in this country, and to find a woman he respected more than most.

The outcome of these stories of the courage of both a simple man named Dickie Short and an outspoken and plain-living woman named Miss Frances would be the framework for redirecting the ever-expanding changes and making people stop and think about what was really important in life.

We cannot stop change, but we can try to make sure that, when it comes, it doesn't ignore past lessons learned, and we can try to find a way not to insult those who paved the way for others. It is here we begin this last chapter of the Chesapeake. What will happen is up to you—us really—and all our friends and all the people who come here. Can we save it? Can we dare to think the dream will live on?

Chapter One

"With all we have to do today, I can't believe you are doing this and fussing about it so much. I could hear you all the way downstairs. Really, Tug? You don't have to fix everything in this house in one year, you know."

"Well, maybe not, but some of the things I really do need to fix haven't been fixed for decades, and, while I love it that Dickie gave us the house after he passed, he had to know it was in horrible disrepair."

"Oh, so now you're going to blame it on the sweetest, kindest man who ever lived?"

"Well, that is your opinion and now that you mention it . . ."

"Stop right there, Theodore Alston the Third. My Uncle Dickie and Aunt Shirley lived in this here house for almost fifty years together, and I love it now as much as I did the day I came into this world. When my mother brought me here to introduce me to them, I tell you I could feel the love instantly."

"Well, that is a miracle, Miss Lindy. No newborn can feel anything except wet and the need to eat, sleep, and poop."

Catching herself from an outright belly laugh, she looked at him sweetly and said, "Why, Tug, how would you know a thing about babies?"

"You might be surprised. The young mothers would bring their babies into the office back when I worked at the *Sun*, and they always smelled God-awful and were screaming to eat. That's how I know."

"Spoken like the egotistical Boston blue blood reporter, writer, and wealthy son of a sports fanatic."

Tug moved across the bedroom wall he was painting—or trying to—took Lindy in his arms, and abruptly kissed her with a smooch that nearly knocked her off her feet.

"What's got into you?" she teased.

"You, that's what. When you go getting your dander up, it turns me on."

"Well, I came up here to tell you that we have to catch the boat across the Bay in an hour, and you know Cap'n Tuck waits for no one."

1

"Holy cow, Lindy. I almost forgot. Today is the island reception for the Congressman and the new Mrs. Charles Lee. And it's a gorgeous July day for it. I'm happy for them."

"I am, too, but go on now and get ready. Put that brush and paint can away and go get showered and dressed."

Tug patted her rear and asked, "Are we coming back tonight?"

"No, we're staying over at Miss Frances's house. She invited us and I thought it was so sweet of her to do so."

"She is something, that woman. How is she doing anyway? I haven't seen her for a month of Sundays."

Lindy smiled and said, "You know, Tug, you are beginning to sound just like us down here. And Miss Frances is just fine. She is writing her own book now."

"Wow, that's great. Who's helping her? I can't imagine she can do it alone."

"She can do most anything she sets her mind to, but Willa is helping her. She comes down on the weekends when she can bear to leave that gorgeous new congressman husband of hers."

"I've been so busy with the house and my own work, I didn't know Willa came that often. Did she buy that old house she was looking at over in Tuckerton?"

"Yes, she did, and talk about work to be done! It really is outdated, but I don't think Willa and Charles care. It looks right out to the water and they aren't in a rush. Sooner or later, they'll get it all refurbished, but not like you, having to do every square inch by yourself, and in such a hurry."

"Makes it all mine this way."

Lindy let out a sigh and walked out of the small bedroom. Suddenly she felt a bit faint, but she didn't say anything because nothing was going to interfere with this weekend. Besides, there was no time; she had to finish packing.

As Tug picked up the paint can, he looked out the window to the water. His mind went back to the days he had spent here in this house and in this room as Dickie's guest. He suddenly felt so alone without that old man. Tug had truly loved him. And he was so happy. He could never have imagined his life would be what it is right now, but he sure was pleased with how it was turning out.

Dickie Short had taught him how to love the simple things in nature, and, now that he was gone, Tug missed him more than he could ever say. He missed all Dickie's country ways that, at times, could aggravate a soul to tears, and yet you didn't seem to mind once you knew him. And Tug knew everyone in Somerville felt the same way. Even if you had a beef with him, you loved him. He had been the quintessential waterman, a throwback to a time when this culture had been in its prime and not in danger of fading away as it was today.

Tug knew everyone felt that way about Miss Frances, too. She was an island woman with a mind all her own and didn't mind speaking it. Lindy always said she was a force to be reckoned with and that was just how people had felt about ole Dickie. The two of them had made a difference. They weren't at all afraid to speak up. Got them in a heap of trouble sometimes, but they could handle it.

Lindy walked back past the room Tug was painting. She noticed him staring out the window holding the paint can in his hand. She couldn't see his face, but his profile told the story. She knew what he was thinking and who he was thinking about. She quietly walked back in the bedroom and stood beside him. She took his hand gently and just stood there with him, looking out to the water, a ways off.

"I miss him too, Tug. I miss him so much at times, my heart could burst."

"There will never be another Dickie Short, Lindy, and sometimes I feel as if I let him down."

Astonished, she turned to face him and said, "Let him down? What do you mean? You fought the land-grabbing developers and made a real change for the better for all of us. And you married me and made him the happiest man in the world. He loved you, Tug, and was so proud of you."

Tug didn't turn to look at her but kept staring out the window with a look that beckoned that old man to rise up from the Bay and come sit in the living room in that old chair of his that Tug deliberately still kept where it had been for years, even though it was shot. It was Dickie's chair and such a part of him and Tug was never going to throw it out, even though Lindy had scrubbed it a dozen times to get rid of that crab smell ingrained in the fabric forever.

"You're right, Lindy, but marrying you had nothing to do with Dickie." He stretched his arm around her shoulder and squeezed. "That was because I fell in love with *you*. You were the best thing that has ever happened to me and that's the truth."

Lindy wiggled her body close to him to show him she was happy, too. She worried sometimes, because she was younger than he, that maybe he would one day wake up and be sorry for what he had done by marrying such a country bumpkin. But it did seem they were in sync with one another and they worked as a team. He always knew when she needed that extra bit of love, as he did now.

All of a sudden, it hit her: they had to get going. "Come on, Tug, we'll miss the boat and the reception. Willa and Charles would never forgive us if we weren't there. They have become good friends now and I don't want to mess that up."

Tug looked at her and smiled. "How could anyone not like you, Lindy? You make the world special for all of us, and I know that Charles and Willa like you very much."

"Willa is so nice, and she actually comes into Virgil's once in a while and has a cheeseburger, and that takes courage for the wife of a congressman."

Tug laughed hard, visualizing Willa, famous author and congressional wife, walking into Virgil's to eat lunch. No doubt they had the best burgers anywhere around, but it was a real man's place.

"I'll say it takes courage. I hope she never asked you where the ladies' restroom was."

"Tug Alston, you're bad. You know no woman would use that bathroom. Even working there, I never use it. I would rather die."

"No lady would, that's for sure. I never have understood why they don't put a porta-potty outside for the women."

"Maybe because they don't have a lot of women going in there. It's a waterman's place; you know that."

Tug was laughing hysterically. He remembered the first time he went in there to meet Dickie Short, one of many adventures he would never forget.

"I love you, Lindy. You know how much you are like Dickie? He could make me laugh like this, and, to be honest, it's one of the reasons I fell in love with you."

"How romantic, Tug. You have a real way with women, don't you? Now enough of this! Clean this mess up and go take a shower."

With that devilish, little boy look he could do so well, he said, "Want to join me?"

"Go!"

By the time Tug got his act together and they had parked at the pier, the Cap'n was pacing, knowing they were coming. Cap'n Tuck could be ornery at times, but everyone knew, deep down, he had a great heart. He also respected both Lindy and Tug and had told them that, straight out one day when he had congratulated Tug on his book.

They really were a very humble couple, and, while Tug's novel, *Reclaiming Our Lives*, had made it to the *New York Times* Best Seller list, he was still the young Harvard graduate who had fallen in love with the Bay and the people who fished it and, most importantly, the love of his life, Lindy Short.

"Whew! I am glad he waited for us, Tug. That's so unusual. He must like us a lot. Why, I do believe he thinks we are celebrities!"

"I know it, and that embarrasses me."

Hurrying to get to the boat, Lindy asked, "I've wondered, if he thinks *we're* celebrities, what must he think of Willa and Charles?"

"Probably hates Charles because he's a politician and a rich one at that. And a famous writer like Willa? We won't even speculate about that."

Lindy laughed at his comment because he was right on the mark. "Very observant, Tug. The Eastern Shore folks are a pretty independent group and don't trust politicians much to begin with. And, as for Boston blue-blooded hotshot writers like you and your dad? Why, you are just lucky they let you live in their universe. Must be because of me."

"And I intend to keep it that way, my dear. Besides, as we speak, Dad is out the door of the *Boston Globe* this year, and so we won't have his title of sports editor to hang around our neck anymore either. Come on; let's get our gear on the boat before Cap'n Tuck decides to take off just to teach us a lesson."

Trying to keep up with Tug, Lindy continued, "Are you ever sorry you didn't stay in Boston and write for your dad's paper?"

"Sometimes I wonder what it would have been like, working in my father's world. But no—I loved working with Max at the *Baltimore Sun*. And, even though he loves my dad, he understood the rough times I had being Theodore Alston's son. Remember, he was Dad's best friend when they went to Harvard."

"Wonder what Max is doing these days. When is the last time you heard from him, Tug?"

"After Dickie died, he called me to talk about 'that old man,' as he called him. However, I think he came to respect him tremendously in the end, even though Dickie—and me, for that matter— about drove him crazy and was, in all probability, the reason Max had to retire from the paper. My guess is his retirement wasn't by choice."

"Well, whatever happened to Max, he turned out to be a good mentor and friend to you, Tug."

Their conversation was interrupted by Cap'n Tuck yelling one last time. "Y'all better git on over here; I am 'bout to get 'er goin'."

"Coming, Cap'n." Tug grabbed their overnight case and he and Lindy rushed onto the boat. As luck would have it, the day was windy, and Tug hated going out on the water when it was blowing.

"How do, Miss Lindy. How are ye today?"

Lindy flashed her broad, sweet smile and said, "Just fine." But she was telling a lie. She really was pushing herself to smile and act fine.

"Hope ye stay that way. The wind's breezin' up some today."

Lindy didn't need Tuck to tell her that, and she was a bit nervous that Tug might get sick on the way over. She also didn't feel great herself, but it wasn't that she was afraid; she was used to the water and living around it. Something else was bothering her, but she was making the best of it, because this weekend was all about Willa and Charles and how happy she was for them and how much fun they were all going to have. For one thing, she had been thrilled when Miss Frances introduced Tug to Congressman Charles, thinking they would get along, and, as always, Miss Frances had been right.

The boat cast off. But, when they got out onto the open water, instead of feeling better in the cooler air, Lindy felt a bit queasy. She had brought a bottle of water and now dug it out of her large pocketbook— big enough to have been an overnight case in and of itself—and took a slow sip. Instantly she felt better.

"Are you okay, Lindy?" Tug asked with concern.

"Sure am. It's the wind. Every once in a while it gets to me when I go over to the island."

"I'm not going to need to get a bucket, am I?"

"Not unless you're going to need it. Now hush, Tug. I have never used a bucket nor have I ever thrown up on the water. I'm not like you. I was

6

born and raised on the water with Dickie. I remember hearing how bad you were when you went out crabbing that first time."

"And am I never going to live that down, either? Wally and Clumpy take every opportunity to tell me just how green I was on that boat, and I can tell you my body hurt in places I had never known existed before."

Lindy began laughing, then noticed Tug wasn't enjoying it near as much as she was. "Okay, Tug, we won't talk about it."

"No, we won't. You have no idea how those guys got on me."

"And you loved every minute of it. They wouldn't do it if they didn't like you."

"Well, you may be right, but, all the same, I felt like a fool."

The rest of the passengers were looking at them but they didn't care. They knew most everyone on the boat, and everyone was in such high spirits that they all joined in, as if they knew what Lindy and Tug were laughing at.

Denny Bradshaw was coming back from buying a whole load of groceries for his store on the island. Lots of people would be coming over for this shindig and he knew that he and Nellie—his wife and Frances's daughter—would be cooking up a storm for the event.

Lindy struck up a conversation with Denny. He was a few years older than she was, same class as Nellie, but she really liked both of them and had been so happy when they got married a year or so before. "Going to make a lot of money this weekend, huh, Denny?"

"Yup. I got in some good steaks for you all. Miss Frances ordered them special for ye."

"She doesn't miss a trick."

"No, she does not. She's so excited about this for Willa that she's about to burst her sides."

"She loves Willa like a daughter."

"You got that right, Miss Lindy. She adores her and is so happy she has bought a house here in Tuckerton. Willa only comes on weekends when she can, but we're all glad to see her when she gets there." Denny smiled and added, "So how are you and Tug gettin' on? Fine, I hope."

"Well, to tell you, Tug is having a fit over the things that need fixing in the house Dickie left us, but he'll survive."

Tug poked her and stage-whispered, "Do you have to tell everyone how unhandy your husband is?"

Lindy chuckled as she turned her head and looked at him. "Tug, I think they knew that already, don't you?"

"Well, you don't have to broadcast it. I want to become like them and be able to do so many things with my hands."

Denny laughed. "Now don't go fussin' with Miss Lindy, Tug. We all like to tease ye. Why, you do things we could never dream of. If you need some help on that ole house, give me a shout. I can help you get it all done in no time. There are a lot of guys who would be glad to join us."

Lindy made a face and said, "See, 'Mr. Privacy,' they love you and want to help us."

"I just wanted to do it myself, maybe to prove to me that I can learn how to do things with my hands and not with my mind all the time."

With a twinkle in her eyes, Lindy leaned over and said quietly in his ear, "Oh, there are a lot of things you do so very well with your hands, honey."

Tug about fell over dead with embarrassment. He was sure every soul on that boat had heard her, but, when he shot a quick look around, they were all busy talking to one another and paying no mind to him.

Lindy began giggling and couldn't stop—and then it hit her bad. She was going to throw up and nothing could be done about it. The boat didn't come equipped with a bathroom so it was over the side for her. She jumped up, turned around, and let it fly. Tug's eyes bugged out of their sockets so far, he looked like a frog. He jumped up and held her long hair out of her face while she got sick, and, although he was doing it instinctively, as any husband would, he began to feel queasy, too.

After she was done, she continued leaning over, gasping for some air, before she stood up straight. She was hoping she would just die right there, and thought she might, mostly from embarrassment.

Smugly, Tug chuckled and said, "And who's the one they will be talking about now, Lindy, huh?"

"Darn you, Tug." With that, the scene repeated itself and there was nothing to do but turn and lean over the rail again. Miss Phoebe, who had sat stone-still watching it all, and had known Lindy all her life and loved her dearly, stood up and walked across the aisle and sat down next to her. Tug moved over to give the very large and sturdy woman room.

Lindy seemed to lean toward her as Miss Phoebe took a hand that was cold and clammy. "Are you all right, Lindy?"

Lindy was red-faced, throwing up in front of all her people. She knew they all had known Dickie and Aunt Shirley and her parents. Come to think of it, everyone knew everyone down in Somerville and out on the island.

"Oh, yes, Miss Phoebe, I think so. I don't know what hit me. I think it's all the excitement and everything. This is such a wonderful weekend for all of us."

Miss Phoebe got up real close to Lindy and whispered in her ear, "Have ye told him yet?"

Lindy gave her an incredulous look. "Told him what, Miss Phoebe?"

"Ye know what I'm talking about, child."

Tug stared oddly at the two women, not hearing a word.

Lindy finally turned beet red. "No, I haven't and please don't say anything. This weekend is about Willa and Charles, not me."

"Point taken, but if I were ye, I—"

"Yes, I know, Miss Phoebe, but you're not me and I beg you to not make any statements. Just let's keep it with us right now, okay?"

Hugging the young girl, the older woman said, "I won't say a word."

"Thank you, Miss Phoebe."

When Miss Phoebe went back to her seat, Tug moved in real close and said, "Okay, Lindy Alston, what's the big secret?"

"Nothing, Tug, really."

"You were fine when we left the house, and now you have upchucked twice and you're telling me it's nothing?"

"Drop it, please. I guess the water got to me today, that's all."

Lindy was so relieved when she heard Cap'n Tuck let out a whoop, yelling, "There they are!"

All heads on board turned to see Willa and Charles coming up aside them in Charles's boat, *The Willa Lee*. Lindy got up with Tug following her lead, and they waved and shouted, "Hey there! How are you?"

The newlyweds yelled back, "Good to be home. See you at the dock."

Tug smiled and had to admit how much he had missed seeing them. Charles was a good man, and Tug's father had done some research on Charles's family in Virginia and told Tug they were a very old, distinguished, and historic bloodline. Tug's dad thought it would be good for him to become friends with Congressman Lee. Miss Frances had made that happen, just knowing they were a match, and because she wanted Lindy to be around more sophisticated people. It would help her grow to like them better and understand where they all came from. Miss Frances knew Dickie, as country as he was, had a pure shore streak of intuition, and he had figured Lindy and Tug would work out just fine. Now she was determined to make sure that Willa and Charles had some younger friends to visit when they came to the island on weekends.

As they docked, Lindy felt sick again but was determined to ward it off; she wanted no more scenes, no matter what it took. She and Tug got off the boat, and, all of a sudden, Tug looked at her, stopped, and gently grabbed her by the arm.

"Lindy, what's wrong with you? And don't push me away this time. You know something, so out with it."

"What are you talking about? Now behave, Tug; this weekend isn't about me."

"Hot damn, girl, we won't have any weekend if you don't tell me what's got you so si—" Tug stopped dead in his tracks. "Oh dear. Oh my God. Girl, you're pregnant, aren't you?"

"Tug!" she said firmly. "Will you please stop this?"

"I'm right, aren't I? You're expecting, so to hell with Willa and Charles and everyone. I don't give a hoot what they think. You're pregnant, aren't you? I don't believe how stupid I was not to see it."

Lindy saw the excitement on his face and couldn't hold it in any longer. "Okay, if you must know, yes, I am. Now, are you going to act like one of those crazy husbands who have to tell everybody, or are we going to keep this under our hats until the reception is over?"

Tug stood there, staring at her, then went to let out a big whoopee, but Lindy covered his mouth. "Don't, please, Tug?"

"Okay, Lindy, I won't, but I am so happy. We'll tell everyone only when you say it's okay."

"Thank you," she whispered. She started walking again, Tug following her with a huge smile on his face. At that moment Miss Phoebe was also walking up the dock; she nodded to Lindy, clearly giving her notice that she was glad Tug finally knew. Lindy put her fingers to her mouth and made that *please don't say anything* sign. Miss Phoebe smiled and nodded, letting her know she got the message.

For all that, Lindy couldn't believe it when Tug took her in his arms and kissed her right in front of God and everyone. At that moment she didn't care. She was in love with him.

Chapter Two

Miss Frances was in a frenzy at the thought of all the people who would be staying with her, but she loved every minute of it. Food was made and cakes were on the way over from her sister-in-law's house, where the smell of all the cakes and wedding pastries were emanating from her windows. No one could bake better than Miss Millie. Her real name was Mildred, but no one ever called her that. She was Miss Millie, and she made the best island cakes anywhere around.

"Now, Jimmy, you go down to Bradshaw's and get me some more eggs. I have used most all I have and will need some more if anyone is to have breakfast this weekend."

"Okay, Franny. Is there anything else while I'm over there?"

Frances thought a minute and said, "Maybe some more milk, if they still have some. I can always use that."

Jimmy walked out the door and Frances heard her guests talking to him as they approached the house. She flew out the kitchen door, She was so happy she could hardly contain herself.

"Hey, Miss Frances. How are you?"

"Comin' just fine, Tug. How are you?"

Tug gave her a big old bear hug as Lindy smiled away, and then she hugged Frances.

Charles and Willa had met up with them and also walked over to Miss Frances's house. She said, "So good to see y'all. Just look at you, Willa. You are the picture of a beautiful bride. And you, Charles, are more handsome than I remember."

Charles beamed at her and said, "Look who's a politician now."

As they began to enter the house, Charles tapped Tug on the shoulder and nodded for him to let Lindy and Willa go on. "Tug, later on, when we get settled and the girls start talking, can you and I walk on down to the water and talk for a while?"

"Sure. Charles, is everything all right?"

"You mean with Willa and me? Absolutely. I love her so much and we're going to be very happy together. No, it's something else. I want your opinion."

"You want *my* humble opinion? Well, I will give it to you if you think it's that important."

"I do indeed, Tug. Willa and I were talking the other day about how odd life is and how we all came together in the oddest of ways and how this land has affected us."

"You can say that again. I think my very Bostonian parents believe I have lost my mind entirely, but having my book make the *New York Times* Best Seller list helped a little to ensure them I'm still in the game."

"Hey, I actually took the time to read the entire novel. Well done, Tug. You transitioned well in your writing from reporting to narrative. That's not at all easy and you're good at it. I know when your book came out, you took a lot of heat for it. Willa did, too, with her special nonromance novel. Many people don't understand you're both trying to find answers that may be able to accommodate everyone. Although that rarely happens."

"Charles, you have said a mouthful there. Some folks are in it for the money and some are in it for all the right reasons, but, in the end, unfortunately, it's the money that takes over and that's what talks."

"You should be a politician. Money is shoved in our faces every minute of the day and it's hard to walk a straight path."

"Unfortunately, you're right, but politics isn't for me. I am enjoying my life down here more than I ever thought I could. My dad thinks I've gone over the edge wanting to live here. I don't understand why he doesn't get it. He used to love to come down to this shore to fish once in a while with Max, and he loved the beach and how kind of 'old-timey,' as he would call it, the people here were. Now all that isn't good enough for his son."

"Who knows what fathers think sometimes? They can be hard on their sons. I know that too well. You think it's easy being a Lee of Virginia? Well, Willa and I love owning a part of this island now, and we love coming here when we can get away from the mad world of D.C. As for my family, they love Willa and they still love me."

"Well, they do learn to get over it because, in the end, we're their children and they taught us to live independent lives and then sent us out into the world to do so. How can they fight that argument?"

Charles shook his head. "I hear you."

Miss Frances stuck her head out the door and said, "What is going on out here with you two? Come on in and get some food."

"Sorry, Miss Frances. Where are our manners?"

"Guess you must have left them back there with all those rascals in Washington."

Tug and Charles laughed, and they each patted her on the shoulder as they walked through her kitchen door.

Lunch for a lot of people was a feast at Frances Evans's home. There wasn't a food group missing on that table. It was a Thanksgiving Dinner replete with cranberry sauce, relish, and jellies of all kinds. Homemade biscuits like no one could make anywhere else filled a huge basket. Crab casseroles aplenty were lined up on a side table and the turkey was carved and ready to go. However, before anyone picked up a fork, Miss Frances looked at Jimmy and gave him a nod.

Jimmy bowed his head and said a blessing, and, as soon as it was over, forks immediately began to dig into that turkey and everything else going around the table. Lindy was having a hard time of it but Tug bumped her leg with his to let her know he was in support and right there for her.

Charles ate like he had never eaten before and Jimmy laughed at how much they were all enjoying his dinner table. "Sure is true, ye can't get food like this in a restaurant."

Frances laughed at him and said, "Eat up now, there's a whole kitchen full of this here food."

Willa looked at Lindy and they both smiled, knowing that if you ate one of everything there, you would gain ten pounds all at one sitting.

Despite hating to eat and run, after lunch Charles and Willa thanked Frances and Jimmy and got up to go over to the house they had just bought.

"Are you sure you won't stay on here a little longer?"

"We would love to do that, Miss Frances, but we would also like to get our things settled in before tonight's bash at the firehouse."

"I understand, Willa, but please make sure you stop on by Nellie's house and say hello."

"Already did. We saw them both on our way here. They were coming out of their store and had a million things to do. Everybody is so wonderful to be doing this for Charles and me."

"You're family here now," Miss Frances said. "See you a little later."

Charles smiled and looked over at Tug and said, "See you shortly, Tug."

Tug nodded as Lindy gave him a stare. "What's that about?"

"I have no idea. Charles said he wanted my opinion on something, and I said I would be glad to listen."

Lindy snuggled up to him and said, "Should we tell Miss Frances?"

"I'm not going to say a word. If I told someone, you would shoot me, and now here you are asking me if you can tell Miss Frances. Women! I'll never understand them."

Lindy giggled and said, "Good. We don't want you to."

Tug got up from the table and said, "I'm going upstairs to unpack our things. Care to join me or are you going into the kitchen to spill the beans?"

"Don't know yet. Can I get a better offer if I go upstairs?"

"I don't think so; I have to go and meet Charles."

Lindy winked at him and said, "I'll remember that, Mr. Alston."

"I'll bet you will, Mrs. Alston, and hold it against me, too."

Lindy picked up some of the dirty dishes and wandered into the kitchen to help Miss Frances clean up the meal. "It was sure good."

"I'm glad you liked it, Lindy, but I saw you didn't eat very much. Are you okay?"

"Yes, I am, but I am having a tough day today."

Frances turned from the sink and said, "Why is that? You and Tug aren't arguing, are ye?"

"No, nothing like that. We are better than fine. It's just that . . ." Her voice trailed off.

"Just that what, Lindy? Tell me, girl, and I'll help you if I can."

"Well, it's just that I am pregnant."

Miss Frances nearly dropped the plate in her hand. "Say what?"

"Hush, Miss Frances. Bad enough Tug almost blurted it out to the whole world at the dock. I had to cover his mouth when he finally figured out why I was sick on the way over. I really don't want to spoil today or this weekend for Willa and Charles. You asked, and you being like my mother and all should know, but I really would like to hold it all down until at least after the reception. I want this party to be the best time ever, and I can tell people later on when I start to show."

Miss Frances immediately glanced down at Lindy's stomach, the way everyone does when they are told someone is pregnant. "I won't say a word until you say it's okay." She hugged Lindy and then added, "Dickie and Shirley sure would have loved to have seen this."

"I know, and I wish they could still be here, but things aren't always as we want them to be."

"They both sure loved you, Lindy. You were the child they always wanted, and I know how much you loved them, especially Dickie."

"He was like my granddaddy, for sure. I know my mother disappointed my own granddaddy, and he and I sure never really connected so much, but Dickie and Shirley made up for it all."

"They did indeed and I think it's so nice he left you and Tug that house of theirs."

"Right now that's a sore subject. Poor Tug is working himself to death on the weekends to fix it all up, but Cap'n Tuck told him he would be glad to help him and could bring some other men to help, too. I sure hope he's not so stubborn that he won't take them up on it."

"That's real nice, Lindy. You can talk him into it. Now that you are in the condition you're in, I 'spect he'll do anything for you. Men are like that."

"I don't know about that, Miss Frances. He's pretty good to me now, so I don't know how much better he can get."

"You go on upstairs and lie down for a while. These dishes are no match for me. Did I hear Tug say he was meeting Charles? If so, you will have the whole house to yourself. Jimmy and I are going down to help at the firehouse for tonight's big doings, so, go on now. Get some rest."

"Thanks so much for everything, Miss Frances."

"I love you, girl, and I have to make sure nothing happens to you or that bundle wrapped up inside of ye."

Lindy walked up the stairs, smiling from ear to ear. She was so happy. Everything she had ever wanted was coming true.

Chapter Three

Charles quietly left their new house while Willa napped before the big bash. He knew she needed to rest. She had been running like crazy lately with her writing and with signing books. Her publisher, Kit, had about driven her into the ground, and Charles wasn't at all happy about that, but it was what she did and he would never dare to change her life. He loved her too much, and, after all, she accepted his life as a United States congressman. Lately, even he had to admit he was pretty drained, but politicians got used to late nights and chicken dinners. It was part of the territory for them, and, if you couldn't keep up, you had to get out of the game—something he was not going to do.

Tug walked slowly down the lane toward the water where he saw Charles sitting on an old weathered bench, staring out to the Bay. While he didn't know what Charles could possibly have to discuss with him, he was looking forward to the exchange. He liked Charles, what little he knew of him, but wanted to get to know him much better. And, now that the Lees had bought a house here on the island, he suspected he would get that chance.

They actually had a good deal in common, coming from similar backgrounds of fame and notoriety and having gone to excellent schools. Charles was the epitome of southern style and grace, while he was a real Harvard man, raised on New England grit and perseverance. He was younger than Charles but still knew the ways of the world. They both had fast-paced jobs, and the one thing they shared the most was that they loved their young wives very much.

"Hey, Charles, it looks to me as if you are a million miles away."

"Not quite, but close. I can truly relax out here in the middle of nowhere."

"Don't say that in front of Frances; she might hit you. This is her home and she loves it and, to her, it isn't nowhere. It's her passion, her people, and, as we know, she will fight anyone, anywhere, anytime to preserve what they have here."

"Don't you feel that way about the island, too, Tug?"

"I do in my own way, but I prefer to live in Somerville and work over there. I think if I lived out here all the time, I might not get anything done. However, the house I have in Somerville is making me crazy. As you know by now, it was a gift from Lindy's family, and, while I don't mean to sound ungrateful, Dickie lived in it all by himself for a while after his wife died, and he didn't pay any mind to what needed to be fixed or done to keep it up to date. To add to that, I was also left his old crab shanty and we won't even go there. I think his real home was on the water, in his boat, and his house really was only for sleeping and eating."

"You own one of those shanties? Tell me about it."

"Well, a shanty, Charles—by the way, can I call you Charlie? Charles seems so formal to call a friend. Everyone down here has been given more casual names, and some have nicknames that defy logic."

"Sure you can, Tug. One day I'll ask you about yours."

"I can tell you right now. When I was little I used to put on these tug-of-war sports events in my family. My dad started calling me Tug and it stuck. Seemed like a great name for a newsman."

"I suppose it does, and it makes sense now that I know."

"They all make sense once you know where the names come from. Down here, no one is known by their proper birth names. James becomes Jimmy and Steven becomes Stevie, and sometimes they go all out and, if you get caught doing something when you're young, you get nailed with a name that lasts a lifetime. Some of them you'll hear will make you want to laugh out loud."

"Go on."

"Names like Cheeseburger and Slugger, Nature Boy, and so on. But to those who know them, it makes perfect sense, and they don't care one bit if they are adults walking around with the nicknames they got as kids. You never outgrow your nickname down here."

"Kind of like they are all Peter Pan."

"Well, something like that, Charlie."

Charles smiled. When Willa called him Charlie, he thought it was cute, but, he had to admit, when grown men called him that . . . well, he wasn't sure about that at all. But he could see, if he was going to make it down here, he would have to make a lot of adjustments and his name might well be one of those.

Tug continued, "Okay, now that we have that all straightened out, let me tell you about my shanty. It's the gift that keeps on giving, but more pain than joy at the moment. You've heard a lot about Dickie, Lindy's great-uncle who was really more like her grandfather? When he died, he left us his house, along with what I fondly call the leaning water shed. And that's because it's so old now, it leans to one side and is sinking a little and takes on water every time the tides come in and then roll on out. Well, that old shanty probably means more to me than anything else he left to us because there aren't so many left, and it's proof of what was once here in such abundance. Men would come in from a day of crabbing and head right to their shanties and do their work in them, shucking oysters or separating the crabs. When it's crab season, someone will stay in there with those critters all night to watch for them to shed their shells."

Charlie stared at Tug. He had caught crabs when he had gone fishing as a youngster, but he'd always thrown them back. He really hadn't known that a whole industry was built around the seemingly simple crustaceans, and he certainly hadn't known about the way of life devoted to catching them. Not until he met Willa and Miss Frances did he learn the real story of the watermen of the Chesapeake. Now he felt as if he knew more about crabs and oysters than any of his friends back in Virginia.

"You know, Tug, you and I were so naïve when we learned about this life, and now each of us is working to help these folks out, you with your words and books and me with legislation that makes sense for everyone."

"That's a laugh, Charlie. Nothing suits everyone. Some group always gets their panties in a bunch."

Charlie smiled at that comment. "You're so right, but we can keep trying. By the way, do you own a house over here?"

"Not yet." Tug grinned. "No, when Lindy comes over, she stays with Miss Frances or Miss Frances's sister-in-law, Millie Evans. She's known around these parts as the 'Cake Lady.'"

"Really?" Charles said. "I am sure I will meet her soon enough."

"At the reception for sure. Will you spend your weekends here now, Charlie?"

"I know Willa wants to, and I will come, too, when I have the time. I am usually so busy even on weekends trying to catch up, and then I do have my own family in Virginia. Plus, I hear there are some really nasty bugs over here in the summertime."

"You might say that. There are some real mean flies. They're green; thus their name—Green Heads. Their bite is as mean as a mule's kick."

"Well, they sound lovely."

Tug laughed and said, "You never get used to them but you learn to live with them."

"I'm not sure about that." Then Charlie sat back on the bench and said, "Tug, I want to talk to you about something a bit more serious than flies that can carry you off and eat you."

"Okay. Let's talk."

"There is another ill wind blowing from D.C. that will greatly affect this area."

"I'm sorry to hear that, Charlie, What is it now that they're up to?"

"To get right to the point, I want to get some information leaked, and, from what Willa has told me about you and your background with the paper, you know the people who can do that."

"Gee, Charlie, the big man I know is gone. He was the paper's editor and the best newsman in the business, but he's retired now, and I think that happened because of me."

"You? How could you destroy a powerful editor like that? Both of us know that all things news or politics are mostly kept in the hands of the senior members who feel they have earned their stripes. Don't take offense, but you were just starting out, weren't you?"

"Yes, I was a cub reporter, as they say, but you have to understand that I went to war over the Eastern Shore and the overdevelopment of this land, and I stood with Dickie Short and the rest of the folks here. The developers, the bankers—some of the paper's largest advertisers—were ruining the entire landscape down here and causing a lot of trouble for a whole bunch of folks. Max Pierson, the main man at the paper, had to play both sides, but the paper's bread and butter was the money from those advertisers. Max got caught in the middle, and I sort of knew he might have to take an early retirement, but he didn't seem to care. He ended up loving 'that old man,' as he called Dickie, and I was the son of his best friend."

"Yes, Tug, sometimes we have to take chances. Do you think it was easy for me when Frances spoke before my committee? All hell broke loose, but sometimes it has to be."

Tug responded, "She was wonderful and so was Dickie, but I paid a price for that. I left the paper and wrote a novel, and I'm proud that it brought to people all over the country word about what is happening down here. But do I want to get back into that crab pot? Well, I might if the cause was big enough. Your hearings did do a lot, and they went a long way to keeping folks civil."

"Tug, the fight is never over. I have to pick my battles and then try to get legislation to really affect those who are struggling. I wish I had known 'that old man' you speak about. He sounds like he was a real mover and shaker for his cause, no less than Frances is right now."

Tug started to laugh.

"What's so funny?"

"You, not knowing Dickie. If you had, you would never have forgotten him. He was the real deal and was both ornery and lovable at the same time."

"My kind of man."

"Let's face it, Charlie, our problems started the day we met our ladies. Lindy and Willa are from two different worlds, and yet they are so much alike and our hearts were lost to them both. And now here we are, from a world away, sitting on this old bench talking about the next adventure."

Charles sat back and looked out to the water. "I guess what some say is true: there really is no such thing as coincidence. I could never believe I would marry a famous writer, have a country nickname, and be getting ready to take on the establishment all over again."

Tug flashed his brilliant, boyish smile and said, "Why not? We're both idealists looking for a new way to do things. I don't know why we don't just rent a band and march into the Capitol and announce a new circus has come to town and the old clowns need to leave."

"God, what a great visual you paint, Tug. Wouldn't you just love to do that?"

"More than anything. So, what is it exactly we are talking about here?"

Charles explained, "This time it's the farmers joining the watermen in a fight to keep what they've had all these years. And it's not just the farmers—it's an entire industry that has been here for a very long time."

"You're referring, of course, to the poultry industry. Holy cow, Charlie, you *are* out of your mind! Count me in."

Charlie was shocked at Tug's sudden response. He thought it had been going to take far more persuasion than one session on an old bench. "Tug, that's great! I didn't think you would go for it."

"Well, it would get me away from that old house and all that has to be done."

"Good point. Though nothing is going to happen for a while yet. But there is some talk of really tying the hands of the farmers, and we have to find a way to get people to the table. And I don't have to tell you how hard that can be."

"This is beginning to sound like a rerun of bad movie, Charlie, but I'm willing to help you on it."

Charles looked down at his watch and let out a yelp. "I can't believe where the time has gone. We're going to be mincemeat if we don't get a move on. Our girls will skin us alive if we aren't home to get ready for this big reception."

"You're right on that. Good to talk with you, Charlie, but now it's all about the fun."

"Thanks a lot for your support, Tug. I really appreciate it. We'll talk again before I go back. Now, let's go celebrate my marriage to the wonderful Willa Carpenter Lee."

Tug smiled. The two men were off to a good start in their budding friendship; Tug liked Charles and could tell the feeling was mutual. As they began to walk back down the lane, Tug stopped and said, "I don't think we ought to tell either of the girls what we are going to be doing right now. Let's let that sit awhile. Lindy will get all over me."

"Willa might not like it so much either, so it will remain between us. Okay?"

"My lips are sealed, Charlie."

"Mine, too. If there's one thing I have learned being a politician, it's how to keep secrets."

Tug stopped and said, "Now I know we're both in a lot of trouble."

Chapter Four

It is said, and rightfully so, that when islanders decide to throw a big bash, there's nothing like it anywhere. They cook up a storm for days and have themselves a big old-fashioned time. And that is no lie.

By three o'clock, vegetable casseroles and salads were flooding into the fire hall. Then came the turkeys, roast beef, and, best of all, the crabs. Crabs by the bushel were being brought around to the back door of the kitchen where they would be put into huge pots on the stoves to be steamed up and served hot and spiced with Old Bay. They were the center of attention, without a doubt. No one could imagine living on the island and not liking crabs. It would almost be sacrilegious. You would be banished forever. The folks in Tuckerton loved their crabs.

The crab was why they existed. Oysters, too, of course, but it was the Maryland Blues that ruled their lives and their calendars. Had been since the island was inhabited way back in the sixteen hundreds. The people worked all winter with the oysters and fixing their crab nets and pots, but, when the crabs began to run and fill up the Bay, there was nothing more important to them. The oysters kept them going through winter, but the crab was in their DNA. The watermen of the Chesapeake had a healthy respect for those mischievous crustaceans; they understood one another.

By four o'clock, everyone on the island had stopped what they were doing and headed to the church to make a blessing for Willa and Charles, their new neighbors. The old Methodist Church was the center of all things for these folks, having seen them through everything in the circle of life. Not only in good times, but bad, too, especially when the storms came through. It was always their refuge in a time of turbulence.

Today was to be a high time, and Reverend Mike, who had now been there quite awhile, gave a beautiful blessing. Then it was back to the fire hall and the party. By now, the pots were at full boil and ready for the crabs, still being brought in for the dinner.

Willa looked radiant, with a quiet sophistication that was so classic and city. She had on a lightweight pale pink blouse with cream pants. She was always a stunner, but, today, she was beaming with happiness. She had told Charles when he got back from his talk with Tug that she was so glad she had taken the short nap he suggested. She was burning the candle on a new romance novel and pushing herself pretty hard. She needed this time with him and her new neighbors.

Charles fit right in and was very happy to be back on the island. In fact, if his wife didn't know better, she would say he was thoroughly enjoying his new home, even though they were going to make major changes and update it entirely. However, they both had agreed they wanted to keep the integrity of it. Just make it more to their liking.

As the happy couple walked from the church to the fire hall, a man smiled at Charles, tipped his hat, and said, "Hey there, Charles. Good to see you back here."

"Good to be back. See you at the reception."

After the man walked away, Willa said, "Who was that, Charles?"

"I have no idea, but it won't matter. There aren't that many people over here, so I can't believe it's going to be too hard to meet everyone and remember them."

"Sad, isn't it, how few folks *are* left over here in Tuckerton? Frances told me that, once upon a time, there were almost two hundred adults and children in town."

"Yes, the culture is changing and changing quickly, but those who are here are all so nice and friendly."

"Spoken like a real politician," Willa said. "Well, here we are. Ready to go in, Charles?"

"Would rather be back inside the house with you alone."

"Later, sweetheart," she said, teasingly.

"I'll hold you to that."

Just then Tug came up in back of them and tapped his friend Charlie on the shoulder. "Hey, Congressman, are you ready to rock and roll?"

"You bet, but first I want to eat me a mess of crabs."

Tug said, "Why, you're beginning to sound just like us down here."

"Thought I would give it a try and see if I can get used to it. Not sure it works for me though."

Willa laughed and said, "You better watch out, or the next time you stand on the floor and give a speech, you won't know what might come out."

"They'd really be all over you then, Charlie." Tug laughed.

Lindy stared at her husband and said, "Since when do you call him Charlie?"

Charles spoke up quickly in defense of his friend. "I told him it would be all right, Lindy. He said it would be what they called me down here anyway. You know—a nickname."

Lindy's mouth dropped open and Willa just stared at the two men. "You know, Lindy, if I didn't know any better, I would think these boys had been drinking down at the water's edge this afternoon while we were sleeping."

Lindy looked at Willa and smiled. "Any other place you might be right, but not here in Tuckerton. They don't take to drinking on James Island."

Charles shot a look at Willa as if this was one thing about the place he hadn't known.

Tug saw it and quickly added, "But you can bring a bottle over with you. Just don't let them catch you."

"Well, at least that is something to be grateful for."

"Come on now, Tug. Let's go over and stand in the buffet line with Miss Frances and Jimmy."

"Hold on, Lindy. Let the guests of honor go first."

The food line was ridiculously long, but half the fun was talking with everyone and seeing what they were scooping on their plates.

"I haven't ever seen so much food, Charles, have you?"

"I used to see this kind of all-out war on one's stomach when I was younger, and Dad would take my sister and me to a real down-home southern church picnic. I don't see it here, but there we always had what they called five-cup salad."

"What in the world was that?"

"Well, I don't remember exactly what each cup was, but it was made with mayonnaise, sour cream, cherries, mandarin oranges, green grapes, and those little jet-puffed marshmallows. Outrageously good."

"That makes six, but who's counting, right, Charlie?" Willa pointed. "I think I spot something like it over there."

Charles responded, "I'll be a son of a bootmaker."

"A son of a bootmaker?"

"Well, I am in the company of ladies, Willa."

"Oh, I see. When you're alone with me, you don't mind letting it go. So I guess I'm no lady."

"Willa, dear, stop teasing me. You are *the* lady to end them all."

Suddenly, the food table line stopped when a woman just inside the door shouted, "WHOOOPPEEEE!"

Willa's mouth fell open and Charles stood stone-still.

Charles whispered to Lindy, "Who's that?"

"I don't believe it. That, my friend, is none other than Miss Ruby."

"Who's Miss Ruby?"

"Wait a minute and you'll see what's going on."

Charles looked a bit shaken. "Are we safe, Lindy?"

Tug started laughing and leaned over to his friend. "Oh, you'll be safe all right, but you'll never be the same."

Everyone watched as Ruby moved aside and in walked a man as slim as she was large. Others joined him, carrying musical instruments.

Willa's mouth was still hanging open when Miss Frances arrived at her side. "It's okay, dear. They've come over from the other parts of James Island to show you two a good time and wish you well."

Charles mumbled, "Holy mother . . ."

Willa chuckled. "Now we're getting closer to the real you."

No sooner had the island gang burst in and started to set up their entertainment, when the door opened again, but, this time, it was a surprise to end them all.

"OMG!" cried Willa. "It can't be." She tore away from the food line and ran to grab her dearest girlfriend, Prue, along with Charles's sister, Verinnia. (Prue had affectionately nicknamed her Vernie. The much-less-a-mouthful moniker had quickly caught on with everyone, and—most important—Verinnia adored it as well.) Willa began crying and so did Prue. Tears of joy ran down their faces, as Charles planted a huge kiss on his sister's cheek, then stepped back and looked at her with great admiration. "You came, Vernie. You came to see us."

"I wasn't going to miss the best part."

"How did you . . ." His voice trailed off as he saw the look on Frances's face. He finished his hanging sentence looking right into Frances's eyes. "Why, you did this, didn't you?"

Frances stood up tall and said, "I sure did, and proud of it."

Willa wrapped her arms around Frances, still crying with joy, and said, "I am so glad you did. I've so missed my Prue."

"Now, children, let's get on with the eating," Miss Frances said. Then she turned to everyone and shouted, "Come on now! Dig in, and there's a mess of crabs to be eatin' and then it's time fer some dancin'."

Whoops and hollers went up from all over the room.

Charles turned to Tug and said, "You know, one time I was in Texas, at a wedding of a college friend, and they had a little something like this. They called it a shivaree, and all the guests got drunker than skunks and carried on all night."

"My God, Charlie, these aren't Texans—"

"Glad of it, too. That poor Texas couple really had a night. I hope these folks all go back home tonight and don't get any ideas."

Tug continued, "—but they might be close in spirit. These folks do like to have fun and fool around."

He then laughed at visions of staid and traditional Charlie getting dragged out in the dark in his underwear, while poor innocent Willa watched it all through a window from inside. He shivered a bit just thinking of it.

The band played on and Ruby belted out some songs of the island they all knew. Everyone was having a great time, including Charles and Willa, who were catching up with Prue and Vernie.

This time it was Nellie who let out a shout: "Hey, everybody! Make way for the dessert!"

Everyone cleared a pathway to the head table where Willa, Charles, Tug, Lindy, Vernie, and Prue sat. Then, with the men shouting a drum roll, in walked Miss Millie pushing a huge welcome cake on a wheeled cart.

Tug said to Charles, "Remember I told you about Miss Millie earlier? She is the cake baker to end them all in these parts. No one can make cakes like Miss Millie. Frances's sister, Rita, is pretty good, but not in the same class as her sister-in-law, Miss Millie."

Millie's husband, Richard, then said in a loud voice, "Congratulations from all of us to you, Willa and Charles."

Millie put the cake in front of their table and the newlyweds came around and stood there while Richard said a few more words, welcoming them officially as neighbors in Tuckerton. Everyone then saluted the couple with a heartfelt "Amen!"

Willa kissed Charles and then Charles had a few words of his own.

"Thank you all for coming today and for making Willa and me feel so at home already here in Tuckerton, I know we will love having a home here and will try to come back every chance we get. Even though I know many of you from past visits, today marks a new beginning for both of us as a married couple, and I would like to say how happy we both are to be a part of such a fine community. There are plenty of wonderful times ahead for us all, and, today, while surrounded by friends and family, I would like to tell you how much I appreciate the support I get from all of you. I hope to continue on in the work of letting everyone know the value of the water communities here and all around this country."

Willa could see Charles had switched into politician mode. She moved closer to him and kissed him again. He got the message and smiled, saying, "See what a good wife does. She knows when it's time for me to stop talking and for us to take our leave. And we shall. Thank you all, again."

With that, Nellie shouted out, "And don't forget to eat some cake and take some home!"

Willa began saying good-night to everyone while Charles and Tug talked for a moment. "I'm leaving tomorrow, Tug—though I've had to hire one of the less religious men from Somerville to come get me because the regular island boats don't run on Sundays. And I'm keeping *The Willa Lee* here on the island. Anyway, I likely won't see you before I go, but I will be in touch and we can continue our conversation on what we talked about."

"I'll be waiting, Charlie. Lindy and I are staying on, so we'll make sure Willa stays safe, and we'll get the other girls back to Somerville safe and sound, too."

"I appreciate that, Tug. I hate to run out on everyone, but I was lucky to be able to get over here for this. But we both know what would have happened if I hadn't come."

"You got that right. Good night, Charlie. Stay safe and call me when you're ready. I will call Max and see what he's up to and how he can help, if at all."

"That would be great, Tug. I guess you and I were meant to be in the thick of it, as they say."

"In the thick of it can be a lonely place, Charlie."

"Especially for a man who has greater plans for himself."

Tug said, "Well, I'll be darned. You didn't mention that sitting on the bench."

"I didn't want to put too much on you at one time."

"Well, turnabout is fair play, I guess."

Charles looked at Tug warily eye. "What?"

"I said turnabout is fair play. I have something to tell you, too. Lindy is expecting. She told me before she came over here, and I'm still trying to get used to that idea."

Charles smiled broadly at the good news. "I'm so happy for you, Tug. You are a great couple. When?"

"I haven't gotten that much out of her yet. I don't think she would have told me at all except she got sick on the boat coming over here. She didn't want me to say anything because this is your and Willa's weekend."

"Well, we both have a lot going on. Willa doesn't know what I'm thinking yet, but I'll tell her and soon. Then you and I will talk, and I'll tell you about my future plans."

Tug said, "I think I can guess, but what you should do is run for the Senate, Charles, in Maryland, and help us get rid of Buddy Dawes. The game of politics is in your blood and it's a family business with you Lees."

"I guess you could say that. There sure have been a few political giants in my bloodline. We'll see how this turns out. One never knows. What you think one minute is a good idea can head south in a heartbeat."

Tug patted Charles on the shoulder. "Can't wait to see how it all goes. Be safe going back to Washington."

Chapter Five

When everyone had finally gone home or back to the mainland, Frances and Jimmy joined Millie and Richard and walked over to the island store for a last cup of coffee. They rolled the borrowed cart along with them, the one that had made a grand entrance to the event, proudly displaying the incredible welcome cake.

"Ye sure outdid yourself with that cake, Millie," Frances said, yawning.

"I haven't baked a cake that size for quite some time. It took some doing. I'm used to the regular-sized cakes I do every day."

"By the way, how's that comin' for ye?"

"Very well, thank ye, Frances. I get more and more orders every day, and there's a lady who is going to open up a new store just for them over by Cambridge, so things are going well."

"Darned if those cakes aren't the talk of everyone these days. People are learning about the island cakes more and more, so hang on; yer in fer a lot of orders."

"But some cakes being sold aren't original island cakes. There are a lot of copycats, but only a few are the real McCoy."

When they arrived at the store, Nellie came to unlock the door for them. "It sure was a wonderful cake, Miss Millie. Your cakes are the best!"

"Thank you, Nellie. Do ye have any coffee in there?"

"Funny you should ask. Denny just put a new pot on the stove. So go on in and get you some."

"C'mon, let's all go in and have a cup and sit a spell."

Denny was just finishing putting all the leftovers away in the big refrigerator in the back when he heard the noise at the front door. "What do we have here? I would have thought you all would be going on home after all the excitement."

Frances looked at him kind of funny and said, "The real excitement was Miss Ruby and her gang from over on Ewell. Isn't she something?"

"I think she's great," answered Jimmy. "She sure brings the life to a party."

"I don't know about that, Jimmy," Millie piped up. "She sure is large and getting larger every day. I watched her eat three pieces of that cake, and I swear I could see her expanding right there on the spot."

"Now, Millie, ye shouldn't go on like that. She's a wonderful lady and you know it."

With no break in her thought, Millie continued, "She wasn't always that way. Way back in school, she was quite pretty."

Richard winked at his wife and said, "Yes, she was, and, as I remember, ye were pretty jealous of her at one time, thinking I took a fancy to her. Now, Millie, ye know ye were always the gal I was going to marry."

Millie stood up from the chair she had just sat down in and looked him straight in the eye. "Richard Evans, you got the best of the bunch and ye know it."

They all laughed as Nellie brought over mugs of fresh-brewed coffee. "Here y'all go. Miss Millie, I am short on your cake slices, so can you please bake me up a couple for the store?"

"Sure will, Nellie. By the way, how is your research going on the waters around here?"

"Thank you for asking. It's going slow, but good. I'm so happy the headquarters let me stay out here to do the work."

Frances smiled at the daughter she was so proud of and said, "Would have been a pretty hard time trying to keep a marriage going that far away, and I would have missed you something terrible."

Denny heard that as he walked over to them. He put his arm around Nellie's shoulder and added, "It wouldn't have mattered where Nellie was; I would love her just the same."

Jimmy smiled at his son-in-law as he pulled a chair out for Nellie to sit in. He liked Denny and had known him all his life. He often went out on the Bay with the young man, and he had always known that, one day, that young boy would grow up and marry his daughter.

Richard sat back in his chair and stretched. "Sure was a nice reception, wasn't it?"

"Sure was," Millie answered. Just as she said that, in walked Tug and Lindy, smiling as though they were the ones who had just gotten married.

Lindy was surprised to see everyone. "What's going on here? Are we having another party, and no one told us?"

"Now don't fuss, Lindy," Frances said. "Just come on and sit down with us. We're just hashing over the big party."

As Lindy grabbed another chair to join them, she smiled and said, "They look so happy. As happy as Tug and me."

Frances wanted to say something about their new surprise, but kept silent. She was so happy Tug and Lindy's marriage was working out so well. She had to admit to herself that, on more than one occasion, she had wondered if Tug wouldn't get bored with country folks and want to go back to Boston, where his kind enjoyed city life. However, as the year passed along, she saw how much he adored Lindy Short and how he had really taken to their lives down here. He had thrown himself into his work, and, even though he complained about that old house of Dickie's, she knew he would never easily move out of it. It was his bond to that old man.

"How's the house coming, Tug?"

Tug's eyes rolled in desperation. "It's a slow go right now, Frances. I sometimes wonder why Dickie didn't fix the things that were broken."

Millie looked at the young man and said, "Because the one thing that was broken the most was his heart, and, when that goes, ye don't fix anything."

Tug knew she was right. "But couldn't he still have fixed some things, Miss Millie?"

"When Shirley died, we all knew he would never be the same. The Dickie Short who went out on the water no matter what, and would stop out to the island twice a week to talk to the men in their shanties, was gone mostly. The brightest spot in his life was Shirley, and I'm not sure he realized how much he needed her and how much he loved her until she died. He was lost. They had an unusual, but good, marriage. Lindy here was their prize in life, and, when you came along, Tug, he was determined to make you fall in love with the way of life here, and with his little girl."

Tug sat silent, thinking about what she had said. He had never thought of Dickie being that clever, but then Dickie had been a mischief-maker.

"You might be somewhat right, Millie, but I think I would have loved this place anyway. I think it was always in me to be by the water and with people whose lives took on a deeper meaning from the day-to-day. People who understood their heritage and would do anything to keep it. And as for Lindy?" Tug looked at his wife and said, "He didn't have to try very hard there at all. She is my other half, and, if I had stayed in Baltimore or gone back to

Boston, I would have spent my whole life looking for her. We think the same thoughts, as odd as that may sound."

Lindy sat there with tears in her eyes. She was so in love with her husband and wondered how she could be so lucky. His fancy upbringing and education never stood between them. She knew he was smarter than she, but she was more practical than he was. That made them the couple they were. She was determined to keep at it and finish her education, but it would come slowly. And now, with a baby on the way, their life together would be absolutely perfect. But she would never give up on her education.

Frances knew exactly what the girl was thinking and hoped Millie didn't make her feel uncomfortable or inferior to Tug. Lindy Short could have had any young man here, but she hadn't wanted that. She had wanted an educated man and Dickie had wanted that for her, too. He may have been a waterman all his life, but he was well aware of what his little Lindy wanted and needed. Frances felt the same about Nellie. Nellie had been determined to get an education and Denny just wanted to be on the water, but the good Lord knows how to put people together, and, when they married, she was well satisfied her daughter hadn't made a mistake. And, one day, maybe she would live to see a grandchild, too.

Millie was tired, as the rest of them were. "Time to go now, Richard. Church tomorrow and then dinner to make, so we all best be heading on home."

Frances sighed and then said, "Yep, a woman's work is never done. Time to go, Jimmy."

Nellie picked up the cups as Denny made sure everything in the store was all set for the next day. "Good night, everybody. See y'all in church."

The group took different paths, so not much was said on their way to their homes. It had been a joyous day and a lot of fun was once again had. They all worked so hard, but, when they had fun, it was always the best.

Chapter Six

The next morning was as beautiful as a July day could be. Charles awoke early and made coffee for himself and tea for his bride. Willa heard him and got up, washed her face, and went into the kitchen. There she snuggled up against her husband, contented and happy.

"Good morning, Mrs. Lee."

"You know it doesn't matter how many times you say that to me, I will just never get tired of hearing it."

"Good thing because I'm not letting you out of this contract."

"Spoken like the good lawyer you are."

"All that money spent on law school at UVA wasn't wasted then, huh?"

Charles went to break off and get his coffee, but Willa held on a bit longer. "I don't want to let go."

"A natural reaction after all the carrying on last night."

Willa blushed and then added, "I didn't notice that you weren't enjoying it."

Now he blushed and did pull away, then reached for the cup and poured his coffee. "Your tea is steeping in the pot over there."

With an overemphasized southern accent, Willa said, "Why, Congressman Lee, I do thank you."

"You know, Willa, you would have given Scarlett a run for her money."

"And I suppose you think you're Rhett Butler?"

Charles smiled, then said in a very heavy drawl, "Why, my dear, I *am* Rhett Butler."

Willa giggled. "We are something. I'm not quite sure what, but we are something."

Charles sat down at the small table and looked around. "What are we going to do with this old house you bought?"

"We're going to fix it up."

"Well, if we're going to do that, can we get an architect? Because I think we should switch the house around so our kitchen overlooks the Bay."

"What a great idea, Charlie. It's dark back here and that would change everything."

"It would be nice to get up every morning and look out on the water. And we can expand the porch some so we can have folks over and sit out there."

"Well, only when the bugs aren't out."

"Oh, you're right, Willa. Good point."

Willa got her tea and sat down, thinking about what Charlie had just said. "You know, you're so right about the kitchen being in the front of the house."

Charlie took her hand and said, "I love you so much, Willa. And now that we are going to have real neighbors here, I will try hard to get out here as much as I can."

Willa smiled at this new husband of hers. "I know you will and I love you for saying that. It means a lot to me. I want us to stay happy together forever."

"You're such a romantic, aren't you? Glad one of us is, but, right now, I have to get going. I hired a man from Somerville to come get me, as everyone here goes to church and the island is on hold until sundown."

"Kind of old-fashioned, but I like it. I remember our Sundays as so special. My father wouldn't work on his comic strip and my mother would cook a Sunday dinner after church. She usually made a nice roast and oven potatoes. I can still smell that dinner when I close my eyes."

Charles saw her sadness, so he hugged her and added his own memory. "I know what you mean, Willa. In the South, we made a big thing of dressing up and going to church, and then the lunch afterward was so good with so many southern dishes. Verinnia and I would eat and then go off, maybe down to the fishing hole, and sit for a couple of hours just talking about everything. Or nothing. We've always been close. Sundays were different from any other day, and I think we lost a lot when we stopped having that special day in the week. We must bring that back in our own home."

Willa nodded and said, "Life moves too fast these days, and people don't get to visit their friends and just sit back and relax. I know I miss Prue so much. I think about all the times we would meet at The Willard and have drinks and talk about all the things that go on in Washington. I was so shocked when she walked in."

"When who walked in?"

Sleepy voiced and still stretching, Prue came into the small kitchen. Willa was surprised to see her so early.

"Prue, you're up. I hope we didn't wake you."

In a mischievous voice, Prue said, "No, that was late last night."

Charles's face turned crimson red. "Prue, I don't believe you just said that."

"Cat got your tongue, Charles?"

"Got me there. Want some coffee?"

"You bet. It smells heavenly."

As he headed toward the coffee pot, Charles said, "Prue, have you heard anything about any legislation on the Hill concerning farmers?"

Prue rubbed her eyes and yawned. "Really, Congressman, don't you think it's a bit early for talking politics?"

"Maybe, but I'm leaving in a little while and thought maybe you had."

"A little inside information for you, Charles?"

"Well, have you?"

Willa rolled her eyes and said, "You two talk D.C. now. But I am going up to check on Vernie and see if she was kept up late last night by our debauchery."

"Okay, Willa, but you could stay here and listen to me tell Charles all the latest gossip."

"You two have at it."

As Willa left the room, Charles said, "Thanks, Prue, for coming. I know how much this means to Willa."

"I almost didn't come because I am underwater now with so much work to do."

"Are you enjoying it?"

"Sometimes, but you know the man I work for now isn't you, Charles."

"But you needed a change, Prue. Besides, you will eventually leave him and go on to a business that works for the government and make three times the money."

"You're right about that and it may happen sooner than you think. I've had offers lately, and, soon, one may be too good to turn down. However, it may not be a business; it may be something else, but I can't say just now."

"I can guess. And let me know if I can help you in any way."

"I will. Now what's this about the farmers? I thought you would have had enough fighting for the watermen and their rights."

"Oh, I'm still at that, but it's coming along. Slower than I would like, but at least now we're all talking. I may have to get Frances involved again. I haven't said anything but she may have to come back to D.C."

"Well, D.C. needs some shaking up, and, if anyone can do it, Frances Evans can."

"But now I keep getting letters from farmers on the shore and they just can't keep up with all the changing legislation that has been passed lately. They are asking if there is anything I can do."

"Well, is there?"

"The people are trying to do it by elections only, but you and I know that elections are only for a cycle and then things can change again. What we need to find is a more permanent solution. I am working with a congressman from Maryland, but it's a slow go."

"I really haven't heard anything, but what seems to be the biggest beef?"

"Well, right now, it's getting people to understand why the farmers need to grow soybeans and corn. It's for the chicken industry."

"That sounds easy."

"I know, but nothing is easy anymore. Too much red tape and regulating, if you ask me."

Prue looked at him a minute and then said, "Sounds to me as if you're heading right back into the frying pan again, Charles."

"I know it, and, right now, I really don't want to do that. I have so much else going on."

Prue laughed and said, "You're right about that. Why not take some time off from the crusades? Work on your own state and your marriage."

"You're forgetting Maryland is my state too now, isn't it?"

"Got me there. Well, I better go see what's going on upstairs with Vernie. Thanks for the coffee. I wish I could have helped you more."

"We'll see how this goes. Right now I need to get dressed and ready to leave my Willa."

Prue said, "That's my cue. If you're leaving, then so am I. I think Vernie is staying on with Willa, isn't she?"

"Yes, Willa begged her to last night and Vernie would never turn down her new sister-in-law. She's wanted a sister all her life and now she has one. The two of them will no doubt get themselves into a lot of trouble here."

"Why would you say that? There's nothing to do here to get into trouble unless they are planning to go out fishing."

"Worse than that, Prue. Willa is going to begin planning how to resurrect this house."

"Oh, you poor man. You better protect your bank account."

"Better yet, she needs to write a new best seller."

Prue laughed and then added, "If you two keep at it, she will be writing from her own romantic experience."

Charles chose to leave that comment alone as he padded out of the kitchen and to their first-floor bedroom.

Vernie and Willa were deep into plotting the overhaul of the house when Prue got back upstairs. She brought a properly brewed cup of tea with her for Charles's sister.

"How lovely of you. How did you know I preferred tea in the morning over coffee?"

"Lucky guess. I think somewhere in the back of my mind I remember my mother saying southern ladies drank tea in the mornings."

"Well, she was right. Coffee seems so harsh on one's stomach when you first get up."

Willa patted Vernie's hand and remarked, "Not much has changed for the southern lady all these years. They still keep so many of their old customs."

"We like our customs," Vernie replied. "It keeps us in touch with our roots and where we came from. It's not that different here, I imagine. These island folks are nearer to being southern than anything else."

"That's the truth. Charles and I have commented on that many times. They speak with a sort of Olde English when they say 'ye' instead of you and a few other quaint things. And, of course, they are descendants of the settlers from Virginia in Jamestown and thereabouts. So, really, you might say they are southern-certified."

"Oh, Willa, that's a stretch, don't you think?"

"Not at all, Prue. Ask them. They'll tell you that their hearts are much nearer to the South than to the North."

"Well, next time I am over here I will do that, but, right now, if I don't get moving, I will miss the boat Charles is going back on."

Willa's look turned sad. "I wish you didn't have to go back so soon."

Prue put her arm around her dear friend and squeezed. "I know; I wish it, too. But that congressman of mine isn't going to think kindly of the fact that I couldn't get into work because I was out here in the Chesapeake having a grand time."

"Aren't they all rascals?" Vernie piped up.

Willa chuckled and said, "Well, next time you visit us, Prue, you'll stay longer and the house will be in better shape than it is right now."

"Charles was just telling me about your grandiose plans for this place. Heaven help that man. Does he know how much you enjoy spending money?"

Willa held up her hand and said, "No, he does not, and, if you say one word, you will feel this hand come down on your head. Besides, I have a ton of money myself, so I don't need to go picking his pocket."

"Oh, I forgot about that," Prue said sarcastically.

"I intend to make this the loveliest, most beautiful house on the island."

"Oh, I'm sure they'll love you for that, Willa. Be careful. These are wonderful but simple people. They might not like you coming in and changing things so dramatically."

"I know that, Prue. I wouldn't ever do anything to make them feel inferior. I love them and wouldn't want Miss Frances to ever think I was doing something to make her and her people uncomfortable. Glad you reminded me of that."

"That's what friends are for, and, besides, I like these folks a lot myself. I have never felt so welcomed to a place. Ever."

"The only other place I ever felt like this was in Maine where my parents and I would head off for the summers. Mother wrote and Father drew his cartoon strips. We all loved it so much. I miss it and them terribly."

Vernie didn't know much about her sister-in-law's background but she could tell there was a story behind this statement. She said, "Well, you have it again now, Willa, and, while I don't know what happened to make you look so sad at those memories, life has worked out for you and my brother. He's such a dream and a wonderful brother. He's had his rough spots, too, especially with our father, but it seems they worked through them before Father died."

Willa smiled at this dear sister of Charles. She could see she had been indulged but not spoiled completely, and she knew that Vernie's husband, Tom, was a true southern gentleman and that she loved him dearly.

Willa realized, here she sat with love all around her. Except she wished Prue would one day meet a man so she could feel the same deep and abiding love she possessed now. She would have to work on that when she got back to Washington. But now she had things to do to help get Prue ready to leave with Charles.

Prue shot to the shower and then pulled a spring green sweater over her head, pairing it with casual black pants. She was a beauty, and, as she dabbed on some light makeup, Willa thought about who she could get to go out on a date with Prue.

"I know what you're doing, Willa. Remember we've been friends for a long time. I'm not interested."

"Not interested in what?"

"In what you're dreaming up. I have a career to mind right now, and you know I'm not stopping until I am president of a company. Or something. I am just using these politicians until my own ship comes in."

"Well, what if that ship's captain is the man of your dreams?"

"Are you writing now in your head, or are you making an attempt to be serious?"

Willa smiled gently and answered, "Both."

Shouting from the bottom of the stairs, Charles yelled, "Prue, you better be ready. We have ten minutes to get down to that dock and I need to see my wife before we do."

Willa turned and flew down the stairs. Charles led her back to their bedroom for privacy. "Willa, I hate to leave you, but you understand what is waiting for me back home."

"I know, Charlie. I just hate good-byes."

"I do, too, so we won't say good-bye." He took her in his arms and kissed her passionately.

Coming up for air, Willa said, "I may not let you go anywhere after that."

"Just remember: if one of these watermen makes eyes at you . . ."

Willa swatted him on his rear and giggled. "Fat chance. I'm in love with you, Charlie. You're stuck with me."

"See you back home in D.C., love. Be careful and I'll call you tonight."

"You better; I'll be waiting. And don't worry about Vernie. We'll have the best time."

He left the bedroom, joined Prue, and they both turned and waved as they walked out the door.

Vernie had come down to say good-bye to her brother and noticed the look of dismay on Willa's face. The young woman who could be as cold as steel in her business was now crushed and beginning to cry, saying good-bye to the man she loved.

"Come on, Willa, let's get dressed, and then take a lovely walk around this island. I'd love to see it through your eyes. And then, maybe, later on, we could think about leisurely naps? Yesterday was a long day!"

Willa smiled and said, "You're on."

Chapter Seven

Vernie was thrilled to be able to spend this time with her new sister-in-law. It didn't matter to her whether they were in Washington or out here on this magical island. The point was that she desperately wanted to get to know Willa, both as a famous writer and also the woman who had been able to catch her brother. So many had tried to get Charles. He had definitely been the most eligible bachelor anywhere in Virginia. To southern girls, he was the catch of all time because he was a Lee. But to Verinnia Lee, he was just a brother and the most wonderful one at that.

Willa was finished dressing and ready to go. It was Monday morning, and she had so much more she wanted to show Vernie before it was time for her return to Virginia.

Willa, in very casual clothes, shouted up to Vernie that she was ready. And Vernie was wearing clothes as close to casual as she had: a pair of light cream cotton slacks with a very expensive knit top to match.

"I must say, you are a bit overdressed for today's adventure, Vernie. Do you have any jeans?"

"I don't wear jeans, Willa. I know that makes me the oddest person in America, but I don't like them, and I never can get a pair that fits me right."

"Sounds like two great reasons to me, but I hope you don't mind if the clothes you have on now get dirty."

"Nooo," she dragged out. "But what are we going to be doing to get them dirty?"

"Don't know for sure, but you can't ever tell when you're out here. We won't worry about that now. Let's just walk over to Bradshaw's and have some of those crab cakes you've wanted to try. Actually, I would have thought you might have had enough crabs yesterday to last you awhile."

"I didn't eat any yesterday, to be honest with you, Willa."

"Should I ask why?"

"Sure. I didn't want to get those pants dirty, and, even if I didn't care about that, watching people picking at those poor things made me feel sorry for them."

"And you want to eat crab cakes today . . . why?"

"Well, there will be the meat, and all mixed up, kind of like shrimp salad. Not all those buggy eyes staring at me just like they looked before they were loaded into the boiling pot."

Willa wasn't going to say another word. Apparently Charles's sister had some odd notions, and she would have to work around them if they were to get off to a good start. Heaven forbid she should ask Vernie if she liked lobster.

They walked up the steps of the store and in. As luck would have it, neither Nellie nor Denny was there, but a young woman was behind the counter.

Willa said, "Hi, there! We have come to order a few broiled crab cakes for lunch."

The woman stared at her, then found her senses and said, "You're her, aren't you?"

Willa was puzzled. "Who's *her*?"

"Oh, my heavens, I've gone and embarrassed myself. I'm so sorry."

"You haven't embarrassed yourself at all, but who do you think I am?"

"That wonderful romance writer."

Willa just smiled as the young woman, now red-faced, turned to get the crab cakes out of the refrigerator. Vernie poked Willa and whispered, "See, you're not Charles's wife here; you're the romance writer."

"Shh, Vernie! I don't want to embarrass her." Then she quietly walked over to the area where the grill was and said, "We'll sit over there, if you don't mind."

"Mind? Why, not at all. Do you both want slaw on the side?"

Vernie answered, "Absolutely, I want the slaw."

Willa leaned over to the clerk and asked, "Who are you?"

"Oh, I'm Willy's wife. Willy Deavers. He's a waterman and I help Nellie and Denny here. Oh, my name is Maude. I get a little tongue-tied sometimes and this sure is one of them. If you are that writer, you should know I have read almost every one of your books and I love the way you write. Will you be writing out here when you come on weekends?"

"Yes, sometimes I will, I'm sure. Were you at the party yesterday? I don't remember meeting you, although I met so many people. I can't remember all their names."

"Oh, yes, I was there, and you were about the prettiest one in the hall. I was helping to get the food out on the table."

"Well, you did a wonderful job. It was a great party."

"Oh, I'm glad you liked it, Miss Willa. Your husband is famous too, isn't he?"

"I guess you could say that." Willa pointed toward to their table and said, "And this is his sister, Verinnia."

Maude peered over the counter and waved at Vernie.

Vernie smiled and waved back. Manners were very important to Verinnia Lee.

"You go on and relax, Miss Willa, I'll bring the crab cakes to you directly."

Willa walked back to sit down, looking, as she did, at all the things in the store. It was really an amazing place. A little this, a little that, including some of her books for sale. Seems Nellie must have made sure they were in the store. She noted that none of them were signed, and she would do that sometime during this visit to the island. And she would thank Nellie when she saw her.

Willa sat down about the same time Maude delivered their lunch.

Vernie took a deep whiff and said, "These smell heavenly."

"They're the best crab cakes anywhere," Maude said with great pride.

Vernie squeezed some lemon juice on the crab and sunk her teeth in. She sat back and munched away, then said, "These are heaven."

Willa agreed. "Yes, they are. I've had them before, and I can attest to them being the best anywhere around."

"Well, you two ladies enjoy, and if you want anything else, I'm just over there. Give a shout."

Willa nodded that she would, but knew that Vernie would never yell out. Oh no, that just wouldn't do.

Vernie seemed to inhale the crab cakes and slaw. She looked as if she wanted another one.

Willa said, "I'll be glad to get you another one, Vernie."

"Oh, I just couldn't, but they are amazing."

Willa stood up and walked over to the counter. "Maude, dear, we would love two more, please."

Vernie's eyes got like saucers. "I don't believe I'm going to do this."

"Live it up a little. I won't tell."

When the crab cakes were devoured and they were truly full to the brim, the two of them got up, paid their bill, and walked outside. For some reason, they both started laughing.

Willa looked at Vernie and said, "What are you laughing at?"

"The same thing you are. We don't believe we ate two of those babies and now we certainly won't want anything else to eat for the rest of the day."

"I think you're right about that, but you never know. Now we're going to take a walk down to the Co-op."

"To where?"

"Start walking and I'll tell you." As Willa proceeded to explain to Verinnia all about the co-op where women picked the crabs, she stopped and said hello to everyone who was out and about. It was so much fun meeting her new community, and she knew all over again that she and Charles had made the right decision in buying a house out here.

By the time they arrived at the Co-op, Vernie understood all about it and was a bit scared, but also intrigued at how women made their living out here. And how industrious Miss Frances had been to establish this place. Vernie was beginning to fall in love with the island, too.

Nellie and Frances were both inside, and, when Willa and Vernie walked in, they shouted, "Here comes the bride."

Willa turned beet red but loved it. "We were just down at the store, Nellie. We missed seeing you."

"I had work to do this morning and then decided to come on down here with Mom. Has either of you ever picked a crab?"

Vernie began to step back as if to hide behind Willa. She tugged at her knit top, signaling that this would be a great time to run. Right now.

Willa couldn't stand there and say nothing, so she answered, "Well, I . . . no, I've never picked a crab, and I don't think Vernie has either. Have you, Vernie?"

Vernie looked like a beaten-down dog. She knew she was in for it now.

"Well then," said Frances, "no time like the present. Pull up a chair and we'll show you."

If Vernie made it through this, she could make it through anything. Willa felt sorry for her. Almost as sorry as she felt for herself right now.

"Looky here, you take the crab and turn her over. Now, you can tell it's a she because her claws look like they have polish on them."

Frances went on like that until, when she cracked the crab open and began picking, Vernie leaned toward Willa and then dropped like a swatted fly. Thud! She was down for the count.

Nellie ran to her, bringing a lemon for her to smell. When Vernie opened her eyes, she was clearly begging Willa to be allowed to leave.

Frances said, "She's back with us. Nothing to feel bad about, child; it happens to a lot of outlanders the first time they pick."

Vernie finally got up and stood there. She took a deep breath and said—very politely, of course—"You must excuse me. I need some air."

Willa watched her dear sister-in-law run out of the building. They all knew what she was going to do and Willa waited a few moments, giving her some time to lose the lovely crab cakes she had just eaten. Then she smiled at Frances, Nellie, and the rest of the ladies, and walked outside.

Vernie was sitting on the grass, looking as if she had been beaten up. Her long, dark hair was scattered all over her head, her expensive top was totally askew, and her cream slacks were stained with grass, slobber, and some of what she had just enjoyed for lunch.

Good grief. She's completely come unraveled.

"Come on, Vernie. I'll take you back home and you can shower and get fixed up. I think we've had enough fun for the day."

Vernie stood on wobbly legs and said, "I'm not so sure I could make it living out here. You are so brave, Willa."

Chapter Eight

While Willa sat on the front porch, still chuckling about her sister-in-law's experience with picking crabs, Vernie was upstairs licking her wounds from the embarrassment. Her shower was going to feel very good indeed, and then she would see what she could do to salvage her clothes.

Willa got up and went into the kitchen to get a glass of iced tea just as her cell phone rang. She looked at the caller's number and her heart jumped. It was Charles. She said, "Hello, sweetie."

"Hello, Willa. I'm almost back but wanted to ask if there was anything special you need me to do here before you get back."

"How thoughtful. I guess I would have to say, don't have any pretty young women come stay with you. But, other than that, I think everything is in order."

"Gee, you're tough on a guy." Charles laughed. "You know better. How are things going?"

Willa hesitated a moment and then said, "Well, I don't know if your sister will ever come back out here."

"I have been gone only a few hours, Willa. What could possibly have gone wrong in that short a time?"

"Crabs, that's what."

"Should I even ask?"

"Why not? I took your sister over to see the Co-op, and, before you know it, she was asked if she wanted to pick a crab—"

"Oh my God, don't even finish this story. Vernie always hated fish, and whenever I would go and bring them back, she would take off screaming. She said she hated looking at their eyes."

"I have to say she was a good sport, but when Frances cracked it down the middle . . . well, that's when she lost it. Fell right over. Passed out. And when she came to, she stood up a minute and then ran out and vomited all over her clothes."

Charles started laughing and couldn't stop. "I can only imagine the scene."

"No, Congressman, you can't. She was sick, embarrassed, her clothes were stained all over, and she looked like she had been at a Texas rodeo all night."

"Oh, Willa, that's too funny a picture to behold. Where is she now?"

"Well, she's still here, but I'm not sure she'll go outside again until she has to leave."

Charles said, "You'll help her over it. And I'm sure those folks have seen it all. Her incident can't have been the first one."

"She'll be fine. She's upstairs taking a shower and that will make her feel so much better. However, I think those clothes may not make it back home. Small price to pay really. She's lucky a crab didn't pinch her finger. Now *that* she would remember for a long time."

"Appears I can't leave you for a minute, my dear wife. You are destined for adventures."

"They make good fodder for novels."

"Miss you, Willa. How long do you think you'll stay over there?"

"How big is our budget for the resurrection of Willa's Cottage?"

"Oh-oh, I think I'm in trouble. You've now named it, but first things first. Figure out exactly what all you want and need to do—with the operative word being *need*."

"Oh, Charles, families lived in this house as it is for decades and decades, so need has very little to do with it."

"I forgot, I'm dealing with a woman, and one who has very good and pricey taste. So do what you want. I mean, you'll just write another book to pay for it, right?"

"You got it, Prince Charming." Willa smiled and then said, "Seriously, I miss you, too, Charlie, so I won't stay out here too long. But we'll talk, and I'll know when I've had enough. You said you were going to be busy this week anyway. Something about farms?"

"Yes, I have some farmers coming in to talk about their businesses and what's going on."

"Well, good luck and let me know."

Suddenly there was silence and then Charles speaking: "What? Willa, are you still there?"

When the sound cleared, Willa was saying, "I hate these things."

"It's the reception out there, not the phone. I love you, Willa. Talk to you tomorrow."

"I love you too, Charlie."

As they ended the conversation, there was a shared emptiness, but Willa also knew her time here was very important and Charlie's time in Washington was, too.

Vernie pushed open the wooden front screen door and walked out.

"Well, don't you look like a breath of springtime?"

"Willa, I'm so sorry I embarrassed you, myself—"

"Stop it, Vernie. No one will say anything to you, nor do they think you're anything but a lovely southern lady."

"I just feel so awful about the entire matter."

"Well, crabs may not be your calling. How about cakes?"

"Cakes? Who doesn't like cakes?"

"Weight Watchers."

"Well, I think they even have cakes you can eat now."

"Probably so. No, I mean would you like to see how they make one of the famous James Island Cakes?"

"Oh, yes, I think that would be lovely. I don't think I would get sick doing that."

"I would hope not. C'mon. We'll walk over to Miss Millie's and see if she would mind us poking around while she bakes some, and find out what time we should be up and over there. Besides, you'll love her home."

"Okay, I think that would be a fine idea. Am I dressed all right to go visiting?"

"Oh, Vernie, it's an island, not a tea party."

Miss Millie was preparing supper when the two of them knocked on her front door.

"Richard, would you go see who that is? My hands are all tied up here with the fixings."

"Yes, dear." When he opened the door, he was surprised but delighted to see their guests and invited them in.

"Hello, Mr. Evans. We're sorry to barge in at suppertime, but we wondered if we could ask Miss Millie a question?"

"You're not bothering us at all, Willa. Come right in and make yourselves to home."

Richard showed them to the kitchen and Vernie's eyes swept around the room. "It's so lovely in here. I would never have imagined it this way."

"I told you it was pretty," Willa said. "Miss Millie and Mr. Richard were childhood sweethearts and have done well for themselves over the years."

"I'll say." Vernie turned to Millie. "You keep your house real southern with a wonderful combination of furnishings, wall hangings, and lots of personal accessories. You know how us southern folks like to do that—pictures of all our forebearers and such."

Willa still was shocked at how southern the Lee family was. She didn't see Charles as being quite so entrenched in this southern way. She certainly saw his impeccable manners and how he treated a lady, but, really, was he this far out? But then, he was a clotheshorse of sorts; everything had to match. And he did like to celebrate occasions. She had never really thought about it until now, as she got to know his sister. Wow!

"You will stay on for some supper with us, won't you?" Miss Millie was always so hospitable. Indeed, the perfect southern lady.

"Supper? I don't think we could impose on you for that, Miss Millie."

"Why, it wouldn't be an imposition at all; you're welcome if you want to. It's just a simple meal of crab soup and some ham."

Willa didn't dare look at Vernie. She smiled sweetly and said, "Well, what we really came for was to ask you, Miss Millie, if we could both come around early tomorrow morning and watch you make your famous island cakes?"

"Why, I would be honored. I have a big order to get out, so you might just be able to help me some with it, if you wouldn't mind."

Vernie was in heaven. She had met a woman who reminded her so much of home. "We would love it, wouldn't we, Willa?"

Willa hadn't seen her this happy before, so she eagerly nodded. "Of course, we would be happy to help. What time should we come?"

"Oh, I get going very early. About four should be okay. I get the ovens started and then we can start with the batter and all."

The big smile started to disappear a little off Vernie's face. Willa caught the look, but Vernie had started this so she owned it now. "That would be fine."

"Oh, good news! Now won't you come on and join us for supper?"

Willa was going to take charge now. "You are too kind, Miss Millie, but I think we'll call it an early night so we can be bright eyed and bushy tailed for you in the morning. Vernie and I have had quite a day already, and I think we'll just get something simple for supper and then be off to bed."

"Well, another time then, Willa. I always want you to feel right at home with us here in Tuckerton. You're one of us now."

"And Charles and I are thrilled. See you in the morning and thank you."

As the two young women walked away from the Evans house, Vernie said, "I can't get my eyes on at that hour, let alone my hair curled and combed out."

"Well, you'll make the best of it, I'm sure, dear. It'll be worth it. I've never seen her bake these icons of the Chesapeake either, so I will get up and get us tea and get us going. Do all you need to do tonight before bed."

Vernie looked at her with a syrupy southern smile and said, "In order to do that, Willa, I will have to roll up my hair, comb it out, put my clothes on, and sleep standing up."

"Hey, whatever works for you."

Willa set out a quick and easy outfit for the morning, her weekend stock-in-trade: a pair of clean jeans and a sweatshirt. Verinnia was going to be another matter. Willa ran up the stairs and, when she got to the guest room, was caught off guard at what she was looking at.

There stood Vernie in front of a long mirror in all her glory, with a pair of bikini underpants and a push-up bra that explained exactly how such a small gal could have a bosom the size of Texas. When she saw Willa, she smiled sweetly and said, "I have given this being ready early a great deal of thought and have come to the conclusion that I might fare better if I looked a bit more like the rest of the people here, so, 'when in Rome,' as they say. Could you be a dear and lend me a pair of your jeans?"

Willa was speechless, not only at the sight of her standing there assessing herself as if she were going up for sale in an expensive New York auction house, but that Vernie had just asked to borrow an honest-to-goodness, down-to-earth pair of blue jeans. Good God, what was the South going to say about this?

"Oh, you don't want to lend them to me? I'm so sorry for asking."

"Oh, Vernie, don't be ridiculous. You're Charles's sister; you can have anything I have. It's just that you made such a big thing out of not ever wearing jeans. Come on downstairs and let's take a look. I'm bigger than you, but I have a belt or two that might solve that problem." While Willa was a stunner, she tended to carry the weight she did have right through her hips. She was always on a diet and exercised all the time, but being a writer had its downsides, and being sedentary a good deal of the time was one of them.

Willa pulled a couple of pairs of jeans out of her dresser and held them up for Vernie's inspection. She had brought a bunch of clothes over after they had bought the house, right before they married. She always wanted to be prepared, and it seemed that this was one of those times it was good she was such a meticulous planner.

"Well, what do you think?"

"I didn't realize that jeans came in colors. They're lovely."

Willa smiled at her. "I wear the colored ones for special activities over here. They don't look quite so much like blue jeans. I do like them a lot."

Vernie looked at each one carefully and then stopped at a particular pair. "This one. This is the one for cake baking."

"How did you come to that conclusion?"

"They're pink and remind me of icing."

Willa looked at her inquisitively, but let it go and said, "Why, yes, that makes sense." She, of course, didn't mean it, but she figured it would be the kind thing to say. "Try them on so we can fit them before we go to sleep."

"Good idea. There won't be an extra minute in the wee hours."

Vernie pulled them on, and, surprisingly, they fit her very well. A belt of Willa's did the trick to make them perfect. "I love them," Vernie cried. "Will you look at me, wearing jeans?"

Willa raised her eyebrows and said, "Miracle of miracles. Wonder what your southern girlfriends would say about this?"

Vernie's head snapped up quickly in defense of her friends. "They would love it. You see, I am the only one left in my gaggle who won't wear them. They will be positively hysterical when I tell them how I came to break my southern vows."

Willa was nearly in tears, laughing so hard. How could Charles, thoughtful man that he was, have such a simple sister? It wasn't that she was dumb, but she sure wasn't a rocket scientist either. Willa put an arm around her. "Vernie, you are one in a million. Here's a sweatshirt to go with

51

them. This isn't anything fancy—just a plain old gray sweatshirt—but gray is the new chic, you know."

"No, I didn't know that, but I can see how that could happen. Gray must be one of those neutral colors my mama used to tell me about. She taught me so much, but then she died, leaving Daddy desolate and Charles and me to go on by ourselves. Now Daddy's dead, too."

Willa stood there silent, not wanting to divulge the intimate conversations she and Charles had shared about his mother's death. He had rarely spoken of it; she knew it was something that had deeply hurt him.

Vernie continued, "We were so very young, and then Daddy met another, much younger woman than Mama. She took up most of his time at first, but, after a while, he came back to us. She didn't like that much but Daddy didn't care. I think he felt very guilty about his goings-on with her. Don't get me wrong, Willa; she warmed to us in time and ended up being rather sweet about it all, but she wasn't our mama. You only get one of them."

Now it was Willa who was noticeably quiet. Vernie felt awful. "I am a fool, and I am sorry if this conversation has brought back sad and sorry memories for you, too. Besides, the other woman—as Charles and I always thought of her—eventually left Daddy for another man. Then we heard she died suddenly, a fact Charles and I found we cared little about."

Willa said quietly, "I loved both my parents very much. It's just that they went so fast in that car accident, and they were together. I had no one except for my aunt and her husband to look after me. And I loved them, but, as you say, 'you only get one of them.' In my case, I lost both of them together."

"Well, we'll go no further with these sad tales of ours. Now, let's get this all ready for tomorrow."

"Done. But what will you do with your hair?"

"Easy peasy—I will do what you do. Plop it up and put it in a ponytail. See? I'm learning to do as you do in any given situation: adjust."

"Charlie will never forgive me."

"Oh, yes, he will. He adores you and so do I. And I love that you call him what I do. He's just Charlie to us. Oh, Willa, we are so blessed."

"Yes, we are, Vernie. Now no more talk. Go to bed."

The sun was not up even slightly when Willa's feet padded off to the kitchen to make a pot of tea. She put the water on to boil and then went to take a shower. That would wake her and then she would tackle Miss Verinnia. As the hot water trickled down over her lovely body, she thought of how lucky she was now, to have both this wonderful sister and the most fabulous husband.

"Willa? Willa are you up?" shouted the sweet voice into Willa's bathroom.

"Wow, look who's ready to get going. Go pour the tea; I'll be out in a minute."

The two of them sat there quietly, in the small but lovely kitchen, sipping their tea. Willa wasn't much of a morning girl, so she was delighted Vernie followed suit. Mornings are to be contemplative, Willa had always thought.

Finally she spoke. "Ready? Shall we venture out to learn how to bake these cakes?"

Vernie said, "I will follow you anywhere."

As the two of them walked the narrow path to Miss Millie's house, the sound of spluttering diesel engines could be heard all around the island. The men were leaving to bring in the crabs for the day. Willa soaked it all up and even stopped momentarily to take it in with her eyes closed. When she opened them, Vernie was staring at her sort of oddly.

Willa explained, "When I want to frame something so I can later put it into words, I close my eyes and imagine it and how it looks and the sounds around it and the people involved in it and nature's noises engulfing it."

"Oh, Willa, how I wish I had your talent."

"You have your own, Vernie. Don't ever envy someone else, because you don't know what else about them you would have to endure as well. The grass is never greener."

Vernie reached over and gently squeezed Willa's hand.

Miss Millie was waiting for the girls. All the kitchen lights were on when they tapped on the back door.

"Good morning, girls. I hope you're ready to go."

Vernie looked around the kitchen in which the counters looked like those of a well-greased bakery.

Millie said, "This is an organized business I run here. I get orders every day either online or in the mail, and they have to be baked, packaged up, and on the mail boat at 7:30 a.m."

53

Willa looked a little shocked. "I guess I hadn't thought of it this way. Makes sense why you have to get up at the crack of dawn."

"Before dawn, Willa. By the time the sun makes her appearance, the cakes will be cooling. Now let's get started."

Millie moved to the cake pans and said, "Each cake I make has nine layers. Some people's cakes have ten, but I find nine makes them easier to handle. And nine makes them my cakes."

Willa shook her head and asked, "Nine layers? I don't think I've ever seen more than three."

"Yes, but you're thinking of thick layers. Island cakes have skinny layers. It's what makes them unique—fresh—and allows for different fillings or combination of fillings."

Neither of the girls looked as if they really understood. Yet.

Millie asked them to grease the pans, showing them how to do it so there was just the right amount of greasing on each one. The girls took to it rather quickly, and Miss Millie began the batter.

"Today most of the customers seem to be in the chocolate mood, so it will be white cake, chocolate layers, and then chocolate frosting."

"What's your favorite, Miss Millie?" Willa asked.

"Not sure. I make a fig one that I'm particularly partial to, but plain old yellow cake layers with white or chocolate is just fine, too."

"The cake you made for Charles and me was out of this world."

"A different kind of cake. A tiered wedding cake with cherry filling and white frosting."

Vernie chimed in, "It was heaven. Of course, I love anything cherry. We have cherry trees on our land back in Virginia. Daddy used to say old George Washington himself would love our cherries."

Millie said, "Cherries are wonderful fruits, Vernie. So much you can do with them and they seem to be a more traditional southern flavoring."

"That must be why we had them and why I love them so. My husband, Tom, planted some around our property in Loudoun County. They are beginning to bloom now and they always mean spring to me."

Willa looked at her and smiled. "I hope to see your home one day soon."

"Charles told me he means to bring you there, very soon. It's so very lovely—though unlike our old, historical family home—but I love it."

"You have a wonderful husband, Vernie. I know how much you two are in love," Willa said.

"Just like you and Charlie."

Millie interrupted. "Okay now, ladies, we have to pour the batter in each pan. Watch me and then you can do it until you get the handle of it. Takes a light hand or else too much batter will spill into the pan."

Millie poured each one for the first batch as if she were holding a baby. Obviously, she had done this for years, and it had become a part of her everyday ritual.

"There, see? Now you try it, Vernie."

Vernie was nervous, but she picked the bowl up and gently poured the batter into a pan. It was perfect. And so was the next and next.

"Go ahead, Willa, you try," Vernie urged.

Willa picked up the bowl and poured too much in the first pan, then messed up the next one, too. She was clumsy and had no knack at all for it.

Millie chuckled at the sight of Willa pouring the batter into the pans. "I see why you write for a living, Willa."

"Yes, you've found my great flaw! I cannot bake a thing. Seems I am not only all thumbs, but have never enjoyed it either. So I will let my dear sister-in-law take over this part and carry on. I think packing them up is more to my talent."

Vernie blushed at the lovely compliment Willa had paid her. "Well, I couldn't begin to put one word next to another and have it make any sense."

While the cakes were in the ovens baking, then cooling, then getting ready for the frosting, the three women sat at the table sipping tea as the sun rose in the sky. By the time all the orders were finished—Willa had been true to her word and packed them up without a hitch—Richard came in and boxed them up to go over to the boat and on to their markets.

The girls handed in their aprons and thanked Miss Millie profusely for allowing them in her kitchen and for sharing with them her age-old baking secrets. They had bonded, these women of different ages and walks of life. They shared so many joys of life together that it didn't matter much about the whereabouts, the how-d'ye-dos, or the who-see-whats. Miss Millie hugged both girls and thanked them. Vernie beamed as if she had found not only a new friend, but a new talent she had never known she had.

Willa turned just before she closed the door and said, "Miss Millie, thank you for this wonderful experience. And I officially dub you the Cake Baker Extraordinaire."

Millie bowed dutifully and laughed. It had already been a good day.

Chapter Nine

Charles was not sleeping well. His mind would just not shut off; a thousand and one things were swirling around. He finally got up and saw that it was the staggering hour of three o'clock in the morning. He knew that, if he tried again to sleep, it wasn't going to happen, so he padded slowly down to the kitchen and started to brew his beloved morning coffee. Then he hit the shower to steam off while preparing for the day ahead.

His weekend trips over to the Eastern Shore of Maryland had brought him many new friends, but with new friends came new problems to solve. After discussions with some of the watermen and a few farmers, he realized he had a long way to go to find lasting solutions. If he were a senator it would be much easier because senators had greater power than congressmen, but he was what he was, so he had to deal with that fact and stop thinking about it. His time would come, and, when it did, he would seize that opportunity.

He did so want to be a senator, though. He knew, with his father's friends in tow with their vast money pots and with the Lee name, he probably could make the jump from the House to the Senate. But it was always a tough transition and not many had done it. When he had mentioned it in passing to his father before he died, he hadn't seemed too keen on the idea. Maybe if he had lived, he might have seen the work his son had done and changed his mind, but now Charles would never know that for sure.

The time would come—he knew that—but he had to get his ducks in a row. And the challenges he was hearing about were in Maryland, not Virginia. Would he stand a chance in a race like that? Others had done it, but not many. However, he *was* now a landowner there.

His mind continued to go round and round as the hot water careened down his body. So much to think about and always so little time.

While Charles was struggling with his mind and the early hour, Tug was already up and going. He always got out of bed early. He and Lindy had returned from the island Saturday night after the party when one of the men had offered them a ride back over to the mainland. Lindy wasn't thrilled—she had been looking forward to staying with Jimmy and Miss Frances—but knew she would be better able to cope with her new condition if she were in her own house and bed.

She wasn't getting out of bed with Tug this morning, though. She'd managed Monday, but now she had begun to get that sudden sick feeling again and Tug had told her to stay where she was. He would bring some tea and toast to her. She smiled sweetly at him, thinking he was the most wonderful man in the world.

"Here you go, Lindy." He set the tray on their very large bed, one they had both picked out soon after they were married. She had always wanted a huge bed, and now she had it.

"I don't feel so good, Tug. I don't know if I can work today."

"You're not going to work today, Lindy, or any other one from now on. You have to get through this part of your pregnancy, and I don't think smelling cheeseburgers and fries cooking on the grill is going to do anything to help this situation."

"Tug, I've worked at Virgil's forever. I can't just up and quit because of a little morning sickness. No, I'm not going to leave them in a bind like that."

Tug slid over next to his wife and rubbed her belly. "I still can't believe we're going to have a baby, Lindy. I know that the way you told me probably wasn't the way you would have liked to, but, you have to admit, it was kind of funny."

Lindy rolled over on one side and faced the sandy-haired husband she loved so much. "Funny? You think I wasn't mortified? I don't think that was funny at all."

"Calm down there, Lindy-girl. No one will think anything of it. Those folks have been through it, you know."

"Yes, they have, and the women didn't up and quit their jobs neither."

"Either."

Now Lindy's dander was way up. "I hate it when you correct me. Makes me feel like a hick or something, It's the way we talk down here, and, as I recall, you loved it once upon a time."

Tug started laughing, and the more she went on, the more he loved it. "I'm just saying that I think you would fare better if you weren't in a restaurant, of all places."

"Well, you can think and say all you want, but I'm not going to quit working at Virgil's."

He had lost the battle, but the war was still up for debate. "We'll see."

Lindy took a pillow and hit him over the head. "We'll not see. It's over. No more talking about it." Just as she was going to assault him one more time with the pillow, his cell rang.

He got up to retrieve it from the dresser, and said, with a grin, "We'll see."

Then he answered the phone. "Hey, Charlie. It's a little bit early for you political types, isn't it?"

Lindy took a sip of her tea, while Tug walked into his office across the hall.

"What's up that couldn't wait?"

"Tug, I need a friend to talk to and I think you're just that man. I've decided to come back to the island this weekend. I think I can talk Willa into staying over there instead of coming back here. Do you think you and I could talk sometime while I'm there?"

"Sure. Just let me know a time that works for you, and we can have coffee."

"Good. I want to get some information so I can ask the right questions. In the meantime, can you ask some of the farmers in that area how they're doing? Especially if they raise chickens?"

"I'll do better than that. I'll head north to Salisbury and snoop around there. That's the mother ship of the chicken industry here, you know."

"Yes, I've heard that. Thanks and see you this Friday. Oh, how is Lindy doing?"

"Right now, she and I are in deep negotiations about her working." Tug had no sooner said that then he saw her run to the bathroom, clearly preparing to lose the tea he had just brought her.

"I better go, Charlie; she's going to need me. Her stomach just can't seem to hold anything down."

"Good luck in your negotiations. Sorry to call so early, but I just couldn't sleep."

"No problem, Charlie. Bye now."

Tug sat back in his chair as Lindy spilled her guts, quite literally, in the commode. He wasn't sure what Charlie was up to or why he would care about chickens. He had been great for the watermen but that was an issue he had been involved in at the time. Now he was going after something entirely different. Or was it? He would dig around a little, and, hopefully, by Friday he would have something to discuss with his friend.

On Lindy's way back to the bedroom, Tug watched her from his office chair. "Are you okay?"

"Not great, but not horrible neither. I feel a bit better now after getting it up and out. I don't understand why this has to happen."

"Don't ask me. I'm only the father bear of this situation. And, by the way, the word is either, not neither."

Lindy made a fist at him and then cracked a smile. "Forget correcting my English, Tug, but don't forget you were the perpetrator of my condition."

"Oh, that's not nice, Lindy. After all, won't I be the one getting up in the early morning and feeding the little tyke?"

"You say that as if the baby will be a boy."

"It will. Won't have it any other way."

"Well, Mr. Alston, what will you do if he is a she?"

"Trade her in." He grinned from ear to ear.

"You men are all the same: impossible."

He got up and kissed her. "Ooowee, you taste like vomit."

"What did you expect?"

"Not that. Hey, will you be all right here alone? I want to go down to Virgil's and talk to some of the guys."

"Sure, and tell Virgil I'll see him for lunchtime serving."

"Lindy, did you hear a word I said to you before the phone rang?"

"Now, let's see, were we talking about something?"

"Women," Tug snarled back at her. "And, by the way, wear a jacket; there's a bit of a breeze today." He smiled at her and, before she could say another word, went down the stairs and out the door.

Lindy did feel a bit better, and decided to pull on some sweats and get some early morning fresh air. She was quite proud of herself for winning round one. Heaven knew what round two or three would bring, but, for now, there was something she wanted to do.

Tug got a mug of fresh, strong coffee and carried it over to the group of men already hashing over the day's events. Those who went out on the water were long gone, but Virgil's always had a faithful crew who stayed on, coming and going throughout the day. These were the men retired from the water, but one never really did totally retire from that life. They were still so used to getting up in the middle of the night to come down here, get their coffee and some food, and then head out, that, when they couldn't do it anymore for a host of reasons, they still kept the same routine. Then they hung around all day until the men came back from the water and gathered to tell of the day's catch. Then they went home for their main meal of the day, made by their wives who were most likely now at their own jobs.

"How ya comin', Tug?"

Tug always enjoyed the greeting, different from the island men who always said "ye" instead of "ya" or "you." There were subtle differences among the Eastern Shore folks that you only learned by living with them.

"I'm doin', I guess. How's it going with the crabs? Look like maybe a good year coming?"

"Might hard to tell yet, but, so far, not so bad."

"We'll all pray for a good year."

"No crabs, no money, and that won't do to pay the bills."

Tug loved the talk. These men knew more about the ways of the world than people gave them credit for. That was part of the problem with the bureaucrats who would come down inspecting everything to make sure no one was out of line with the regulations about crabs and fish that got pulled from the Bay. They always spoke to these men as if they were a bunch of dummies. But they were the only dummies because they had no real understanding of the waters around the Bay. These men had gone out all their lives, and they had learned from their fathers and grandfathers and from way back before men even paid attention to the years gone by.

Tug turned the topic from the water to the land. "What do you all hear from the farmers around these parts?"

"What do you mean, 'hear from the farmers around these parts,' Tug? Are they having any problems with anything?" Slim Carson, an old-timer, sat back in his chair with his thumbs stroking his suspenders up and down. "Are you fixin' to get yourself in some more trouble there, boy?"

"Is there trouble to be gotten into, Slim?"

"There's always trouble iffen you go lookin' for it."

Another retired waterman said, "There's some truth to that, Tug. What are ya lookin' for?"

"I don't know. I thought I would just ask."

Cap'n Tuck was sitting next to Slim and said, "The farmers are having a hard time with all the regulations and taxes being put on their farms. And then there's the matter of this fertilizer thing. The Baywaters Commission blames them for the fertilizer runoff they say is damaging the Bay."

"Wow," Tug sighed. The Baywaters gang was a familiar group to Tug's ears. They were the ones who had been all over the watermen about their problems in the Bay, accusing them of polluting it with their diesel boats. It was Miss Frances who had raised a fuss about that mess, while Dickie was fighting the developers over their practices. "Seems everything interacts with the Bay down here. A fragile ecosystem to be sure, but the farmers have been farming here for years."

"Yes, indeed," piped up Slim, "and that's why they want to go after them because of all the poultry farming and the fertilizers they say wash into the Bay."

Tug shook his head. "What a nightmare all this is."

Cap'n Tuck said, "A nightmare for us who have to make a living here. Some folks are watermen, some are farmers who grow corn or soybeans, and some raise chickens or other livestock to sell at the market. I mean, that's what we've done for years and years."

"Where does all this lead?" Tug asked.

"Leads to a mess of trouble," shouted Virgil from behind the counter. He was always working, but that man didn't miss a word of what was being said.

Tug said, "I can see why so many people here keep themselves upset so much."

Slim said, "No use in getting upset, Tug. We have to live with it and come up with answers. The only problem is that the state and federal government just keeps spinning out more and more regulations every year, and we don't know how much longer we can all hang on. There's only so much money to go 'round."

Tug took a last swig of his coffee and said, "How right you all are. Well, I think I have enough to stew about right now. Guess I'll wander back home. Oh, before I forget, Virgil, Lindy said she'd see you at lunchtime."

"Yes, she always does, Tug, so what's so different today that you have to mention it?"

Tug blushed and knew he dared not say a word. The gossip mill would tell everyone soon enough and then the teasing would be almost unbearable.

"I don't know; just thought I would, that's all." He rushed out before his mouth got him in any more trouble.

Virgil said, "That boy is hiding something from us, boys, sure as shootin'. Wonder what it is?"

"Well, if he is, it won't keep long in this town. We know everything about everybody."

"You got that straight, Slim."

Chapter Ten

Tug walked back to their house and immediately noticed that Dickie's old truck was gone. Only one person had the nerve to drive that thing. He never had understood why Lindy had wanted to keep it. However, he had to admit, the memories of riding in it with that old man were priceless—and hellish. He much preferred his new Jeep Cherokee.

Where was she? The last he had seen her, she had just finished retching over the commode. *Better go and find that girl.*

Lindy had one destination when she had to sort things out. She had pulled the old truck up to the one place she loved almost as much as she loved her husband: Dickie's shanty with its weather-beaten gray shingles. It belonged to her now, and, as she walked out on the half-broken planks, she was careful not to trip or fall. She had a baby to be mindful of, and not just any baby, but Tug's child deep within her. She wanted this so much and knew he did, too.

She couldn't recollect how many times she had come out here. Dickie always seemed to have known when Lindy needed to be alone and think, and this was certainly one of those times.

She opened the creaky door carefully and realized she would never tire of that sound. The door was special because it was warped and old now, mimicking its master before he had left in such a hurry. She walked inside and it was just as Dickie had left it. She and Tug had never moved a thing.

She could feel her beloved uncle's spirit wrapping around her the way his arms had when she was a little girl and he would kiss her gently on the cheek. Tears began to puddle in her eyes as all the memories came flooding back. When she was barely out of childhood, she would come out here and sit all night, watching the crabs stirring, about ready to shed their shells. When they began, she would scoop them out and separate them from the others until they did the same. She never minded staying up all night to help her old uncle out, and she had loved hearing him walking those loose planks in the wee hours to join her in this glorious chore all crabbers have to do. Their talks lasted for hours as they worked away. And, when daylight came, they would be done, though Lindy would have fallen asleep by then on the old cot he kept there for her. He would lean over and kiss her good-bye, waking her just a little, as he went out on the Bay for another day.

Dickie, I know you're here with me. I can feel you. It's a nice feeling, but I just wish you could come back, even for a moment, and really be with me again. I need your advice. Tug wants me to stop working at Virgil's, but how can I? I've been working there for years now and been going there longer than I can remember. I know I feel sick now—it's a good sick, though!—but this will all go away, and I want to make some money now, money for our baby. How I wish you could be here for that. What a party you would throw for that announcement. Oh, dear Uncle Dickie, what should I do?

Now Lindy broke down and cried, loudly and passionately. She had been so attached to him, and this old place brought everything to mind again. Through her tears, she began to feel a little sick again, but this time she was determined not to throw up. She would show this baby who was boss long before he or she made its entrance into this world. The tears kept coming as if she needed to cry more than anything. Sometimes it's like that, she remembered her Aunt Shirley telling her; sometimes a woman has to "bust open and let it all out."

She sat in an old rocker next to the cot and did exactly what she had been told to do; she let it all out. As the rocker moved forward and back, she did not hear the man she loved so very much walk quietly through the creaking door. But, when he gently touched her shoulder, she did not jump. She knew it was him. It was the touch of comfort that comes only from one who knows you deep down and so well; only their touch can heal your heart.

"Are you going to make it, Lindy? I think you've needed to do this for a very long time."

"You're right, Tug; I have needed to do this. I'm not crying out of sorrow really, but rather for everything and yet nothing. Does that possibly make sense?"

Tug chuckled softly and whispered, "Of course it does. You're still young, Lindy, and I'm not sure you wanted to have a baby just now, but we are. We can't go back in time now."

Lindy turned to look at him. "Would you want to? Do you really want this baby?"

"More than anything, and I can't wait to tell my parents. They will be so happy, I think. Mom maybe more than Dad, but he will get used to it. With him retiring soon, I think he might like to play with a child again."

"That's comforting, to know they would take an interest. I really love them, but I am afraid they will think I am trapping their son."

"Trapping me? I don't think so. They know what you mean to me. They've seen the balance you have brought to my life. I think Dad was jealous of Dickie for a time, but then he saw that old man and why I would love him so. Dad was forced to take stock of our relationship." He smiled. "I'm so glad my brother is done at Salisbury University now, and has taken a job down here. That's just more assurance that they'll be here a lot."

Tug moved to sit on the old cot across from her. As he sat down, he chuckled and said, "Do you remember the first time you brought me out here, Lindy?"

She smiled demurely and said, "I sure do. And you fell through the boards and had to dry off."

Tug cleared his throat, his male pride somewhat offended. "I didn't mean that. I meant the first time I kissed you. Or didn't that make quite the impression that my falling through those damn old boards did?"

She was going to string this along; she so rarely got the best of him. "Really, did our first kiss happen out here? I thought it was out back when Dickie was steaming the crabs." She could see he really looked upset. He was trying so hard to be romantic! She knew she had better stop teasing him. "Oh, Tug, how could I forget that? I had been waiting so long for you to do it. And, if my recollection is clear, we both lay down on this old cot—"

Blushing, he stopped her. "Yes, I know, Lindy; you don't have to go on."

She laughed and looked at him tenderly. "I love it that you're still kind of a little boy about intimate things."

"Well, some things are best kept quiet even between the two people involved. They don't have to say it; they just know what the other is thinking."

"Willa and Charles have all this to look forward to. They make such a beautiful couple, don't you think?"

"Yes, I guess they do. Charlie is a great politician, and yet he doesn't seem he would lie about anything the way most of them do."

"Sad, isn't it? The people we should be able to trust the most have let us down the most. And I don't think they know it or care about it."

Tug said, "Well, I will do all I can to keep our new friend from turning into a Washington politician, but it won't be easy. The old guard goes after the young ones and eats them alive, teaching them that, if they want to play in their town, they have to follow certain rules. I hope Charlie stands his ground."

"Just what is going on with Charlie, and what did he want to talk with you about?"

"I don't know, really, but he reminds me of me when I got going with Dickie and the developers. He seems to be on to something."

"Well, that turned out to do a lot of good."

"Somewhat, but it's too tempting for them not to overdevelop the shore. The only thing that really stopped them was a dip in the market, but, with it coming back now—well, you can see for yourself—they're at it again. Good for some folks, but not good for all."

"Tug, I'm sorry I snapped at you before. I think I need to work, though, until the baby comes."

"I'm sorry, too, Lindy. How about we compromise? As your time gets nearer, maybe you could stop and take some time for yourself and the two of us? It's going to change when the baby comes."

"I know that, and you're wonderful to understand. I think that'll work. We'll see how it goes."

Tug looked at her, knowing she was happier with this compromise, and that made him happy.

He patted the cot and said, "Wanna come on over and lie down for a bit?"

Without hesitation, she got out of the rocker and walked across to him. As she lay in his arms, they giggled between kisses, and she just knew Dickie had a hand in all this. His spirit was still there and always would be when she needed to talk with him. But, for now, she would talk with her husband in a language they both knew so well.

Chapter Eleven

Charles had begun reading up on some past farm bills and especially ones in Maryland. He had received letters from farmers on the Eastern Shore, asking him to take a look, but his responses had always been the same: while he empathized with them, he represented the Commonwealth of Virginia, and so on.

However, now he was a Maryland landowner, and that fact had gotten out thanks to the media. One of the style magazines had done an article about his wedding to novelist and trendsetter, Willa Carpenter. The article had mentioned where they had bought a home, and he wasn't at all pleased about that. Charles Lee was a very private man and he thought where he lived with his wife wasn't anyone's business. But Willa was a celebrity, and sometimes he had to remember that, especially when she spent many evenings signing books and doing meet-and-greets at department stores. One illustrious store even wanted her to do a spread on her fashion sense and make an appearance at the store related to that. This was getting a bit out of control, but he didn't want to say anything right now. He wanted to see where all this was going to lead.

After Prue had left as his trusty assistant, he had hired a new one, Steve Allen. Charles was extremely pleased so far with his work, though he still chuckled a little at his name, remembering the entertainer from another age. Steve, of course, never really got the joke; he was too young. However, he had Googled it and been surprised to learn of the original.

None of that mattered. Steve knew how to keep his opinions to himself, unless asked, and that was essential in a town where loyalty was in short supply.

Charles was reading documents when his phone buzzed. Steve never allowed calls to go directly to the Congressman, so this had to be a constituent or someone from the Hill. Charles picked up his phone and heard Steve's voice: "Hold, Congressman. I have Senator Richardson on the line."

Charles was stunned. Senator Richardson had "retired" after an ethical and legal mess some time back, and they had not parted friends, even though both were from Virginia and Richardson had been a good friend of his father's. But Richardson had been making money off the watermen, a fact discovered when Charles's committee had brought Miss Frances Evans in to testify.

Senator Rennie Richardson had come to despise Frances and never ceased to refer to her as "*that* woman," but even he'd been forced to admit she had fought the better fight. There had been a grueling investigation, and, in the end, Richardson was forced out of the Senate in disgrace. He had been lucky not to go to jail—though, in D.C., that rarely happened to one of their own. Still, the man had been beyond salvation.

Now there seemed to be a familiar drum beating, but, this time, the issue was different. It wasn't about the watermen, but the farmers, and the man going after them appeared to be Senator Buddy Dawes, a friend of Rennie Richardson with the same corrupt way of doing business. And Dawes was from the great state of Maryland, Charles and Willa's new home, when they could get away.

"Good morning, Senator. To what do I owe this honor?"

The minute Rennie heard the voice of the young hotshot who had done him in, he tensed up. He really hated this young weenie, as he had been known to call Charles, but Charles's father had been a heavyweight in Virgina to whom Richardson had gone more than a few times for contributions to his senatorial campaign coffers. He didn't need the money anymore. What he needed now was information.

"Why, how are you, Charles? It's been a long time since we've had a chat. You got married, last I heard. Congratulations, son."

How Charles hated it when Richardson condescendingly called him "son." The bloviating sonofabitch was hard enough to stomach under any circumstances, but, when he put on that overdone Virginia drawl, it made a person want to puke.

"Why, yes, I did, Senator. Willa and I were so sorry you weren't able to make it to our reception. It would have been a pleasant memory of your friendship with my father. I know he would have liked that." *God, it makes me sick to kowtow to this overinflated ego, but I'm a young man compared to the senator, and manners—especially when it comes to one's elders— are always in style and always demanded from a Lee.*

The senator was clearly annoyed by the young whippersnapper, but he had to play the game just as much as Charles did. "I know, Charles. It was a hard event to miss, and may I say how sorry I was to hear of your father's sudden passing? We all respected him greatly. Tell you what; when you are home down here, why don't we go on out to lunch so I can make it up to you?"

What was Charles going to say now? The old fox was trying to corner him. "Well, that isn't necessary, Senator. But you called about something?"

"Yes, I did, didn't I? Well, I heard a rumor—and you know I don't put much stock in them, but I heard it all the same—that you were asking a lot of questions about farming over there on the Eastern Shore. Could I be so bold as to ask why? You know that farming was one of my priorities."

"Yes, I seem to have heard that. You worked closely with the Secretary of Agriculture."

"Yes, that's true. I sat on the agriculture committee, as well as a few others that you know of."

"Well, Senator, there's nothing really concrete going on . . . yet, but, when there is, you will be the first to hear about it, I'm sure."

Little shit, Richardson thought. "Well, I would very much appreciate that. And, if you have any thing you need, please don't hesitate to get in touch." Then he chuckled. "You know you can't fool an old fox. I might be able to help, so let me know."

Charles knew the old man was trying to game him, but he wasn't going win now any more than he had won before. "I will do just that, Senator. Thanks for the call." With that, Charles hung up.

The former senator immediately made another call, this one to a good friend and another senator who had not retired. When the man's office assistant answered, Richardson told him he needed to speak to the senator immediately. In moments, Senator Dawes came on the phone. Rennie informed him that Lee was sticking his nose into things and Dawes needed to keep a close watch. Then they agreed not to get in touch through office phone lines anymore. Too risky.

Senator Dawes informed his assistant to strike that incoming number from his logs permanently, and, if Congressman Lee called this office for anything, the senator wanted to know immediately, and wanted a full report of what he had wanted. Then he asked his assistant if he understood that order clearly.

The man nodded, turned, and left. The senator from Maryland wasn't one for small talk with his staff.

The very fact that Rennie had called told Charles he was on to something. You bet he already had a lot of questions about the onerous taxing and regulations being put on the farmers, but now he knew something else was afoot. The former Senator Richardson would only have called this early if he didn't want anyone messing around in his business, and why would that be? The senator was retired, so why would he care about any of this? Charles didn't like what his mind was thinking, but then the games of power and wealth never stopped in this town The bigger question was, could he keep himself honest and above the fray? And was it even possible to do that if he ran for Buddy Dawes's seat? He hoped he knew the answer to that question, but he would keep on praying that he could hold to it and succeed with his long-range plan. Which might not be so long-range anymore, given that phone call.

Steve buzzed him again and this time it was Willa. He picked up immediately.

"Hey, how are you out there all by yourself?"

"Well, I'm not exactly all by myself. I am with all the islanders and your sister."

"Correction accepted. How are you two doing? Yesterday Vernie had a run-in with crab picking. What has happened today?"

"Why do you think anything happened? That doesn't say much for me."

Charles sat back, smiling. He missed her and loved to tease her. "No, no, it doesn't, but you can't say I'm not telling the truth."

"Come to think of it, you're right, Charles, although it pains me to say that. Today is pretty good, so far. We got up at three o'clock this morning."

"Three o'clock this morning? Good heavens, you didn't go out with the crabbers, did you?"

"I've not completely lost my mind, Charlie. No, today, Vernie and I went and baked island cakes."

Charles shook his head. "What in tarnation are you up to, Willa? Killing my sister?"

She laughed and shot back, "The thought had crossed my mind, but I love her too much. She's so much nicer than you."

"Got me there. I have no snappy retort to that. She *is* nicer than me. Baking pies, huh?"

"No, cakes. There's a huge difference. And, I might add, she is great at it."

"How hard can baking a cake be, Willa?"

"What's with you today? Are you in the mood for putting down women in general, or just your sister and me?"

"I'm not putting you down; I was just making an observation. I guess I'm getting myself into hot water, so I'll keep my mouth shut."

Willa couldn't tell if he was teasing her or if he really meant it. Suddenly the mood had changed between them and she didn't like it at all.

"I have to run, Charles. We'll talk at another time. Something's got you all stressed out and I'm not enjoying the conversation."

"Willa, wait; I'm sorry. I do have a lot going on right now, but that's no excuse. Forgive me?"

Willa waited a moment before answering, then said, "Maybe. But I am enjoying myself with Vernie and all the others here. I am so glad we bought property on the island, and I can't wait to start on the house. Can we do that soon?"

"Yes, if it will make you happy. Any idea for an architect?"

"I don't know, Charlie. I think you and I could design it ourselves and save that money to hire a really good builder. There are some really talented men here who could do this, and they could us the money."

"That sounds like a win-win. Why don't you start asking around? And, oh"—Charles laughed—"have fun whatever you and my sister do for the rest of the day. Be sure to give my love to Vernie, and, as for you, young lady, I love you."

Chapter Twelve

Willa walked out to her small front porch and sat down to start thinking about what she really would do to this old house to make it more up to date. She wanted to start as soon as they could come up with a plan.

Vernie walked out and plopped into another chair. She had so much to say that she could hardly contain herself. "You know, I really loved being with Millie this morning, and I loved baking with her and listening to her go on about the island and the people who live here. Do you think I could go over again before I leave?"

"I don't see why not. When do you have to go back, Vernie?"

"I don't think I have a set date but I don't want to stay too long. You need to work on your book and begin plans on your house, and there is no doubt my brother will be back as soon as he can break away from his pressing duties in Washington."

"He just called me and said he sends his love."

"I do so love my brother. We had as near perfect a time growing up as two children could. I know he had his spats with our father, and neither of us really liked his new wife, but I think, on balance, it all worked out."

Willa smiled at her and said, "I think it has. Charlie always needs to settle things within himself. He likes things in order. I drive him a bit nuts with the house talk and the mess I make when I'm writing. Papers and notes scattered all over the place, since authors need to get a thought down the minute they think it."

"Well, your own office should be on the top of the list when you begin to design: Willa's Writing Room."

"I used to have that in Washington, but that seems a lifetime ago now."

"Well, you should have it out here then. A writing room, one that overlooks the water. I should imagine you could write anything with that view."

"Yes, I agree. Great idea to put the office upstairs so I can use the water for inspiration."

"My goodness, you may as well tear this one down and start all over again."

"We may have to, but I wouldn't want people to think of us as one of those they call 'come heres.' They're the ones who come here because they love it, but, when they get here, they want to change it all to suit them."

"You have a point. So, in other words, you will have to keep the nut but ditch the shell."

Willa looked at Vernie and started laughing. "I can't say I have ever heard that expression before, but it sure hits the mark straight on. Is that one of those down-home southern sayings?"

"Probably. I've heard it all my life, so it must be."

"Strange how you got all the southern genes and Charlie didn't."

"Charlie used to, when we were kids, but, when he went away to college, even though it was in Virginia, he tried really hard to incorporate many of the other students' cultures within himself. I think he was always on the fast track to politics. As you know, it runs in our Lee blood."

"Yes, I think I've heard that before." Willa chuckled. "Now, about this cake baking thing? Just walk over to Miss Millie's and ask her. I have a feeling she enjoyed having us there. You know the schedule she keeps; she must get lonely in those early hours."

"I don't think I could ever do it. I just want to have her help me perfect some of my old family dessert recipes. You know, a southern girl always has to be prepared."

With a sweet smile, Willa said, "Why, of course you do."

"Willa, do you ever think you and Charlie will have a normal life?"

"What do you mean by normal? I think we already live a normal life! Doesn't everyone get up and go to Congress to work every day, while the other one goes into a room and drives herself crazy playing with words?"

"Willa Lee, you are teasing me, aren't you? I mean normal like Tom and I have."

Willa saw she was being serious and knew what she was really asking. She wanted to know if she and her brother were going to have a family and a home out in Loudoun County, Virginia. In other words were they going to have a happily-ever-after?

"I don't think so, Vernie. Charlie has other dreams and so do I. I want to spend more time with my readers and traveling, signing my books and speaking. We still have to work all this out and learn about compromise."

"You want babies, don't you?"

There it was, right out in the open. Vernie wasn't going to let this drop until she got it out of her.

Willa paused and then said, "I'm not sure I want children. I know that sounds selfish of me, but I lived a life that always seemed different from other children. When my parents died, I realized I was on my own. To be totally honest, I wasn't really looking or wanting to marry, but then life changed after Charlie and I met. I love him so much, and, right now, I do not want a baby, and I know, deep down, Charlie doesn't either. Too many other dreams to fulfill."

"That's a dreadful thing to say, Willa. Everyone wants a baby to care for and love."

"Then I'll get a dog. I don't mean to upset you, but you and Tom can have the kids. Charlie and I will have a different life together, I believe."

Vernie smiled sweetly and said, "We'll see. You know, sometimes things change."

"Maybe, and, if they do, we'll handle that when it comes along. But, for now, I am a new bride and the last thing I want is to have to get used to being a new mother. I want to be Charlie Lee's wife and soul mate. As it is, we have our hands full with this house, his politics, my writing and traveling, and living in Washington, a town that demands more than you will ever know."

"Okay, then; that settles it. I will go home and make babies, while you and my brother make the Lees even more famous. However, I am not doing that today. Before I collapse in bed, I am going over to Millie's to see when I can bake with her again."

Willa stood up and looked at this lovely new sister of hers, so sincere in her life and her ways. She wrinkled up her nose in a funny, familiar sort of face and said, "I'm so glad you're in my life, Vernie, and you can look forward to your future plans. But remember to have some fun, too. So, as you make and bake cakes, you can dream of making babies."

They walked into the house with smiles of sheer contentment on their faces and a feeling of love found only in strong and adoring families. Willa was so happy to be one of them now—part of a real family.

Charles couldn't settle down. He was annoyed with the call from Rennie and he missed Willa terribly. She was always his comfort zone. He had never before been attached to a woman long enough to establish a real, meaningful relationship, but Willa fit so easily into his life. She had kind of settled in gradually; then, as the days and months went on, she had made a place in his heart that could never fully be explained. It was true love for sure, and he was as hooked as a man could be. He didn't quite know what to make of it, but he knew he liked it a lot.

Restless, he looked at the clock and decided he was done for the day. He picked up the phone and called Prue. She was the closest he could be right now to Willa, and that's exactly where he wanted to be.

"Hey, welcome back to the wonderful world of Washington."

"Hi, Prue. Right now I don't feel like it's so wonderful. I was wondering if I could entice you to come out and play with me at The Willard. Like old times. Scotch Bar?"

Prue heard something in his voice that raised a flag. He was upset and needed to talk. "Sure, but I have about an hour's more work here."

"Perfect. See you in an hour and a half."

"Care to give me a hint as to what's up? I can hear it in your voice."

"Never could keep anything from you, but would rather spill it enjoying a glass of something nice."

She was concerned. Charlie wasn't given to explicit words; he usually was more measured. She had learned to read his signals working for him for over two years. "This better not be about you and Willa," she blurted out quickly.

"Oh, no, Prue. I'm sorry if I made you think that. I have some issues to run by you, but I do miss Willa terribly. Hate to admit that. I need to be more focused."

"You're a newlywed, Charles. Cut yourself some slack. We will talk. See you later."

Steve walked in just as Charles hung up the phone. "Sorry to tell you this, Congressman, but you have a visitor out in the office. He says he has to see you. It's very important."

"Steve, people don't just happen by to say they want to see a congressman. They make appointments."

Steve tried to search for the right words, then decided just to go for it. "Sir, this man is, shall we say, a bit 'provincial'?"

"What? A bit provincial?"

"Well, yes, sir. He's not a city man, if you know what I mean. I don't know how else to put it."

The bulb went off in Charles's head and he bolted for the door, leaving Steve standing there like an idiot.

Charles stepped into the outer office and looked at the man, at least six and half feet tall, with a huge frame to go with the height. One would have to say he was larger than life and definitely not a city man. Charles extended his hand and said, "Good afternoon."

The man took off his green John Deere gimme cap, the kind farmers and watermen all count among their necessities and treasures. They weren't exactly baseball caps, but a kissing cousin. Then, holding his cap in one hand, he extended the other and said, "Sorry to bust in on you like this, Congressman, and, frankly, I'm amazed I even got in here and that I'm doing this at all, but I am mad as all get out. Think the security man must have a relation who lives on the shore and is a farmer so he let me pass by. I do thank you for seeing me."

Charles liked him immediately. There was something about him. He was, without a doubt, pure shore, and he obviously had something to say, especially if he had this kind of nerve.

"Please come into my office." Steve had quietly walked back to his desk and was keeping a wary eye on this behemoth of a man. As Charles walked into his inner office, he gave Steve a wink to let him know all was well and that he could handle this. Steve was a good employee and assistant, but it could never be said he wasn't a bit of a snob.

"Please sit down, Mr. . . . . I'm sorry, I didn't catch your name."

In that Eastern Shore twang Charles had grown to love, the man said, "Oh, I'm sorry, sir. Buster . . . Buster Talbot. Buster wasn't always my name—my mama named me Owen—but Buster is all I ever remember being called. I don't know why and it doesn't seem to matter much, so I let it alone and have carried Buster around with me for all my life."

Charles shook his head firmly. "Buster is a good name. No doubt some family name from way back when. Now, what can I do for you, Buster?"

Buster was still trying to get comfortable in his chair, and Charles couldn't make up his mind if he was just too large for it or if he may have been trying to let some hot air out slowly and quietly, so as not to embarrass himself. The congressman didn't want to think about that and so just smiled at the man politely until he got his position all straightened out.

"Well, then, what is it you need to tell me, Buster?" Charles was having a hard time keeping a straight face, but he kept telling himself it was the chair positioning and not the other.

Finally, Buster began. "Well, Congressman, I see it this way—someone has to fight for us and I was talking with a group of farmers and we all remembered how you have been fighting for the watermen and wondered if you might help us out, too."

"What exactly is going on, Buster? I've heard some rattling about onerous regulations and perhaps some that might truly hurt the farmers over there, but you do know I can only do so much, right? I represent Virginia. The watermen situation came before a committee on the Bay and the Bay is also part of Virginia, not just Maryland."

Buster thought a moment and then answered, "Well, not anymore, really. Didn't you buy a place on the island?"

"News travels fast over there. Yes, I did, but it's a weekend kind of place. My real home is in Charlottesville, Virginia, and, of course, here in D. C."

"Nice town, Charlottesville. Went there once to visit Tom Jefferson's home."

The way he said it you would think Buster and the writer of the Declaration of Independence were good friends.

"Yes, it's a wonderful town. The Lee family has lived in several places in Virginia, but I love that part."

"Are you related to Robert E. Lee?"

Charles smiled gently with a look of nostalgia. "I am, sir, but he lived in Alexandria as a child."

"Well, I'll be."

For a minute, Charles thought he was going to stand up and salute him.

"Would you look at me, sitting in this fancy room, talking to one of General Lee's descendants? This will make for a big story when I get home."

"Where is home for you, Buster?"

"I live smack-dab in the middle of the shore. I live in a tiny town called Secretary, but I farm lands away from there. The original farm belonged to our father, but my brother lives in the old house. My wife wanted a newer one, so we moved a little down the road from it, but it's not a bother."

"Well, I've never heard of that town."

"You should come over one day and eat at Suicide Bridge."

Half smiling, Charles said, "Interesting name. Should I be nervous?"

"Yeah, we got some doozies over there, but the food is real good."

"Tell me, Buster, what exactly you want me to do. I still don't quite understand."

"Iffen they pass these regulations prohibiting certain fertilizers and things, we won't be able to farm the land. Crops would die off from the insects. And then the chain would break from there. I mean from the farmer of the crops of soybeans and corn, to the chickens that need that to feed, to the producers of the chickens. So many folks are affected by these cussed regulations."

Charles sat there, listening to this old-timer. He may not have had a formal education, but, like the watermen, he knew more than any Washington bureaucrat could ever hope to.

"I see. I get it, Buster. I really do. I want you to leave your name and phone and address with my man Steve out there. I will see what I can find out. And that's all I can promise you— that I will do that and I will report back to you. Have you gone to your own congressmen?"

"Yes, sir. The ones over there are real good to us, but they don't have the power. Buddy Dawes pretty much has that. Go talk to him and see what he has to say and you'll see: we're in a bind if this matter goes south. Our farms are all we got, just like the crabs and boats are to the watermen. But some folks, who don't know much about anything, have blamed us for everything that goes wrong in that Bay, and we're trying to do our part to clean it up. But it's not all any one person's fault. There's a whole bunch of things that have gone wrong out there on the Bay, and some of them— many of them—are beyond anyone's control."

"Sounds to me like the farmers and the watermen have their hands full."

"Times are changing, Congressman Lee. We know that and we know our kids, many of them, don't want to stay and farm anymore. But they would if we could get the government folks off our backs. We are getting pushed from every which way."

Charles stood up and said, with absolute determination in his voice, "I will check on it and see what I can find out. Thank you so much for coming, Buster."

With a wide grin on his large face, Buster shook Charles's hand again, and, this time, it was so hard, Charles felt as if it might break every bone. "Thank you, and I'll wait to hear from ya."

Charles opened the door, and Buster Talbot, after placing his old, worn-out cap on his head, walked out of the office.

Steve stared, stupefied. "What was that all about?"

"Oh, a man who needed to be heard." Charles was not about to go on about what Buster Talbot had wanted, No matter how much Charles trusted Steve, his assistant was still subject to the arm-twisting of those like Senator Dawes and his staff. Best to keep one's own confidence, or share such things only with those you trusted implicitly. *Good grief, I'll be late for Prue. But won't she love this story of the farmer and the congressman?*

Chapter Thirteen

After Charles walked through the door of The Willard Hotel in the heart of D.C., he headed straight to the Scotch Bar. Prue was already sipping a cosmopolitan to help her forget a fast-paced and difficult day.

"I'm sorry to be late, Prue, but you won't believe what happened to me as I was getting ready to leave."

"Oh, I could believe anything after the day I've had. Why don't you order your drink while I dump my pain on you and then you can return the favor, okay?"

"Fair enough. Go on."

"Well, first I had to deal with a little problem in our government that might have caused the entire downfall of Rome. That began my day—I was still drinking my first Starbucks. The budget thing is out of control and getting worse every day. It's beyond any of us how to deal with this unless we cut everything and start from square one, and I don't want even to be on this planet if that should occur. Then there was a woman who threatened to sue the government and run to the press over some crazy notion that we were solely responsible for the killing of whales in the ocean. Okay, Starbucks number two. After I settled all this with calm aplomb, I had to go to the floor for a while and deal with a runaway gaggle of press people. I gave up on the Starbucks and am now here medicating with something a bit more satisfying."

"Good God, Prue, and I thought my day was a train wreck. Is there a full moon?"

"If not, then we are surely at the end of time. I tell ya: people—they're the worst."

"I like that saying of yours, although I'm not sure I totally understand it."

"Give it a moment. It'll come to you."

"I've missed these sessions here at our favorite watering hole. It's such a nice place, and it's so good to see some things never change."

"Yes, it is, but it's not quite the same without the acerbic wit of Willa Carpe . . . uh, Lee. Caught myself, didn't I?"

"And don't you forget it. I have been away from her three whole days and . . . well . . . by the time I reached D.C., I was already itching to get back there."

"Would that be to Willa or the island?"

"Funny, Prue. By the way, she's been doing things with Vernie that will change poor Vernie forever."

"Like, what kind of things? I mean, how much trouble can one get into over there?"

"Easy for you to say, but my sister isn't very worldly. Her world is the South. No, even more defined: the spoiled South."

"Does she know how much you think of her?"

"I adore my sister and she knows that, so stop teasing."

"Oh, hit a nerve, did I?"

"Not really, but I do love her very much. She's my only sibling. Protective brother thing, I guess."

"Well, what in the world is our dear Willa doing with her?"

"She took her to the crab-picking co-op and a lady started to show her how to pick a crab. Vernie is sensitive, you know, and she passed out, and, when she came to, I guess she ran outside and threw up all over herself."

Prue started to giggle as Charles went on. "She was mortified, as mannerly as she is. Willa calmed her down and then they went home and to bed. Next morning, they got up before God and went off to bake cakes."

"Now this is disturbing. I get up early, but not before the sun rises. Before that would kill me. What in heaven's name were they doing baking cakes, and at that hour?"

Now it was Charles laughing hard. "Well, the woman who made that wonderful confection for us at the reception—remember?—was teaching them how to bake some special cake that is famous over there. She has a little business doing that and people order them from all over." He shook his head. "You know, those folks are simply born with an entrepreneurial spirit."

"Well, that makes sense, and that cake was out of this world, but that didn't upset your sister, did it? I mean she didn't get sick there, did she?"

"No, but I know my sister and how intense she gets. The next thing I am going to hear is that she wants to be like this woman and bake cakes back in Virginia. That will set off quite a conversation with her husband, who expects Vernie to be his genuine southern wife, sweet and a little bit sassy. And not a cake maker, up before the sun rises."

Prue chuckled, then said seriously, "You don't want Willa to change, do you, Charles? If so, your marriage won't last a year."

"Into a genuine southern wife? No! I don't think that's Willa's style. Wonderful—absolutely—and bright and charming, but she's not syrupy sweet. As for the sassy . . . well, let's say, doesn't every man want that from a gal?"

"You're all alike, aren't you?" Prue laughed, then said, "Now, how 'bout telling me what's really eating at you. I don't think it's your sister baking cakes."

"Oh, right. Well, Steve came into my office and said a man wanted to see me, and that the man wasn't up to his standards. I didn't understand at first."

"So, the man was different? How? I mean, not security different, I hope."

"No, nothing like that. I agreed to see him, and, when I did, I understood our snooty Steve's description. The man was a giant of a guy, heaven knows how tall. And he wasn't dressed like he was coming to see a congressman."

"How so?"

"Well, he had on a clean flannel shirt and denim jeans. In his shirt pocket, he had one of those plastic pencil carrier things. God knows what you call them, but they are utilitarian, I suppose."

"Go on. I'm hanging on every word."

"He also had on one of those mesh baseball cap kind of hats. It had John Deere on the front, but he did remove it when I asked him his name."

Prue almost fell off the barstool, laughing. She was near hysteria already when she asked, "What was the man's name? Bet it was Bud."

Charles cracked a smile and answered, "Better than that. His name was Buster. Buster Talbot."

Prue could no longer speak; she was shaking uncontrollably.

Charles said, "I asked him into my office—under Steve's watchful eye, of course—and he turned out to be the nicest man. And, when he told me he was from the Eastern Shore, I immediately liked him."

"Watch out, Charles. You're becoming one of them right before my eyes."

"I'm not sure I wouldn't like that. They are all really great and honest people." He looked thoughtful, but then shook it off and continued, "Well, anyway, he's a farmer, and, as we talked about before, they have their gripes too about what is happening to their world."

"Charles, farmers have been complaining for some time now. You know that, and you also know that, without farmers, we don't eat. What did you tell him? I mean, you aren't involved with that committee."

Charles answered, "Don't forget: I wasn't involved with the watermen before either, and look what happened with that."

"Yeah, you ran off and fell in love with my best friend and then you married her."

Charles smiled and said, "That wasn't what I was referring to, Prue."

"I know. Look, I feel really bad about a lot of things, but I can't save everyone and neither can you. Please don't tell me that you're determined to jump on the *Crusader Rabbit* train again?"

"*Crusader Rabbit* has a ring to it. They could call me Crusader Lee."

"Have you spoken to Willa about this? I mean, it wasn't this man that got you thinking about this. I saw it in your face already at the island. Something's going on with you, Charles."

"Well, yes and no. I haven't said anything to Willa. She has a lot on her plate, too, right now. And I am letting her enjoy the island while she is deciding what we are going to do with that house."

"And what's the yes part, Charles?"

"An old 'friend' of ours called me. Remember Rennie Richardson?"

Prue spluttered, "Rennie Richardson? But he's supposed to be out of the picture now."

"I know. Which is why I am 99% sure he was calling on behalf of someone else. I know the name Buddy Dawes means something to you."

"That man is the bane of my existence. Along with Richardson, who was supposed to behave and then go quietly into the night. Instead, the old snake seems to have decided to slither on for a while longer, and he's just plain trouble to everyone. Not the least of which is my boss."

"So, how *do* you like working for the Speaker?"

"Let's just say that Alexander Tisdale isn't you. We get on well enough, but the workload is a killer."

"He's third in line you know, so what did you expect?"

"I know. My father wanted me to do this in order for me to get experience so I can run soon myself. He's put a lot of pressure on me not to go the corporate route, but to stick to politics. Like with you and yours, it's in the Harding family genes, and having a nearly direct ancestor who was a president puts me in a small club indeed. Beats out the Lees," she teased.

Charles said, "I really miss you, you know, but your lineage was a real resume-builder for the Speaker when he knew you were looking for a job."

Prue gazed down at her drink. "Charles, I wonder what my ancestor, President Harding, would have thought of things today."

"He's probably rolling over in his grave, just like all the rest."

"Well, you're probably right, but that doesn't help you with whatever is eating at Richardson and, more importantly, Dawes."

"Dawes smells something, Prue, and, when that man smells something, it's usually trouble."

"Well, I guess I can say I will help if you need it. However, he's, unfortunately, a powerful senator and that makes him a tough man to beat."

"Miss Frances beat Rennie Richardson—made him eat his words!"

Prue laughed. "She should run for office. Then we'd have some fun. Can you imagine what would happen if honesty and trustworthiness came into Washington?"

"It would be something, wouldn't it?"

"You know, Charles, farmers have a lot of friends in Congress. We are still a nation of folks whose families farmed or lived near farmland, so you may have more friends than you know. With whatever it is you're on to."

"You're right, Prue. I don't really know yet what's going on, but, if there is any way I can help them and get people together, then I will."

"That's your specialty, dear Charles. Now, on another topic, when is Willa coming back, or isn't she?"

"I've decided to go back over there for the weekend. I think Vernie will then come back with me, but Willa will stay on for a time. She is determined to do this house right, and doing it right means you have to be on-site."

"Are you going to fly over? If you are, let me know who does that for you. Then, one of these days, I'll go back when she and I can have some girl time."

"I know she would welcome that. And then you can spend my money, too."

"Knowing Willa, it will be mostly her money she spends. She's got it, and, if she can find the right builder, then she can go on and keep writing her next romance novel. The world needs them, or at least we girls do. Give us hope and dreams."

Charles looked at her seriously and said, "Are you interested in ever meeting someone? I mean, you're a fabulous catch, Prue Harding."

"Well, I didn't catch you." She winked. "Seriously, I have too much to do yet to get all tangled up with love. I can still remember all the women trying to beat your door down when I was the gatekeeper."

"And a damned good one. I have to admit, those were the days. But, once I got hooked by Miss Willa, I was done. Who would ever have guessed I would marry the queen of hearts and romance?"

"She's an interesting and wonderful lady. I love her, and she's been through a lot of sadness in her life, so you best take good care of her, Charles Lee, or you'll answer to me."

They both checked the time and started to gather their things. Charles paid the bill and said, "You won't have to worry about that. I'll give our girl your love."

"Oh, please do. And keep me posted on your farm adventure. And be safe this weekend, and, for heaven's sake, bring your sister back in one piece."

Chapter Fourteen

Driving back home to the Eastern Shore, his favorite country music playing in the background, Buster Talbot smiled to himself as he thought about what he had just done. *Did I really walk into that congressman's office and tell him what was on my mind? You're a fool, Buster. There are probably FBI agents following you right now.*

He looked into his rearview mirror and didn't see any giant black SUVs. He looked up at the sky and no black helicopters either. Safe! Reassured, he began his ascent of the big, long Bay Bridge, a bridge that made many folks real nervous. He never did have a problem with it. Maybe his size helped him handle it better than most. He didn't know, nor did he care; it wasn't his problem.

He wondered if he would ever hear from that nice, young congressman and knew it was a long shot. But you had to take long shots these days if you were to survive. Farmers had been a target for a long time. Environmentalists were constantly on their backs for causing the Bay's pollution problems, but this wasn't exactly the way it was.

There would always be circumstances to make people point a finger, but, when that young reporter, Tug Alston, stirred the pot, calling out the overdevelopment of the shore as one of the main causes of harm to the Bay . . . well, everyone went crazy. As Buster saw it, it was like everything else: there was enough blame to go around. The question that no one could answer very well was, how do you feed your country without messing around in the dirt and fertilizing your crops? Farming had evolved to a great degree over the years as it was, but you can only go so far and still grow crops and raise livestock.

Time would tell what, if anything, could be done. The Eastern Shore was in the cross hairs for a whole host of reasons, but Buster Talbot felt as if he had to have his say about things. This young congressman would learn just who Buster was—one of the leaders of the farmers who had been raising awareness for years.

He'd deliberately gone to D. C. dressed as a farmer out in the field. That is who he was and he was not going to change. He'd known it might offend the congressman, but, when he took the measure of the young man and looked him square in the face, he knew he might have a good relationship with him. Charles Lee had a strong handshake and a direct eye. This was a good sign and might just produce something. It had to, because the farmers were on the edge.

The next day, Tug was eating a late breakfast at Virgil's. Late meant it was eight o'clock in the morning, but, at Virgil's, this was really late. Virgil's got jumping about three to four in the morning when the watermen came, got their breakfasts and snacks they needed for the day, and then were off. All left now were Tug and a few old-timers.

He liked to come down here sometimes, just to think things through. For some reason, he could do that in only two places: here and inside the old crab shanty. Today, he wanted to think through Lindy's condition and the baby who would be coming along. He had to tell his parents, and he thought they would be over-the-top happy, but, at the same time, he had reservations. Just an odd feeling, but they were there.

What parents wouldn't be thrilled to know they were going to the logical next step, being grandparents? He needed to throw off the odd feeling and go forward, but there was also the matter of Lindy being so sick right now. He really didn't want her working here, but he could see that was a subject best to stay away from. His life would change now. He hadn't expected to have a baby so soon, but wasn't real upset about it either. It was just going to be different.

He sat quietly. *I sure wish Dickie were here to give me some of his nutty but wise advice. He would probably tell me to go on out to the garage with the boys and drink until we were all drunker than skunks.* He would never forget the first time Dickie had taken him out there, and he'd seen the fun the men had in that big, old garage. And he loved the fact that it was for men only—no womenfolk allowed. He smiled.

Lost in a million thoughts, Tug was startled when his cell rang. It was Charlie. His daydreaming was over. He hoped nothing was wrong with Willa.

"Hi, Charlie! To what do I owe this honor? I hope nothing's wrong out there on the island."

"Oh, no, Tug. I just wanted to hear a friendly voice and talk to you."

"Well, glad you consider me to be that friendly voice. Washington getting to you?"

"I think Washington gets to everyone, but I have a favor to ask of you."

Tug said, "Name it."

"Well, I had the most unusual visitor come to my office yesterday. As it turned out, he was a farmer from the Eastern Shore. A small town named Secretary? You ever heard of that place?"

"As a matter of fact, I have."

"I believe he said something about a place with suicide in its name, but I really didn't get all that. I had a hard time understanding him, to be honest with you."

Tug chuckled, knowing exactly what Charlie was going through. It had taken him a long time and a diary of local words to finally understand what Dickie Short had been saying. "Yeah, I've heard of the place. Suicide Bridge. It's supposed to be a great restaurant with super food."

"Yeah, that's it; that's the one. Boy, you've been down there too long."

Tug laughed. "You may be right, Charlie. Well, what do you want me to do?"

"I want you to do a little detective work on the man. His name is Buster Talbot and he's a farmer."

"The plot thickens; tell me more."

"He was all spun up about the problems the farmers are having, and I wondered if you could find out who he really is."

"That's no big deal. Sure, I'll do that. As you asked, I've tried to get some info down here about farmers, too, but I'm just beginning. Whenever I've said something, the watermen just kind of steer away from the conversation. Think they have their own troubles and don't want to mess into yet another problem."

"The truth is their problems are somewhat the same. This man, Buster, said they are having difficulties with the regulations and the costs of farming. Sound familiar?"

"It's happening all over the country, but I have to say that I don't get it. In this state, as everywhere else, farming is as old a way of life as fishing. I don't understand why the state folks would want to destroy a food chain like that. With the watermen, it's crabs and oysters, and they brings in millions of dollars to the state. With the farmers, it's the poultry industry and the same thing."

Charles said, "I don't get it either, Tug. Sometimes I just don't get what politicians are doing."

"Well, you are one, and you have to figure this all out. There must be money in it for them somewhere. It's always about following the money."

"Yes. You're spot on with that, and I have to start there and learn exactly what is going on."

"There you go, Charlie. Keep on that train and it will take you to the right stop."

"You know, you sound more like those shore folks every day."

"And you envy me for it, too, Charlie, don't you? Watch out; it's catching!" Tug laughed, then said, "Why are you taking such an interest in this anyway? Did all the hearings with Miss Frances get to you? And now you own property here and your feet are getting deeper and deeper into this culture. What gives?"

Charles chuckled. Then he decided to drop the bomb on his friend. "Wait until I run to be a senator from Maryland."

His comment was met with stunned silence; Tug was in shock. "I'll pretend I didn't hear that. The Old Dominion is your home. It's where your family has been for generations."

"Just like yours was in the blue bloodline of Boston. Times change, friend. Times change."

Tug was shaking his head. "When are you headed this way again? Tomorrow? I think we need to have a long conversation."

"Yep, tomorrow. I miss my bride and I think I better get my sister off that island. She fancies herself a cake baker now, I understand."

"Didn't Willa warn you that the island is magical and a little mystical, too, it seems? You better watch out."

"Indeed. Look at what's happened to you and you aren't even on the island."

"It was the crab shanty that got to me, Charlie; not quite as romantic as an island."

"How is Lindy doing?"

"She's hanging in there."

"You ready for a baby? That will change life considerably."

"Well, I wasn't expecting it or anything, but I can't say I am sad about it. I love Lindy and having a baby will be a good thing. Now I'm hoping my parents think it's as nice as I do. And—did I tell you?—my kid brother has taken a good job down here. So, who knows? Maybe the blue-blooded Brahmins of Boston will all come to Somerville."

"Good grief, Tug! Don't say that. If so, we're all doomed."

Tug chuckled with his new friend. "Maybe so, Charlie. Maybe so."

Chapter Fifteen

When she heard the tapping on the door, Willa was upstairs measuring room sizes. She wanted to have a plan in place when Charles arrived. She knew it would be easier to have him agree to all the changes if she had them laid out. Then they could get a builder. This was going to be only their getaway for a while, but she hoped that, one day, it would be their full-time residence.

"C'mon in," she shouted down the stairs. People out here never worried about who it might be. They knew most everyone, and, besides, they were surrounded by water, so no one wandered in accidentally.

"Hey, how ye comin'?"

"Miss Frances, I'm so happy to see you! Let me put up this old measuring tape and I'll be right down."

"I'll put the teapot on."

Frances knew this house like the back of her hand. It had belonged to a good friend of hers who had died recently. The woman's husband had gone to live with one of their children on the mainland, and she was saddened by that because she knew he wouldn't last long living with any of his children.

Willa walked into the kitchen. "There, that's done."

"What are you doing, Willa? Thinking of expanding one of the rooms to a nursery?"

"My God, Frances, don't you even think about that. No, I'm going to reclaim this house for my own, and that means the whole house will undergo a transformation."

Frances looked a little shocked, and a little sad.

Willa walked over and gave her a bear hug. "Don't worry. I'm not going to make it a mansion or anything like that. I want it to look on the outside like an old Eastern Shore waterman's house, but the inside will be completely modernized."

Trying to make the best of the change to her old friend's house, Frances said, "I'll bet that will be right purty, Willa. You have a fancy eye for things. I'm just a plain woman, with plain tastes."

"Well, nothing is going to get done until Charles and I agree on the plans, and then hire a builder to see if all my ideas even can be done."

"You should remember some of the men over in Somerville, Willa. The ones who build boats. Some of them might need the extra money. A lot of them build houses, too."

"Charles and I already talked about that, Frances. But how can I find out who's good and who's available?"

"Ask Lindy about it. She could find out. That girl knows everyone in that town and most of them come into Virgil's."

"Great idea. See? Things are falling into place now, as if it was meant to be. Told you that you weren't a plain woman. You are a fountain of resource for all things."

Frances laughed. "I don't know about that, but I'm not much on the fancy things."

"Oh, I wouldn't say that. You love pretty things. And that reminds me—pour the tea, please. I have something for you."

Willa went back to her bedroom and retrieved a small gift box from the closet. When she returned to the kitchen, she set the box down, lifted her cup, and took a small sip. Then she said, "Ah, this tea is just what I needed. Here, Miss Plain Jane."

Frances hesitantly took the box. "What's this about? I don't recall it's a holiday or anything."

"Just open it, Frances."

Frances's eyes got as big as the saucers under the teacups when she pulled out the most exquisite silk scarf.

"This is beautiful, Willa, but why? And where will I wear this?"

"When you come to Washington to visit me."

"When am I going back up there?"

"When I ask you, I hope, and that won't be too long. I want you and Jimmy to come stay with us for a long weekend."

"Well, I don't know if Jimmy will come, but I'll be there when ye ask." Miss Frances changed the subject. "By the way, where's Vernie? Did she run off, embarrassed about that crab incident?"

Willa laughed. "No, she is past that. She's over at Miss Millie's house, learning how to bake cakes."

"Good Lord. Why on earth does a fancy girl like that want to bake cakes?"

"She's southern? I don't know, Frances. I think she's got a notion or two about maybe starting a business in northern Virginia. As she and I talked the other night, I could sense she needs something to do, and she sure took to cake baking when we went over to Miss Millie's Tuesday morning."

"Well, we'll see how long that lasts. Millie works herself to death doing that. But she loves it and we're all glad of that. She's the best, no doubt of it. My sister, Rita, learned how to bake cakes from Millie and the two of them help each other out sometimes."

"I remember going to Rita's house that first time, and the smells that came from her kitchen were nearest thing to heaven. How's she doing anyway?"

"Ah, she has her spells lately and says she doesn't feel so good, so we'll have to see what all happens. She's been down awhile now, and that's why she didn't come over for your reception."

Willa took her dear friend's hand and said, "I liked her a lot, but not nearly as much as you. You, I love. Do you like the scarf, Frances? If not, I can get you something else."

"I love it. Looks kind of Chinese. I will treasure it, Willa. It'll be warm when it gets cold out here. Look at me, with a silk scarf all my own."

"I love Chinoiserie. It's kind of a southern way of decorating. They mix traditional with a bit of Chinese influence and it comes out really well."

"I like that. I just never knew they had a name for it. I will have to remember that word, Willa."

"I've missed you so much, Frances. Funny that we can be on a small island and yet not see one another much."

"It's like that here, Willa. Small as we may be, we all have our lives to live. We kind of catch up when we go food shopping over to the mainland, but sometimes it can be awhile before we see one another. That's why it's good to go to church every week. If one of us doesn't show up for a while, we send out a search party." She stopped for a moment and then added, "And there are some of us who have homes over on the mainland now, since some of the men stopped fishing. We are getting smaller and smaller in number."

"But then you have people like Charles and me who buy here."

"Yes, and that's good. We want to see new folks come to the island."

In a lighthearted tone, Willa said, "Who knows? Maybe one day we will live here year 'round."

"I don't think you fancy folks will ever want to do that."

"Maybe, but I love it and would like to come as often as I can."

"Well, between fixing this place up and writing, I don't see how you are going to get it all in."

"I will have to find the time, won't I? Nellie does."

"Yes, but she lives here full time."

"Well, maybe this is where I will write. My apartment in D.C. is expensive to keep. Charles and I haven't talked about that. We're now living in our fancy Georgetown digs, but, when I write, I still go over to my old place. I am thinking of letting it go. So many memories there, though. One of the compromises one makes when they get married, I suppose. However, I really think it has to be sold."

"So many places to worry about. Too much for this old gal. But you do need your own space and this house is perfect for that."

"Yes, but we really want you and Jimmy to come visit in Georgetown. You would have your own space there. And we have an elevator. We had it put in because the stairs are narrow in those places, and we do have guests who come to visit."

"An elevator, Willa? Well, I'll be. Can't imagine that. We'll see about it. I best be going now. I had Denny buy me some meat when he was over to Somerville, so I want to go pick it up and cook it for supper."

"What are you making?"

Frances laughed and said, "Hamburgers. Nothing very fancy like your Chinwooser something or other."

Willa hugged her and then said, "Chinoiserie. Try using that at your Ladies' Aid meetings."

"They'd run me out of there, quick as look at me."

"Nah, you'd all be laughing your pants off. Say, Charles is coming back over for at least part of the weekend. I know he adores seeing you, so we'll have to get together."

"Maybe he'd like some of my cream of crab soup. I'll make some up."

"I'm sure he would and I know I would, too. We'll talk. Bye, Frances, and remember I love you."

"I love you, too, girl."

Chapter Sixteen

Finding Buster Talbot was going to be a whole bunch easier for Tug than fixing the back door he was walking through. It had had that squeak for a long time, and he didn't think it was going to surrender anytime soon, even to someone who actually knew what they were doing.

Right now the squeaky back door was the least of his concerns, even though knowing the man's name and where he lived was going to make this a piece of cake. That's all you needed to know on the shore to find anyone. Besides Buster wasn't a young man, even though Charlie hadn't told him that. He just knew this was a much older man, for a younger man would never have had the kind of guts this one did, to just head on up to the Capitol Complex and bull his way in.

He couldn't help but hear Lindy talking to someone on the phone, but he couldn't quite make out who it was. Her tone of voice was a bit strained. When she saw him, she waved him over. She put her hand over the mouthpiece and mouthed the words, "It's your father. Please take it."

His father liked Lindy, but Tug knew he would have liked it so much more if his Harvard son had come back to Boston and married the daughter of one of his old friends. Shandy Lee Atkinson was her name and she was a piece of work. She and Tug were good friends, but she'd always been more than he could handle.

Shandy lived up to her rather vivacious name, a cross between that of her mother, Sharon, and her father, Andy. Why they decided to do that to her, no one would ever know, but she was old-line wealthy, Wellesley-graduated, and the spoiled darling of her daddy. There was nothing Shandy Lee Atkinson didn't have . . . except for Tug Alston.

She had laid claim to him from the time they had first splashed around the club's swimming pool. As they grew, Shandy chased other girls away. He was hers, all hers, and, when she found out he had married a girl from "crab town" (as she referred to Somerville), she had wanted to die. Her whole life had been planned around their getting married, and the Alstons and her parents had just assumed it would happen one day. Tug's father was trying to make the best of it, but Tug also knew his big shot, celebrity father would have preferred he had married Shandy.

Tug took the phone. "Hi, Dad. It's been awhile. How are you?"

Lindy left the room. She was always nervous around or talking to Tug's dad, and with good cause. She was perfectly aware that he thought her people were hicks. After she and Dickie had gone to Boston for Thanksgiving that one year, she had known it was going to be hard for him, especially, ever to fully accept her. However, she was a bright girl, now taking college courses, and determined to graduate, then maybe be an artist or a decorator, her secret desire. Willa's friendship was good for her; it made her want to keep moving forward.

Tug's voice was always so strained, too, when he spoke to his father, and that made Lindy sad. They had overcome so much, but it seemed his father was slipping right back to his old self. Tug's mother was a living doll, but Lindy didn't see or hear much from her. She prayed her kindness hadn't been a show for her son; it hadn't felt that way.

"I don't know when I'm coming home, Dad. Have you heard from Mikey lately?" Tug was trying to deflect the conversation.

"No, I haven't, son. In fact, I thought you might be able to enlighten me as to the whereabouts of my younger son. Neither of you keep in touch very often. Makes your mother unhappy."

Tug hated when he did that, always using that tired old guilt-thing about how much it hurt his mother. He knew it was a crock because he spoke to his mother on a fairly regular basis. Whether she shared that info with his father was anyone's guess. Honestly, he wouldn't blame his mom if she up and left him. He was always at the office or the club or who-knows-where. Maybe she did blame his dad and that's why she was so sad.

"Dad, there is something I would like to tell you and Mom. Is she there? If she is, tell her to pick up an extension." He would take the coward's way out and do it over the phone, so, if they weren't really as pleased as he hoped they might be, at least he wouldn't see their faces.

He heard his father calling to his mom. *Good. I can get this message over with.*

"Hello?"

"Hi, Mom! I wanted to tell you and Dad something. Glad you were home."

"Tug, how good to hear your voice. What is it? I hope it's something good. Everyone all right?"

"Yes, Mom, Lindy and I are doing fine. I heard from Mikey not long ago, and he seems to be doing okay, too. Haven't seen him for a while, though."

"Well, out with it, boy," his father urged, sounding rushed.

"Okay. I want you to know that you're going to be grandparents. Lindy's expecting."

His mother shouted, "That's wonderful! I'm so happy, Tug Were you two planning on this so soon?"

"Well, kind of," he lied. He didn't want to say they weren't. That would only cause more conversation than he wanted right now. And still no response from his father. Tug was pretty sure he knew what was going through his dad's head, and it wasn't at all what his mother was verbalizing at the moment.

"Ted, isn't this good news?" his mother urged his father.

In the coldest voice Tug had ever heard, he answered, "Yes, yes it is. I guess." Then he did something so unexpected that Tug was glad he wasn't standing in front of him. His father said, "By the way, Tug, I saw Andy Atkinson today, and he said you should come on back up here and play some golf this summer."

This was such blatant code. His father was saying he should leave Lindy and go on back to his home, his way of life, and Shandy. His dad had deliberately ignored what he had just been told.

"Really, Dad? That's your response to what you just heard from me? I don't believe it. This time you've just gone too far. I don't know when Lindy and I might get to Boston, but that doesn't matter now, does it?"

There was dead silence on the line. Then his mother jumped in to try to salvage things. "Well, I think this is wonderful news, Tug. Is Lindy doing okay?"

"It's early on, but she's sick on and off, Mom."

"That will stop. Oh, I am so excited about this! Please give her a hug from me. I've got to go now. Father and I are off to the club for the day."

"Thanks, Mom, and you two have a good time today. I'll talk to you soon. Take care." With that Tug hung up.

He had been deeply wounded. Why couldn't his father cut him some slack? Why couldn't he stop trying to break apart his marriage? He had thought this was all over—the games between them—but it seemed it would never be done. *If my baby is a boy, I am going to do my best to have a relationship with him that is the complete opposite of what I have had with my father. I am not going to make my son suffer as I have.*

Lindy saw the torment on his face as she came back into the room. "Your mom was thrilled and your dad was not. It doesn't matter, Tug. He'll come around after the baby is born."

"I doubt that, Lindy. There's something wrong with that man. He's in a different world and time."

"Gee, maybe that's what he thinks of you?"

Tug embraced her. "How did I get you, Lindy-girl? You are so much smarter than most people I know."

"Most? Well"—she hesitated and smiled—"I guess you know a lot of smart people, so I won't take offense."

"Mom is over-the-moon happy, though."

"Well, that's half the team. Don't worry about it, Tug. We're going to win the game."

While he wasn't at all sure, he loved her spirit and said, "That's my girl."

Chapter Seventeen

Tug's mother was furious at her husband when she hung up the phone. She walked down the stairs and confronted him in their den.

"That was awful, Ted. What you just did to our son was unforgivable."

Ted looked at her with disgust. They had been married a long time, and he knew that tone of voice. She was out for blood.

Defiantly he said, "I can't say what I don't feel."

"You can't say what? About a new baby? Our first grandchild?"

There was history between these two: she, a genuine American blue blood whose forebearers were on the Mayflower, and he, a genuine Irishman, whose family was proud and stubborn. He was true to his clan's ways and drank a lot, and, though he had a quick wit, he also had a bad temper to go with it. When they fought, it was to the death. Thankfully, that didn't happen often, but this one was not going to end well.

"What has our boy done to himself, Kay? He went down there to that Godforsaken place and lived with that old man who took his brain, turned him around, saw a good thing for his little girl there, and, the next thing we know, our Tug has thrown out his Harvard pedigree, thrown out a damned good job at the *Globe*, and married that, that—"

"You stop right there, Ted Alston, if you ever want me to speak to you again."

The fire in her dark green eyes was flaming now, and her beauty was even greater when she got truly mad at him. She always reminded him of Maureen O'Hara in *McClintock*! when she would get into it with John Wayne. Wow, what a woman!

"Kay Ann Hastings Alston, stop it. I have a right to my opinion. Tug made his bed, and now he has really made it, and he can live in it. That doesn't mean I have to embrace it."

"What has she ever done to you to make you feel this way about her? You sure put on a good act when they got married."

"By then, it was too late and I could see she had bewitched Tug."

99

"Dear God, you would think you were talking about Salem. Pull your head out of that nasty arse of yours and give me a break."

"She's trapped him for good now."

She walked around him and stood right in his face. "I swear to you, if you do not call him back and apologize, I will leave you, Ted Alston. I've put up with your fits and bar fights and even a woman or two you thought I didn't know about, but I won't put up with this. That child will be my little one, and, if you cannot abide that and join with me in our blessing, then we are over."

He had never seen her like this. He hadn't always been the most faithful or best husband, but, on balance, over the years, they had enjoyed a wonderful life together. He loved her, but there was something about the way Tug was living his life that he could not forgive.

She shook her head. "I see you now very clearly, and what I see, I don't like. Your stubbornness has split us apart. Then so be it." She turned and walked out of the room.

He stood there like a statue. He couldn't imagine why he didn't say something to patch this hole from tearing apart completely. Then a horrible thought occurred to him: maybe he didn't want to. Maybe he was tired of trying so hard to keep it all together. He loved her, no doubt, and he wanted her the way a man wants a woman, even at their advancing ages, but there was no more fight in him anymore to bring her back, to make it right. He knew she meant every word she had said, and now he would pay the consequences for his stubbornness.

Kay Alston was now determined to leave her marriage. They had a home on Cape Cod that was year-round suitable, so she called a mover and was fortunate enough to find someone who could come the next day. She packed up some of her things while Ted was at the paper. They hadn't really spoken after the fight, and the odd thing was, this time, neither felt the need to do so. She was heartsick, but knew Ted. He was determined in his behavior, and, this time, she didn't think he would come to a peace table with her. This had been coming for years, but, to have it come over their son's happiness and a beautiful and innocent unborn, was almost unbearable.

She waved as the movers went down the walk for the last time. "I think that's it, guys. We have it all. I'll meet you at the address in a couple of hours. Be sure to treat yourselves to a good lunch."

As she turned and looked at the old Boston house she had loved and cared for, she realized how empty it really was. It wasn't just empty of things now, but of spirit, too. This had been the home she had been brought to as a bride and she had loved it. Now it dawned on her that it had been empty for a very long time. The boys had been the glue that had held it together, but they were gone now. She had to move forward with her life. And that life would not include Ted Alston.

The house on the Cape had always been her heart and soul anyway. She loved the ocean, and now she would wake up to it in the four seasons and that was a very comforting feeling. She was so close to Tug and had always defended him. Her Mikey was an athlete, and his father had adored him from day one. She loved them both, but, deep down, she had to admit that it was Tug who gave her inner joy. Seemed almost fitting that it would be over Tug that she and her husband would end the charade of a good marriage.

Her cell phone rang, and, with tears in her eyes, she answered and heard that voice of joy.

"Hi, Mom. I just wanted to talk to a friendly voice. I had a feeling you and Dad were going to have at it when I hung up yesterday."

"Hi, Tug. How perceptive you are."

"Who drew the first blood?"

She chuckled softly. "Well, if I tell you I am sitting on the stairs looking around the house and saying good-bye, would that give you a clue?"

A long silence fell between them and then he said, "I was afraid of this. That is why I really didn't want to tell you, but—"

"Oh, Tug, we all know Dad and I were washed up when Mikey left for school. With the two of you gone, the house got bigger and bigger and colder and colder. I'm so sorry you got so hurt. He had no cause to do that to you. I thought he had come around with you."

"I had, too, Mom, but I see now that he hadn't and never will. He feels I failed him. How he wanted me to live my life came between us. I think it really started the day I went to work for Max."

"Ah, Max. I haven't heard from him in a long time. He adored you and was so happy to have you along with him down there in Baltimore."

"I love Max, and I will always be grateful he was able to give me that job. But I'm also sorry because I think he lost his when I stuck my nose into that business with some of his biggest advertisers."

"Max is a big boy, Tug. He could always take care of himself, and he was probably glad to go, if he ever would admit it. He needed to retire and find a new adventure."

"I always thought he loved you, Mom. He never married and devoted his whole life to the paper."

"Well, maybe he did a little, but your father won that dogfight. Ted Alston wasn't going to take no for an answer."

"Sorry now? I mean, where are you going?"

"My special place, the house on the Cape. I love it there, and I'll be happy there. And so will my new grandchild!"

"Oh, Mom, I'm so sorry it's going this way. Maybe you and Dad—"

"Stop it right there. There's no me and Dad now. We said our piece and it's done. Should have been a long time ago, but a man who can't accept and love a grandchild, who still holds on to the past, is not a man I want to end my days with."

"Lindy and I love you, you know."

"And I love Lindy. You, I'm not so sure about," she said teasingly.

"When will you go?"

"Right after I hang up with you. Now, is Lindy still getting so sick? Tell her it'll let up in a while. But nasty stuff, morning sickness."

"Good for getting the husband to wait on you hand and foot, though. You women have it all figured out, don't you?"

"Well, now that you say that—" She stopped and her tone turned serious. "Be happy, Tug. Don't let your father rob you of this joy. You are a wonderful writer with more books to come. You are a wonderful husband and will be a wonderful father. No mother could have asked for a better son, and I love you so much."

"That goes two ways, Mom. Let me know when you are settled."

"When I am, I'm going to head down there for a visit with you and Mikey."

"I'll hold you to that."

Chapter Eighteen

Tug decided the time was right for him to drive up to the small town of Secretary and have a talk with this Buster Talbot. Some of the Somerville men had heard of him, but none knew much other than he was a farmer "up to Secretary," as they put it.

"Lindy," he called up the stairs. "I'm getting ready to go. Is there anything I can do for you before I leave?"

Lindy came to the top of the steps, while putting another roller in her hair. "I don't think so, hon."

Tug looked up at her and became a bit puzzled. "Why are you fixing yourself up to go to work at Virgil's?"

The truth was, Lindy was now eager to get something done with their house—especially, adding a nursery—so she was on her way over to see Clyde Shaw in his office. She had called her old high school friend to set up an appointment while Tug was busy with his own work. She was so happy for Clyde that he was doing well enough now to be a builder all the time instead of working on the water all day and doing the building he loved only on weekends.

Now she knew she needed to tell Tug about her plans. It wouldn't be much, and her drawings for it were very simple—nothing at all like the ones she'd been doing for the dream house she wanted them to build one day. But that was a topic for another time.

She walked carefully down the narrow stairs.

"First off, I want to give you a kiss before you leave, and, second, I want to tell you something. And I don't want you to get mad at me."

"Oh, boy. What are you getting ready to do now, Lindy Short?"

"I'm Lindy Alston now, and you only pull that 'Lindy Short' thing on me when you think I'm about to do something you won't like."

"Well, are you? I know you, girl, and I know how you work me."

"That's so not nice, Tug, but I do want you to know I'm going over to visit a man named Clyde Shaw. He's a builder and we grew up together."

"A builder? For what?"

Lindy didn't want to get too particular with Tug at this point; she knew he already had a lot on his mind. "I am going to talk to him about fixing up a nursery and a few other things in this house. The baby will be in college before you finish it, and then it won't matter."

"I don't believe this. I don't believe you don't have the confidence that I can do it."

Lindy wanted to giggle, but thought better of it. "You're wrong. You can do anything. *But* you don't have the time to do it. You are working on a new novel, doing some project now for Charlie Lee, and you are being the best husband ever. So— please—let me do this."

Tug retreated for a moment. He didn't want to fight with her; he loved her far too much to do that. He took a deep breath and said, "Okay, Lindy, I trust you and you're right about my not having the time. But where do you think the money to do this is coming from?"

"Well, we aren't exactly poor, Tug, with your writing and advances and all. But that isn't where I'm getting the money anyway."

"What? Are you a rich girl, Lindy, and hiding that from me?"

"Well, not rich by your standards, but I do have money. Dickie left me quite a nice sum. I just never told you."

"Dickie left you money? I don't understand."

"Because he gave it to me before you came here. I was in high school."

"What?" The look on Tug's face was one of sheer shock.

"Yes, he gave me a barrel of it and told me to save it, so I did. I never really needed any of it. As you can see here in this house, Dickie and Shirley didn't spend much on anything. They didn't see the need, so Aunt Shirley, who had a job at the bank for years before she retired, had a big savings account. They lived off Uncle Dickie's crabbing and oystering and he was one of the best watermen alive. So, now that I want to have better for my family, I first half-thought I would sell this old house and move out to the island, but I didn't think you would ever go for that."

Tug sat down in Dickie's old recliner. He couldn't even imagine the words coming out of her mouth. "How much exactly did he give you, Lindy?"

"Well, there are several accounts, and I haven't checked on them lately, but I should imagine way more than half a million dollars."

"I don't know what to say. I'm—"

Lindy interrupted. "Well, there was never a need to talk about this, so I didn't, but now I want a little better home for my baby."

"I'll bet you do. This really is a shock, Lindy. Tell you what. Go talk to this Clyde man, and you can tell me all about it when I get home, and then we can talk about what we really want to do here."

Lindy sat down on his lap and screeched, "I love you so much." Then she gave him a long and loving kiss.

Tug finally pulled back. "Lindy, if we don't stop here, I won't get to Secretary and you won't get to your builder friend."

She smiled and hugged him tight. "I know, but it might be fun."

"Go on now. Make yourself prettier than you already are, but don't let that man get any ideas. You're all mine."

"Forever. Be safe and I'll see you at dinner. I'll work at Virgil's after my meeting."

Kissing her lightly on the check, he said, "Behave."

Tug drove off, still thinking about their conversation. Lindy was such a gem. Here she had had all that money and saved it and never touched a dime of it and never saw a need to tell him. She was a true innocent, and he knew that was part of what had attracted him to her in the first place.

They did have a lot of decisions to make. Living over in Tuckerton, though? He didn't know if he could do that. It really was remote, a completely isolated life. He wouldn't mind buying a small place over there, though. His mind ran in a thousand directions. How funny it would be if both he and Charlie ended up there—Harvard and Congress on the same, small island. Preposterous really. Or was it? He couldn't wait to tell his new friend this tale.

Suddenly his mind jumped to his mother and father and what had become of them now that his mother had moved out and to the Cape. Life was so fragile and unpredictable, and he knew she was so right: it wasn't the baby news that had ended it. Their marriage had been in trouble for years. He'd known it, but he wasn't sure Mikey had. That was another conversation he would need to have.

He had done some legwork and found Buster Talbot's phone number and had set up a meeting at the Suicide Bridge restaurant. He couldn't wait to see this place. If all else failed, he would at least eat lunch and meet another fine Eastern

Shore character to add to his file. He could tell he was in for something special, just in the short conversation he'd with the man while setting up this meeting.

When Tug walked in the restaurant, he couldn't miss Buster. He appeared even taller and bigger than Charlie had described. He was Goliath, and Tug had never considered himself that short.

"You Tug?" the man said as he walked over to meet him.

"Yes, and you're Buster Talbot."

"Yep." The hostess, seeing the size of the men, directed them to a table for four so they could spread out a little.

"This is beautiful here. What river is that?"

"That's the Choptank. She runs aside of Cambridge down a ways. She's a big one, all right."

Tug never tired of the regional speech. He loved it, actually.

They looked the menu over, and ordered. Then Buster looked Tug square in the eye.

"What exactly are you here for?"

Yes, directness was a shore strong suit. "Well, I'm not totally sure, but my friend is Charles Lee—Congressman Charles Lee?—and he said you went to see him. You had some grievances and asked him to help."

Buster leaned in to Tug and whispered, "I'm not in trouble, am I?"

"Not unless you threatened him." Tug chuckled. "No, you're not in trouble. I'm just trying to find out some things and then let Congressman Lee know."

Buster sat back, a relieved look on his face. "Okay, then. Ask away."

"First of all, I wouldn't recommend you go visit the congressman like that again. You're lucky they didn't lock you up for being crazy."

"Yeah, I know, but I think the guard was a shore man himself."

"Well, just the same. Charles tells me you went to see him about farmers. I live down in Somerville with watermen, and they seem to have the same problems and challenges you do. Would that be fair to say?"

"Some might say that. I guess maybe we do. The government is making it so hard on us to farm or fish, for that matter, that a lot of us are giving up and selling our land."

"Tell me more about that, Buster. Why aren't your children taking over your farms?"

There was an intermission of sorts when the server brought their lunches. The smell of the crab cakes was heavenly. "Boy, does this look good," Tug said.

"Sure does, but I prefer the beef. Never did like crabs so much, but don't go back to Somerville and say that."

"Your secret is safe with me."

Once served, Buster wanted to get to it and eat, and Tug could see that, until his guest had taken a few bites out the mammoth hamburger in front of him, he was best to hold his thoughts for now. Tug knew that men eat very differently from women. They just eat and feel no need to talk until their palates catch up with the taste. Then they again come up for air and find their tongues.

Buster finally came up for air and said, "So what do you want to know, Tug?"

"Well, I'd like to know just what all is going on with the farmers and why it was important for you to speak with Congressman Lee."

Buster wiped his mouth on a huge, white, linen table napkin. He politely belched into it and then said, "There are things that just don't make sense. And the legislators want to pass laws they don't even understand."

"Why don't you educate me?"

"Well, they want to ban phosphorus and that's what makes fertilizer. They don't understand anything. If they do that, we can't farm our fields."

"But the last election sort of helped that, didn't it?"

"Yes, for now. But, I tell you, they just won't stop until they put us all out of business, and then who is going to feed the people and the livestock? And who is going to pay the taxes?"

"Well, I don't know, Buster. It was the same with the watermen and now it's with you farmers."

"The way these scallywags operate, you have to stay way ahead of them. It's like they lost their common sense and have no idea of how to get it back. The lawmakers and that Baywaters Commission keep on blaming the farmers for the runoff pollution in the Bay. It is a whole lot bigger than that, and the farmers keep adjusting things, but it's never enough for them."

"If it's really that bad, how far do you think they will go?"

"All the way, if they can. They have no common sense and they don't understand how the food chain works."

"What do you mean?"

"Well, if they close down the grain production—because you can't grow anything without fertilizer and bug treatments—then they close up the poultry business because the chicks can't eat. And, if they do that, the poultry moves somewhere that isn't as nuts as these folks, which closes down the farms and everything associated with them."

"I get the picture now, but do you think they will really do that?"

"They will if people don't find their brains and put them back into their heads."

"You know, Buster, none of this makes sense to me. I just don't understand why a state would want to kill off its income. The same is true with the watermen. Why?"

"Nothing seems to make good sense anymore. It's all become an argument about the Bay, and there are plenty of differing opinions on that, so why not wait and see? If the watermen don't fish out there, the Bay will surely die anyway. It's all a cycle of life. The chicken business is, too. I mean, how do these folks think that farmers can raise chicks and take them to market without feeding them, and how do they think we can feed them if we can't raise our crops?"

"Maybe there is a different kind of feed that can be produced without fertilizer?"

"If you know of any, please tell us farmers, won't you, Tug?"

"And you want what kind of help?"

"Well, now that you're here, it wouldn't hurt none if you could write some articles for a newspaper presenting our side."

"That would be a neat trick. Who would print it? The papers seem to side with the Baywaters Commission. I've been through this before, you know."

"I do know, Tug, and, well, you're respected in these parts. So why not start with our local papers? They would print what you said."

"That may be true, but I have to have a lot more than this to go on. No disrespect, Buster."

"That's okay with me. I understand what you're sayin'."

"You know, I really just want to settle down and write my books and enjoy a quiet married life."

"Wouldn't we all? But some people have talent to grow things, some people have talent to fish, and you, my son, have talent to say things."

Tug sat there and finished his crab cake, thinking about what Buster had just said. Buster was right, and he knew it, but did he want to jump back into the fray? Hadn't he had enough?

"Look, here's what I'll do. I'll talk this all over with Congressman Lee and research what you've told me. And then—and only then—I will see if there's enough to write about. I can promise you this and nothing else right now."

Buster broke out in a great big smile and said, "That's more than I expected to get."

"I find that hard to believe. I thought you would want me to go slay the dragon, too."

"Not right away, but, sooner or later, I think you might just do that."

Tug grabbed the check before Buster could lay his big hand on it. "This one's on me."

"I pay for my own, Tug. Let me have it."

"Not on your life. If I come up with something and can slay that dragon, then you can pay the next one."

"You got yourself a deal. Thanks."

Chapter Nineteen

Lindy showed Clyde the drawings she had done, both of her ideas for Dickie's house and for the dream house she had not yet mentioned to Tug. She was a very good artist but had never really pursued it, and now she was wondering why.

"These are really good renderings, Lindy Loo."

"I haven't heard that name for years. Since I last saw you, I guess. What did you call them?"

"Renderings. That's what architects or builders have to have in order to build or fix anything."

"Wow, you learned a lot away at school, didn't you, Clyde?"

"Yes, I guess I did. Took long enough, but I'm glad to be back here now."

"I'm glad you're back, too. You haven't met my husband, Tug, have you?"

"No, I haven't, but I've heard he's a real nice guy. I'm looking forward to it. That is, if I get the job."

"Honestly, I wonder if it's worth it on that old house. The only reason for keeping it is because it was left to us by Dickie."

"My mother told me, Lindy. We all loved that old man, you know, and nothing will ever be the same in town or on the water now that he's gone. He was an institution and the best example of what a waterman is truly like."

"Thank you, Clyde. You know how close I was to him and Aunt Shirley. But the old house is quite a mess!"

Clyde took his gimme cap off and said, "I can only imagine."

"What do you think? Is it worth it? I want a straight answer now, Clyde."

"Well, you put me in a spot, Lindy Loo. I'm a builder, and so—honestly—I would suggest you rent out that old house after you build a real nice one over there on the point where you and your man can look out to the Bay and the islands. But I understand about your house being a gift from ole Dickie."

He continued, "So, what about this? I could do some fixes to the old house that will make it more livable for you and Tug, and then we could work on plans for the dream house you've been drawing until we get them just right. I believe both of you would rather live on the water and closer to the old shanty. I've heard that shanty means a lot to Tug."

Lindy said, "I love it, too, so very much, Clyde. Those old boards have seen some history." She smiled. "Thanks for telling me what you really think. It has helped me make up my mind. I will blame it on you, of course, when I tell Tug."

"Now, I don't want to go getting Tug mad at me, but, if you think it's easier that way . . . well, just go on and tell him, Lindy. I want to see you happy, too." Clyde grinned at her and said, "You know, I had such a crush on you."

"Get out of here, Clyde Shaw. You did not."

"I sure did, and, to be honest with you, when I heard you had up and married Mr. Ivy League, I wasn't any too happy about it."

"He isn't at all like that, Clyde. He's different from his folks up in Boston."

"That's what I hear, so I'll give him a fair chance when I meet him. Now that you say you've decided, Lindy Loo, what's your pleasure?"

"Lindy Loo isn't sure, but Lindy Alston has made up her mind. Until I can really talk to Tug—he's so busy right now—I want you to plan to fix some of the things in the house. Will that work for you, Clyde?"

"Yes, it surely will. I'll start by helping you with the drawings for the nursery."

Lindy flipped her long hair and said, "Renderings, remember?"

"Oh, yeah. Right." Clyde smiled.

Lindy said, "I will talk to Tug soon and then I'll get back to you. You know, I feel settled about this. I think it will work out really nice. And, if we do build out on the point someday, I will be very close to the shanty, and I want to fix that up, too."

Clyde laughed and said, "Maybe that project Tug can do. With a little help, mind you."

"Oh, Lord, Clyde, you don't have enough life in you for that job."

On the way home, Tug called Charles. Steve picked up the private line and said, "Hello. Congressman Lee's office."

"Hi, Steve, it's Tug Alston. Is Congressman Lee in? He gave me this number to call." Tug wanted always to refer to his new friend Charlie as Congressman Lee in front of others. He never wanted to diminish Charles's position.

"Yes, he is. Hold a moment, please."

Real uptight guy. But working in that world was different from anywhere else, so maybe that's how it was supposed to be.

"Hey, Tug, how ye comin', as Miss Frances would say?"

Tug laughed, and said, "I be fine, Charlie. Hey, I just had lunch with your Buster Talbot."

Charles then laughed, too, and said, "You did? God bless you, Tug; that was fast. What do you think?"

"He's a real Eastern Shoreman, and, as it turns out, a well-known and respected farmer. He's held high positions in the farming community and seems to understand the way of things in Washington. But there is no doubt he's a character. Reminds me of that great columnist, Baxter Black. I would like to tell you more about our conversation and maybe come up with some ideas, if you still want to be involved in all this. So are you still planning to come down this weekend?"

"As a matter of fact, I'm flying in tomorrow and going over to the island."

"Miss her, do you?"

"Have to admit it: yes, I do. And I have to get my sister off of there before she turns into one of them. Her husband, Tom, is very traditional, and he's going to have his hands full when she gets back to Loudoun County, Virginia."

"What does your brother-in-law do?"

"He's an attorney, from a long line of Virginia attorneys. Semi-retired and part time now. But he's southern proud all the way."

"I see. And you don't think he would appreciate his wife catching crabs or skinning muskrats?"

"Oh, God, Tug, forget the muskrats; he'd skin her alive."

"Well, she'll be okay. The island is magical, but not everyone is cut out for it. Actually, most people aren't cut out for it. I couldn't live out there all the time. Once in a while is really nice, but full time would drive me insane."

Charles said, "I know what you mean, but, I have to tell you, it's a tonic for Willa. When she's out there, she calms down, and, when she's here, all she wants to do is go back out there. She's hooked. Willa is a lonely soul, and I understand why. Writers are an odd lot, and need a lot of quiet time and spaces that can let them imagine."

"I can't argue with that, Charlie. If I were to go back to Boston, or even back to my life in Baltimore, after now having been here for a time, I would wither up and die."

"Well, you have Lindy. She's wise beyond her years."

"All I can say is, when I met her, I was done. So I know what you're going through with you over there and Willa on the island."

"Tell you what, Tug. I'm still hoping we can get together while I'm there, even though I can't stay as long as I want. By the way, who's Baxter Black?"

"He's a legend. Look him up and hope to see you soon, Charlie."

Tug made a note to put together a paper outlining what he and Buster had discussed, both for Charles's use and for his own, if there were to be articles and other follow-up. Now, to stop and pick up some food for supper so he could have it in the oven when both of them got home. *I sure hope she can keep it down.*

Chapter Twenty

Frances had gone down to the tiny post office on the island, and she knew she would be there for a while. This was where the women seemed to meet up in the mornings when they didn't have chores to do back at their houses. She wanted to mail a package back to Sears. She had ordered a new bedspread and it wasn't quite right. Her previous one had lasted over thirty years, and she knew this one wasn't going to go that far. But, for that matter, neither was she. The mail boat would take it over in the afternoon when it went to get the folks waiting after doing their shopping. They had left at 7:30 a.m. Another life cycle for island folks.

Willa was just beginning to stir, not realizing that Vernie had been as quiet as a mouse when she had slipped out to go over in the wee hours to see Miss Millie and learn more about those wonderful island cakes.

Willa yawned as she padded to the kitchen and put on a teakettle. She then walked over to the small nook that was the dining area and looked out to the water. Charles was so right: the house needed to be turned around. She stood there in deep thought about it, until the kettle whistled. She was getting a vision of what she was going to do that would still preserve much of the outside style.

Her cell rang and she picked up to hear Charles's voice on the other end. "Morning, sexy."

"You wouldn't particularly say that if you could see me right now."

"Up to your ears in *the* project or in writing? I know how you look when you do that, but I would still say you were pretty sexy."

"Good thing love is blind. The fact is, I just got up."

"Willa, are you all right? You're the one who bounds out of bed in the early morning."

"I'm fine; I just needed a few extra winks. Funny thing is, Vernie isn't up yet either. I'll wake her when we are finished. Is anything on your mind, or is this just a call to say how much you love me?"

"Well, now that you mention it . . . But, no, I am giving you a heads-up that I'll be back over there sometime today."

"That's fabulous, sweetie. I miss you so much—so much, I was considering coming home—but I really want to get a plan together for the house, and I think I'm getting a vision. You're right: we need to turn the house around."

"See? I'm good for something."

"A few other things too, I believe, but that will have to wait."

"I am meeting Tug for coffee when I first land, but then I have a boat arranged to bring me over."

"What are the two of you up to? Getting into some mischief?"

"I guess you could say that." Charles paused and then said, "I had a drink with Prue the other night."

"How is my dearest? I really miss her."

"She's fine, but I wouldn't be surprised if she was on the verge of getting ready to run for office. She'll eventually have to leave the Speaker's office to do that and go on back home."

"Oh, Charlie. She would be great, but I thought she was headed for the corporate world. Still, I know it's in her genes."

"She would be great in Congress, but it's a leap, even for a gal with the last name Harding. One thing I know for certain: you two will see each other."

"Do you think she has a good chance of winning?"

"Absolutely. She has smarts, experience, incredible good looks, and a good bloodline. That all adds up to a win, I think."

"When would she leave? I mean, the election isn't for another year, but I know it takes a long time to ramp up."

"I know she has been moving some of the chess pieces into place while she is working, but that has put a real strain on her."

"Prue thrives on stress. She's well suited for the political game. Much as you are. I would rather write novels about it, myself. I wouldn't last a minute in that game."

"Speaking of that, we are going to have to head down to Virginia later this summer and do the picnic BBQ circuit."

"That sounds kind of fun."

"Will be hectic for us now that we are married. Everyone will want to see us both— me the politician and you the famous writer."

Willa said, "I see. Well, we will make the best of it. Fame has its price, you know. Now to the most important thing: when will you get here?"

"As soon as I am done speaking with Tug. Are you actually working on the plans yet?"

"As I said, I'm getting a vision."

"Bet that vision is expensive."

"I'm going to pay for a lot of it, Charlie, but you will love it. By the way, tell Tug to tell Lindy, she can always use our house when we're away, if she wants to. I know she goes to stay with Frances, but maybe they would like to have some place that is a bit more private."

"That's nice, Willa. Now go check on Vernie. I'll be there soon."

When she discovered Vernie wasn't to be found upstairs, Willa knew exactly where to look next. By the time she reached Millie's kitchen, the other two women were well on their way to being done baking. The kitchen was an almost unrecognizable mess. Willa walked in. With all the racket, no one would have heard a knock on the door anyway.

"Vernie?"

Vernie looked up and she was covered in white icing, actually dripping down her pretty face.

"Hi, Willa. You won't believe what a time we've had."

"Looking at your face, I think I can believe anything right now." Willa walked over and swiped some frosting and licked it. "Mmm, this is good," Willa purred. "What flavor is this?"

Millie laughed at the two of them and said, "It's a secret concoction of mine, but no one else is around to overhear us. It's vanilla fig."

"Vanilla fig? That's unique. I don't think I have ever eaten anything like this anywhere."

"That's because it's unique, dear."

Willa smiled and said, "Got me, didn't you?"

Millie said, "I experiment all the time with new flavors, and figs grow right here on the island. I know that sounds odd, but it's true. We have lots of things people would never guess would grow out here in nowhereland."

"Hmm," Willa said, thinking for a moment. "We could write a cookbook and call it *Recipes from Out Here in Nowhereland*."

"Watch out, Willa. I might just steal that from you."

"It's all yours; just give me credit. Better yet, I'll write a review for the first page."

"Maybe one day, huh?"

Vernie finished washing her face in the kitchen sink. "I had the best time today, Miss Millie. You are simply one divine southern woman, even if you aren't from Virginia."

"Well, I'm glad you won't hold that against me. I'd be heartbroken. We gals over here really are more southern than anything else, but with the English thrown in."

Vernie hugged Millie. "Thank you so much."

Willa took her turn at embracing the island baker and said, "I don't know how I'm going to return her to her husband after she's been here with you."

Millie turned to Vernie and said, "Well, guess you'll have to bring him over here with you next time."

Vernie said, "I don't know if he would like it over here so much. He's a real Virginia boy and his passion is the mountains. I must say, there isn't anyplace much more beautiful than the Blue Ridge."

Millie responded, "I've seen those mountains and couldn't agree with you more. Well, except for the Chesapeake."

Willa said, "There's so much beauty in this country. I love the coast of Maine and have many wonderful memories from my childhood up there."

"Do you ever go back, Willa?" Millie asked.

"Haven't for a long time, but think I may have to do that one day soon. But now, with my own house here, I'm sure that will keep me busy. Do you know of any good builders in these parts, Millie?"

"Actually, I do. There's a young man over to Somerville. He's kind of new at it, but I've seen some of his work and it's simply good work at a fair price. His name is Clyde Shaw. I think he was in school when Lindy went. Ask her about him. He's a real nice boy."

"Thanks, I will. You take care now, Millie."

Vernie hugged her new teacher again and said, "I've had the best time being with you, Miss Millie."

"I enjoyed it too, Vernie, but please call me Millie. Miss Millie makes me think of my mother-in-law."

"Okay, but I know I will forget. It's how I was raised."

"Bye, girls, and don't be strangers."

On the way home, Vernie couldn't wait a moment longer and burst out, "Willa, I'm going to open a cake business when I get home. Don't tell me no; I'm going to do it."

Willa stopped dead in her tracks and said, "Are you out of your mind? Tom will kill you first and then come hunting for me. He will be positively furious, thinking I did this to you."

Quite suddenly, Vernie's delight turned to anger. "What do you mean, Tom wouldn't be happy and would be mad at us? I found something here I love and I am going to pursue it. Don't you dare try to rain on my parade, Willa Lee."

For the first time, Willa saw the spoiled streak Charles had warned her about. Vernie's claws came out as her eyes narrowed. The bitch in her was on full display. Willa treaded carefully.

"If you would calm down a minute, Vernie, all I am saying is that you need to plan this out so that, when you tell Tom, he won't hit the roof. You've told me he likes having you home and being a southern lady. Not, perhaps, a businesswoman."

Vernie not only knew Willa was right, but she also was horrified at how she had spoken to her sister-in-law. "Oh, Willa, can you forgive me for being so mean? I didn't mean it. I really *found* myself in Millie's kitchen. I can do this. Help me plan this out."

"I told you this island is magical, Vernie. Outsiders get thoughts they never had and dreams come to them that they never imagined before. First thing you have to do is go home and bake a cake in your own kitchen and see how that goes. And feels."

"You know, Willa, you're absolutely right. I will have to buy a whole new set of pans and bowls, but I think this is my calling."

"If it is, I'll support you to the moon."

Vernie jumped up and down like a little girl. "Thank you, Willa. You're such a dear."

Frances was walking back from the post office when she saw the two girls. "Hey, there! Hang on, you two."

Vernie whispered to Willa, "I love Miss Frances; she's the best. You aren't going to tell her how mean I was to you, are you?"

Willa shot her a look as if to ask, what? Frances was up to them by then, so she just smiled at Vernie.

"What are you two up to? Fussing like that with one another. I could hear you clear down the lane."

Vernie turned beet red but Willa recovered the ball immediately. "Fussing at one another is what sisters do, isn't it, Frances?"

A devilish smile crossed the woman's face and she said, "Well, when I think about it some, Rita and I would get into some pretty bad scuffles. Still do, if you want me to be honest."

"We were just exploring some employment opportunities for Vernie here."

Frances gave Willa the eye and then looked at Vernie. "What kind of opportunities? Out here?"

"Oh, no, Miss Frances," Vernie said. "I was just telling Willa that I want to go home and bake cakes like Miss Millie."

"Well, no harm in that. Your husband will love that."

Willa poked her and said, "Maybe he won't."

"Oh, I didn't realize the cake bug bit that fast. It's a hard life, Vernie, and why do it if ye don't have to?"

"Well, I can see neither of you really support this idea, but you'll see: I'm going to become the best cake maker in Loudoun County."

Not wanting to set her off again, Willa announced, "Well, look out Sara Lee."

Suddenly completely serious, Vernie drew herself up and stared at Willa. Then, in that gentle southern drawl, she said, "I don't know about anyone in our family named Sara Lee. We do have a large family, but no Sara."

Frances looked at Willa in stunned amazement. All Willa could say was, "Don't worry about it. She's from a different tribe than yours."

Chapter Twenty-One

Lunch on the weekends was one of Lindy's favorite times of the week. Tug liked to cook and was good at it. Yes, he was a keeper. Today, she was particularly glad. After working the early shift at Virgil's, she was already dog tired.

"Hey," she said, as she walked through the kitchen door to see Tug popping something in the oven.

"How's my girl?" he said as he walked over to give her a hug.

"Oh, pretty good. Work was the same, but I think it's finally time to share some news with you."

"Okay. Why don't we go into the living room? Lunch won't be ready for about thirty minutes."

"Smells good in here already. What are you making?"

"A casserole. I am becoming quite good at them these days. Chopped meat and vegetables, not complicated, but real comfort food on a chilly day."

"Sounds good to me. I can't tell you how nice it is that you cook. I really appreciate it, Tug. Another reason to love you."

"Doubt that. You fell for me before I began to cook."

Sitting down on the sofa, she said, "You're right. Must have been another of your many charms, like your smelly socks."

"I don't have smelly socks, Lindy."

Playfully she answered, "I'll have to think what is was then."

"Okay, what's the news?"

"Well, you know I went to see Clyde Shaw yesterday morning. Sorry I was not feeling well enough to tell you about it last night, but he loved my sketches of the house here and told me I was quite good at it."

"Did he now? Since I haven't ever seen them, I couldn't tell you."

"I thought you would think they were kind of amateurish. Well, anyway, when we started talking, Clyde said he would do the job, but he also suggested that we might want to build a new house and rent this one out. That way we could keep Dickie's house here but also have a house better suited for us."

At first Tug felt a twinge of anger he didn't understand. Maybe it was jealousy. He should have been the one making that decision with his wife.

"He did, did he? What did you say? I can't imagine you would want to do that after all you've said about this old house."

"That's true, Tug, but, after we spoke a bit, I think he's got a point."

"Maybe he does. I know the little I have done here has shown me how much more needs to be done. It's a financial sinkhole."

Lindy laughed. "I think we should build a new house out on the point where we can look out to the water and be nearer to the shanty."

Tug sat there, thinking about it. He knew in his heart she was right. This house was going to tear them apart before it was done, and it would cost a lot of money, too. "Do you really want to, Lindy?"

"This is way too easy, Tug. I thought I was going to have to promise you the moon to get you to see it."

"Not really. These older houses need work and I just can't do it. Look, you're lucky I learned to cook. Well, cook a little."

Lindy flew off the sofa and sat down on Tug's lap in Dickie's old recliner. "You are the best husband anywhere. I really do want to do this. I think it would be all right and that Dickie would say to do it."

"You do, do you? I think he would say we were crazy, but he was crazy too, right? So why not? We would have to buy the lot first."

"Clyde can take care of that after we decide exactly where we want it to be."

Tug sat up and moved Lindy off his lap. "I better get that casserole or it will be burnt." As he walked toward the kitchen, he turned to her and asked, "What will we do with this place?"

"We'll figure it all out as we go along. Over lunch, you'll have to tell me about your day yesterday, too, up in Secretary."

"It was an experience, but it went well. Come on now; let's get ready to eat."

Lindy went upstairs to change her clothes and wash up. She also wanted to do something else. Something she had been putting off for a while.

Kay Alston was imagining the finishing touches she would like to put on her newly permanent residence on Cape Cod. She stared out the large window that ran along the back of the house from the living room to the dining room. It looked out to the sea, which had always brought her peace and solace. She and Ted had refurbished the old house over the years, and, as the boys had gotten older, she'd actually been able to bring in some less rugged pieces that she knew would survive two more mature, if still very active, sons. Now, as she stood there, it was all so quiet. She was alone—truly alone—for the first time in almost forty years.

Kay was a beautiful woman, now with mostly salt-and-pepper hair. She had been the catch of the century when Ted Alston had come along, and no one, including her parents, understood how he had won the hand of their pride and joy. Now, she wondered just why she hadn't listened to them, except, of course, that her gift from the marriage was two fabulous sons. They were wonderful to her, especially Tug, her secret favorite.

Mikey had always been the jock and running around with cheerleaders and doing everything he could to drive them all crazy, but he held that special spot as the baby. He'd always been his father's favorite, so it had seemed to work out that each boy had a champion. Still, Tug had taken the brunt of his father's mean streak. He'd always had to deal with that, and the present episode was only the latest in a long line of horrible moments for him.

She didn't regret moving out. It had been long overdue, and now she could do things Ted had never wanted her to do. He had held her back and now she was free.

Kay was so caught up in her own thoughts, she barely heard the phone ringing. When the sound finally penetrated, she hurried out to the kitchen and picked up.

"Hello?"

She almost fell over to hear the sweet voice of her daughter-in-law.

"Mrs. Alston, it's Lindy."

"Hi there! But remember: you should call me Kay, dear."

"I know, but it's still difficult for me to do that. I'll work harder on it."

"It's good to hear your voice. How are you feeling?"

"It still comes in waves, but I think it's a bit better. Tug told me you moved, so I wanted to check on you."

"How sweet, Lindy. Yes, it was time, and one day you and I will talk about it and you'll understand."

"You don't need to explain anything to me, Mrs. . . . . Kay, I mean."

"Good girl. I want us to be good friends, and I can't wait to see my grandchild. I can't believe I'm saying that! I've waited a long time to see this and now I will."

"It was a surprise, but it isn't like we weren't trying either."

"I understand, dear. Most of the world is a surprise. But, so long as you both are happy about this, then all is just right."

"I have a favor to ask you, Kay. I was wondering if you could come down here."

Kay hesitated for only a moment before saying, "Why, yes, I would like that, Lindy. I could fly into Salisbury and see Mikey, too, while I'm at it. Now that he's started his new life down there, I need to see what my youngest is up to."

"Wow, that's great. I have to ask Mikey, too. You see, I want to surprise Tug. I think it would be fun to have a party for his birthday."

"Wonderful! Well, I won't say a word to Tug." Kay loved Lindy's youthful enthusiasm. Maybe that was what she liked so much about her. She herself hadn't been much older when she had had Tug, yet now that seemed so very young. "I'll talk to Mikey and see what works for him and then e-mail you the answer so Tug doesn't see it. Are there any days Tug will be gone?"

"I know he's working on a project, but, when you find out what dates work, I will make sure to have Tug around the house."

"Wonderful, dear. I'm so excited to see you all. I hope you're feeling better by the time I get down there."

A little hesitantly, Lindy said, "By the way, I'm really sorry about you and Mr. Alston. I don't know what to say."

"It was coming for a long time, Lindy. Please don't think it was the baby that got him going. I'm afraid Ted has a lot of rethinking to do about his life. So, I will be in touch soon. Do take care of yourself."

"Thank you, Kay, and see you soon. I am so happy!"

Chapter Twenty-Two

Charles had made the arrangements for his trip home. When it was personal, he preferred to do it himself rather than assign Steve the task. He wanted to have some sort of private life away from the spotlight of any workplace gossip, and, while he trusted Steve, one could never really completely trust anyone around Washington.

He was interrupted suddenly by his assistant, telling him Senator Dawes was on the phone. Charles's face twisted in annoyance. "Put him through, Steve." He was never prepared for Buddy Dawes, who spoke out of two sides of his mouth, but especially not on a Saturday morning when he was just trying to get out of the office as soon as possible.

"Why, good morning, son. Sorry to bother you, but I was at an agriculture meeting recently and one of the underlings in the department made mention that they were getting some heat from a man who had been seen coming to your office. I wanted to check this out and see if there was even a morsel of truth to it."

The only reason Charles took Dawes's calls was because he was seriously considering running for his Senate seat, and he wanted to keep the man close to him—all while he mistrusted him.

"I see a lot of people every day, Senator, and I talk to a lot of people, Senator. Is there a name to this man?"

"I believe there is. Let me see here. I wrote it down on a paper and it's somewhere."

Charles could hear the shuffling of papers as he waited.

"Oh, here it is. The name is Buster Talbot. Have you ever heard of him?"

"Yes, I have, Senator. He did come to see me not long ago."

"Well, then my information was correct. What did this man want?"

Discussing a private conversation with a constituent was really out-of-bounds, so Charles answered, "It was a private matter, Buddy. That's all I'll say. You understand: confidentiality."

Charles could tell Dawes was fuming at his unwillingness to play ball with him. "That's it, son?"

Why can't this man go away? Charles knew he was up to something for sure. If he could only make his mind up about running, then Dawes would know his intentions and think twice before pissing him off. And calling him "son." The way he said it was sheer put-down.

"That's all I'm going to say, Buddy. He came, paid his respects to me, and left."

"You're not going to cooperate, are you?"

"I don't think there is any cooperating about this. The man came to talk to me and that is confidential between me and him. Or do your spies report something different?"

Senator Dawes had got enough out of Charles to know that he was meeting with farmers. But why? He had to find that out. The powers that be on Congressional agriculture committees weren't going to like this young upstart interfering with their issues, or whatever he was sticking his nose into. They liked things quiet and peaceful. They didn't want anything to stand out because that's when trouble starts with the voting public.

Of course, he didn't know Charles was already twisting some committee arms in order to know what was going on, and the rest of his information was coming directly from farmers.

"Be careful, son. The big boys don't like surprises, and it seems you're always involved in blindsiding them with these shore matters. Farmers have always complained. They're as bad as those watermen, and they have to learn to obey rules and regulations without complaining all the time."

Charles was now seething. He hated the prejudice this man had toward the farmers and fishermen of this country. He couldn't hold back any longer.

"You know, Senator, I respect you and your service to this Congress, but, sometimes, do you ever think you might be wrong? I mean, do you think there are two sides to any given situation?"

"You've stirred things up for a while now, Charles. Your family is well respected, but there are rules for you, too, and taking your complaints through proper channels is one of those rules we follow—"

Charles cut him off. "I *stirred* things up, as you say, and it turned out to be the best thing I ever did. Watermen and state and federal officials are now communicating with one another. Do our crabbers and oystermen like all the things they are being told to do? No, they don't, but it's better to talk face-to-face than to shove things down their throats, not allowing them their grievances. Frances Evans was one of the most well-received people to come to the Hill and you know that. I think you and your friend, Richardson, even admired her spirit and the information she gave."

Bristling and ever the snake, Dawes answered, "Okay, son, I'm going to assume you're going to do the same thing with the farmers, but be prepared to get some pretty stiff incoming on this. There are powerful groups who want to rein these farmers in over the way they farm."

"First of all, don't threaten me, no matter how you try to dress it up. And, second, don't you think farmers are aware of the issues and already trying to solve the various challenges set before them?"

The senator from Maryland was fed up with this young pup. "I'll tell you again, son: be careful."

"Don't you worry about me, Senator. We've had arguments before, and I see we're going to have another round. I'll be just fine. Good day, sir."

With that, Charles slammed down his phone. Then he called Prue. She could give him an outsider's opinion, and she could help him with people in the Department of Agriculture. It was clear—he had to make his decision soon.

Prue was just about to head home when she got his call. She would always take his call.

"I can't play today."

"But can you have a quick lunch with a friend?"

"You sound positively . . . I don't know what. There's a tone in your voice and it scares me."

"How about Yitzi's Deli in thirty minutes?"

"Okay. Their chicken soup cures anxiety, too, you know. I think you need some."

Charles cleaned up his desk and got ready to go immediately. He was relieved she had said yes.

"Will that be all for the week, Congressman?"

Curtly, he said, "Yes, that's all, Steve."

"Then I'll see you Monday morning."

Steve left and shut the inner office door. Charles, meanwhile, wanted to throw one of his prize paperweights at the wall, but they were treasures, picked up all over in his travels. Now his collection had become so well known that many were gifts from others close to him. The one Willa had given to him before they were married was the most exquisite piece of swirled art he had ever seen.

Prue was right on time and so was Charles.

The restaurant/deli was so well known, it was always busy, but they did have a back section with privacy booths for those who wanted privacy, and they got one. This lunch was to be very private.

Prue started, "Okay, we've ordered, so what's up? Or can I guess? From the look on your face, I would say Senator Asshole."

"Yep, that's what's up. That old bastard threatened me today."

"So what else is new? That's his MO, Charles, and he gets away with it, so why should you be so upset about this time?"

"You know, Prue, he could have been so great, but he chose to be such a low-down shit. It's embarrassing. I hope people don't judge the whole state of Maryland on his behavior."

"Charles, people all over judge the entire Congress as low-down dirty shits. They do that because the ones you see and hear from are exactly that, and the folks who come here to actually do the people's business gets shoved in the background. They don't sell newspapers. It's political theatre that turns the powermongers on."

"Wow, I didn't know how strongly you felt. Do you view me like that?"

"If I did, I wouldn't have stayed very long in your office. And then you fell for my best friend, so out with it."

"Hey, Prue, you're on the fast track and you'll be on the top one day soon. You have it, Prue. You're a wonderful, intelligent person, and you have that killer instinct, too."

"That's it," Prue barked. "Watch it or you're paying."

"I always do anyway. First, tell me how much you knew about Steve when you suggested I hire him to replace you."

"What's wrong with him? I thought you really liked him."

"What's wrong is I suspect him of playing both sides."

"Wow, that hurts. How do you know it's Steve?"

"Buddy Dawes wouldn't go any lower. He would only have the person nearest to me to make sure he got the right stuff."

Prue thought a minute and said, "You're right. I only know what Steve's credentials were and I went on that. He's very good-looking, a Princeton grad with good connections, and a pretty tight and perfect résumé. What's not to like?"

"Do you think Dawes planted him there, knowing I would hire him?"

"Snakes are snakes, so your guess is probably spot on."

"Damn, I don't want to be right, but I really think I am. That old blowhard bastard would want to contain me if he and his friends were up to something over on that shore. I smell corruption and the stink is coming from something down there."

Sarcastically Prue said, "Charles, are you suggesting kickbacks? Our senator from Maryland? This story sounds like a rerun of a bad movie."

Charles laughed out loud. "How naïve am I?"

"You're one of the good guys, and you know what I told you about them."

"Do you really have the stomach for this, Prue?"

"Daddy and I were just discussing that, and you know what Daddy said? I will make a wonderful congresswoman for Ohio. So that ought to tell you what he thinks of me."

"Boy, you political dynasties are something."

"And I could say that to you, too, Charles E. Lee."

"Touché. But who says I am all that easy and nice? You've seen me go back at people, and I won that round last time with Rennie Richardson."

"Yes, you *and* Frances Evans, and take my word on this: the party big shots will never forgive you for that."

"Well, if he's getting kickbacks from the bureaucrats over in Maryland, I'll find out and he will pay. Damn, Prue, don't they ever learn? It's why people are so angry at Congress. It's men like that who will bring down the entire system eventually. And, if our Princeton hotshot sitting outside my office is involved, he'll pay, too."

"If you look closely, Charles, where you find one snake, you'll find them all. My guess is he's flying under the radar with this one. Be careful with Steve, too. Get him to confess before you boot him out. Set him up, and then make sure he doesn't get to Buddy until you can prove it."

"You're right. Thanks for being such a good friend."

The server arrived with their meals. Prue had ordered her favorite from their menu, a corned beef on rye, and Charles was about to stick his spoon into the biggest bowl of chicken matzah ball soup anyone has ever seen.

"As always, I appreciate your advice."

"You're too close to something, Charles, and with Dawes probably involved, too, who knows what can happen? By the way, I see you took my advice about dinner, too, huh?"

Charles smiled and said, "I need this soup. It will soothe my soul. Isn't that why they write books about it?"

Chapter Twenty-Three

Charles had a lot weighing on his mind. He hoped the island would help bring clarity. Willa's keen intuition about him made their bond strong. She knew when he needed space and when he needed to be with her.

Vernie was very excited to see her brother. She always relied on his advice, and, heaven knows, she needed it now. She wanted to feel relevant in her life, and, while she adored her husband very much, she envied the quiet, sensual life her brother had with Willa. They just fit together, and she and Tom needed to remember how to do that. They had at one time. Maybe he would think better of her if she had her own business.

"Hey, Vernie! Come back to earth," Willa teased as she passed by on the way to a big old wicker rocker with her cup of tea.

"I'm sorry, Willa. I was lost in thought."

"I can see that. Excited about big brother coming out tonight?"

"More than you know. I need his support in what I want to do, and I have no idea if he'll give it or think I'm a silly little fool."

Willa sipped her tea, studying Vernie's face to find out her what her sister-in-law needed. "He'll adore your idea, even if he doesn't agree. You know that. He adores you and only wants your happiness."

"He adores you, too. I have never seen Charlie so intensely passionate with a woman."

"I thought we kept that part of our lives under the sheets, so to speak."

Verinnia let out a loud protest. "Lands, Willa! I wouldn't ever pry into something that personal between you and my brother, but you two are just . . . well, you're a together couple."

"I guess you could say that. I'm still amazed we met and fell in love. I wasn't looking for that at all, but Charlie was different from anyone else I had ever known."

"He is that, Willa. And you're the best thing that has ever happened to him. I know how proud he is of what you do and who you are."

Willa noticed a faraway look coming back into Vernie's eyes. It made her suddenly sad; here she thought this girl had everything.

Vernie saw Willa staring at her and blushed at showing her deepest feelings so clearly. "Oh, listen to me. I'm being so foolish today. I must be homesick for Tom."

Willa leaned over to her and took her hand. "What's wrong, Vernie? Do you want to talk?"

"Why, Willa, I would tell you anything. Thomas is different from most people. I've known him forever, and I think I fell in love with him when we were but eight years old. He kissed me out by the old swimming hole and swore me to secrecy for fear Daddy would skin him alive."

"Go on."

"Everyone wanted us to marry. It was accepted and over with. It's just that Tom always kept something back and never gave me his whole heart. I used to be able to break through once in a while, but now it's just harder. That's all I know."

"There's something else, too, Vernie, isn't there? Something deep down."

Vernie looked away. She hadn't realized how much she needed to talk this out with another woman, and now here was the chance to do it with someone she loved so much. She never did understand things hidden inside of her.

Willa saw Vernie's hesitancy and said, "Keep it then. You'll tell me when you're ready. Know this, though: you can trust me and you certainly can trust Charlie. He would walk through fire for you."

With that, tears flowed down Vernie's cheeks. She sobbed for a moment and then abruptly said, "I can't give Tom children, Willa. He wants that more than anything, and I can't have children."

Willa's eyes widened. She searched for just the right words, feeling the irony that, here she was, not only a writer but a writer of romance, and she didn't have words enough to console her. She had heard Vernie say she had the perfect life and wanted children and one day they would. Why had she said that to her, knowing she couldn't have them? Willa felt frozen, unable to gather her thoughts. This wonderful sister of the man she loved so intensely was struggling for help and here she was, stuck. *Please help me console her, Lord.*

Willa found the words. "Vernie, sometimes the very thing someone wants, they can't have. They think they want it more than anything, but it's impossible. I'm sure you've searched the possibilities and they aren't there. Tom loves you. I've seen you two together and I can tell, but maybe he just doesn't know how to tell you it's all right. Maybe he's afraid that, if he tells you that, then that dream of your perfect life dies forever. But there are other dreams the two of you can have."

Vernie sobbed even harder. Then, when she was done, she looked at Willa and said, "Sometimes dreams just die, Willa. Love can die. And, worse than that, a person can kill love."

"I know that, but I know you and Tom still have a deep and abiding love for one another. Do you want children? If so, adopt a child."

Vernie squirmed in the chair and then said, in a moment of complete and utter honesty, "No, I don't really want a child. I never did. I wasn't like all my friends who wanted to grow up, marry Prince Charming, and have babies all around them. I want to be the center of a man's affection, totally, and, when my doctor told me I couldn't have children, I was, in a way, relieved, Willa. Thankful even. I now had the justifiable excuse I had wanted all my life. So how do I tell the man I am married to, and who wants children, that I lied to him? I love him so much and I will lose him."

"Love makes us do and say things we aren't often honest with ourselves about. But things change, and, maybe, if you just tell Tom straight out, he can handle it better than you think he can."

They both sat there, caught in the moment, communicating with one another through their silence.

Willa thought about how she and Charles had spoken one time about having a child, but, somehow, that conversation had gotten lost, and they had never talked about it again. She never wanted a child to feel the loneliness she had when her parents were killed in a car accident. She too was determined to be the centerpiece of her husband's life, and the conversation she was having now with his sister was one she feared to have with him.

Charles had called ahead to Cap'n Tuck, who did private charters for him. He needed Tuck to be at the dock in Somerville by five so they could then set off for the island. In the meantime, Tug was waiting for his arrival so they could talk before Charles went over.

The small plane from D.C. was having an awful time with the winds, always a hazard on the shore. For Charles, who received an unexpected phone call along the way, it was white-knuckle time in more ways than one. When they arrived, Charles thanked the pilot and also shot a silent prayer of thanks to God that they had arrived safely. Tug was waiting for him.

"Hey, Charlie! good to see you."

Charles shook his friend's hand and said, "Are we going to go to Virgil's?"

"No, I have a better idea. Hop in and I'll show you."

Charles got into Tug's Cherokee and away they went out to the main road.

"How was your week, Charlie? You folks spending our money faster than it's coming in?"

"That would be funny if it wasn't true. It's unreal what goes on in that town."

"Yeah, I know. Politics is a dirty business. It has seeped so far into our lives that you can't do anything or go anywhere you don't see its effects."

"Where are you taking me, Tug? I have to meet ole Tuck at the marina at five."

"Don't worry. We'll be close."

Charles looked around and couldn't for the life of him understand where Tug was headed. Then the Jeep turned down a narrow lane and they wound back through the woods to a huge open field.

"Okay, here we are. Come on and get out. I made some coffee for us. I want to take a walk."

Charles followed, but wondered what this was all about. Tug handed him a cup of coffee out of a big thermos.

"Look at this land, Charlie. It's beautiful. It belongs to a friend of mine."

"Pretty piece of property."

"He rents it out now to be farmed."

"Why doesn't he do it himself?"

"He got old, but didn't want to give it up entirely. He lives in a house that sits in the woods over back in there. His wife died a few years ago, and he told me he wants to die right there in his boyhood home."

"How did you meet this man?"

"He was a friend of Dickie Short, the man I talk about all the time and Lindy's great-uncle."

"How's she doing, by the way?"

"Still throwing up, but it gets better every day."

"I'll bet you're excited."

Tug chuckled. "It was a shock, I'll say that, but we're ready, and we love each other so much that having a little one who belongs to us will be fun."

"Well, Willa and I are just getting started and that isn't in our plans right now. Now, why did you bring me out here, Tug?'

"I want you to see this land, feel it, breathe it deep inside of you. It's what most of these men do if they don't go out on the water."

"I think I'm getting your message." Charles stood there, sipping his coffee, then walked a few steps away and took a deep breath. The ground smelled so good in the summer. It was the earth, full of itself.

"The farmers are right behind the watermen, you know, Charlie. They won't make it here either, with all the new regulations they put on these properties. Buster was a font of knowledge for me. You need to go meet with him again."

"I want to. While completely unorthodox in his ways, he was an honest man who came to me to fight for his land. And you were so right when you told me he was like Baxter Black. What a character that one is."

Tug laughed. "I told you. Black and Buster would have gotten along well with Dickie. He was another man fighting for his culture and everything he knew. Times are passing here and I understand some of it is the fact that change is hard to accept, and has to happen, but what happens when we mess with our food chain?"

"Explain," Charles said.

"Crabs, oysters, chickens—it's what we all eat and a lot of what we export and it's all part of what this area has been forever. Now some want to get rid of it all."

"I see what you mean. When you spend so much time inside that hateful Beltway, you lose sight of what America is really all about."

"That's what the island will bring to you, Charles. Going over there, you will see things and learn about an ecosystem so vast you can't imagine. You will get to know people whose families have been here since John Smith came up this way. It puts people like us back in touch with our country's roots."

Charles stood still and stared directly into Tug's eyes, and then said, "Are you sure you don't want to run for office? You just gave a mighty powerful platform, if you ask me."

"That's your business, Charlie. I'd rather write about it. You have a great future if you never lose touch."

"You're quite a guy, Tug, You do Harvard proud."

"To be honest with you, my friend, living down here, surrounded by nature and real people, Harvard seems a million miles away."

Charles glanced down at his watch. "Holy cow, I have to get to that dock. Thanks, Tug. You've given me a lot to think about, just coming to this piece of land.'

"Anytime, Charlie. Anytime. Bet Willa's anxious to see you."

"No more than I am to see her. She is going to change everything about that old house we bought, while still trying to keep it looking like the island. I don't know how that's to be done, but, if anyone can do it, she can."

"I like her so much. And it sounds like you and I are going to be going through the same thing. Lindy has spoken to a guy in town, a builder, and I think we are eventually going to build a new home here in Somerville, on the water and looking right out on the Bay."

"What are you going to do with the one you're in?"

"Lindy's talking about renting it out, but I'm not sure right now. Besides, she also thinks I can fix up the old crab shanty with my two left thumbs! I do have some ideas, but someone else will need to help. And I'm too busy anyway. I do want it to be my writing space someday. Maybe Willa will be able to come over sometimes and use it, too. I think that would be neat."

"What a great idea. I'll tell her Lindy has a builder and maybe she can go meet up with him and they can talk."

"Yep, you and I are knee-deep into the domestication act now, Charlie."

Charlie was now off to the island and Tug was looking forward to getting back home and relaxing. It had been a hectic day and so much was on his mind, as was also true for his good friend Charlie.

When he walked in the door, he heard Lindy upstairs and instinctively knew something was very wrong. This time she wasn't throwing up—she was crying.

He raced up the steps and into the bathroom to find Lindy slouched on the floor next to the toilet bowl, just staring. He sat down beside her. "Lindy, talk to me. What's wrong?"

"I can't speak, Tug. I just can't say a word."

"What do you mean?

Her swollen eyes looked at him and she whispered, "I lost it. I lost the baby."

A cold shiver went up Tug's spine. "What are you saying, Lindy?"

"Look in the toilet. I lost the baby."

Tug couldn't bring himself to look, but said, "Come on, Lindy, let's get you into bed. I'll call your mother."

Lindy grabbed his arm and said, "No, don't do that. We'll do it together and then I want to sleep."

Tug knew he couldn't back out of the gruesome task. "Of course. We'll do this. Then you lay down, and I'll call the doctor, to see if there's anything more we need to do."

At his strong and understanding tone, she grabbed hold of his neck and began sobbing.

"It's okay, Lindy. We'll have other babies. This is supposed to be the way of nature."

"You're right, Tug, but I so wanted us to have this baby. We were preparing everything for this."

Tug's thoughts ran together, but then he pulled her up and into his arms. "We're going to be all right. And we're going to go ahead and build that house over on the water, out by Dickie's shanty. We'll go on."

They cleaned up the bathroom and then lay down together on their bed. In moments, they fell asleep in each other's arms, and didn't awake for a couple of hours. When they woke, they both cried a little together, and then agreed their life had to go on and they would tell their families whenever the time was right.

Chapter Twenty-Four

Kay was thrilled with the thought of going down to see Tug, Lindy, and Mikey. She hadn't been to the Eastern Shore for a long time, and now, given the circumstances, she really needed to see her youngest son, Mikey, and talk with him. Plus, she truly adored Lindy and was so happy when the young girl had reached out to her. And she knew Tug was keeping a lot bottled up inside about his parents' situation. But this visit would show him that it really was all right.

Looking into the large mirror hanging over her bedroom dresser, Kay suddenly felt old. She leaned into it, pulling her skin a little to try to mask some of the lines that lately seemed to grow overnight. *Where do they all come from? How many more will be there tomorrow?*

Standing back a little, she assessed herself. She tried to smooth her body down a bit, thinking she needed to take a few pounds off. More exercise was clearly required. So, she would now walk routinely, thankful again to be near the beach, where the narrow, back road paths were so delightful. She would watch every bite that went into her mouth and try to stem the tide of advancing age. It could be done. She had been doing it for years, but, if she were honest, she had to admit she'd lately been indulging a bit too much in selfish delights. That had to stop.

As she stood there, lost in silly thoughts of age and wisdom, the phone rang.

"Hey, gorgeous! Whatcha been up to?"

How she welcomed this voice. Her greatest fan. "Max, you old dog, how are you? I haven't heard from you in ages."

"Oh, I've been fine. Was doing a lot of sailing for a while, and now I'm thinking about taking off for Arizona for the winter. The old bones aren't what they used to be."

"Funny you should say that. I was just doing a major age assessment."

"No way it didn't come out with a perfect score. You're a beauty, Kay, and always were. I think you get better as the years go by."

"You sure make a gal feel good." Suddenly she wondered if he knew she needed a friendly voice. She said softly, "How did you come to call me out here?"

Max nervously cleared his throat and she knew right then he had talked to Ted.

He never had been a man given to intrigue, so he dove in with both feet. "I spoke to Ted, Kay. He told me you were staying out on the Cape for a while. He said no more, but I caught the drift. How bad is it this time?"

"Permanent damage, I'm afraid. We're done, Max. We should have been done years ago, but the boys . . . well, you know."

"You were the best wife for him, Kay. We all know he's a bear, but are you sure?"

"Are you working overtime, Max?"

"No, not really, but he knows I've always been close to you in a way he never could be."

"Yes, that's true. I could talk to you. Ted was always too busy being Ted and playing the big boy sports editor. It got a little crowded in all that jockstrap territory."

Max laughed out loud. "Gee, Kay, I didn't know you thought like that."

"Well, now you do."

"How are the boys?"

"I take it Ted didn't say a word to you about them?"

"No, he was too busy crying in his beer about how his wife took off for the Cape and left him to fend for himself."

"Wow, that sounds so familiar. Poor Teddy. Yuck! Well, the boys are doing great. Seems they both may be destined to live on the Eastern Shore of Maryland."

"No kidding! How do you feel about that?"

"Happy if that's what they want. Mikey has now started a big job down there, doing something I don't understand at all, and Tug . . . well, Tug is going to be a daddy!"

"Well, I'll be damned. He loves that little girl, doesn't he?"

"Yes, he does, and so do I. She's having a rough go of it right now, but that passes. Hey, I have a great idea, if you're game."

"What's that, Kay?"

"Well, Lindy called earlier and she's giving Tug a birthday party. I'm going to pick up Mikey and we're heading down to Somerville to surprise him. Come with us, Max."

"I don't know, Kay. I mean—"

"I know what you mean and forget about Ted. Come with me. The boys adore you and you would make Tug so happy. He was just asking after you, as a matter of fact."

"I do miss him. He was the brightest young reporter I ever had, and then that old man came along."

"You sent him down there as I recall, and, as I also recall, you ended up falling in love with that old man."

"Yes, I hate to admit it, but Dickie Short will be in my heart forever."

"I'm leaving the end of this week. Now, what excuse can you give me?"

"None that wouldn't sound like an excuse, so, yes, I'll go with you. There'll be hell to pay with Ted, but who cares?"

"That's my Max. We won't tell Ted and then you won't catch hell."

"You always were able to wind me around your little finger, Kay. When do we leave?"

Kay was floating on air. Max's call had made her heart soar with a sudden energy that had been evading her for a while. She had always adored Max and loved his sense of humor. She walked to her closet, and her choice of outfit told the story of how badly she needed the attention of an old friend who cared.

While Kay was already finding that life alone can hold some wonderful surprises, Ted was not. He was becoming even more sarcastic with his colleagues at work and demanding more and more from the younger ones—all just biding their time until he retired: sooner rather than later, they prayed. As the sports editor of the *Boston Globe*, he held sway over everything in that department, and his seniority was becoming an impediment to progressing into the age of modern technology. He balked at every turn, and some of the really good young folks had already left because of him.

He slammed his office door and grabbed his desk phone and made a call he knew was going to put him in a worse mood. Hearing Tug answer, his blood was already warming to a boil.

"Tug, it's your father."

Tug felt sick. "Hello, Dad."

Ted fumbled with his phone cord and then said, "Have you spoken to your mother?"

"Yes, I have. She told me she's moved to the Cape."

"Well, she'll come to her senses and come back home soon."

Tug knew better. This time, his father had gone too far with his mother. And with him.

"Dad, what goes on between you and Mom is your business. I'm a man now and have my own life to live. You will be glad to know that Lindy lost the baby, so now that's one less thing for you to hate about me. Though you might try to appreciate my wife. She is a great gal with many talents. Whether you do or not, that's your choice. I really don't care, so let's leave it at that."

Ted was stunned at his son's frankness. Maybe he was right maybe they should leave it alone. But, still, there was a part of him always searching for a way back. "I'm sorry about the baby, Tug. But guess it's too little, too late with us."

"Let's just leave all this behind, Dad. Maybe one day you'll wake up and stop feeling so sorry for yourself."

"Maybe, but I do know this: she isn't one of us."

"I don't know what that means, Dad. She didn't finish in some fancy school—no, she did not—but she is almost done now at a local one, and she is so artistically talented. Can't you come down from Mt. Olympus one time to live among us mortals?"

"Tug, don't speak like that to me. I've given you everything."

"Yes, you have, Dad, but you need to give more now. You need to give me your acceptance of the life I have chosen. I don't want to work for a newspaper, especially now when they are on the edge of major change. And I don't want to be your 'sonny boy.' I'm a writer, and apparently a good one, given my first novel and how well received it was. Can't you just accept me for what I am?"

Before Ted completely lost it, he drove one more jab into his son. "I hear Mikey is down there now. He's found a really good job."

Tug felt sick to his stomach. "That's right, Dad. Always run back to Mikey and how proud you are of him. Please do me at least one favor, and don't call me anymore. Or not, at least, until you can accept my life the way it is. I thought you had, and now something ugly has gone off in you again. Just leave me alone, won't you?"

Ted never got a chance to answer Tug. The phone went dead on the other end, and, in his heart, he knew he had deeply wounded his son, his brilliant Harvard son, for the last time.

He sank into his big leather chair and his thoughts went back to swimming in the ocean off the Cape while his boys splashed in the waves. Mikey would venture out to join him but never Tug. Tug had played it safe and returned to his pail and shovel and dug for gold in the endless hole both boys had made, knowing its end was in China. He wasn't the adventurer his father had wanted; he was the son who used words to express his feelings. And, right now, his father would give his fortune to have his son write the words to express how and why he had lost his family.

Chapter Twenty-Five

Cap'n Tuck was a good captain and experienced navigator of the Bay waters, and Charles had gladly used him many times. Since the old waterman liked doing private charters for the congressman and was always happy to see Charles, it worked out fine.

"Hi, Cap'n. I know I'm a little late, but I got held up with something."

"No problem, Congressman. Are you ready to go? It should be a good sail over this evening. The water's slick cam today."

"And I know what that means, Tuck. Calm is always a welcome thing when one is out on the water."

"Yes, you're becoming one of us, Congressman. How's Miss Willa?"

Charles smiled. He still wasn't used to being married, but he was glad he was.

"Willa's just fine. She loves living out in Tuckerton and I'm beginning to wonder if she'll ever come back to D.C."

"The island has that effect on some people, but they have to connect with it. It's a different life and most wouldn't go near it."

"Connect—that's a good word for it. Well, I'm half-connected myself. It's truly beautiful."

"Better when them greenheads aren't flying around and the mosquitos, too."

"Every place has its drawbacks, Tuck. Perfection is nowhere to be found."

"Well, out here is close to it."

Charles sat back and enjoyed watching the sun set, so beautiful as it slipped down quickly behind the straight horizon, creating a magical and otherworldly afterglow.

He could easily stay out here forever, but he would also miss the world he was now a part of and all the hustle-bustle he had grown accustomed to. Politics had been in his family for generations in one manner or another, and now he had a decision to make. And he had to have Willa onboard with it or he wouldn't win. He couldn't have the distraction of an unhappy mate; that would be hell on earth. He had seen too much of that and how it tore at couples when they weren't both moving in the same direction.

Yes, he would have to tell her soon whether he was going to run for Buddy Dawes's seat.

"We're almost there, Congressman," Tuck said, interrupting Charles's thoughts. "When do ye want me to come back and get ye?"

"Unfortunately, I need to leave tomorrow, Tuck. I know you don't like to work on Sundays, but I really do have a lot going on. Can you come around three or so? Why don't you call me on my cell?"

"We just got to hope the cell reception is working then."

"Oh, I forgot about that. Let's settle on three then, and, if there's a change, I'll get word to you. My sister will be coming back with me, too."

"Miss Willa will be staying on the island again?"

Charles laughed. "She will. She's on a mission with that house we bought."

"Changing it, is she? Women do that sort of thing once they have us on the hook."

"Yes, they do, but the old house does need to be updated and expanded some. She's working on the plans now."

"Who'll do the work for ye?"

"I don't know. Tug Alston said he and his wife were maybe going to be building a new home and she had a good builder. Do you know Tug?"

"Why sure. We all know Tug. He's a regular Somerville man now that he's married Dickie's little niece, Lindy. I wonder who she's using?"

"I don't know, but he said he was a friend of Lindy's."

Tuck laughed and said, "I'm not really being nosey, Congressman. We just like to know what's going on with our neighbors. I'll bet it's that young guy, Clyde Shaw. They all went to school together, and, if that's the feller, he's supposed to be real good."

Charles chuckled. "See? You know more than I do. Won't Willa be surprised I knew a good local builder before she does?"

Once Cap'n Tuck had brought the boat up at the Tuckerton dock, Charles grabbed his overnight bag and shook Tuck's hand. "Thanks again for another safe passage. See you tomorrow at three."

"Yes, sir, Congressman."

Charles turned to see his sister and his beautiful new wife standing at the end of the dock, waiting to greet him.

"You're one lucky man, Congressman. Enjoy the weekend."

Charles smiled and walked away and was soon in the arms of his wife, who seemed as if she were never going to let him go.

Tug held on to his phone and said, "Well, I didn't expect to hear from you so soon. What's going on?"

Buster cleared his throat and answered, "The farmers around here decided to have a meeting on Monday. Any chance you might be able to join us?"

Tug let out a breath, thinking of how much he didn't want to leave Lindy, and the work he had yet to do on both his new books, but he knew better than to blow this man off. "Well, I think I can. What time are you going to meet?"

"Four o'clock in the afternoon. Before our suppertime."

"Your timing might be perfect, Buster. Congressman Lee is down on the island this weekend and will be heading back to Washington. I don't know exactly when though."

"Well, can you ask him and get back to me? One thing we don't do is meet on a Sunday though, Tug. That's our day of rest, so, if you can see if he can find a way to be here Monday, it would be great. We might be able to change the time of the meeting, but I would have to know pretty soon."

Tug became a bit uncomfortable with this man who was now trying to push a congressman's schedule and life around. *A bit ballsy.*

"Well, I don't know. I'll try to get hold of him, but no promises. However, I'll come, and I will do my best to get the congressman to join me."

"Fair enough, Tug. You're a good man. And I think, if the congressman can come, he might understand the challenges we are having a bit better."

"I said I'll try, Buster. I'll get back to you."

Tug looked at his watch and knew he couldn't call right now. This was Charlie's night on the island, and Tug did not want to interrupt anything that might mean. On the other hand, time was of the essence, if he was to have any chance of getting the congressman to meet with the farmers on Monday. He'd have to call sometime . . . .

As the three of them walked off the dock, Vernie just kept smiling. She couldn't contain herself. "I'm so happy to see you, Charlie. You look so good. How's Washington? Same old stuff, different day?"

"You might say that, Vernie. A good way to put it. Washington moves slowly, so slowly that hardly anything gets done."

"You sound a bit frustrated, Charles."

"And you might say that, too. Some things and people never change, and I don't like that aspect of it at all. Why can't people try to be civil?"

"Not happening in today's politics. Those days seem over and long ago now."

Now Charles turned from his sister to his wife. "Have you been writing, Willa?"

"No, not really." A mischievous look crossed her face as she looked at Vernie. "Your sister has been keeping me company, and we've had such a good time. I'll miss her terribly."

"I'm so glad you two have become such good friends. Would be awful if you weren't."

Vernie pinched her brother's cheek as she stepped ahead and added, "I would have hated you for life, Charlie, if you had married some dreadful girl like Felicia Pemberton."

Teasing her, he said, "Good thing I didn't then." He watched Willa carefully to see if his sister's remark had affected her. It hadn't. She was just like that—not a jealous type.

As they finally reached their house, Willa stopped short. "You see? That front porch just has to be bigger. More like a southern porch."

"So you haven't been writing, but I'll bet you've been drawing."

"Yes, I have. Vernie's been baking and I've been drawing."

"Should I be afraid?" Charles asked cautiously.

"No, I think you'll like it very much. I just have to get a builder to work through some of the challenges."

Charles turned to Willa and kissed her. "I know I will love it *and* I may have a builder for us."

"You do surprise me, Charlie. Who is it?"

"Tuck told me about a young man named Clyde Shaw."

Willa laughed. "And Millie told me about a young man named Clyde Shaw!"

Charles just shook his head. "I knew I couldn't beat you with a bit of shore knowledge." He chuckled. "I met Tug briefly before I came over, as you know. When I mentioned your project, he said he and Lindy were thinking about someday building a new home over on the point. He said maybe you could speak to Lindy and get their builder's name. And then, on the way over, Tuck got talking and he mentioned Clyde."

Willa's eyes rolled. "Stop. Don't go further. I know how these shore conversations go. This place is like playing one gigantic game of telephone. Somebody tells somebody else something and then it goes from there."

"Kind of like the old days."

"This place *is* the old days." Willa grinned, then said, "But that's exciting to hear about Tug and Lindy. I really like her so, and this will give me a good excuse to get to know her better. You and Tug seem to be two peas in the same pod lately. What's going on?"

"Oh, it's kind of a long story and I don't want to waste my time with it right now."

Willa grabbed hold of his arm again and said, "I don't mind at all, but it's funny how one conversation can help everything fall into place."

Charles looked at her, winked, and walked up on the porch and through the front door. As he did, the smell of what the girls had been cooking hit him.

"My God, whatever is cooking smells heavenly. Who made dinner?"

Willa said, "We both did, so take your stuff back to the bedroom and get settled. Dinner is in twenty minutes, give or take."

Vernie moved over to one of the small counters and picked up the ten-layer delight she had baked in honor of her brother's visit. She proudly smiled, then whispered to Willa, "Where can I put it? I want to bring it out later with some fanfare."

Willa grinned at her. "You southern girls all love the drama. I guess it's what makes occasions so special. Put the cake upstairs in your room. Charlie won't go up there."

"You're right." And, as she took the cake out of the room, she turned and said, "Southern girls just think all occasions are special, Willa."

Willa had to admit Vernie was right. She was learning that each day is a gift and one that may never come back again. She was more and more ready to reach out and enjoy it, even if it meant embracing a little drama along the way.

146

Chapter Twenty-Six

The table set and the simmering pot roast ready to serve, Willa called everyone to come and eat. Charles was reading in their small den. As he got up to go eat, his cell rang. It was Tug, so he took it.

"Charles, I didn't want to disturb you, but Buster Talbot called me earlier this evening and his farm group is meeting on Monday. When I told him you were out here for the weekend, he wondered if you could join them, too."

Charles said, "Gee, I don't know, Tug. Tuck is coming to pick me up tomorrow at three, and I don't know what his schedule would be for Monday. And I'm not sure of my Washington schedule either."

"I think this meeting is important, Charlie. It could give you the information you've been looking for. I tell you what: if I can get Tuck to pick you up Monday around eleven, could you change your schedule around?"

"But how will Vernie and I get back to D.C.?"

"I will take you."

"Oh, I can't let you do that, Tug. That's way too much to ask."

"No, it's not, Charlie. I'm going to be at the meeting too, remember. The only problem I see is your sister's boredom sitting through this farming session."

Charlie thought fast. He knew Steve could have his schedule cleared for Monday. In a way, this was actually better, as it would give him more time to think about Steve and what he suspected. And, of course, more time with Willa.

"Okay, but you'll talk to Tuck? I'll clear my D.C. schedule."

"Not to worry. I will text you and let you know, but plan on going back Monday and not Sunday."

"Boy, Tug, this Buster guy is something else."

Tug said, "I think he sees you as a friend, and that counts big down here. I'll get back to you. And Charlie? Before I get off the phone, I should tell you that Lindy lost the baby earlier today. We are dealing with it and want to move on with not a lot of talk about it. Okay?"

"I am so sorry, Tug. Please give Lindy our love."

"And give my best to Willa and your sister."

Willa walked in just as Charlie was hanging up. "Who was that? Come on now; dinner is ready."

"That was Tug. Seems you're going to be stuck with me an extra day, woman. I'll explain at dinner."

Vernie had cleaned up for dinner. Gone were the jeans Willa had lent her, and in their place was a pair of black slacks, paired with a lovely black and red lightweight sweater. She looked lovely. Verinnia Lee had always been a stunning young woman who could have had any man she wanted, but she and Tom Hibbons had loved one another since they'd been children. That had been settled business long ago.

"Oh, Vernie," Willa exclaimed, "you look so gorgeous. Doesn't she, Charles?"

"She always does—a real southern lady."

Vernie said, "Oh, stop it now, you two. Let's eat. I'm sure you're starved, aren't you, Charles?"

"I must admit I am. What is it that smells so good?"

Willa answered, "A pot roast, dear, and I hope you like it."

Charles smiled as he looked across the table at his wife. "As I recall, you don't cook, Willa, so what's this all about?"

She smiled sweetly at her husband and said, "A naked attempt to get something."

Full of her new business idea, Vernie babbled on through dinner and hardly let Charles get a word in edgewise. Finally she took a breath and Charles took the opportunity to jump in.

"Can I say something, Vernie? I know you're excited about this cake business, but I haven't had a moment to share my good news."

Vernie looked a little deflated at her brother's reproach, but couldn't stay annoyed for long. "Good news? Oh, tell us, Charles."

"Well, Tug called to tell me about a meeting on Monday over here on the shore that I really should attend. It's on our way home, Vernie, so you will have to join us, but then Tug will drive us on home to D.C."

Willa smiled broadly. "Gee, an extra day with you? How will I stand it?"

Charles loved her quiet sense of humor. It equaled his. "You'll have to try real hard."

148

Vernie squealed with delight. "Oh, I am so happy, although I don't like meetings. What kind is it, anyway?"

Charles knew this wasn't going to go down so well, but he breathed deeply and said, "A farmers' meeting."

Vernie's mouth dropped open. She was speechless.

"You can do it, Vernie," Willa said.

"A farm meeting, Charles? What in the world?"

"Look, Vernie, this is important, and you can have a cup of tea or something and endure it, do you hear me?" This was a command, and Vernie knew, when Charles spoke in that tone, there was no room for negotiating.

"Oh, okay, I'll behave and be so proud that my big brother is a fancy congressman and all."

Willa laughed at Vernie's response. As she took another bite of pot roast, she winked at Charles, knowing he had won this round with his sister.

"My God, this roast is good, Willa. You know, if you did this more often, you might be surprised at the results."

"I doubt it, but shortly you're going to be very surprised."

"What does that mean?"

"You'll have to wait and see, Charlie. It's all about the dessert."

Charles's eyes widened. "Just what's been going on out here on this island?"

Vernie couldn't stand it any longer. She excused herself and ran upstairs. Willa shook her head at Charles and said, "Be nice."

Within moments, Vernie was slowly coming down the stairs and into the kitchen carrying her magnum opus.

"Why, what do we have here, sister?"

Vernie placed the cake in front of him and said, "What we have here is my new business venture."

"A cake?"

Impatiently, Vernie said, "Charlie Lee, listen to me seriously now. As I've been telling you, I am going to bake cakes and sell them all over Loudoun County. Miss Millie taught me how to do this and I think I can make a go of it."

Charles moved his big plate out of the way and brought the confection in for a closer look. "So, you've made a James Island Cake, have you? Sure looks good."

Willa brought the smaller plates and Vernie cut into her masterpiece, giving them each a slice. "I just can't wait to hear how you like it."

Willa took the first bite and slowly let it melt in her mouth. Then Charles took his bite. Vernie never moved her eyes off him.

"Well? Well, what do you think? It's yellow cake with mocha chocolate icing and filling."

Charles turned his lips down and made a look that wasn't pleasant. He grabbed his throat and pretended he was going to get sick.

When Willa saw how distressed Vernie was getting, she said, "Charles Lee, you stop that right now. You're breaking your sister's heart."

Charles swallowed and started laughing. Then he reached over to Vernie and took her hand. She was about to pull it away, she was so mad, but then laughed and said, "You're awful, Charlie. Why, no girl ever had a worse brother."

Charlie couldn't stop laughing, even as he leaned in and kissed his sister on the cheek. "I love it, Vernie. It's amazing." He took another huge bite. "I just can't believe you baked this all on your own."

"Well, Miss Millie helped me some, but I have the hang of it now. Isn't it divine?"

A knock came at the front door, and then a voice. "What's all the ruckus about?"

Willa got up and answered the door. "Speak of the devil herself."

"You say what, Willa?"

"Come on in, Millie. Vernie was just trying her cake out on us guinea pigs."

Millie walked in, waved to Charles, and patted Vernie on the back. "Is your brother putting you through the wringer, girl? Brothers are like that."

Willa smiled as as she pulled up a chair for their guest. "Even if they are big shot congressmen."

Millie only stayed a short time. She had known what Vernie was up to and wanted to make sure all had gone according to plan. She was very pleased it had. She stood and said, "I have to be getting home. Good to see you again, Congressman. It's going to take some getting used to, you know, having a congressman out here on the island. I think everyone is excited about that. I know Frances is thrilled to have her Willa here."

Willa said, "Speaking of Frances, she called before and wants us to come over for a while sometime this weekend, Charles. Now that you're staying on a bit, maybe we can? Maybe still tonight?"

Vernie popped up out of her seat and said, "Y'all go on now. I'll clean this up and enjoy some peace and quiet."

"Thanks, Vernie. That's so nice of you. We won't be long."

"Take your time. I have a great book by Willa Carpenter that I've been trying to read, so now's as good a time as any."

With a twinkle in his eyes, Charles said, "I hope it doesn't put you to sleep."

Millie laughed and said, "Oh, I don't think she'll sleep. They're kind of racy and that's why we women love them so much."

Willa shot her a smile and said, "Why, Millie, what a compliment!"

Chapter Twenty-Seven

On the way over to Frances's home, Charles and Willa were finally alone and could catch up with one another. He loved his sister, but he and Willa were still on their honeymoon. Both of them were public people, and they knew it would be hard for them to have much privacy, but, still and all, even on this small island, in their own home, they still had too many people around them.

He took Willa's hand and said, "What was Vernie talking about back there? Should I be afraid?"

Willa squeezed his hand and giggled. "Not unless you are going into business with her."

"She's serious about this cake baking thing?"

"I'm afraid so, Charlie. Millie got her turned on to something, and it turns out she loves it. *And* she's good at it."

"God help Tom. He wants a stay-at-home wife, with a house full of kids running around. He wants her driving to soccer games, and *not* while delivering cakes to half the team's mothers."

Willa was slightly irritated at his description of what Verinnia's role should be in her marriage. She wondered if that's what Tom had said to him or if it was his own idea of what the perfect wife should be. Obviously, he didn't know that his sister couldn't have children; of course, neither did Tom know his wife was keeping a rather big secret. Pity Vernie when the day came for truths to be told, but Willa certainly wasn't going to betray her.

"Well, you never know, Charlie. She might start off like gangbusters but then tire of it. I, for one, think it's good for her to give it a try, She seems to need to do this, so don't discourage her. Frankly, the whole thing shocks me because she's been so indulged all her life and starting a business isn't going to be easy."

Charles picked up something in his wife's voice. Was it defiance, or was she just defending his sister? Either way, it didn't really bother him. After all, he well knew Willa was her own person and not one to take orders from anyone, including him. That independence had drawn him to her in the first place. He dropped the conversation and stopped walking.

"What is it, Charlie?"

"With all fuss you two had made with supper tonight, I didn't think it was a good time to tell you that Lindy lost her baby. Tug seemed to not want to make a big thing of it, and so we won't. I know the two of them must be devastated, but it's over for now. You might want to tell Miss Frances in a quiet moment."

"Yes, I will, Charles. They were so happy about it, but nature has a way of doing things like that."

Charles looked at his wife and smiled. She was always the one to say something so sweet. He leaned down and kissed her gently. No one was around, so why not? "I love you, Willa."

Willa snuggled up to him for a moment and whispered, "I love you, too."

Frances was in the yard, pulling some weeds she had never gotten around to in early summer and now with winter coming on sooner than she would like, she didn't want to have to look at them in the rain and, possibly, snow. She did all the work around the house, especially since Jimmy had had his heart attack.

"Hey, Frances, need any help?"

"Oh, my gosh. A congressman pulling weeds? I don't think so."

"You should let him do it, Frances." Willa laughed. "I would love a picture of that for the *Richmond Times*. If that wouldn't make the front page: 'A Lee Pulling Weeds'!"

Charlie poked her and said, "You'd do it, too, wouldn't you?"

"What's up with you two lovebirds?"

"Oh, not much. We wanted to take a walk and stopping by to see you just seemed right."

"Well, c'mon in and sit a spell. Jimmy's gone down to the crab shanty to check on things. He can't wait to get out there on that water. We're nearing the last days of the season, you know."

"Just like farmers."

"Yep, just the same. Their minds are always on the fields and what needs to be done now and in the future." Frances slowly got to her feet and then said, "I made some fresh coffee for supper. Want some?"

Charles said, "I think I'll pass, Frances. It'll keep me up all night."

"Then iced tea it is."

"That sounds great," added Willa.

Frances finally stopped fussing in the kitchen and sat down at the table. "We could take it in the living room."

Charles sat back and stretched his arms. "I'm very comfortable here. How about you, Willa?"

"I always like a table."

Frances looked at Charles and knew something was on his mind. "Charles, I know something's gnawing at ye. Get it out."

Willa looked at Charlie and saw an odd look on his face. He *did* have something he wanted to say.

"Well, as usual you're right, Frances." He looked at Willa and then went on, "I want to tell you both something and it has to stay quiet for now. I have made a big decision, and, frankly, my wife is going to be mad I didn't tell her when we were alone."

Frances said seriously, "Maybe you ought not say it then, Charles."

"No, I need to say it." He then looked at Willa and stumbled a little in his words. "We just haven't had any time alone, Willa, so I thought it would be good to share it while the three of us are together."

The look on Willa's face went from disturbed to bewildered. Slowly she said, "Okay, Charlie, what is it? I know you tried to say something back at the house before Vernie went on and on about her cakes."

"Well, you're right about that. But that was about Tug and Lindy."

Frances looked inquisitive. "What about them?"

There was no sense now waiting for a time when Willa could tell her, so Charlie said, "They lost the baby and don't want a big fuss about it."

Frances shook her head. "That's so sad, but it's the way of things. They're young and will have more. I will try to help Lindy if she comes to me. Now, what else do ye have to say, Charles?"

Willa was still staring blankly at Charles, a little miffed he had not shared this big news first with her.

Charles knew there would be some fence-mending necessary with Willa, but he went on. "This really came as a shock to me, too, but I got a call from some of the big shots in the party—you know, the high-powered senators—in the plane after I left Washington. They said they were looking for a candidate who might run in place of Seth Pullman. He may have to withdraw. Naturally, this is all very hush-hush."

Willa looked at him and said, "Why would the party's candidate for Buddy Dawes's Senate seat withdraw?"

"Apparently he has cancer, but he wants to take his time in making any announcement."

Willa said, "Go on, Charles. Now you're going to tell us you are thinking of saying yes?"

"I am, Willa, particularly given the shenanigans I think Buddy Dawes is into. I may have a good shot. I think I could beat Buddy."

Frances looked very serious. "I think ye could at that. The folks here love ye, and, now ye're one of us, go for it."

Charles looked over at his wife, waiting for her to second that motion. "Well, we do live in Maryland now. What do you think?"

"This is all so new. I think when it sinks in, it will all be okay. When will you know for sure?"

"That depends on Seth. I don't think anyone wants to rush him, poor guy. But, when he's ready to go, the party wants to make this a seamless transition. I imagine it won't be too long from now."

"The Maryland primaries are already over, aren't they?"

"Yes, so I won't have to go through that. The party will take a little time and then just announce me as their new candidate. I must have passed muster with the who's who."

"I hope Seth is all right."

"I do, too, Willa, but you're all right with this change in plans?"

"Yes, I am, Charles; yes, I am. But the people of the Commonwealth of Virginia will be mad, won't they?"

"I suppose they will, but I have a cousin who might take my place and run for my seat in Congress. There are always Lee men or women to go around." He paused, then said, "Most important, Buddy Dawes is a crook and I want to take him down."

Frances said, "Lots of folks here can't stand Buddy Dawes; they have always suspected him of something not quite right. He isn't any different from that Richardson man the watermen had to deal with."

"You're right about that, Frances, and, to make it worse, I think he has a plant right in my office."

Willa's eyes narrowed as she said, "And that plant would be Steve?"

Charles jerked his head around to look at her. "How did you know that?"

"He's too perfect. In my books, I always make perfect men the ones who end up being the biggest jerks."

Frances's eyebrows furrowed and she said, "That's awful." Then, looking at Charles, she said, "She does do that, Charles."

"Yep, it's a darned good formula, so why change it?"

"Good Lord," sighed Charles. "I should just have asked you what you thought of the guy. By the way, is that what you thought of me when we met?"

"Are you perfect?" Willa asked.

"Maybe not perfect, but close to it."

"Well, next time, just ask, why don't you? And, as I recall, I was too busy falling in love with you to make any serious observations."

Charles blushed. "Willaaaa," he muttered.

"Well, it's true, and Frances watched the whole thing happen anyway, so why are you blushing?"

Charles swallowed the rest of his iced tea and then asked, "Anyway, what do you think?"

Willa smiled and remarked, "Is that to one of us or both of us? I think it's fantastic."

Frances leaned over and took his hand. "I second that."

"Then it's settled. We will have to keep this quiet, though, okay? I have to do a lot of legwork, plus try to help the farmers at the same time."

"You have my word, Charles," Frances said. "I won't say anything, especially to Jimmy, but can I tell you how exciting this is? We've never had a senator live on the island before."

"Could be rough sometimes with the extra notoriety, but, as my wife is going to revamp the house anyway, we can have some additional security installed at the same time."

"I didn't think of that." Willa was surprised at how much he had already thought out. "I guess the honeymoon is over, and I better get cracking at that house."

Frances stood up, sensing these two needed some private time to talk things out. "Thanks for coming, both of you. What a wonderful surprise, and, at my age, one doesn't get a lot of surprises."

Willa said, "Come over sometime to say good-bye to Charlie and Vernie, Frances. They're leaving on Monday."

"Aw, I'm going to miss Vernie. I like her so much."

Charles said, "Tug roped me into a meeting, so we leave Monday instead of Sunday."

Willa slid her arm through his and said, "That suits me fine."

Chapter Twenty-Eight

Max felt a little like a traitor going with Ted's wife to see Ted's kids, but, the truth was, Ted had hardly been in touch with him since he had retired. And, he had to admit, he'd always known this could happen. Ted was rough with everyone. He had always wondered why Kay had married him, and had been both sad and jealous when she had. She was so much better than Ted, but she had never known it. All that athletic prowess had overwhelmed her and swept her off her feet. And now, almost forty-odd years later, look at where it had gotten her. Well, he wasn't going to miss the chance to be with her now. Hadn't he waited long enough?

Kay was putting the last few things in a canvas tote when she heard the car pull up to the front door. She admitted to herself she was a bit nervous about this trip with Max, and yet excited at the same time. She had always enjoyed the company of Max, and he had often been a better father to her boys than their own father.

"C'mon in! The door's open," she yelled when she heard the knock. She really felt like a schoolgirl and was giggling at that notion when he came into the kitchen. He leaned over and kissed her lightly on the cheek.

"Hi, Kay. You ready to go?"

"Yes, I think I've managed to stuff it all in these two bags. Aren't you proud of me?"

"Proud isn't the word; impressed is more like it. I can't believe any woman can bring just two large tote bags for any trip. I see the pocketbooks these gals bring to the market and they're more like suitcases."

As Kay laughed, her head went slightly back. Her teeth had always been beautiful.

"They don't call them pocketbooks anymore, Max."

"I don't doubt that," he said. "More like steamer trunks."

"Good Lord, they get bigger with each adjective! They call them purses or handbags."

"Handbags? Hell, one hand couldn't hold those beasts. Why, I should take up being an orthopedic surgeon in my retirement. I could make a fortune fixing ladies' shoulders."

"Now I can't argue with you on that. Some days I feel as if I were carrying around the weight of the world inside mine."

Max chuckled. "Point taken. Here, I'll take the big, heavy one, and you grab the rest. I don't want you to get a pulled shoulder now that we have put that thought into our heads."

Kay took another look around the place and smiled. Everything was just the way she wanted it. Max turned in time to see her doing it and then remarked, "Happy, Kay?"

"Very much so. It's been years since I've been this peaceful."

He looked out the large windows. "With that view, who wouldn't be?"

"Got that right. Let's go. I can't wait to see my boys."

On the drive to the Cape, Max had stopped and bought a bagful of goodies to eat on the road. They had decided to make this an adventure and would stop the first night near Baltimore. He figured, as long as he was down this way, he would stop in at the paper and see how everyone was doing. By now he figured the overzealous Roger— one of Tug's good friends—would probably be well on his way to taking the paper over. Good grief, that young man had ambition.

"So, where are we going first, Max?"

"Well, when you told me that Mikey was tied up and could only do dinner, I decided we would stay around Baltimore tonight, and then push on over to the shore tomorrow afternoon. We can have dinner with Mikey, stay there in Salisbury, and then go on to Somerville the next day. When's the party?"

"Lindy said it will be Tuesday, so your plan sounds perfect." Then, nervously, she asked, "We *are* getting separate rooms, aren't we, Max? I mean—"

Max reached across the car and took her hand. "Of course we are. Not that it wouldn't be fun, but, yes, we will get separate rooms."

Kay let out a sigh of relief. "Well, that's settled."

"Were you really worried about that? I mean, after all these years and so much water over the dam?"

"Well, it's just that everything is so messed up right now."

"Have you heard from Ted?"

"I try to keep it at a minimum. He calls every day, but I don't answer every day."

"Is it really over, Kay?"

"Ah, a serious question. Yes, it's over, Max."

"He never deserved you, you know."

"We had a good run, Max, but we all know what Ted is capable of and how he treats others, including his family. I guess I just didn't know how to say good-bye."

"Well, no more serious questions. Only happy things this trip. Do you think Tug will be surprised?"

"Well, I think Lindy told him I was coming down, but he will probably go into a coma when he sees you and then Mikey."

"You have great kids, Kay."

Looking out the car window, she answered, "Yes, I do." She didn't want Max to see the tears forming in her eyes. She couldn't have told him why they were; she didn't even know herself.

Chapter Twenty-Nine

Even though the three Lees had managed to get in an extra day together, good-byes would always be hard for them. Charles yelled up the stairs, "Vernie, get a move on! Tuck will be at the dock soon."

"Do you really have to leave?" Willa asked as she stretched out her body, raising her arms in the air.

"If I don't, things will pile up back in D.C."

"Doesn't sound as if it's going to be fun when you get back anyway."

"You're right on the mark there, sweetheart."

"Are you going to fire Steve?"

"Not right away. I'd like to, but Prue's right: I have to find out for sure he's working for Buddy, and then I have to figure out how to deal with that. There are others involved, too. Maybe I will get a clearer picture from the meeting this afternoon."

"Be careful, Charlie. Men like Buddy know how to survive."

"Well, the one thing I do know is, when I get this all figured out and have a solid plan, he may not be able to run."

Willa kissed him tenderly, then passionately, before whispering, "Be careful, Senator."

He looked lovingly into her eyes. "You're with me all the way in this, then? Right?"

"All the way to the moon and beyond."

"That's my girl."

Vernie came down the stairs and put her suitcase on the floor. She slumped her shoulders and said, "Do I have to go?"

"Yes, you do, little sister. Tom will send the big guns after me if I don't get you back home."

"Oh, all right. I'll miss you so much, Willa."

Just as Willa went to hug her sister-in-law good-bye, the door opened and there stood none other than Miss Millie.

161

"Now, hold on there, girl. You're not going anywhere until I can say good-bye and give ye a little something."

Vernie looked at the medium-sized wrapped box and said, "I love surprise gifts. Can I open it now?"

"Don't see why not."

Vernie tore into it as if her hands were on fire.

"Hold on there, Vernie," Willa said. "Let me help you so the box survives."

Vernie lifted out of the box ten shiny, new, round cake pans. In the first one was an instruction sheet for how to make island cake the way Miss Millie did. Vernie started to cry, then she squealed and gave Millie a big hug.

"Oh, Charlie," Vernie, said, wiping the tears from her face while still staring at the pans Millie had given her. "I can't believe how wonderful these people are, and especially you, Miss Millie. Look at these pans, and a recipe to guide me."

Charles smiled at the joy in his sister's face. Even with so much else swirling in his head, these moments meant so much.

He said, "This is so special, Miss Millie. Vernie will talk about this all the way across to Somerville."

Willa gave him a knowing look, sending him the message that she knew where his mind was. She looked on fondly as he hugged his sister.

Charlie finally looked down at Vernie and said, "Now, come on. We have to go. Tuck will be at the dock soon, and he doesn't wait for anyone."

"Oh, I want to stay, Charlie. Please?"

"Now, Vernie, you know you can't. Please say your good-byes. I can't bear anymore of this!" He grinned as he and Willa walked out to their front porch.

They both stared out at the water. Finally he spoke. "Take good care of yourself, Willa. Let me know what you find out about the house. I know you will be on that quicker than I can blink." Then he took her hand and whispered, "I'll miss you."

She smiled, then said, "You know what I was thinking? How much you need to be careful with this Buddy Dawes. Never forget he's a powerful man."

"We have our work cut out for us, don't we?"

Millie walked on to the porch and patted Charles on the back. "Take care, Congressman. We all love ye."

"I love all you folks, too, and I'll see you again soon. In the meantime, look out for Willa, will you?"

"Between me and Miss Frances, this girl will be just fine."

Tuck was right on time, of course, and they quickly boarded the boat and were off. Vernie had a hard time holding back her tears, but she knew deep down it was time to go back home. She really did miss Tom and was excited to share this new idea of hers with him. Even if he wasn't so keen on it, she would go forward anyway, and, eventually, he would get into it, too.

When they reached Somerville, Tug was there to pick them up. So far, everything was going to plan, and that always meant, to Charles, something was going to go wrong. He hoped he was wrong, but the feeling was there anyway.

Tug looked in the rearview mirror and said, "Did you have a good time, Verinnia?"

"Yes, I did. The most wonderful people live over there, and I could spend my life on that island."

"You say that now, but, after a tough winter or a hurricane out there, you might change your mind."

"I hadn't thought about that, Tug. I'll bet that's fierce."

"Yes, it is. But they all look out for one another, so, most times, it all works out okay."

Charles said, "Do we need to talk about anything before we reach this meeting?"

"I don't think so. We'll let them take the lead and see what they want, what their grievances are, and how you might be able to help."

"Don't forget they want you to help, too, Tug."

"Yes, I know. I'll probably have to do some sort of writing for them, but I don't mind. You know, Charlie, there are so many parallels between the farmers and the watermen. It's so odd to me that a government could deliberately want to mess things up over here. I mean, it doesn't make any sense."

"I know, Tug." Charles smiled. "It's hard to figure out a politician, isn't it?"

"Well, I didn't mean you. I admire you for stepping in with the watermen and, now, for your willingness to help the farmers. They trust you and that's no small thing. They keep a lot to their own but they have let you in. That's pretty much the battle right there. People are so frustrated because they can't trust anyone. The politicians dribble from their mouths, and everyone knows darned well they're lying when they do it."

"Seems that way, doesn't it? And, when I return to D.C., things aren't going to get any easier for me. I have to take care of a . . . certain matter, but I need confirmation before I do."

"No one better hurt my big brother," Vernie piped up from the backseat of Tug's Jeep.

"Family is everything, isn't it?" Charles turned around, looked at his sister, and said, "And, as far as you're concerned, little sister, you never heard this conversation."

"What? What were you saying?"

Charles laughed. They had used to do that all the time when their father would ask them to tell the truth. They had long ago made a pact to see nothing, hear nothing, and say nothing. He was glad she remembered that.

Tug said, "Family can be great, but it can hurt you deeper than anything else." Charles heard the telling tone in Tug's voice and turned the conversation in a different direction. "So we may be headed into an adventure. What do you think, Tug?"

"With Buster Talbot leading this group, it's anyone's guess. He's pure all right. Pure shore."

Charles looked thoughtful. "I like that: pure shore."

"Says it all, doesn't it? If you're down here long enough, you understand that expression completely."

"I am learning that, Tug. Well, I'm actually looking forward to this meeting. Glad they could change it to one o'clock. That way I can make it back to Washington and still do some work at the office."

Tug laughed. "I'm impressed! But I do know what it's like to fall behind. My publisher is squawking at me to get him the first draft of my new novel. I told him I would stay in touch."

"Bet he loved that."

"Yeah—a whole bunch. They're a crazy lot of people. Willa understands how tough it can be when a publisher is leaning on you."

"Yeah, hers is a woman named Kit, and she's a dragon lady."

"Is Willa working on something right now, Charlie?"

"Sort of, but her main project right now is the house. And making me a poor man. When that's done, I'm sure she will begin writing again.

She says the break will be good for her. She's written so many books, but contracts are contracts, and she can only hold her publisher, Kit, back for so long."

"Willa's a huge name in the business and no doubt a real money-maker for the publisher, so they aren't about to let her retire. Besides, she's way too young."

Charles turned serious. "Well, she might have to make some real adjustments soon."

"Can I ask you why you said that?"

"Off the record here, Tug? You probably remember our earlier conversation on this topic, but I am almostly certainly going to run for the Senate seat here in Maryland."

"Wow, Charles. But is there really one available?"

"There very well might be, sooner than you think, but that's not for public consumption. By the way, you should be prepared because, if I run, I'll need a professional writer to help me."

"That's something, Charlie. No one will hear a word from me. I won't even tell Lindy."

"I appreciate that, Tug. And you, Vernie"—Charles turned around— "you never heard a word of this either."

"A word of what?" They all laughed. Then she continued, "I understand. Why would I interfere? It's your decision and career. I would love to see my big brother a U.S. senator. Although I was always sure it would be from Virginia. You know how we Lees try to keep that seat going."

"Well, time for change. Everything changes, and, when opportunity knocks, you have to go with it. Please, Vernie, don't say anything to anyone."

"I won't. I promise."

Tug looked over at Charlie and, with a sheepish grin, said, "Let me ask you one question. Were you thinking about this when you bought the house on the island?"

"No, not really, but that house does make it official that I live in Maryland."

"Yes, and Frances can tell everyone about your relative, good old Bobby Lee, and how he surveyed that land way back when."

Charlie laughed. "Yes, she can, and so can the ladies down at the post office. But this has to stay quiet, seriously. Before I left, I told Frances and Willa, of course, but no one else until I have my ducks in a row."

Tug nodded, and, while Vernie was a bit put out he hadn't told her, too, she leaned forward and kissed her brother on the cheek. "I'm so proud of you, Charlie Lee. You'll make a truly wonderful senator."

Chapter Thirty

When they walked into the meeting, Buster was pacing like a lion waiting for his next meal. Charles went right over to him.

"Hi, Buster. Good to see you once again. Looks like quite a turnout."

"Yep, it is, and I'm sure glad you could come. You'll hear a lot today, but there is a slight hitch."

"Oh?" Charles said. "What's that?"

"Well, the hitch is standing over there with his back to us, speaking to one of the most influential farmers around here, Robert—or Bobby, as we call him—Henson. He owns thousands of acres of good farmland."

"And who's the hitch?"

"Said his name was Roy Davis and he was joining us today from the Baywaters Commission. He told us he wanted to have a listen to what we were saying. He's from Washington and you know I don't trust any of those folks."

Charles looked straight at Buster.

"Oh, I don't mean you, Congressman Lee. We all trust and respect you. You have proven yourself to the folks here."

Charles smiled gratefully, then took another look at the "hitch" and saw that Buster was right. Buddy Dawes couldn't have known that Charles had seen this man sleazing around Rennie's office more than once and knew he'd long been a lapdog for the highest bidder in the Virginia statehouse. Funny how some guys just hang on and keep on taking the taxpayer's money.

"Well, this is an interesting turn of events, Buster, but it won't make any difference if Mr. Davis is here or not. We have to get to the bottom of it all and we will."

Buster's eyes narrowed as he stared at the man. "He's a rat, that one. You best steer clear."

Charles smiled at his newfound friend and said, "Think I'll wander over there and mingle a bit before you call this meeting to order. How long until we get started?"

"I see you got a plan, Congressman. How 'bout you give me the high sign and then I'll get it started. Just be careful."

"Yes, I will, Buster. I'm hoping his memory isn't as good as mine. While it didn't end well last time, it wasn't me who got in his face, so we will see."

As Charles walked away, several farmers shook his hand and spoke with him. They recognized him right off the bat and were very happy he was in attendance. They all remembered this young congressman as a man of honor, and one who had helped the watermen. They only hoped he could help them as well.

After sharing a few lighthearted words with his admirers, Charles broke loose and crossed deliberately into Roy Davis's path. He was almost there when another farmer caught his arm and shook his hand. "Glad to see you here, Congressman. We're all glad you could make it."

Charles flashed his signature smile and then kept walking, straight into the fire. "Hi, there. I hear you're a guest here today from the Baywaters Commission. Glad to see you. I'm Congressman Lee."

The other man flashed a quick smile and extended his hand. "Yes, I'm here to listen to what's going on over here with these farmers. I often drop by and poke around to see if there's something we can do for them."

Charles looked him straight in the eye and tried to get a read. If Davis remembered Charles, he was not letting on. The poker face was in place and the game had begun. Charles would be careful to tread water lightly for a while. Until the man made a mistake. The liars always did, and so Charles would wait.

"Well, they do need our help so glad we could both come and join them." Charles looked over to Buster and raised his eyebrows. The sign had been given and Buster didn't waste a minute heading up to the podium.

In his casual manner, he tapped the mic to make sure it was working and then said, "Could you all take a seat so we can begin our meeting?"

Buster motioned to Charles and Tug to come sit in the front row.

Charles knew if Dawes had sent this man on a specific mission, it would come out in the Q&A, and then he would find out for sure just how much was at stake and whose payroll Davis was on. And, when he returned to his office, he wouldn't only have a session with the senator but with the person he suspected of leaking his schedule. He couldn't believe Steve Allen didn't know that in Washington there are no secrets. It all comes out . . . eventually. When Buster began the introductions, Tug got up and went to the side of the room to snap pictures and take notes. Everyone seemed to know Tug, and, it was obvious from their reaction to him, they liked him a lot.

A very tall man walked to the front. He was a sturdy and obviously fit. When he opened his mouth, there was no doubt he was Eastern Shore born and bred. He was also clearly a local farmer who wanted to say something. This was Robert Henson, the man Buster had pointed out.

"Hello, neighbors," he began, and then, without any introduction, he bellowed out a list of grievances to be aired in the meeting, not the least of which was to be a heated discussion over phosphorous and its side effects for the Bay. And then there was a huge tax Washington was entertaining to levy on the farmers. The list went on, and it was far more extensive than Charles had been told.

As Bobby Henson spoke to his farmer neighbors, it became crystal clear why Roy Davis was in attendance. Buddy never did anything out in the open; he always used people to do his dirty work behind the scenes. That's how he had stayed in power all these years. However, the one thing neither the senator or Roy Davis knew was that what was now being talked about was exactly what Charles was going to use to destroy Dawes and all his henchmen.

The meeting went on for a very long time. The phosphorous fertilizer issue seemed to be the one getting the most attention, and Charles quickly could see how this issue could undo the shore's entire chicken industry.

Time and again, the farmers spoke on alternative methods being tried, but all these experiments would take time to come to fruition. In the meantime, they were increasingly aware of the pressure to be environmentally safe with their farmland, but no one could stand what the government meddling was doing to the farmer. And not just on the Eastern Shore, but everywhere. Farmers all over were under government attack with regulations unimaginable in scope and reach. Onerous costs and fees were directly affecting their profits.

Their problem was a war of ideas. The farmers had farmed this land for eons and taken darned good care of their fields and property, but it seemed now that, every time they turned around, another attack was impeding them. The industry couldn't sustain itself at this rate, and the future was beginning to look like a nightmare for the agricultural environment of the shore.

By the time Charles was finally asked to say a few words, he had been unnerved by what he had heard. If only a small part of this was true, their industry was going the same way as the watermen's. He would have to choose his words carefully until he could find out exactly what was happening here.

Charles rose slowly after his introduction was over. The farmers clapped, regarding this man as their friend and someone with the welcome arrogance to stand up and fight for them.

Looking straight at Roy Davis, Charles took a deep breath and then began. "These rules and regulations cannot stand if the state of Maryland is to sustain even a small piece of its agricultural heritage. Maryland was all agriculture once upon a time, and now that culture is under siege all over the state. Something must be done to hold on to what we have now and keep it going forward into the future. Each issue must be addressed one by one, and you, the farmers, must keep standing up and doing what you're doing. It's clear that the chicken is the focus, and also clear are the desire and intentions of the state government. They want the poultry industry gone for the most part, or, perhaps, entirely. The Baywaters Commission isn't helping either. They have their view, but the chicken isn't the be-all and end-all of Bay pollution and we all know that." He stopped here to survey the crowd and see who had been most aggravated by what was being said. He wasn't at all surprised to see Roy Davis's face lit up like a fireball at Charles's clear and outright salvo. Now let him carry *this* back to ole Buddy; then the war would begin.

Roy squirmed in his seat, his face revealing the disgust he had for this young congressman. *Just who did he think he was? This young stud had no idea how many years Buddy had been working his schemes on these farmers. Now, when they're where he wants them, this asshole thinks he can waltz in and undo it all. Never! Buddy was going to win, and, if the farmers fought him, he would destroy them.*

Charles knew exactly what Buddy's stooge was thinking, but what Davis didn't know was that soon he was going to fry, and so was his boss. Buddy had been living large and on the edge for years, and it was becoming obvious how he had been able to do this. Bribes were a nasty business that can come back to haunt a person. Charles would do whatever it took to help these farmers, as he had the watermen, and Buddy was going to pay the price for his greed by being forced out of Washington in disgrace, never to return again. Charles loved the Eastern Shore and was going to help all these people, be they watermen, farmer, or businessmen—they were the backbone of this state, historically and economically.

Smiling at them all, Charles brought his remarks to an end. "I have heard you today and will stay in touch. This I pledge to you. Your words and concerns touch me deeply and you will soon see how much. Thank you, again, and please continue to keep doing your good job of providing so much to us in the state and those around the country. After all, it is true that, if you ate today, you can thank the farmers and the fishermen of this nation!"

Buster yelled, "Here, here!" and the farmers stood and cheered the young man who none knew would likely soon be standing with them in his run to rid and replace Buddy Dawes.

Vernie, who had been very patient sitting in the back, came to life hearing her brother. She was so proud. She had never heard her brother speak like this before and found herself standing and cheering with the men. She so wished Willa could have heard him today. But she also was aware Willa knew exactly whom she had married, and that he was going to be a great senator.

While Charles was taking his bows and enjoying his five minutes of fame with the farmers, Buddy was enjoying a different kind of moment. He was digging for something, something he could hang on that young Lee's head and choke him off before anything got out of hand. The congressman's office boy, Steve, was his way to that information.

"I tell you, boy, your boss isn't going to last long in this town. Glad you are there, working for me now. When I finally get him, you will have a great job working for me over here in my office. I bet he doesn't have a clue what's going on, does he?"

"No, Senator, he doesn't, but something is going on with him, too. I don't know what it is, but something is up with Congressman Lee."

"How's that, Stevie Boy?"

Steve hated it when the senator called him Stevie Boy; it was so patronizing. His name was Steve. He sighed inwardly. He had wanted this job, and had worked very hard to get it, even to the point of being a fake friend of Prue Harding. So he would play along with this overstuffed jerk until he had reached his goal, and then he would straighten him out.

"I'm not exactly certain, but it's a feeling I have. He's been meeting Prue Harding once in a while. They always talk politics, and I overheard him saying that he wanted to talk something over with her and it was very important."

"Come on now, Stevie Boy. That could be a million things."

"No, I don't think so. I have a sixth sense about things like this. He has something definite in mind."

"Well, we'll know more when Roy reports back in. *My* sixth sense tells me Charles Lee is going to get in the way of something I have been planning for years, and, if he jumps in to play savior with the farmers, he will find out just how much power I have."

Steve didn't know what that comment meant, but he knew enough to understand that Senator Dawes played hardball to the point that people were truly scared to death of him. Dawes kept everything close to the vest, but, despite his personal reservations, Steve sure admired this giant of a senator, a commanding-looking man with a full head of silver hair and a way about him that made women swoon. He was an old-fashioned southern boy who played to win no matter who or what got in his way.

Congressman Lee was young and maybe not in that league at all, but one thing was certain: Charles had played hardball before with another high-and-mighty senator—and won. Steve knew Charles wouldn't hesitate to get into the fray again. Steve also knew what could happen to him in this game he was playing. There were grave consequences, but isn't that what the game was all about? You had to put your neck out if you were going somewhere in this town, and Steve Allen intended to go somewhere.

Chapter Thirty-One

Kay breezed into the breakfast room of the hotel in Baltimore where she and Max had spent the night, separately. Max was already seated and drinking his morning coffee. He watched as she walked toward him and enjoyed the looks people were giving her. She was still an outstanding-looking woman, and now, after having to keep his feelings to himself all these years, he was free to truly enjoy this lady.

"Good morning, Max. Did you sleep well?"

"I did indeed. And you?"

"I died. I think I'm not so used to all that driving anymore. We used to do it all the time when the boys were young."

"Yes, you did as I remember. I loved hearing the stories of your adventures on vacation."

"Well, I have to say Ted knew how to travel and actually relaxed when he was away from all the hustle and bustle of the sports world and newsprint."

"I know what that's all about."

"You didn't go away much, did you, Max?"

"No, I was married to my job, and most of my travels were in conjunction with that. I did manage to add a few days on here and there to go fishing."

Kay beamed at him and half-teasingly said, "Some woman missed a good man."

Max didn't answer, but, oh, how he wanted to tell her she was that "some woman." After the server came to pour Kay's morning tea and take her order, Max smiled and said, "So today we see Mikey. I sure miss that one."

"Ah, come on. Tug was always your favorite and you know it."

"I never showed it, did I, Kay?"

"No, you were a great diplomat, but I knew. Mikey had all that personality and curly hair. Tug was the scholar who took life so seriously."

173

"Yes, he did, and now he's a good, solid writer and is living in another world. I envy him for reaching out to life and taking what makes him happy."

"Would you ever have believed he would? But, yes, he is truly happy there and loves his Lindy."

"I have to tell you, Lindy is a gem and she's pretty as a picture."

As her food was placed on the table, Kay laughed and said, "I haven't heard that old expression for years."

"Well, I'm old and use those expressions. We don't use our language anymore and that's very annoying to me."

Kay enjoyed the banter and tapped him on his hand, then asked, "You mean, you wouldn't want to be called 'dude'?"

"God forbid, Kay! What's with that?"

"Oh, Max, the world has changed while we were whirling on the dance floor not that long ago, I'm afraid."

"Now *you're* talking like an old lady. Whirling on the dance floor? Who even dances anymore so it's recognizable?"

Kay burst out laughing so loudly that people nearby looked at her. "Oh, my, I am forgetting myself."

"It doesn't matter, remember? We're two old farts trying to make it to the end."

Kay sipped some more tea and smiled at him. Her smile was meaningful and he caught it.

Finally he said, "So, when will you be ready to start out?"

"Give me a half hour. Is that okay?"

"Call my room and we'll be off and on our way to see Mikey in the hub of Delmarva. But do you think we should call him 'Mike' now that he's all grown-up?"

"If you think it's time for you to do that, go ahead," Kay said. "However, he will always be our Mikey, and I'm not sure he will ever fully grow up."

Mikey was pacing nervously around his apartment. He was excited to see his mother but didn't really know what to say to her. What does a kid, of any age, say to their parents about breaking up? He knew she must be heartbroken.

He loved both his parents in different ways. A mom is a mom and accepts a child on every level, but a father was a whole different situation. He had witnessed the trouble Tug had always had with their dad. And he had always felt guilty that he had the main stage with the old man. Tug had been competing with him for attention, and Ted Alston was a tough act to follow for any son. Tug had tried to do everything his father had wanted, including almost killing himself to go to Harvard while being constantly compared to the great *Boston Globe* sportswriter and alum of the prestigious Ivy League school.

But Mikey hadn't wanted any part of that and had made that known very early in his life. He could still remember telling his dad that he loved sports but hated school. When he elected to go to Salisbury University, he'd known his father would be sore at him, but, as the baby, he always got what he wanted and he didn't regret one minute of what he had done. He did adore his big brother, and, when he learned Tug was going to stay down here, he was all in with staying down here, too, even if they didn't see each other very often.

The car pulled in the parking lot as Mikey was looking out the window, and he felt a little homesick. He hadn't realized just how much he missed his mother until he saw her face. He dashed to the door and ran outside.

"Mom, you made it!" He hugged her tightly.

Max stood there, enjoying their reunion. Finally, when Mikey came up for air, he realized who was with his mom.

"Hey, Uncle Max! How ya doing, dude?"

As they shook hands, Max glanced at Kay and winked. She winked back. "Dude" belonged to this generation, no matter how highbrow one was.

Max stood back, looked him up and down, and said, "Would you look at you? All grown-up and a working stiff now. How do you like it, Mike?"

"I love it, Uncle Max, and don't think I didn't notice the Mike instead of Mikey, but you can still call me Mikey if you want to. Mom will 'til the day she dies. I'm surprised to see you, but so glad you came with Mom. How have you been now that you're retired?"

Relieved that Mikey didn't mind the name change, Max answered, "I love it. I'm enjoying doing nothing, and doing nothing anywhere I want."

"Hey, that's a great line." Then Mikey looked at his mother and, in a changed tone, asked, "How are you, Mom?"

She realized what he'd been thinking the minute he'd seen Max and she wanted to correct his misimpression immediately. "I'm just fine, Mikey. I am all moved in at the Cape, and Max stopped by recently and he said he missed you and wanted to be in on the surprise for Tug's birthday. So we decided to split costs and come on down together."

Her son seemed satisfied for the moment, as he smiled and hugged her again.

Max was a little uncomfortable at all the hugging and emotion, but that was so Mikey, and he had always envied Kay's boys being like that with her. Sometimes he wished he'd had sons like that to love and share. He knew Ted could be a real bastard with his boys and had tried to make up for it, but it was too little, too late.

"Okay, so what are you hungry for? We stopped to take you out and you can have anything you want."

"Yep, and I've saved up an appetite, too. There's a great place down on the river, so let's go there. But, first, I want you to see where I live."

He took his mother by the arm as they walked into his apartment. He wanted her to see he really could keep a place clean and neat.

Kay looked up at him and said, "I've missed you and your brother so much. What do you think of the news?"

"You mean about Lindy having a baby? Well, Mom, there's something I have to tell you."

"What is it, Mikey? Has something happened?

"Yes, Mom, it has. Lindy lost the baby. Tug called and told me, and I said I would tell you so he wouldn't have to make another call. They're really sad, of course, but he said Lindy is doing okay."

"Oh, dear God. I just spoke to Lindy recently and she was so happy. Those things happen, I know. And at least they're young. You didn't tell Tug we were coming down, did you?"

"I haven't spilled the beans. In fact, I haven't really spoken to him in a while just because I didn't want to spill the beans. Besides, he's busy working on two new books. He's really a good writer, Mom."

Max piped up. "You can say that again, Mike. I hated to lose him from the paper, but it was time. He had so much else to do besides run down stories and get kicked around at the paper. I needed to go, too."

"Uncle Max, the paper isn't the same without you. They lost a giant in the industry."

"Thanks, Mike. That means a lot to me. So, how do you like what you're doing?"

"Love it. I get to meet so many neat folks around here. Working with farmers is wonderful. I didn't realize how much an agricultural state Maryland was until I took this job and began traveling around the peninsula. My job is to sell farm machinery, but what I learn in return from them is amazing."

"How did you get that job anyway, Mikey?" his mother asked.

"It was sheer luck. I took a bunch of ag-related courses in school and some of them were about the machines used on these big farms down here. I liked it and it seemed a natural fit when I heard about the job. It's sales, really."

"And you would be perfect for that. The Alstons were always good at selling themselves, so you have found your thing."

"Gee, Mom, that sounded a little like a shot."

Kay felt a little ashamed of herself for letting her guard down. "Well, maybe a little, but I didn't really aim that at you."

Mikey changed the subject, encouraging his mother to look around. As she did, he brought out some fresh sweet tea he had made and poured it for them.

"I'm impressed, son. You've finally grown up." Kay held her glass up and said, "Cheers!"

Chapter Thirty-Two

Charles and Vernie thanked Tug for driving them so far out of his way, but insisted on calling a driver to go the rest of the way from the Bay Bridge.

"Thanks so much, Tug. I learned a lot today at the meeting and I learned a lot about who's in this fight against us. I intend to deal with one of the main sources of trouble tomorrow morning and then see who crawls out next."

Sarcastically Tug said, "Not that you don't know who that will be, Charlie. You are one wily man, and I, for one, wouldn't want to do battle with you. Now, what do you need from me?"

"Thanks for those supportive words, Tug. What I need from you is to write a continuing narrative of what is going on down here. One we can use to leak to the press when the time comes. Can you do that? I know you are working on your next book, but I really need this and I can trust you. Can't say that about too many people."

"Appreciate your confidence, Charlie. Yes, I can do that. I'm so mad about what the government is doing to this state." Then, scratching his head, he added, "Makes no sense at all to destroy a complete heritage and such an important one at that."

"Does the government make sense these days, Tug? It's upside down, and no one knows if it can be fixed, but we have to try to do what's in front of our faces."

"I'll get started on it soon as I get home. You'll have it when you give me the word."

Vernie hugged Tug and smiled. "Give our love to Lindy. She's so sweet."

Tug's face changed and he said, "I will do that."

Vernie saw the look, but didn't know what it meant. Still, she knew he seemed as if he could use another hug, so she gave him one and then looked at Charles, ready to leave. She could see he was uncomfortable, too, but wanting to let it drop. Maybe he was wishing his wife were going to have a baby, too, but Willa had said he really didn't want one. She was confused, but it did no good to try to guess what was going on in anyone's head. Including her own.

Charles said, "Bye now, Tug. Take care of yourself and do give our love to Lindy."

"Thanks, Charlie. I will."

Tug drove away, and, while they were waiting for their driver, Vernie said, "What was going on here with Tug and then you?"

"Tug didn't want to make a big thing about it, but Lindy lost the baby. So I was hoping you wouldn't go on about it, and you didn't."

"That's too bad. How's Lindy doing?"

"He says she's doing okay and they are moving forward."

The drive out to Loudoun County to drop Vernie back home seemed endless. The fact that she rattled on about the cake business she was going to start had given Charles a bit of a headache, but he indulged his sister. He adored her and hoped that Tom would go along with this new venture—or there might be hell to pay. Tom was a saint most of the time, but Charles didn't know how a start-up cake business in his knockout new home was going to sit with the guy.

Finally back in D.C. and their Georgetown townhouse, Charles went right to the fridge and pulled out a beer and then sat down to think through what he had to do in the morning. Apparently Buddy Dawes had cast a huge net to catch him, and part of that net was right inside his office. He would have to get rid of Steve before he leaked anything else, and then he had to make plans for the likely event Seth Pullman withdrew from the race. He had to be ready to go.

As he drank his beer, he looked around and smiled at all the womanly touches Willa had brought to make this their home after they moved in. He loved everything she had done. Then he thought of what was going to happen to that simple, humble house on the island. She was going to tear into that, and it would surely be the finest home ever seen over there when she got done with it.

He missed her terribly when they were separated, something he knew any couple had to get used to when their jobs took them away from one another. At least her career was within her imagination, so she could live or go anywhere. But her readers loved her and she needed to feed that following at least once a year. Thinking of her made him miss her all the more. He couldn't stand it. He had to call her. He had to hear her voice.

Charles's voice was low and sexy. "Glad you're up late, Willa. I needed to talk with you."

"Missed me, huh? Well, I couldn't sleep without my best friend next to me, so you got lucky. Glad you made it back to D.C. safely."

Charles could hear the sheets rustle as she moved in bed. He wanted so much to be with her. She had stolen his heart when they met, and he loved her almost too much to bear their times apart.

"Dropped Vernie off and she was on cloud nine thinking of the cakes she was going to bake."

Willa giggled softly. "Poor Tom. I hope he goes with this or we could have a permanent boarder on the island."

"No, we will not," Charles snapped. "That's our private space and an occasional visit is fine, but that's all."

Willa knew that tone. He needed her right now and her body responded to his call, but they were so far apart. She was crazy in love with him, but knew she had to accept the absences or be condemned to a life of frustration. All she could do to fill the void was write stories that reflected their deepest thoughts and expressions of love. She was so happy how tight they were, and it satisfied her to know he felt the same way.

"I agree, my love. This is our home now, and, when I am done with it, we will be so content to spend whatever time here that we can. For my writing, it's perfect, and, when you're here, we will shut the door and keep the rest of the world out."

"Sounds good, sweetheart," Charles whispered gently to her. "Willa, I need you so much and want you to know that."

"I know, sweet Charlie. But please keep going. You aren't changing your mind about becoming a senator, are you?"

"No, I'm not, but it won't give us much time together."

"You're needed right now. Our country is in trouble. We have no real leaders; people who will stand for what's right are in very short supply. So, see? You have no choice."

"You're right, my dearest friend, but we should be greedy with every moment we get together. Once Seth pulls out and I announce and begin the campaign, it's going to be catch-as-catch-can."

"I've always liked that dish," she teased, trying to lighten things up.

But Charles was not in a light mood. "I have to deal with Steve tomorrow. What a dirty dog he turned out to be. Buddy must be paying him a fancy amount on the side to betray me."

Willa sighed. "Yes, it would seem that way. I'm sorry it worked out that way, Charlie. It would seem that, in no place more than in D.C., garbage smells a long time after you take it out."

Charlie laughed softly. "No doubt you're a writer. Who else but the famous Willa Carpenter could turn a phrase like that? You present a clear and distasteful vision."

"Does Prue know any of this?"

"She knows I have always had greater plans, but she doesn't know yet of this new development with the party bosses. I haven't had time to tell her, but I guess I should." He thought more about what Willa had just asked. "You know you inspire me, don't you, Willa? I'll call her in the morning before I deal with him. She always has good advice and her ears are to the ground in this city like no one else's."

"I am the worst friend. Since I've been here and working on the house and my next book, I have all but neglected her. Give her my love and tell her I'll call soon."

"She understands. I know she's working hard behind the scenes on her run for Congress now. She did zip me an e-mail to tell me her father is so happy she has finally decided to enter the fray."

"Well, that's going to make *two* great leaders in Washington. I am so impressed to know and love both of them."

"I love you, Willa. Sleep well, my darling."

"I love you more, Charlie Lee. Good night. Let me know how it all turns out."

Very early, Charlie was already up, coffeed, showered, and dressed. He gathered his papers and the thoughts he had worked on after speaking to Willa and was just about to call Prue on his cell when his other phone rang, His home phone, the number of which hardly anyone knew, except for his sister and Willa. What was wrong?

He immediately picked it up. "Hello?"

"I wanted to tell you before you left this morning that I got a call late last night from Roy Davis."

Charles was stunned. *How did he know how to reach me?* "How did you get this number, Buster?"

"That isn't important right now, but this is: Roy Davis came on like a frog in heat. He demanded I get you to stop all this fussing about farmers and their problems. He said, if this didn't come to an end, farmers would see just how hard it can get for them. And then he had the balls to ask if I caught his drift."

Charles, furious, kept his cool, but was still wondering how his new farmer friend had gotten his home phone number.

"Buster, I don't know the extent of all this—yet—but I can assure you, I'm going to get to the bottom of some of this manure today. I can't believe Roy would be this obvious, but what *is* obvious is that someone is very afraid of having their applecart turned upside down. I have to run right now, but thanks for the heads-up. You won't hear from Roy again because I'm about to pounce on the man who's behind this. I intend to find out what's really going on."

Buster's voice changed and he quietly said, "Your sister."

"What does my sister have to do with this?"

"You asked how I got your number. I asked her politely and she told me. I said it was very important."

Charles smiled and realized he should have known. Vernie trusted way too easily. "Well, it's a good thing I trust you, Buster, but please don't give it out to anyone else."

"I promise I won't, Congressman. If you need anything—anything at all— you call me. The farmers trust both you and Mr. Alston to handle this and help us out."

"Thanks for that vote of confidence, Buster. I'll be in touch."

Chapter Thirty-Three

Tug had been up practically all night working on the notes he had taken at the meeting the day before. He had fallen asleep at his desk just before the sun showed its face, which really wasn't anything new for Tug. But he seemed to be doing that a lot lately, just to get caught up.

Lindy, sleepily, padded quietly down the hall and saw Tug sleeping sitting up—a scene way too familiar to her. She did what she always did: tiptoed in, kissed him gently on the forehead, and, when he stirred, helped him off to bed. She loved him so much, and, even though there would be no baby this time, there would be another time. She had always been taught to accept what was given. That advice from her Aunt Shirley was now what was keeping her sane.

She glanced out the window of this small upstairs room Tug used as his office. She caught catch a glimpse of the Bay and, even farther out, James Island in the distance. She loved her friends over there and would love to do what Willa and Charles were doing and build a home one day in Tuckerton. Maybe someday they would be able to do that and still keep their home in Somerville as a backup. Many of the folks on the island did that in case they needed to leave the island for a variety of reasons like bad storms or freezing winter weather. But now she had to get this old house fixed up and then think of what she wanted to do with it once they could build. Maybe it could be a small guesthouse? She could never sell it outright; that would be like killing Dickie's memory forever, and that was never going to happen.

Tug had not been able to go back to sleep when he hit the bed, so he got up and headed back into his office. There he saw Lindy staring out the window. He loved to watch her when she did this and try to imagine her thoughts. Probably about Aunt Shirley and Dickie. He quietly walked over to stand behind her, then put his arms around her shoulders and kissed her gently on the neck. It was one of those moments that didn't happen nearly enough for a woman, but, when they did, the world stood still.

Snuggling in the comfort of his embrace, Lindy said, "Hmm. This is nice, isn't it, Tug? Want some coffee?"

"You know what I want, love."

"Well, that's not going to happen now."

Tug released her and laughed softly. "Why not?"

"Because I say so. Today is going to be a busy day."

"Too busy for your husband?"

"I'm afraid so. Now go sit down and I'll get your coffee."

"I fell asleep again at the computer."

"You're burning that candle at both ends. It worries me."

"I know, but I want to do this for Charlie. I admire what he's doing so much. He is going all in on this, Lindy."

"What do you mean?"

Suddenly Tug remembered he had promised Charlie not to say a word about what he was going to do, and that included to Lindy as well. And he kept confidences; he had learned that at the newspaper: you never broke a confidence.

"I just meant he is going to finish this battle of his with some of his colleagues in that corrupted sewer we call our capital. It's such a shame it's gotten so bad. The founders weren't perfect, but they would die all over again if they could see it now."

Lindy sat down carefully. "Yes, it is, but, right now, I want you to drink your coffee and then take a shower."

"Why the rush? I still have a lot of—"

She leaned over and put her fingers to his mouth. "Hush now. Do as I ask and we won't have to make up about this matter later on."

He kissed her fingers softly and said, "I like making up with you, girl."

"Go on now. Just do it."

Tug swallowed the last sip of his coffee and headed off to the shower, having no clue that, in a short time, he would be reunited with his mother and brother, not to mention his former boss and dear friend, Max.

Kay was up early and had gone to the hotel's indoor pool to take her morning swim. Kay loved the water and turned to it when she needed to think. This time she needed to understand that funny little stirring inside her when Max was around. *What is that all about?* The water hit her face as she did her many laps, and, the harder she pushed, the more she thought of him and how he amused her with his witty stories and how he had been so wonderful to come with her to surprise Tug for his birthday. And had she noticed a slight change in him, too?

He had been in her life, it seemed, forever. Or at least during the years she had been with Ted. Max was Ted's best friend. They had met at Harvard and became fast friends and that friendship had stuck through the years. She had always been close to him but had never felt this particular feeling before. *So many changes since I left Ted.* Was this just another, or was this because she was free to laugh with someone who was kind and caring? Not at all like the husband she could no longer stand to be around.

Max was dressed for the day ahead. He knew where Kay was but didn't want to disturb her during her daily swim. He knew how important it was for her to get her head clear for the day. Funny how he was noticing things about her now that he hadn't dared to before. He had always thought she was too good for Ted and had put up with way too much guff from him.

Kay rushed out of the pool and dashed upstairs to get ready for the day ahead. As she jumped into the shower, she smiled, thinking of how like a schoolgirl she felt trying to put an outfit together in her head. She had never done this for Ted—at least, not for years—but, suddenly, she wanted to look just right for Max.

Max left his room feeling quite good about himself. He had dropped some weight, and a man knows when he looks good and is back in the game.

Kay finished quickly because she didn't have to fuss much. She just put her hair up in a twist and clipped it, dashed on minimal makeup, pulled on some Talbots slacks with a lovely blue sweater. There. She looked at herself in the mirror. Not bad for a woman of a certain age. She leaned into the mirror for a closer look and whispered, "You can still cut it, Kay."

Max stood up in the dining room and waved her over. Now it was him having an odd, but nice, feeling inside his stomach.

"Good morning, Max. You're looking fine today, and I notice you've lost some weight."

"Yes, I have, Kay. Nice you noticed. You always look fabulous."

"Thanks, Max. What's on the agenda?"

In a slow, full-on drawl, he said, "Well, I thought we would go on down to visit Tug for his birthday. What do you think?"

"You always make me laugh, Max! I can't wait to see the kids. I know Lindy might be having a tough time, but we will make her feel better. There will be other babies."

"I'm sure she's okay, and it will be great fun when Mike shows up."

"Yes, it will. To have both my boys there with me—what a joy! And, by the way, Max, I noticed you went ahead and are calling him Mike now. He didn't seem to mind. You really adore that kid, don't you? But I thought Tug was your favorite." She grinned.

"You know I don't have favorites." He grinned back. "I respect and really admire Tug a great deal, but, you have to admit, Mike takes your heart sometimes."

Kay laughed, flashing her perfect smile. "Yes, he does. I'm so proud of both of them."

"I would never have guessed Mike would end up in something to do with farming. Athletics, yes; farming, no."

"Well, would either of us have thought Mr. Harvard would end up a novelist and married to a wonderful country girl and live at the end of the world?"

Max raised his eyebrows. "Guess you never know what turns people will take. They both seem to be so happy and they love what they're doing, so all is well."

Kay gave Max a long stare as their coffee was being poured. "You know, you are right about that. I would never have believed I would one day have had enough and walk out on Ted."

"I know, Kay. I wouldn't have believed it either, but you have blossomed since you did. You've proven to yourself that you can live without all the negatives Ted brought into your marriage."

Kay was completely taken by surprise at Max's keen insight into her life. She'd thought she had hidden that away from the entire world, including her boys. Maybe what she hadn't seen was that everyone else *had* seen the misery she was living in—everyone except her.

"What gave me the strength to do it, Max?"

Max took a moment before wading into such an intimate subject with the woman he admired more than any other. "I think it was time, and you had had enough. Sometimes two people work as hard as they can not to show the world the side of their lives that is really tearing them apart."

"You mean Ted was miserable, too? He never acted that way to me."

"Did you act that way to him?"

"I see," said Kay quietly. "You're a very observant man, Max."

"I care, Kay. I care deeply."

Kay became flustered. She didn't know how to answer; she wasn't ready to accept these new feelings about Max.

Max saw the look that was all over her face and reached his hand across the table to take hers. "It's okay, Kay. Nothing historic is going to happen between us today except two old friends going to enjoy a wonderful guy's birthday."

Kay looked straight into his eyes. "Thank you for saying that. Right now, I have a long way to go to figure this all out."

"Of course you do, Kay. You are a wounded bird at the moment. So let's just enjoy our wonderful friendship. And who knows? Maybe it will take us up someplace we hadn't expected. Now, here comes our breakfast. Let's eat and then let's go enjoy Tug's big day."

Kay beamed at this dear, old friend. She knew he was so right. Destiny would lead her where it would, but today? Today was for celebration.

Chapter Thirty-Four

Charles processed his most unexpected early morning conversation with Buster for a few minutes before finally grabbing his cell. He wanted to speak with Prue, as Willa had suggested.

A groggy voice answered, "Hello, Congressman. Don't you think it's a bit early for phone calls?"

Damn caller ID! "Not really. Aren't you up yet anyway? You're the early bird."

"Well, I spent some late-night time on my campaign strategy. You know how that goes. What's up? Everything okay with you and Willa?"

"Yes. She said she'll call you. She feels awful she hasn't done it sooner."

"Last time I spoke with her, she said she was about to tear your house apart. Has she begun?"

"About to commence shortly. But that's not why I've called, of course. I have to ask you some questions, Prue, about Steve Allen. I need to be absolutely sure before confronting him. I don't want to make a bad mistake."

"Oh-oh. So you're really thinking he's in Buddy's pocket? As I told you before, to be honest, I didn't know a whole lot about Steve when I hired him. He came highly recommended and had a great resumé. I had been in his company several times. He impressed me. That was it."

Prue had gotten up and was now putting a cup of water in her microwave to make tea. "I had a hunch something wasn't right in your office, and I should have seen this coming. You should have buried that little mole sooner, Charlie. You've been too good to him. He hasn't learned yet, you live or you die by the rules of the game in D.C."

"Are you ready to play that game, Prue?"

"You bet, or I wouldn't have made the decision I have. And I wouldn't be talking to you at 5:30 a.m."

Charles looked up at the kitchen clock. "God, Prue, I'm sorry. I really didn't know it was this early, but you're wrong about me and you should be the one person who knows that. When I know someone has betrayed me, I'm very capable of destroying them. Buddy Dawes is going to pay."

"Keep talking. You have my interest now. What are you planning to do with one of the most powerful senators in Congress?"

Charles bit his lip and hesitated a moment. Then he told her what was going on. "Prue, I need to tell you something in confidence. The party bosses called me Saturday afternoon and told me Seth Pullman may very well pull out. Apparently it is cancer, and it's not good. Well, anyway, they want me to step in and run in his place. After talking with Willa and Miss Frances, I said yes. I'm going to run for his seat in the Senate."

Silence. No snappy retort. "Well, Prue, what do you say to that? Naturally, that information is in complete confidence. Only Willa and a few others know."

"What did Willa say? Being a senator's wife isn't easy. But she could do it. In fact, she could do anything she wanted. And will, if it's for you."

Charles said, "She is amazing, and said she thought it was a great idea. But, right now, I need you to think hard. Is there anything else about Steve?"

"Well, if he's a good snitch, then he would come at a high price. And Buddy does have the money to buy him. Happening a lot these days. No loyalty. Lots of assistants in congressional offices are being bought off to produce 'facts' that can be used at appropriate times when a bill needs to pass or fail."

"That stinks, but it's what I think, too. I think Steve's on his payroll."

"Bingo."

Charles went on, "As you know, I'm now working with farmers on the Eastern Shore, and I went to a meeting yesterday with Tug Alston. A man named Roy Davis was there. I'm sure he's up to his ass with Buddy, too. That bastard has more informants and they're all over. Tug's going to prepare a fact sheet to use when the time's right. The farmers are getting hit with so much these days."

Prue sighed and said, "Ah, the new crusade. Remember, the last ones were awful touchy for you and Tug."

"Lesson learned, Prue, but we need the farmers to produce or we don't eat, and the threatened interruption to the food chain is enormous."

"Those are nice reasons to step forward, Charlie, but there is something so much bigger going on here. I can feel it."

"It's got to be money and lots of it, Prue."

"That's also a bingo. So, how are you going to find out exactly what Buddy's doing?"

"I'm hoping to get that information soon enough."

"I'm behind you all the way, Charles." She chuckled. "By the way, it's still odd calling you by your first name. Now, when are you going to announce?"

"That's coming as soon as Seth pulls out and the party heads say it's time. Buddy will go ballistic, but we'll know exactly what he's doing by the time he hears that news."

Prue took a sip of her tea, yawned, and said, "Give my love to Willa, and remember: I'm with you all the way to Washington, the Senate, and beyond."

"Let's just get me to the Senate. Thanks, Prue. I appreciate your time. If you should hear anything else, please let me know. And you're going to make a great congresswoman."

Tug was still thinking of how he wanted to go about this project for Charlie. He had a frame built around the issues, but he needed Charlie to find the smoking gun. Why were the farmers getting such heat from the government? There had to be something or someone driving this.

A shower would help get his mind going. Though he wondered why Lindy had been so adamant about moving him along this morning. He loved her to the moon and beyond, so knew he would just go with it. He stepped into the shower and let the hot water do its magic.

Lindy quickly finished picking up and making sure the house was ready for the company arriving very soon. She had prepared a lot of food but put it in their extra refrigerator so Tug wouldn't see it. The cake her Aunt Rita had made took up most of that room! Now Lindy just hoped she could keep the surprise until they arrived.

Tug felt so good after the shower. He quickly slipped on clean jeans and a tee shirt, his best working clothes. He was eager to get back to his computer. He heard Lindy moving all around downstairs. *Was that the vacuum going? What is going on anyway?*

When he sat back down at his computer, he glanced at the calendar. That's when it hit him: today was his birthday. That's when, being the smart man he was, he knew something was up. However, he wasn't about to spoil anything for his wife if she had gone to the trouble to do something for him. Nope, he would stay put until he was called. So back to work he went, a huge smile on his face. He didn't notice the two cars pulling up two houses down, or the people who got out of them and were now walking around the back of his house.

Mikey had driven his own car so he could leave quickly after Tug's surprise party. On the drive down from Salisbury, he had used the time to think. Lately, he'd wondered briefly about a lot of things, but, with his new job, he hadn't really had much time to reflect deeply on anything else. Now these other issues were front and center.

For one thing, he couldn't help but see how easily Max and his mom got along. He would never have believed anything would come from that because Max had been a part of their family forever. Why now would that relationship turn into something more, something completely different? He couldn't even bring himself to think about this, and yet . . . he had seen the way they looked at each other. Something was going on there.

The excitement at being with his brother and family was overwhelming. Except his father wouldn't be here for this birthday celebration, the first one since his parents had split. It was an odd feeling. Would they get back together or just spend the rest of their lives angry at one another?

His father was a tough and stubborn man, so Mikey thought he knew the answer to that question already. Life as they had always known it was now over forever. But, somehow, he knew that didn't mean there wouldn't still be good times ahead for them. He and Tug had to accept this situation and deal with it like adults. But even adult kids hurt when that family bond is broken.

Lindy heard the slight tap on the back door and hurried to answer it. There they stood, her wonderful new family, and she was so happy to see them. She waved them in while putting her finger up to her mouth to signal that they should be as quiet as could be. Kay looked at her and then gave her a reassuring hug. Mikey grabbed her tightly, whispering in her ear, "Hey, Sis, you look great." Then Max hugged her and said, "Hello there, doll." No one said a word about the loss of the baby, and that was a relief to Lindy.

They all quietly entered the kitchen, and then Lindy called upstairs, "Tug, I need you to help me with something in the kitchen. Can you please come down?"

Tug's mind was deep in his notes and his writing, so he unsuspectingly yelled, "Sure! Down in a minute."

The minute seemed like an hour by the time he walked through the swinging doors into the kitchen to see four wonderful faces and hear their greeting: "Surprise! Happy Birthday!"

He hadn't realized how much he had missed seeing his mother. When her hands went out to hug him, he rushed to her, with a look of total surprise and happiness. He hadn't expected this.

"Mom, I have really missed you," he said with a hug that was pure love. Then he saw Max. "Good Lord, did this ole scallywag come with you?"

Max first extended his hand, but then hugged his former employee and good friend. "Hey there, Tug. I know I was the last person alive you expected to see, but I'm glad to be here with you."

"You got that right, Uncle Max. How the hell are you?"

"I'm fine, and being back down here sure brings back some memories."

"I'll bet. Like memories of Dickie Short?"

"That old coot about drove me into an early grave. Kind of miss him, though."

Tug laughed. "I miss the heck out of him. So does Lindy." He put his arm around his wife. "He was family, and we really miss him every time we go out to his crab shanty. We're fixing it up now, sort of. You and I should take a walk later and see it."

Max realized that was Tug's way of saying they needed to talk. He answered, "He helped change things, that's for sure, Tug. And gave you a very pretty wife. She looks great."

Tug blushed. "She sure does."

Then Tug turned and hugged Mikey. "Hey there, little brother! You were in on this conspiracy, too?"

"Guilty as charged. But it was a great excuse to see Mom. I had no idea Uncle Max would tag along, so that's all the better." What wasn't said between them was understood, loud and clear. Their dad's absence was felt strongly, but they would leave that alone for now.

"Yes, it is. It's just great to see all of you," Tug said, as he guided everyone into their small living room.

Lindy stayed in the kitchen to get some coffee and tea. Tug walked back in, took her by the arm, and hugged her. "You sure got me this time, Lindy. I'm overwhelmed to see all of them."

"I am so happy you are happy, Tug. I wanted to see your mom anyway, and this seemed like a good time."

"Wish things were different and Dad was here, too, but that isn't going to happen. What's with Max coming with Mom?"

"Don't overthink it, Tug; just enjoy it. Hearing you talking to Max about Uncle Dickie really made me wish he was here with us, too. I miss him so much."

Tug continued to hold her in his arms. "I know. I miss that old grouch so much. He would have loved to be with us, but his time had come, and now he is in that special place in heaven with all the other old watermen."

Lindy wiped a tear from her eye and then pushed him away. "Now go on in and enjoy. I have a ton of food and our time with them isn't going to last forever. So, go now and have fun."

"Did I tell you this morning I love you?"

"As I recall, you fussed with me over my suggesting you take a shower."

"Wait until tonight, Miss Lindy, and I will thank you properly for this get-together."

Lindy, with a bright smile and girlish giggle, turned and walked to the other fridge, saying, "Promises, promises."

Chapter Thirty Five

Charles was in his office before Steve arrived. He was so glad he had called Prue and discussed the situation. He missed her terribly as his chief of staff, and especially today, when he had to confront this young man who had used him like a wet rag. *Were there signs I missed?* This wasn't going to be pretty but he had to know everything Steve was up to, and, beyond that, what Buddy was doing.

He made the coffee, poured a cup for himself, and waited for Steve to walk in. His assistant was thrown completely off guard by the presence of his boss.

"Well, good morning, Congressman. You're in the office early this morning."

"When you're settled, could you please step in here, Steve?"

"Yes, sir. I see you made the coffee. Sorry about that. This coffee system can be pretty temperamental."

A few moments later, Steve entered Charles's office. *The little weenie has no idea what's coming. Good. Look at him, fussing about as if nothing has changed.*

In a cold voice, Charles directed him, "Take a seat, Steve."

Steve knew immediately something was wrong; the congressman had never before asked him to take a seat. He nervously did as he'd been told.

"As you know, I made the most interesting stop yesterday on my way back to D.C. I met with a large group of farmers on the shore."

"Well, you said you wanted to find a way to break through to them. I'm glad that man—what was his name? oh yes, Buster Talbot—came through for you."

"Good memory, Steve."

"That's my job, isn't it, Congressman?"

As Charles leaned forward, Steve wiggled a bit in his chair.

The congressman said, "Comfortable?"

"Yes," the young man lied.

"Well, Steve, I think you and I need to have a conversation about trust and confidence. What do you think?"

By this time, Steve was pale and not looking so good. He knew Charles knew something, but also that he had to play this out.

Charles continued, "Okay, Steve, we can do this the hard way or the easy way. How much is Senator Dawes paying you to be his stooge in this office?"

Steve swallowed hard. He felt bile rising in his throat. He had been found out, but how? Stammering, Steve groped for words, though he knew it was probably too late. "I don't know—"

Charles slammed his fist down on his desk. "How much and when did you turn?"

"Please, Congressman . . . please don't do this."

"Please don't do what? Blow my stack at the fact that my right hand has just cut my throat? Did you think for one minute I wasn't going to uncover this act of betrayal? Well, I have, and you can thank Roy Davis for that. He was as transparent as water. I hate liars and deceivers, Steve. Aside from being fired, before you walk out that door, you're going to tell me all I want to know, or you won't work anywhere on this planet ever again. And if you think Buddy Dawes will come to your defense, think again."

Steve's face said it all. He had been caught and he looked as if he were going to pass out. Charles got up, pulled a bottle of water out of the small office fridge, and threw it to him. "Here. Take this, gather your feeble, lying wits, and start talking."

Steve took a long swallow and then sat up straight. This was an entirely different man than he had known. "All right. Yes, Senator Dawes offered me quite a sum to tell him what was going on inside this office.

Charles sat on the corner of his desk so he could be as close to Steve as he could stand. Then, leaning down into his face, he said in a steely tone, "Now, tell me, Steve, what exactly is Dawes up to? What is he doing to the farmers of that state?"

Steve knew he had no choices here; he had to tell him. When he began speaking, at first the words came out all jumbled up. He had never before seen this side of the congressman and was a bit scared. Finally, he quit babbling, took a minute to collect himself, and started again. He had known the risks and taken them anyway. His luck had just run out.

"Go on, Steve, I'm waiting."

"Well, it's not exactly the farmers he's targeting. He wants their farmland."

Charles snickered. "What's he going to do with all that?"

"He wants to get legislation through at the state level to grow marijuana and make wine."

Charles wasn't at all prepared for that answer. He was stunned at the scope of Buddy's vision and his greed.

"Marijuana and wine?"

"Sure. With all the marketable fruits on the shore, he sees a huge potential wine industry that could be developed over time. But, for the immediate future, cannabis growth would bring in millions in taxes and be a huge industry—all regulated, of course, and for medicinal purposes only. The people would love him and he would stay in office until he died."

"I see. His plans make him look so magnanimous and as if he's the savior of the sick people of the state. But then he would expand on that once he got it going, right? The entire state would become a cannabis farm. And when and how is he going to strike at the unsuspecting farmland?"

"Soon, Congressman. He knows you are on to something over there, but he doesn't think that you know just what. He figured Roy's appearance would tip you off, so he has to rush with this as much as he can."

"Before someone stops him? Does that tell you anything, Steve?"

"Yes, sir. That's pretty much the idea."

Charles got up, walked back to his chair, and sat down. Steve didn't move a muscle. He just waited for the congressman to say something. Anything. Just to get it over with.

It was a few minutes before Charles opened his mouth. He was seething underneath, but kept as calm as he could. His plan had changed.

"How much is he paying you, Steve?"

Taken off guard, he said, "What, sir?"

"How much did it take to turn you?"

"Twenty thousand over what you are paying me."

Charles shook his head. "Seems a small purse, doesn't it?"

Steve looked at him in stunned amazement. "I have to have that money for my already overdue student loans. The government is threatening me."

"Well, now, Steve, life sure is crowding in on you, isn't it? Now, I will tell you what deal *I* am going to make. I am going to help you with your loans, and you are going to stay here and help me find out every move that man is going to make. You will report to me every step, every thought, every move. Do you understand me?"

Steve's head was mush. He looked like a bobblehead as he nodded at every demand Charles was making of him. "Yes, I understand, sir. You're not going to fire me?"

"Firing you wouldn't get me what I want. I want justice for these farmers, and nothing else will do. They aren't going to be turned against each other in some hideous bidding war Buddy Dawes is about to instigate. They are good, decent, American people, and our government has already squeezed every dime, every inheritance, every good hope, out of its people through its own corruption and greed. This must end, or we won't have fishermen or farmers anymore in this state. Or anywhere else for that matter. That, Steven, is our food supply he's playing with."

Steve was both relieved and disturbed at the same time. Still shaking, he said, "The senator will find out what I'm doing, you know."

"By that time, other matters will be playing out, I can assure you. I promise to protect you, Steve, but hear me now: if I find out you are playing both sides again, you won't want to know what I can do to you."

Steve stared right into Congressman Lee's eyes in stunned disbelief. He had never heard the man speak like this before. Wobbling, he stood up and said, "I believe you, Congressman, and I'll do this and I will do it with an apologetic heart. You're a good man and I don't deserve this second chance. Can you ever forgive me?"

Charles took a deep breath. *How sad a state of affairs these days that young people can be so easily bribed to lie and betray.* He stood up to put Steve on an even playing field.

"Right now forgiveness is not the issue. I need to be able to trust you again, and, this time, don't disappoint me. You have to act as if none of this happened, or Buddy *will* know. And, if you think I'm playing hardball, you haven't seen anything until you see what that man is capable of."

Now Steve was afraid, very afraid, but he had to make the congressman trust him again. "I won't let you down. I promise. I am sorry, but I will make it up to you."

"You remember that statement, and, for the love of your country, don't disappoint those farmers."

Steve was dismissed. As he walked out of the large office, all he could think of was his family, his debt, and how he was going to fool Buddy Dawes.

Chapter Thirty-Six

Tug nudged Max, leaned over to him, and whispered, "I need to speak with you privately."

Without any telling expression, Max replied, "Where?"

"Come on with me."

As the men walked toward the kitchen, Lindy said, "Just where do you think you two are going?"

Tug turned around and said, "I want to show Max Dickie's old shanty."

Mikey could see the look on his brother's face, so he stood up and said, "Hey, you know me—I eat and run on you folks all the time. I have to get back to work."

Tug smiled at his kid brother, then walked over and gave him a bear hug.

"Thanks for being in on this surprise party. And don't be a stranger."

Kay had tears in her eyes watching her two sons together. She loved how they had always stayed close, no matter what. She joined in the family farewell. As she hugged Mikey good-bye, she couldn't hold back any longer and the tears flowed.

"Can we stop on our way home? I mean I hardly spent any time with you and I don't know when—"

"Mom, stop. Call me when you're leaving and we can have lunch together."

Max went over, took Kay by the shoulders, and said, "We would love that, wouldn't we, Kay?"

The scene was weird for both boys, but they didn't say a word. Maybe it was the smile on their mother's face.

"I will do just that, Mikey, and please be careful going home."

Mikey gave her cheek a light kiss and said, "Some things never change, I guess: once a mom, always a mom."

Lindy chimed in. "You better believe it." Then she bravely added, "And I will feel the same way one day."

Mikey smiled back at his sister-in-law and said, "You take care, girl, and I will check in on you soon, just to make sure that big brother of mine is treating you like the princess you are."

At the very last moment, Mikey turned back to his mother and smiled his always boyish smile. Then he walked out the door.

Lindy broke the silence. "Well, the party part of this day seems to be breaking up. Could you help me in the kitchen, Kay? I think Tug and Max want to escape for a while."

Kay smiled sweetly, then walked over and gave her daughter-in-law a warm embrace. "I would be happy to help you, dear. What a wonderful time this has been, with all my favorite people."

Tug tapped Max on the shoulder and they walked through the kitchen and outside.

"Were you really surprised, Tug? If you weren't, don't ever tell that lovely girl; you would ruin it for her."

"I can't tell a lie, but I won't tell Lindy. I did suspect something this morning, but I never suspected you would be here. That's the real surprise."

"Miss ole Uncle Max, do you? Well, I've missed you two boys terribly. This whole mess with your father and mother has taken a toll."

Tug didn't answer at first; he just kept walking. Max knew what that silence meant. Tug had always been the quieter of the two boys, and, growing up, he'd had a really hard time with his father. Ted Alston had expected way too much of his firstborn son. Mikey turned out to be the real athlete and got away with murder. He was still a good kid though.

Tug stopped suddenly. Looking Max squarely in the eye, he said, "How is the old bastard, really? We don't speak much. He wasn't real happy, as you know, when I married Lindy. He faked it for a while, but I don't think he never truly understood Dickie and why I wanted to live down here with 'those people,' as he called them."

Max smiled and said, "He loves both of you, you know. He just can't show it. That's why he finally lost your mother. She is the best woman any man could ever have, and he treated her like she was invisible."

The two men started walking again, as Tug said, "And I thought you never saw that. Now I know you were watching her all the time."

"Watching *out* for her, Tug. There's a difference."

"You're in love with her, aren't you, Uncle Max?"

Shocked, Max took a deep breath, then said, "Now, Tug, let's not go there. Yet."

"You are, and I noticed the way she was looking at you. Now wouldn't that be something?"

"Don't, Tug. Any man would be honored to be with Kay, but she is still hurting and licking her wounds. She isn't nearly over Ted Alston, and I know he isn't over her. He's hurting, too, and so let's take some time and see where all this goes."

"He's lost her, Max. I know that. I know my mother better than anyone. She and Mikey are close, but not like she and I are. She understood me. And she will never go back to Dad. Well, doesn't matter right now because we're here. Come on."

Max followed Tug along the new planks that led to Dickie's old shanty, planks a friend had put down for him and Lindy. Right now, the building was clean enough for the two men, since Tug had thrown out old garbage and organized a few things. Still, it was a ways from what he envisioned when it was finished.

However, when Tug opened the door, Max peered in and couldn't believe it. "This is fantastic, Tug. I mean, it has good bones and great potential."

"You can stay here anytime. Go fishing. Would do you good."

"Maybe tomorrow, eh?"

"Maybe. But, for today, there is something I wanted to talk over with you."

"Figured."

Tug retrieved the bottle of good whiskey he kept for special moments. Sheepishly, he said, "I keep it around, hidden from Lindy. She would kill me."

"My lips are sealed," Max said, with an understanding look.

As Tug poured, he looked at Max and began to tell him what was on his mind. "You see, it's a matter of salvation."

"Oh, no. Not another crusade? The last one almost killed us all. You and that danged old fisherman."

"Waterman, Max. They are watermen. And, as I recall, you liked him at the end."

"Yes. I know. Well, what is it that's got you going this time?"

"Farmers."

"Farmers?" Max said, looking a little astounded. "What in hell is wrong with them?"

"Nothing—right now—but they are beginning to struggle with their farmland and what's coming."

"And just what is it that's coming, boy?"

"The same thing that's worrying the watermen. Their children. A lot of them want to go on farming their land, but will they be able to? That's the question."

"I'm not getting it, Tug. Why wouldn't they be able to?"

"In short, it's the chicken and its ability to stay here. There are some who want to get rid of the chicken because they say it's damaging the Bay and other shore waters by the use of their droppings for fertilizer. The farmers are cooperating with officials and using all kinds of different methods to fertilize their fields. Their techniques improve in quality every year, but things take time. If the wonks accomplish the abolition of the chicken, then the poultry business leaves and that impacts the grains grown here as well. The impact to the whole shore will be enormous."

"Ah, yes, it is another crusade. Don't you get tired saving all these folks?"

"No, I guess I don't. Congressman Charles Lee, who's become a good friend, is getting very involved with this. He recently married Willa Carpenter—you've heard of her, I know—and they bought a house out there in Tuckerton, on the island."

Max took a long sip of his whiskey. "Are you sure you want to get messed up in whatever it is you think is going to happen?"

"No choice. Charles—Congressman Lee—has asked me to, and he's my friend, so I won't say no."

"And you can't be persuaded otherwise, right?"

"Right. And I need your help, Max, to help me get the word out."

"I'm retired now, Tug. You know that. So what makes you think I can do anything? You know what happens when the big dog leaves."

"I know you were deeply respected for the stands you took. And I know you can help me. Don't say no; just trust me and say you'll help."

Max breathed deeply, then let out a loud sigh. "I knew I shouldn't have come down here."

"You're not mad, are you, Max?"

"Not mad at all. Quite the opposite, actually. I think I just found a way to stay relevant in my retirement. I mean, I can't spend all my time chasing rainbows in hope that your mother will come to her senses."

Tug held up his glass in a toast. "I sense she already has, Max. Gee, what will I call you?" He chuckled. "But, seriously, thanks. I need you in on this with me."

Max took another sip of the whiskey and smiled. "Just don't call me stepdad. Besides I don't want to lose your dad; he and I are like brothers. Let's just let this play out. Okay? For now, as always, your mom and I are good friends."

"Then you'll help me help Charles, right? That's great. He is going far in D.C., you know. I can't tell you all, but—trust me—Charles Lee is going far."

"Proud heritage those Lees of Virginia have. I can't wait to meet him."

"Well, you can meet his wife tomorrow. We're going over to the island for lunch. Great crab cakes at Bradshaw's Market."

"Is that island woman over there?"

"Didn't think you knew about her."

"Your mother told me about her. Said she met her at your wedding."

"She's amazing and a real scrapper. You two will get on fine."

As Max stood up to go back to the house, he hugged Tug. "I've missed you, Tug. Things were never the same after you left the paper. I always felt I didn't do enough."

"What are you talking about? I fell in love with the most wonderful girl in the world and decided Boston wasn't for me and neither was Baltimore. This is where I belong. I love the people, the land, the heritage. And, by God, I am going to do my best for them."

"That sounds like another book for you."

"Right now, I'm actually working on two—another novel that my publisher is already bugging me about, and a sort of photographic coffee-table book about the seabirds here and their great migration in winter and fall."

Trying not to laugh too loud, Max said, "Sounds fascinating."

"It's a metaphor, Max. It will show the nature of the people who live here and the natural cycle of life that surrounds them, and how they both ebb and flow with the seasons. You'll see."

"You're a pretty interesting guy, Tug. You always have been, and I think that might have made your father a bit uneasy. It was easier for him to relate to Mikey and his world with the sports and all. I'll help you any way I can."

Tug smiled as he put the bottle away. Max had always been on his side.

Max took a last look around. "This is paradise right here in this small shanty, looking out on that beautiful Bay. I see why you love it so much. Conducive to the word flow."

"You understand, Max. Not many back home can. They think I have lost my way, settling down here, away from the hustle and bustle, so to speak. Well, you will see another paradise tomorrow on the island."

"Can't wait. Oh, by the way, Tug, don't say anything to your mother about . . . well, you know."

"Now it's my lips that are sealed, Uncle Max. I can see the deep affection between you. I just want her happy and not getting hurt anymore."

Max took one last look as he shut the door and left the little shanty on the bay. "I will make sure of that, no matter how this goes."

Chapter Thirty-Seven

"I don't know how Miss Millie can do this each and every day," Vernie shouted in complete frustration.

Tom, finishing the morning paper, bolted from his chair and walked into the kitchen. Mornings were his quiet time to get acquainted with the news and everything else going on in the world. He was an intellectual and had spent his life being both a country lawyer and sharing his brilliance in D.C. think tanks. He loved his life and his wife. In fact, he had been in love with Verinnia since the day he had met her at a backyard barbecue in Charlottesville. But, if asked, he would tell you she confounded him more than any other woman he had ever met. That must have been the glue that held them together. That, and the fact she was a Lee. That meant something in Virginia.

Tom entered the kitchen, half afraid of what he was going to encounter. "My dear, what is going on in here?"

"I can't do this, Tom. I thought I could, but I just can't. I don't know how Miss Millie gets up at the crack of dawn every morning and bakes these cussed cakes."

Tom walked over and put his arms around her tightly. "Does it mean that much to you, dear heart? You have been in a tizzy since you got back home from that island. I'll bet Willa doesn't even attempt to make these cakes."

Vernie hissed a little and put on her pouting face. "Willa's too smart to do this. She has no interest in baking. She's a writer and my brother is a congressman and soon to be a—"

She stopped before she spilled the beans. Tom looked at her and said, "And soon to be what, Vernie?"

"I'm not supposed to say a word, and here I am, not even able to keep a secret."

"You and I aren't supposed to have secrets, are we?"

"Well, no, sir, we're not supposed to. But I promised Charlie with my life."

"Then don't say another word. I don't want to lose you."

Vernie stopped her tantrum and kissed him passionately. "I don't know how you can love me, Tom. I am pigheaded and not very smart, and—"

Tom kissed her back deeply. The kiss said let's just leave this now, shall we? He took her by the hand and led her out of the kitchen and up the winding staircase. The cakes would wait, or maybe never be made at all, but this was so much more important.

The dog days of summer were in full swing, which meant Frances and Jimmy had some work to do that had been put off with all the celebrating. Crabbing was in full gear and going good this year. The oysters were doing their thing and wouldn't be back in the game until late fall. Yes, she and Jimmy had lived this cycle all their lives, loved it with all their hearts, and knew what it was like not to be prepared. It wasn't good.

Willa was walking down the path and now saw Miss Frances's house. She never tired of walking or riding her golf cart all around the tiny island. When she spotted her good friend working outside, a smile crossed her face.

Frances came up for air and a sip of water and spotted Willa and waved to her young friend. She was so happy that she and Charles had decided to have a home here, even though she knew Willa missed the city sometimes. Lately, however, it seemed that was less and less. She was turning into an island girl.

"Hey, how ye comin'?

Willa smiled and gave Frances a hug. "I'm just fine, Miss Frances. How are things with you and Jimmy? Just wanted to pop over and see."

"Then ye will come on in and we'll have a cup of tea."

"How did you know that was exactly what I wanted?"

"Women need tea from time to time. Keeps their heads on and their tongues waggin'."

Willa laughed. She often thought this island woman should be on the stage with her quaint sayings and notions of things. These people simply knew so much more than the average person. They just had "smarts" and a savvy that city folk would never understand.

The two went into the house and Willa was reminded of how much she loved Frances's kitchen. It said home in a way that everyone loved felt deep down in their hearts.

As Frances put on the pot, she said, "I see you're going great guns on your house. I know how upsetting that can be. Ye are welcome to sleep over here if ye need to."

"Thanks so much, Frances. It's going to get a lot worse, but at least they should have the most of the work done before winter comes."

"Excuse me for being nosey and all, but how are you going to write with all that noise going on?"

Willa laughed. "Easy. I'll be in D.C. with Charles! He needs me there anyway. The summer season is upon us with the barbecues and mint juleps and all. There's always a party to attend. I'll come back when I'm needed. Clyde knows exactly what I want, so it should be fine. I adore Clyde Shaw."

"He's a great guy, and you're lucky to have snagged him. He usually goes out and crabs some, but, I guess with your job, he won't need to, unless it's for his own personal eating."

"I'm such a lucky girl. Charles is everything I could want in a husband. I just wish he weren't so busy all the time, and, as you know, right now he's going through a tough patch with that Steve who works for him. He betrayed Charles. It's such a dirty game-playing place."

"Makes my blood boil over. They play games while we pay the bills and have to work harder to pay the taxes. I tell ye, it isn't right. Charles is one of the good guys, but he's in the midst of pure evil."

"You might say that, but he's sorting it out, and I am sure he will come out on top when he's done."

"I have no doubt. So, how's the new book coming? I can't imagine you have much done with all the things you have to take care of. I know the women here love your books."

"I really haven't begun at all yet. I will do that when I get to Washington, but I do have a good plot going on in my head."

Frances laughed and said, "Ye are beginning to sound like us girls here on this island. We always have plots in our minds. Some of them actually work out."

"Tuckerton is paradise and I love it. I'll miss being here all the time."

"Ye don't have to worry none. We'll all keep watch and nothing will happen when ye aren't here."

"You seem to read my mind, Frances."

"I have this sixth sense. Now, how's your sister-in-law doing with the cakes?"

"Not well, I fear. She sunk a small fortune into bakeware, and *my* sixth sense tells me she isn't going to get most of it broken in before she gives up. She had such high hopes of a grand venture into the business world. I love her so much."

"I know ye do, and Millie loves her, too. Doesn't make a difference as long as she's happy. It takes a bit to get the hang of it. Then watch out; she'll zoom ahead."

"From your lips to God's ears."

Chapter Thirty-Eight

Buster had just about had it with the neverending regulation of farmers. It seemed every week the government was cranking out some new one to make them spend more money on their farms while complying with restrictions that would make farming more and more difficult. Farmers worked hard enough already. And now they were seeing what they had done for generations being not only restricted, but, in some cases, almost completely overridden by laws telling them what land could be farmed and where homes, schools, hospitals, roads, and communities could be developed. The Talbot family had been here for more years than he could remember and had always farmed the same way. Now everything was different. The Baywaters Commission was overreaching and standing in the way of any progress farmers could make. His head was spinning by the time he put in a call.

"Congressman Lee, please."

"May I tell him who is calling?" Steve asked, rather curtly.

"You just tell him Buster is on the phone, will you, son?"

Who was this person calling him 'son'? Another Buddy Dawes?

It wasn't a moment before Charles was on the phone. "Hello again, Buster. What's up?"

"What's up is all hell's breaking loose over here."

"Why don't you tell me exactly what's got you all riled up?"

"I guess it was that meeting, Congressman. Something's just not right. I had a man come by this morning, and he wanted to know all about my farms and how much land I have and what I raised. When I asked him who he was, he just looked at me kinda queer-like and said, 'I'm from the state.'"

"Bet that didn't sit too well."

"No, it did not. I told him to get off my land and that I wasn't going to answer any of his fool questions. Can the government do that? I mean, just show up at your door and start firing away?"

"I've never heard of doing business like that, but I've just learned that someone or some group wants your collective lands for another purpose, and I'm working on that now. Just calm down and I'll get back to you when I know more. Thanks for calling me."

When Charles got off the phone, he called Steve in to his office. This would be Steve's first test of loyalty.

"Yes, Congressman?"

"First of all, I want to make sure that every time that man calls me, I get the message or you put him through to me immediately, understand?"

"Yes. Yes, I do."

"That was Buster Talbot. That's all you need to know right now, other than that he is important to me."

Steve caught his drift and knew not to push the good congressman any further. "Is there anything else, sir?"

"Yes. Please call Senator Dawes and ask when he and I can have a meeting. Can you do that, Steve?"

"Immediately, sir, and I'll let you know. What will I tell him you want to meet with him about?"

"Nothing. Just make the meeting, will you?"

Steve quietly turned around and left. The bait was now out there. Charles would see if Steve could talk Buddy into a meeting and also find out if he had told him about Buster. He wasn't at all sure Steve could handle this whole situation. He meant what he told Steve, though: if he couldn't play Charles's game, then Steve was no longer going to work in the world he seemed to love so much. He shook his head and called Willa.

Willa was on her way back home when her cell rang. She checked and saw it was Charles. "Hey, what's up? You don't usually call during the day."

"Well, that's the way to say hello to your husband. Should I hang up and we can try this again?"

Willa giggled. "Sure. Go ahead and see if I answer the call."

"What's got you so spunky today, hon?"

"I don't know. It's what you do to me." Then she turned serious. "Really, Charles, is something wrong?"

"Not really. Well, maybe a little. I dealt with Steve and that wasn't fun, but we sorted it all out."

"Oh? How did you sort it out?"

"Well, I'm keeping him on for now."

"You're what?" she shouted.

"Willa, I know what I'm doing. I want him close to me so I can get to the heart of what's going on. Buster Talbot, that old farmer, called me twice already today. He's even more exasperated at what the state is doing to its farmers. I know Buddy Dawes is up to something, but have to know exactly what."

"I'm sorry, Charlie. I know how many things are pressing in on you. Are you sure you want to take this on?"

"Some people just don't give up. They just keep going until they make people do things they would rather not. But, in his case, Dawes is asking for it."

"I'm so sorry. Are you coming back soon?"

Charles smiled listening to her voice. "Miss me, huh?"

"Yes, I miss you. And I've realized I won't get anything written while I am out here with Clyde really working on the house. So, maybe it would be better if I came back there."

"Oh, Willa, I would love that. I miss you not being with me. This is going to get rough with Buddy, and I could use your loving guidance through this mess."

"Then it's settled. I will be back this weekend. And I'm going to try to get Prue to stay with us in the townhouse for a few days, just for fun. And because I really could use her wit and wisdom."

"Tell you what, my love. I'll call her and tell her you're coming back to Washington for a while and that you could use some company. I'll see what her schedule is. I know she'll come if she can."

"You're an angel, Charlie. Keep me posted on the dread Senator Dawes."

"I'll call you tonight. And say hi to Clyde for me. By the way, have you seen Frances lately?"

"As a matter of fact, I'm walking back from her house now. I told her I was going back to D.C. for a while, and she said she will keep an eye on our house."

"No doubt she will. Poor Clyde and his men."

"Hey, they know this territory. It's great to have such peace of mind leaving here."

"Yep. No shoes, no shirts, no worries."

Charlie called Prue immediately. He was so happy Willa was coming back. He needed her there, especially now. And he couldn't say he'd be unhappy if Prue would come and visit for a while, either. He trusted her instincts. However, he knew she would be busy in the middle of planning her own campaign; she might not be able to get away.

"Hello. Prue Harding here."

"So official with your best friends?"

"Hi, Charles. What's up?"

"I just spoke to Willa and she isn't getting any writing done out there, so she's coming back to D.C. And she wants to see you and spend some time."

"Now, let's see: spending time with me and us doing some serious visiting—how does that help her write anything?"

"I think she needs you, Prue. I don't think anything is particularly wrong, but I could tell she needs to be with you. She'd love for you to come and see the townhouse, and stay with us for a day or two."

"Enough said. Let me know when. After all, I need to spend time with Willa, too."

"That's great. You're going all the way, Prue. I know it! But save some time for me, too, okay? Not just all girl talk. By the time we see you, I will be knee-deep in my own campaign. I hope we'll be able to announce very soon."

"All sounds good to me. How did it go with Steve? Bet that wasn't easy."

"We'll talk. All I'll say for now is that I kept him and am paying him more than Buddy is."

"Ah, the old *Godfather* thing: 'Keep your enemies close . . .'"

"You know, I think that is the only line anyone remembers from that movie. But, yes, those are my sentiments. I'll let you know exactly when Willa will gets back here. I'm going to be one lucky man. I will have both of you all to myself. Well, at least for a while."

Chapter Thirty-Nine

Buddy needed to get this ball rolling and tie up some of the loose ends. He had really gotten to despise farmers. Every piece of legislation he had tried to push through via his friends in the state legislature had gone down in defeat, thanks to the farmers. Now he had to move on his self-serving plan even more quickly, before Congressman Lee's meddling found out too much about the proposal, and so he could retire off the massive profits he stood to make on Eastern and Western Shore farmland.

He needed to call his point man on the shore. Roy Davis was very good at putting pieces together and in place.

"Roy Davis here."

"Roy, I have to find out what Lee is planning on doing over there with those farmers."

Roy, a cautious man, was reluctant to wade into these waters before everything was in play. He knew only too well how vicious the senator could be when he didn't get what he wanted.

"I'd be careful, Senator."

"Careful? Careful, you say? What the hell for? I need answers, and, if you can't get them for me, well then I can always find another who would like to make a lot of money."

"Slow down, Senator. There's no reason for you to go and get your pants in a wad. I told you what I heard at that meeting. I even sent a man over to Buster Talbot's place."

"And what did that man find out?"

"Well, in point of fact, nothing. Talbot kicked him off his farm."

"And you tell me to go slow. These cussed farmers are no different from those blasted watermen. They think they own that shore."

"You have to remember their families have been on this land for generations. They are not going to take kindly to you wanting them to change what they're farming or give their farms over to the government all together."

"If they would just cooperate, some of them could make fortunes."

"You don't understand them at all. They won't turn on each other. They are a family, just like the watermen."

"Well, it's time for the family to have a fight. Are you with me, Roy, or are you going to sit on the sidelines?"

"I'm with you, Senator. You know my loyalty. I have been with you for a good while now, so don't question me."

"Or what, Roy? Are you threatening me?"

"No, just warning you to be careful."

"Senators don't have to be careful, Roy. They just have to use their power and money."

"What do you want from me?"

"I want you to find out more about this Buster Talbot. He's close to Charles Lee, and so that makes him our enemy."

"How about that weenie who works for Lee?"

"Stevie Boy? He's in my pocket. No problem with him. Don't you worry."

"It's my job to worry, Senator."

"Well, while you're worrying, go find out just how close these farmers are. I want to know of a few who might turn and either take money for their land or grow crops that could make them rich men. And us a whole lot richer."

"I'm on it!"

"Good man. Keep in touch."

No sooner had Dawes hung up when he received a call from Steve. "Hello, Senator."

"Well, Stevie Boy, your ears must have been ringing."

"How's that, Senator?"

"I was just telling Roy Davis how much I admired you. Now what can I do for you?"

"Congressman Lee wants to meet with you. When is a good time?"

"Do you know what this is about?"

"No, I don't, sir."

"You better not be holding back on me, Stevie Boy. I need to know what's ahead of me."

"Yes, sir, I understand." Steve really didn't like this man, especially when he called him Stevie Boy. But, when he had thrown money at him, he had figured, what the heck? Now Charles was paying him extra, too. Working both sides for his own financial gain was a dangerous game in this town. Especially if Senator Dawes uncovered his chicanery. Bad enough the good congressman had. *I did apologize, however, so my conscience is clear to dislike both these men. If all else fails, I can always work on the outside as a consultant. No end to the goodies in this town.*

Tug was upstairs working on the first article to be released soon in the local farmers' newspaper. The series would start out slowly and build in intensity. He wanted the target audience to understand that their problems were shared around the country. Maybe not all situations were alike or to quite to this extent yet, but that would change. The farmers needed all the support they could get.

However, he needed to speak with Buster again before he could build a case for what he saw coming down the road—and what he hadn't yet shared with his friend Charlie. He didn't want to sound any alarms until he had proof, and Tug knew Buster was just the man to help him get that proof.

He wanted to make this important call before Lindy, his mom, and Max returned from buying out the local food store. It was so good seeing his mother again, and he was happy Max would watch over her as she worked through this mess with his father. Tug knew Max had long loved his mother, but that love had always been held in reserve because of his father. He prayed it wasn't too late for them.

Dialing Buster, he put all thoughts of his family on hold.

"Yeah, Buster Talbot here."

"Hi, Buster. Tug Alston. I need to ask you a few things. Do you mind?"

"Nope. Been waiting for you to call."

"Really. How's that?"

"I figured, that's all. You're a smart Harvard boy, aren't ya?"

"I guess I am, but I don't know that that qualifies me as a great inquisitor."

"Don't go using those fancy words on me, Tug; you're one of us now."

"I suppose I am."

Buster said, "What can I tell ya?"

"For one thing, have you heard anything about using farmland for mass production of marijuana? I've heard some rumblings, but wanted to know what you have heard."

"Those rumblings might be more right than wrong," Buster acknowledged. "Where did you hear this?"

"From a friend." Tug wasn't going to rat out his brother. Mikey heard a lot, now that he was selling machinery and equipment to farmers. Tug and Mikey had had a good conversation when alone in the kitchen. Mikey could be a real help to Charles, and even more so to Tug as he wove the story of what was really happening to area farmers and how the government meant to use their land.

Buster said, "Okay, fair enough. What else?"

"Have you ever thought about what you're going to do with your farms when you pass on?"

"Yes. In fact, I think of little else these days. I'm worried for my son, who just wants to continue being a farmer and do it the honorable way."

"What does he farm?"

"He raises soybeans and corn in rotation on some of my land. Does a little tobacco, too, but that's not for public education, if you catch my drift. At one time, Maryland was a huge tobacco producer, but those days are long gone."

"I won't say anything, but—really, Buster—will your land continue to be used for these products if the state carries out its threat to tax chickens and whatever else they have in mind to drive the poultry business out?"

"Listen to me, Tug. If the state bureaucrats had their way, they wouldn't have anything here but housing developments. Although I don't know where the folks would come from when Delaware is so much more invitin' financially than this state." Buster laughed. "But, anyway, I suppose they might get into the marijuana business big-time if they had millions of acres and no farmers to oppose them."

"Buster, you hold on to your land. If we can get enough farmers to take a stand publicly, we might make a real difference."

"We have to keep that hope, Tug. We are working on alternative fertilizers and other farming techniques, too. Hydroponics is coming in big; that saves a lot of space. Farmers want to get better, and their kids have got a much better agricultural education than we ever dreamed of. The Farm Bureau is so much more today than it ever was, but we *cannot* fight the government if they stand against us and use environmental issues to make us look bad. We are trying our best, but all these changes take time, research, experimentation, and money."

"You're a wise man, Buster Talbot. You have given me so much to think about. I would love to take a trip and tour some of these farms with you, if you have the time."

"Name your time. I will *make* time for you and Congressman Lee. You'll see so many things being done today that we never dreamed possible years ago. And young farmers want to carry on, but they need money and support to do it."

"Is tomorrow too soon?"

"You're on. Come early and stay late. I like you a lot, son, and I like Congressman Lee. He's a decent young man who wants to help us."

"Yes, he is, and he now lives here, so this means even more to him."

"See ya tomorrow."

"I'll be there right after my mom leaves. And thanks, Buster."

Chapter Forty

When Max and Kay returned to the house after some sightseeing, Lindy was hard at work preparing their last supper together. Tug had spent his day upstairs, writing and on the phone. He knew better than to disturb his wife when she was in the kitchen, hard at work.

Taking a deep whiff as she walked into the kitchen, Kay asked, "What's that heavenly smell, Lindy?"

"It's crab cakes from an old recipe of Uncle Dickie's. Plus vegetables southern-style, biscuits, and a few other side dishes."

Giving Lindy a hug, Kay said, "I know why my son married you. He loves to eat."

Lindy laughed. "I hope there were a few other reasons besides my cooking abilities! Actually, I've been doing this since I can remember, so I ought to be good."

"You're perfect, my dear, in every way. I couldn't be happier to have you as my daughter-in-law."

Lindy looked away, then said, "I wish Tug's father felt the same way."

"Who cares, Lindy? Tug loves you with all his heart, and I'm not sure Ted doesn't like you. He's a complicated man."

Lindy smiled lovingly at her beautiful mother-in-law. They had taken to one another from the start. "I know his dad wanted him to marry Sha . . . ndy? Is that her name?"

Kay laughed out loud. "Tug was never going to marry Shandy. That was all hatched because they grew up together and we were good friends of her parents. Tug and she were always thrown together. Now, forget about Shandy Lee Atkinson and let me help you with this dinner."

"Supper, Kay; we call it supper down here. We normally eat our big meal midday, but, when I married Tug, even that changed. But I still prefer to call it supper."

"Traditions die hard. I will make a note of the proper name for the evening meal. Actually, I rather like the idea of eating big in the middle of the day; that way you eat less in the evening." Looking around the kitchen counters, Kay added, "However, tonight is not what I would call a light supper."

Lindy turned to the sink and began to mash the potatoes. "Why don't you go on upstairs and tell Tug supper is almost on the table." She sensed Kay needed some alone time with her son. It would be hard to say good-bye in the morning, but it had been a lovely visit.

As luck would have it, Tug was heading downstairs already. Kay guessed smelling all this good food had made him hungry. She walked into the living room, took his arm, and they both sat down.

"I will miss the heck out of you and Lindy."

"I know, Mom. We'll miss you and Max, too." He took a deep breath, then said, "By the way, what gives with you and Max?'

Kay stared at her son for a moment before saying, "I don't know. Maybe we both need companionship at this stage of the game. I know he's been lonely over the years, and we have always been close friends. It could become something more, but not now. Now I need to get through this mess with your father."

"Are you sure that you and Dad won't get it back?"

"I know that, no matter the age of the children, they always want that. Who knows with these things, Tug? But I think we just wore each other out. Too many issues, too many nights with him coming home very late from bars, smelling like . . . well, with liquor on his breath." She didn't want her son to know his dad had also been a serial lover. "We'll see how this separation goes. I adore being with Max, and we both understand where we are right now." After a momentary pause, she added, "But I wouldn't be unhappy if it went further. Does that help? I suppose not."

Tug grimaced the way young boys and girls do when they see their parents or other adults kiss. "Mom, too much information. I'm still in the wishing you and Dad could get back stage."

"Be prepared for that not to happen, Tug. Too many bridges crossed, too many lies told. How do you think Mikey is doing with it all?"

"Mom, to be brutally honest, I don't think Mikey thinks. Though he has changed since his graduation. He's focused now on his work and maybe finding a southern girl to settle down with. He has only said a couple things about it, but nothing that would lead me to believe he is terribly broken up. Which, I have to say, staggers my imagination as he and Dad are so close. Mikey was the son he wanted—no, needed—to feed that ego of his."

"Interesting how it all turned out. You're such a deep thinker, Tug, and Mikey is the aggressive wonder boy. I love you both so much, in such different ways."

"Okay," Lindy shouted, "dinner is ready. Tug, go call Max. he's outside watching the sun set."

Kay touched her son's hand and said, "I'll go get him. I love the sunsets as much as he does. I think one does as you age. You appreciate the beauty of life, as you know it has to come to an end."

Tug smiled at this woman, his champion all his life. He wondered if a lot of the battles she'd fought with his father were times she had come to his defense. It didn't matter now. She was on another journey. He wasn't at all amazed at the depth of her wisdom. She had taught him those things from the time he was born.

Kay found Max on a bench, staring out into space, waiting for the giant orb to find its way home for the night. He was at one in these surroundings and completely peaceful.

Kay stopped in back of him and put her arms around his neck. "Majestic, isn't it?"

"They always are. I've seen sunsets from just about every place on this planet and that old shiny hunk never disappoints." He patted the seat next to him.

"We should go in. Lindy has dinner on the table."

"It'll keep for a few moments. Please?"

Kay moved around the bench and sat down. "It's going to be hard leaving the boys and Lindy."

"Oh, you'll be back, Kay."

"Not soon enough, Max."

Max took her hand gently and Kay settled her head on his shoulder. "Nice, isn't it?"

"The sunset or something else, Kay?"

"I can't deny we have chemistry, Max."

"We always did. I never told you this, but that's why I took the job in Baltimore all those years ago. Ted was my best friend, and the one thing a best friend doesn't need is someone hanging around mooning over his wife."

Kay snuggled a bit closer to him. "That's so sad, Max. We both missed all these years."

"Not really. You were lovestruck with Ted and his big job at the *Globe*. He took you places you never would have gone with me. You loved the club life and his celebrity, until you figured out what all of us in the fraternity knew: he wasn't a faithful soldier."

"Why didn't you ever say something?"

"Because, whether you would admit it or not, you were in love with the man, beyond the stars, and you would have hated the person who told you that. I couldn't ever let that happen."

As the sun set slowly, neither of them moved. No more words were spoken, though they both knew they were headed into something unpredictable that could crush them if a wrong move was made. Dinner was waiting, Tug and Lindy were watching them from the kitchen window, and, yet, they didn't seem to notice or care.

Chapter Forty-One

Steve had been able to set up a meeting with Buddy sooner than later, and Charles was ready for what he knew would become a major confrontation with this bastard. He had to shuffle quickly to get his information and facts right. There couldn't be any mistakes with Buddy Dawes. He knew what could happen if he didn't hit the mark. He wanted Buddy bloodied when this was over. Then he would take his Senate seat.

Charles called Willa. He simply had to talk to her once more before taking Dawes on in person.

Willa said, "Are you sure you should go at him head on?"

"Yes. Yes, I am. The farmers are agitated; they are getting pushed really hard. They don't deserve this. His tinkering with their land and lives has to stop."

"He's a powerful man, Charles, and he could really hurt you."

"Well—not to put too fine a point on it, my dear—I'm becoming a powerful congressman, too, and I'm from a very powerful, old family. He wouldn't dare come at me with too much. Besides, he has really outdone himself this time. He has to be found out. What happens to him will be his own fault."

"Do you think he could spend time in jail?"

"Maybe, though I don't put much stock in his colleagues going that far. You know how this town works; it's always protecting the party and not the people."

With a sigh, Willa said, "Be careful. I don't want anything to happen to you. Please!"

"Willa, this isn't a game for crybabies. I have to protect the people."

"But, until this battle is won, you have to protect the people from Virginia, Charles, not Maryland."

"Well, I'm a member of the United States Congress, so that makes me care about all the people. This issue goes way beyond Virginia or

Maryland. This is an issue affecting all the farmers of this country in one way or another."

"I have to trust you. And I do, dearest," Willa said. "All I know is that I'll feel better when I am over there with you."

"Yes! It will be so nice to have you next to me every night and at breakfast every morning. Anything new with the island house?"

"Oh, it's going to be something fantastic when it's done! Miss Frances will be watching out for us when I'm in D.C., but Clyde and I are on the same page. He knows exactly what I want to do with it."

"And God help him if he doesn't do it! You're a very determined young woman, Willa Lee."

"Yes, I am, and I am in love with the most wonderful man—a man who is about to become a *very* powerful man, even more than now."

Charles laughed.

Then Willa said, "Now, can I change the subject? Have you heard from Vernie lately?"

Charles laughed again. "I got a quick call yesterday. She is, shall we say, rethinking her position on cake baking."

"Can't wait to hear that story. Oh, I gotta go. Clyde has a question."

"I love you, Willa Lee."

"I love you, too, Congressman."

"Start writing, Willa. You need to do that, too."

"That will be my main occupation when I get to D.C. Well, except for spending time with you and—oh yes—when is Prue coming?"

"Whenever you want her to."

"Can't wait to see you both. You more than anything."

"Be careful, Willa. Don't want anything to happen to you."

"Love you, too, Charles."

One more time, Charles was going over the facts he'd assembled in preparation for his meeting with Dawes. Then Tug called.

"Hi, Charles. I'm over here with Buster, meeting some of the farmers. They're really spun up this morning. Seems Roy Davis has been around with all kinds of questions about their farmland."

"Really? What about their land?"

"He's asking them if they want to keep on farming, or if they'd sell off some or all of it."

"Sell it to whom?"

"A corporation called Mixic and a subsidiary, Medgro. They grow marijuana for medicinal uses."

"I've heard of them. Dawes must be upping his game and fast. He smells we're on to something."

Buster took the phone away from Tug. "Hi, Congressman. Buster here. Tug is telling you the God's honest truth. Roy Davis and some other men came to my place at the crack of dawn this morning wanting to know the same thing."

"Interesting. Well, you and Tug stay on it, Buster. I'm meeting soon with the man I think is behind all this—and who stands to make a ton of money from it."

Tug took the phone back. "Charles, so far the farmers aren't budging, but whoever is behind this is really pushing."

"That isn't in our favor, for sure."

"We'll keep you posted. One of the farmers said they were approached yesterday by a company that wants to buy their land for winemaking. Might be coincidence. I don't know."

"I don't think anything is coincidence when it comes to how far Dawes will go to destroy those farms and get what he wants."

"Good luck with him and let me know. My first articles will be coming out later this week. Max Pierson is in on this with me. He still has contacts at the paper."

"Great work, Tug. Knew we would make a good team. We'll find out just what is going on and how we can help the farmers. I have to go now. Talk to you soon."

"Good luck again. It's going to be tough, I know. I remember dealing with some rough characters when I was helping Dickie, and it's never fun."

Charles answered firmly, "Right will win out in the end. I know it."

Buddy was waiting for Charles in an out-of-the-way room in the Capitol. Over the years, Buddy had done a lot of deals in this room, away from all the "newbies"—young staffers who liked to listen in and get some nugget for future use. Dirty game this politics is.

Charles was on time, but knew Buddy would already be there. That was Buddy's style: make the opposition feel guilty about being late. Didn't much work on him.

"Good morning, Buddy. Glad we could find a time and place to meet. Haven't been in this room for ages."

"Good morning, son. Steve, your man, said you were keen to meet as soon as possible. What's up?"

Charles put his files on the long table, sat down directly across from his adversary, and took a deep breath, all in preparation to go into battle with this old fox.

"Yes, well, I think you and I both know where this conversation is going and how it ends will be up to you, Senator."

Buddy smiled at him as he took the measure of the young man across the table. He didn't like what he saw.

"Well, as long as we're using a more formal tone here, Congressman, I will assume this is serious business."

"Your assumption, Senator, is correct. This *is* serious business. We have locked horns before when you and Rennie were fighting it out with me over watermen's issues. This time it may be as bad, or even more egregious. It has come to my recent attention that something untoward is going on in terms of a strange, maybe coincidental, attention to farmland, in Maryland in particular."

Buddy leaned forward with his hands together. He knew Lee would get his message. In a stern voice, he said, "Get to the point, Congressman."

"The point is, I know it's you who's poking around farmers' property, and I know that Roy Davis didn't just 'happen' into the meeting I attended with some Maryland farmers. And I am beginning to see a picture forming in my mind. Not a good one, I might add."

Buddy sat back and stared at Charles for a bit longer than comfortable. "Out with it, Charles. I don't like innuendo."

Charles was now the one leaning on the table, fully prepared to go the distance with this big dog. "How many years did it take you to put farmers in such a place? How long, Senator, have you been working on stealing their land and using it for your own profit?"

"Careful, Charles. Be very careful. You better have more than accusations from some half-witted farmers who allow that big oaf to speak for them. What's his name? Oh, yes, Buster. Now, how could a man of your caliber be taken in by a man with the name Buster?"

"Senator, with all due respect—"

Buddy cut him off. "Don't give me any of that 'with all due respect' horseshit. If you have come here to say something and have proof of what you're saying, then, by all means, proceed. But don't waste my time with unsubstantiated crap."

"You know very well what Roy Davis has been doing this morning, Buddy. He's spending time with farmers, feeling them out about a buyout. By the way, he didn't get a very warm reception to that idea. Nor, of course, did he bother to mention who was really going to own that land. I know all about Mixic and Medgro—which I'm pretty sure could be traced back to you, by the way. The farmers are already riled up over what's happening to them and they aren't about to sell off. They're so much smarter than you give them credit for. In fact, you don't have one idea of who these people are, and, as with the watermen with their boats and the Bay, you gravely misjudge their love of their farms."

Fed up with Charles's sanctimonious attitude, Buddy pushed his chair back and yelled in the congressman's face, spitting out, "I think you're crazy. That's what I think, Charles Lee. I think you want something else. Now what could that be, I wonder? Do you think I got here being an idiot? I know when a rat's in the barn."

Charles didn't move. Just listened to the senator's rant. He knew the man had guts and political smarts, but he wasn't about to take a backseat in those departments. He came from feisty stock. Finally tiring of it, Charles stood up and faced him squarely.

"I don't think about you at all, Senator. I think about people who have had their farms for generations and how you want to swoop in and offer them little to nothing to grab their land and use their farms for raising something that maybe only a few want on their farms. These are good, solid people who don't want the cannabis that would be grown for far more than medicinal reasons. Most of them are strongly opposed."

Changing his tactics, Dawes now spoke in a quieter tone. "What an incredible imagination you have, Charles. You and I know that the only reason it would be grown at all would be for providing relief to sick folks. What in God's name were you thinking it would be used for?"

"You really make me sick, you know that, Buddy? You can put on this sanctimonious act all you want, but you and I know that you are the power behind—way behind—the bill that will go to the floor soon in Maryland approving the legalization of marijuana for a much broader use than just medicinal. The state is in deep debt and this would move them out, based on what they're seeing in states that have already passed this sort of legislation. Instead of cutting unnecessary programs and waste, it's just easier to turn into a drug state. Well, the people over on the shore clearly don't want that."

"How do you know what they do and don't want in the long run? The game is just beginning, and my guess is that farmers will take the offers, which aren't chicken feed, if you will excuse the pun. The power of money trumps all, Charles. I thought you would understand that clearly, coming from a family that made its early fortunes in the tobacco industry."

"Have the snappy retort for everything, don't you, Senator? That was a long time ago. We've changed our farming a whole lot since those days, but I don't think that's the end of this story. God knows what else you want to do with that beautiful land. You don't care as long as the money keeps on filling your bank account. You've seen what has already happened to the land over there with the onslaught of development. Now farmers want to keep what's left of their farms for their children and children's children, on down the line."

Buddy laughed sarcastically. "Their children, Charles, don't give a shit about farming. Like the watermen's offspring, these farm kids don't want to work that hard anymore. They want better than their families have had. They don't want to work morning 'til night. It's a different world."

"That may be the case, but shouldn't they be given a choice, rather than greed simply sweeping away their land? I'll beat you on this, Senator. You're up to your eyeballs in this, and, somewhere in the background, you are making a whole lot of money. That's not legal, you know. Not in your position."

"'In my position' being the operative phrase, eh, Charles?"

"What are you getting at, Buddy?"

"Back to first names now, are we? Well, son, I hear you have great ambitions and that might include becoming a senator one day. Maybe even want to run in Maryland now you're a landowner there? Is any of this true?"

"I don't know where you heard that, but that doesn't alter anything."

"Really? It doesn't? If you were to run against me and win, I would go back home to my lovely mansion on the river and become one of the great unwashed. Then I would be free to buy anything I wanted and do with it as I pleased, as long as it was legal."

Charles realized the old sonofabitch had it all planned out. He'd been at this for a long time, plotting his personal course to undo the entire state's agricultural system on the shore and turn it into a huge mess. No more chicken farming, no more need for soybeans or corn—the land would become an experimental petri dish full of marijuana and who knew what else. Housing costs would spiral because of influx populations and the Eastern Shore would no longer exist as it ever had been. An entire history gone for good.

It was sickening to think about and Charles's mind was spinning. He had to stop this man from what he and his cronies were about to do. He would find a way and Tug would help him. They had to preserve something of what had made the state so great in the first place. Yes, the world was changing, but not all for the good.

Charles decided not to continue this any further until he could think. "We'll see about all this, Buddy. At least we know where we stand on these issues."

"Yes, we do, Charles. Glad it's pretty much all on the table now. Just remember one thing, son: you have to get up pretty early in the morning to fool an old fox like me."

Chapter Forty-Two

Charles fumed all the way back to his office. He was thoroughly disgusted with Buddy Dawes and his ilk. They were the ruling elite, and they were as far from working for the good of the people they represented as the man in the moon. They had become a legislature of people who had fought and lied their way to the top. Then, when they got there, they raked in money for themselves like fall leaves in a barrel.

Charles was not going to end up that way. He swore an oath to himself and pledged to stay as far away from them as he possibly could except when absolutely necessary for his work. Buddy's last words kept running through his mind: "fool an old fox like me." Where had he heard that before? He had to remember, but right now there was a far more pressing issue at hand. This issue had a name and it was Steve. And he was toast.

Charles needed to go through some papers before doing anything else. Steve picked up the congressman's mood as he brushed by him without so much as a hello. He walked into Charles's office to see what had happened.

"Here are some messages for you, Congressman. Your wife called a few minutes before you walked in. She said to call her as soon as you had a chance. The rest of your messages aren't pressing. Nothing that can't wait until you get settled in. How was your meeting with Senator Dawes?"

Charles couldn't believe the balls on this guy. He had known what would happen if he got caught this time.

"Well, I'll tell you how it went, Steve. It didn't go well, but we now know what is on each of our minds. We got it out and it was ugly."

Steve saw the look on the congressman's face and knew this was not a good time to say one more word. As turned to leave, Charles stood up.

"Don't go, Steve." He walked over and closed the door. The other staffers in the outer office didn't need to hear what was coming.

"It seems someone told Senator Dawes that Buster Talbot was upset this morning, and you would be the only one who would have known about that call as Buster called me here in my office."

Steve could tell from the look on the congressman's face what was coming.

"You and I are done here, Steve. Get your things and get out of this office right now, and don't look back. Don't try to find work anywhere on the Hill because I *will* make sure they know just how bad a weasel you are. Oh, and if you think Buddy will save you, he won't. He's done with you, too. That's just the way it rolls here."

Steve stood his ground momentarily. "How do you know that?"

"Just a hunch, but you can go crying to him and see for yourself. Don't say I didn't tell you. His kind use people up and spit them out."

"Well, I didn't think I could pull this off anyway, Congressman. Remember: you were paying me, too. That doesn't make you pure as the driven snow either, now does it?"

"Get out, Allen, and never contact me again."

Before leaving Charles's office, Steve said nastily, "See? You can't fool the old fox." With that he walked out, knowing he was done working on the Hill. But maybe not in Washington.

Charles sat down in his big leather desk chair. He was drained. Steve was right; he had paid the young man money to play ball. That made him no better than the rest of them. He felt sick and ashamed. What would Willa or Prue or Frances think of him now? He could never do anything like this again, regardless of the situation. He had to take those words to heart.

Then he repeated Steve's last words: "See? You can't fool the old fox." The young man had no idea what he had given Charles. He had reaffirmed the extent of involvement Rennie Richardson had with this whole stinking mess. This was so much bigger than he had guessed. He had to stop them. He had to forget the sting of Steve's words about being as bad as the rest of them. Now, he *had* to win this election if Pullman pulled out and gave him the chance.

As always, Willa was eager to see Charles. She always missed him from the minute he left until they were together again, and this long absence, while she had stayed on the island, had been particularly difficult. So difficult that she had moved her planned trip to D.C. up by a day. Now she would wait for him to come home. This was a nice feeling.

He had called her back, so he knew she was at the Georgetown townhouse. And she had heard some of the Steve Allen mess. But she couldn't help noticing something in his voice that bothered her. Now he would be home shortly, and she could find out what was going on.

Just moments later, the door opened and she rushed into his arms. Their embrace said it all. As happy as he was to see her, there was something slightly off with Charles. She could just tell.

Charles stepped away from their long and passionate kiss and smiled at his beautiful wife. "Well, I must say this is a nice welcome home, Willa."

Willa took his coat. "Yes, it is, and we will revisit that kiss later on."

"I certainly hope so, my love."

"I have a bottle of wine chilling in the kitchen. I want to hear all about what is going on, and if there's some way I can help you." She didn't mention that she could see something was troubling him. She knew he would tell her. They didn't keep secrets.

Charles followed her into their gorgeous Georgetown kitchen, redone by his wife, no less, in yellows, whites, and pops of nautical navy. Very tasteful. "How is the island house coming along?"

"I have made it crystal clear to Clyde that all the walls are to be knocked out and the new walls up as soon as possible. He didn't think that would be a problem. He is using one or two men from the boat yard who said they would like to help out."

As Willa poured the wine, Charles put his arms around her. "Well, I'm happy because all that pounding means you'll be here for a while."

Willa wiggled in his arms and then handed him his wine. "Yes, I will be. I don't want to hear any rap-tap-tapping while I am trying to write."

"Well, you won't get a whole lot done for the next week or so."

"And why would that be, Charles?"

"Prue phoned me on the way home. She'll come on over tomorrow."

Willa threw her arms around Charles and nearly hugged him to death. "I'm so happy she's coming so soon. My novel can wait as long as it's because of Prue, but I suspect you two have business to do anyway."

"Yes, we do have some work, but, Willa, I want to tell you something first before we talk of anything else."

Willa sat down at their large, round kitchen table, lit now by lovely candles. "Okay, Charles." She sensed his tension.

"My dearest, I had a bad day today with Steve and Buddy called right before that meeting with some interesting information that was truly unreal. After it was all over, I made up my mind to talk to the party heads and tell them what I know—and that we need to get on with this if Pullman is pulling out. When I do announce, if that chance comes, Dawes will go ballistic, and heaven knows what the fallout will be. But one thing is for sure: it will get pretty ugly."

Willa sat still and stared at him. This was all happening more quickly than she'd expected.

"Well, aren't you going to say something, Willa?"

"Yes. Yes, I am, Charles. I was just thinking. What has happened to make you want to push in so quickly?"

"Buddy Dawes happened, that's what. He's such an arrogant asshole, and, before he can do anything more, I aim to make him suffer in the mud he has stirred up. He is so corrupt . . . well, it's hard to believe. He's planning some ugly things for the Eastern Shore, so I want to make him pay for what he is doing."

"Remember, Charles: cornered animals are very dangerous."

"I know that, but, now that I know what he wants to do, I have to be part of stopping this madness."

"And just what is he planning to do?"

"He's planning on buying many of the farms over there—undoubtedly for pennies after he ruins the poultry industry—and then turning some of them into cannabis farms while making others into development towns, feeding off that, too. He will use tax benefits and scams to induce people to move there."

"I really have to think about all this, Charles. How can he do this?"

"He's working to make sure that the state legislature backs proposals he is working on to make it easier to buy the farms by preventing the farmers from carrying on what they have been doing for generations. He wants to finally get rid of chicken farming. That will destroy the entire shore economy."

"Oh, my God. Everything over there is related to the chicken farms, except for the fishing industry—which they are destroying, too."

"Nearly the entire agricultural system of the Eastern Shore of Maryland will be destroyed. They will be left with fruits, vegetables, and maybe some livestock, but many, if not most, of the farms will be sold off."

Willa was stunned. "Charles, this is such a pessimistic view. Are you sure of this?"

"Yes, and my hunch is he only confessed to some of his plan. Naturally all this will take time and in that time, he will continue to build his own empire through taxpayer dollars."

"But why would he do this? To his own people?"

"They aren't his people, Willa. He may have been born there, but he left long ago for the city and he hates farmers. To him, they are an ignorant lot, just like the watermen. He doesn't care. They're all a means to his end and that end is to leave the Senate a very wealthy man."

"Can he do this, Charles? Please tell me he can't get away with this."

"That is why I have to tell people, and soon, Willa. I will have to begin the campaign almost immediately after I announce. He has to be flushed out, and people have to know about it, so he can be held accountable for this. He has been bribing and blackmailing people in power to get this done."

"I don't know what to say, Charles. These are very strong accusations you are making."

"Yes, they are, Willa. But I'm not in this alone. For one thing, Prue knows how bad this town is, and she wants to help make it better."

"But how can a few good people ever clean this sewer? What has happened to this place?"

"It's diseased, Willa. Greed, avarice, and arrogance have come to live in too many hearts and pocketbooks. Our leaders have corrupted themselves beyond anything people can possibly imagine."

Willa sat there looking at him. How proud she was that he wasn't like the rest of them. "What makes you so different? Why don't you just go with them and become a vastly wealthy man, Charles?"

The look on his face told the story. He had felt so guilty espousing how disgusted he was at the establishment and how corrupt they were. Wasn't he as bad? Hadn't he paid Steve to get information? What made him any different from Buddy or Rennie? He couldn't sit there and let her believe he was so pure.

"Willa, I have to tell you something. It will kill me if I keep it from you."

She saw the tormented look on his face. "Tell me then, Charlie. Get it out. I knew there was something more that was bothering you."

"I am one of them. Or, at least, I am beginning to become like one of them."

"No, Charles, stop it. You aren't. You couldn't ever be."

"Willa, listen to me. I have to confess, but only to you. I care what you think. I didn't fire Steve at first, but kept him on and paid him a lot of money to spy for me and not tell Buddy. He couldn't carry it off, and, in the end, I fired him—but not until today."

Willa sat, frozen in place. She couldn't say anything.

"Willa? Talk to me. Please, talk to me. I know what I have done and it makes me sick."

"I understand what you did and why. You're trying to uncover the schemes of Buddy Dawes and help a good many other people. I don't think that's so bad, and I know you learned from it and the pain you must be feeling, but, if that's the worst you ever do, I would say you came through it okay."

Tears puddled in Charles's eyes. She had forgiven him and, in her own way, given him absolution. This was punishment enough, to know how he had disappointed her. And yet she had still forgiven him.

"I can never tell you what those words mean to me. You are truly forgiving and wonderful."

"I didn't do anything you wouldn't have done for me. We all make mistakes, but it's when we realize we're wrong and seek to change that we know we're on the right path. There's nothing to forgive. I love you and you will make a great senator. Maybe we can't change the world, but we can change a little piece of it."

Charles moved near her and hugged her tightly. "I won't become like them, Willa. I promise. With you by my side, I will stay the man you fell in love with."

"Let's not talk anymore about this, Charles. I've missed you."

Willa softly blew out the candles and took his hand. They walked slowly out of the room, united in another world and both so in love.

Chapter Forty-Three

Miss Frances was feeling lonely without Willa. She loved that child, but knew she needed to go home for a while to be with Charles, especially while Clyde tore into their house. She had promised to keep a watchful eye and that's exactly what she was doing.

"How ye comin', Clyde? I told Willa I would be comin' around each day and keeping ye in check."

Clyde chuckled. *Was there anyone who didn't love Miss Frances?* He doubted that. "I am going to knock that blasted wall through this week, so, if ye do come over here, make sure you keep safe. Some of the boys will be here from over in Somerville. They're bringing the big equipment. I want to get the outside framed and the walls up before Willa returns."

"Looks to me as if ye are making a good stab at this here room. It's going to be big, isn't it, Clyde?"

"Well, she is a celebrity writer and Charles is a U.S. Congressman, so I reckon they need a bigger home than what we all have."

"I know she wants to make it bigger, but they really are a modest couple. Just love 'em." Miss Frances knew Charles and Willa likely had an even bigger destiny than anyone else knew, but she kept those thoughts to herself until the Lees wanted to make it public. She had a strong sense about the couple, and Willa seemed almost as close to her as her own Nellie. Who, she just remembered, was expecting to see her about now at their island store.

"I just dropped by to check on ye, Clyde. I best be getting a move on. Nellie is expecting me over to the store."

"Okay, Miss Frances. Always a pleasure. You be careful on your way now and give my best to Nellie and Denny. They sure are great people."

"Yes, they are, Clyde, and I'll give 'em your best."

Charles quietly walked downstairs to make the morning coffee as Willa slept on. Their reunion had been beautiful. Retrieving the coffee from the cupboard, he thought how much he loved Willa and how lucky he was to have met her. He wished they could have more time together, but there was so much to do now. As his vintage percolator bubbled along, he grabbed his cell, walked into his den, and sat down at the large mahogany desk.

He made a call and, after two rings, Tug answered. "Hey, Charlie. What in the world are you doing up so early? I thought you politicians slept 'til noon."

"Very funny, Tug. Can you hear me laughing?"

"Not really. What's up?"

"I had quite the disagreement with Senator Dawes yesterday and have decided to push the party bosses so I can announce as early as they will let me."

"What? This is unexpected, isn't it, Charlie? It's a bit earlier than you expected."

"Exactly, Tug. I want to be prepared before that fox can do any more damage."

"What's he intending to do, Charlie?"

"Well, we got going and most of it came out. As we had figured out—partly thanks to your brother, and please do thank him for me—he's about to buy up a lot of farms using his sham companies, Mixic Pharmaceuticals and its subsidiary, Medgro. And he has been working with the state legislature to ram through some legislation that will legalize cannabis farming. The bastard intends to control the medical marijuana production—and more, of course, because that's not all that will be legalized."

"Wow. Seems you hit the mother lode."

"Guess you could say that. He really wasn't interested in beating about the bush with this; he wanted to come at me head on and so I gave him a good fight. On the way back to the office, I decided it was time to get started and use this information against him as soon as we can corroborate."

"There's more to this than you're telling me, Charlie. What is it that has you so completely nuts?"

"I mentioned to him that what he was doing was illegal—that didn't seem to bother him in the least, but he intends to keep this operation going long after he retires and continue to buy up as much land as he can get his hands on. His plan is so much bigger that anyone can imagine."

"Okay, but how does your announcing early solve any of this?"

"I can expose his deals before he can cover everything up."

Tug took a moment to process all this new information. Then he said, "I can do this, Charlie, but it will take a few days. I want to talk with Max first. He offered to help me in any way, and I suspect this is the 'any way' I need him for."

"Perfect. You take your time, but there is something else, too. When we do announce, I want to do it from the shore and with farmers all around me. The optics will tell the story. Can you arrange all this?"

"Can't your guy Steve set up the meeting for you?"

"Steve is no longer with me, Tug. A long story best told over a glass of Jack."

Tug laughed. "Sounds good."

"Not good. Really. Very disappointing. I don't think anyone over here is loyal or honest."

"Well, I know one and he's my friend."

"Thanks for the support, Tug. So, you think we can pull this together and get it out?"

"Sure will try, Charlie. You know I'll do anything to help you. I will also call Buster. He can make this happen. What should I tell him about you?"

"Tell him I'm running for the Senate against Buddy Dawes. I will be on the shore in a few days."

"Are you kidding me? He will go bananas over this news. But do you want me to tell him to keep a lid on it for now? He will, if we ask; he's an honorable man."

"I know he is. So, yes. Ask him to keep it under that ols hat of his for now."

Tug laughed. "He'll say this is the best dern thing to happen over here since Dickie Short."

Charles sighed. "Wish I had met that man. He must have been one heck of a fellow."

"You can say that again. I loved that old man and miss him every day. No one will ever be like him again. I will get back to you, Charlie, once I speak to Max and get a first draft going."

"I'll be waiting, Tug. I have a million things to do to get ready for this. It's a big step, but one I have wanted to take for a long time." Charles added, "Oh, there is one more thing. I think you will be particularly interested in this piece of the puzzle. Rennie Richardson, our old pal from Virginia, now living the life of an 'ordinary' man, is in over his head with Dawes."

Tug could hardly believe what he had heard Charlie say. "The crooks stick together through thick and thin, eh? Now that I think about it, I suppose I can't say I'm really surprised, given the time he gave you and Miss Frances. So I say, bring it on. You'll make a great senator, and you will do so much good. We'll talk soon."

"So long, Tug and thanks."

Tug wasted no time. He got Buster on the phone and told him everything. Buster was "pretty derned happy" to hear Charles would be running in Maryland, and for Buddy Dawes's seat. He also promised to keep quiet. He would tell the others just that Charles wanted to meet and give them more information. "They'll come. They like and trust him."

Second phone call was to Max, just back in Boston after his trip to the shore.

"What's going on, Tug? Is everything all right?"

"Yes, yes, it is. I just need some help."

"I'm all ears. Shoot!"

"Well, my friend Congressman Lee is almost certainly running for the Senate, and for a seat currently held by that very powerful man, Buddy Dawes. Pullman is going to leave the race due to health problems, we think. Charles is getting all the info today or very soon. He's been talking with the party bosses anyway, so I think it's time."

"This story has all the makings of a movie script, Tug. So what's up?"

"He wants make his announcement just as quickly as possible in order to catch his opponent off guard with some real bad stuff he is doing. Seems Dawes is knee-deep in money from places he shouldn't get money. This isn't going to be pretty."

"Gee, why doesn't any of this surprise me? They all have something going. Okay, you start writing and I will get on the phone."

"This will be quite a fight. Kind of two dynastic families going at it."

"They usually are. Send me a brief description of the situation, and I will see what I can do with it. Sounds like fun, actually. Back in the old saddle again."

"Thanks, Max. When you have that part done, I will get this up to you. By the way, how was your trip back?"

Max knew what Tug was fishing for, but wasn't going there. "It was wonderful. Your mother is the best company and she has a lot ahead of her, too, now that she's left your father. He, on the other hand, isn't doing too well, but he's too proud to say it."

"Dad is going to lose the best thing he ever had, and I agree: he has too big an ego and too much pride. I should know. It took him until I was grown to even recognize me and that I was my own person."

"He has always loved you, Tug, but he's not a man to show it. And this time—you're right—he's going to lose everything. Kay is a great lady."

"And you love her, Uncle Max, whether you admit it or not."

"I always said you were a genius. I'll get back to you soon, Tug."

Chapter Forty-Four

By the time Prue rang the doorbell at the Lee townhouse in Georgetown, she was more than a little excited to see her girlfriend. Willa ran to open the door and the two of them stood outside hugging, making quite a display for the neighbors.

Half crying, Willa chirped, "Where have you been, Prue Harding?"

"Well, Willa, I've been a tad busy of late. I'm sorry, but I'm here now."

The two pushed through the doorway. Willa waved an arm and said, "I'm pretty much done decorating, but I'm hoping you'll help me pick out some things while you're here."

Prue stood absolutely still and looked around the townhouse. The look on her face said it all: she loved it. "These old places are so full of charm and elegance, and, from what little I see, you're doing it justice. This must have cost a small fortune, and then there's the island house."

Willa smiled at her dear friend. "Yes, it did, but what am I going to do with my money if not enjoy it? Charles's apartment was okay, but, as you know, we needed a proper home, and, in Georgetown, and it needs to be fine and special. The island house will be our place to escape to, and for me to write. That is, when it's done. Clyde is simply the best builder."

Prue chuckled.

"What's so funny, Prue?"

"I'm not laughing at you, Willa, but thinking how much like Jack and Jackie you two are."

"Oh, Prue, go on! If I looked like Jackie, I'd be on every cover of every magazine."

"You pretty much are now, and you will continue to be, for sure, when Charles becomes a senator. People will see the comparison. You wait and see."

"You think he has a real chance?"

239

"Oh, sweetie, he's as good as in there already. Buddy Dawes has gone one trick too many this time, and Charles is ready to send him packing—in disgrace and maybe to jail."

"Charles Lee? My husband, a United States senator?"

"Yes, that Charles Lee. He's a good man and a fine congressman, but Buddy has pushed Charles and the people he's supposed to be serving too hard. Charles really wants to serve and his time has come."

Willa put her arm around her girlfriend and said sincerely, "And you will make a great congresswoman, Prue. How proud your forebearer President Harding would be. You will be carrying on the family name and business, so to speak."

"I suppose I will, Willa. I think it's either in your blood or it's not."

"Yes, you're right. But come on now, let's get you settled."

"Do you have a walk-up attic? So many of these places do. I love them."

"Yes, we do, but so many are not used or finished. Ours is in the middle of being finished now."

Shaking her head, Prue stopped in the hall and said, "How are you doing all this and writing, too? I mean the house on the island and this big old place?"

As Willa opened the guest room door, she said, "I have the all-time perfect craftsman and builder on the island and Miss Frances—plus probably about a dozen other interested women—watching over that project. This one is all mine."

Prue gasped when she walked into the room. "Oh, Willa, you've outdone yourself. This is straight out of *Southern Living* magazine. The black toile and pops of Granny Smith lime really give it a classic look, but with a little attitude. And look! It has its own bathroom."

"Did you think I would have guests walking down the hall to pee?"

"Well, no, but seeing all this may make me want to stay with you two for a long, long time."

"Wouldn't that be grand? We would love it. By the way, Charles said to call him when you got in. Why don't you unpack and soak in the experience of the Old South, and then come down for lunch."

"Lunch by Willa? What's up with that? You didn't used to cook."

"I still don't, but I can use a phone and I did. Called Yitzi's. If nothing else, I'm a very resourceful woman."

Prue squealed. "Yitzi's? You've thought of everything." Hugging her good friend, she said, "I'm going to have such a wonderful time here, Willa."

Willa walked toward the door, then turned. "Exactly. See you in the kitchen."

By the time Willa hit the kitchen, a young man was knocking on the back door with a box full of food. *Perfect timing.*

"Bring it right in and set it on the island, please." The young man did as Willa asked, and, before he could turn to leave, Willa handed him a very respectable tip.

"Why, thank you, ma'am."

"Thank you, and please tell Yitzi that Willa and Prue send our love."

Smiling, he looked at Willa and answered, "I sure will. Enjoy your lunch."

Yitzi's Deli was one of the hottest spots in D.C., everyone's choice for deli and chicken soup. They made the best and Yitzi himself was the best. He knew his business well and was also very discreet. With a clientele of senators and congressman, aides and lobbyists, he had learned to *see* everyone while never *hearing* anyone. Knowing how to play the game had made Yitzi a wealthy man.

Prue breezed through the kitchen door, then sat down at the large white French country farm table and looked around the cavernous space. "Is there anything you've forgotten?

"I hope not. Do you like it, Prue? Be honest with me."

"Like it. Well, really, I love it. As a matter of fact, when, and if, I win my election, I want to enlist you to help me decorate wherever it is I live."

"Done," Willa answered as she made up their plates.

"I can't believe you're having lunch, Willa Lee. You never eat much."

"This is a special occasion. And, besides, Charles gets home late these days, so it won't be until then that we'll get a light supper."

Prue snickered. "Should I ask who is catering that meal?"

"Ha, ha. I was thinking of Chinese. Seriously, Charles is so tired when he comes home that going out is nearly always out of the question. And I imagine you two have much to discuss."

"Okay, if Chinese will be the theme, then we can take a walk later and buy some plum wine to go along."

"Great idea."

They both took their first bites of their respective sandwiches, then wiped their mouths and sighed. Prue finally spoke. "God, this is heavenly. Nobody makes a warm corned beef on rye like Yitzi's."

"Tell me about it. I can't get deli like this on the island. Just something about the great breads and meats you can only get in a big city. That has to be what it is."

"Don't know, but this sure hits the spot."

By the time Charles hit the door, the two girlfriends had settled in and were enjoying one another's company. He heard them upstairs, fussing and giggling like little girls in school.

"Willa! Prue! I could hear you all the way from the sidewalk. Come on down."

The two young women jumped off the small sofa in Willa and Charles's room where they had been admiring the wedding pictures and sharing memories of that day not that long ago when they had all celebrated Willa Carpenter's marriage to Charles Lee. Willa was glowing, and, as they walked down the narrow but gracious staircase, she saw that same look on her Charles.

"Hey! There are my girls." He gave Willa a modest kiss, then hugged Prue tightly. "So glad you're back here."

"I am, too. I didn't realize how much I missed all of us being together."

"Well, this calls for a glass of wine, and then we can plot where you two ladies would like to go for dinner. Bet I can guess."

Willa giggled softly and said, "Bet you can." She winked at Prue.

Charles said, "I suppose you two have been conspiring all day about this. Does The Willard sound familiar?"

Willa hugged him. "Charles, you are too good to us. Beats Chinese takeout anyday." She looked at Prue again, who, this time, winked at her.

Charles handed glasses of wine to each of them and took his own. Then they all took seats in the lavishly decorated living room. Flowing gold sateen drapes were tied back with black tassels. The furniture was black lacquer and covered in the same gold fabric as the drapes. Around the room were pops of black and a hint of Chinoiserie here and there to, again, give it that southern touch from the old homes of long ago. All was elegant—and so different from their island home.

They lit a fire in the carved fireplace and sat back to enjoy. Willa noticed a weariness in her husband's eyes that would not be noticeable to Prue. She knew he had likely done battle again that day and wanted to hear about it, but wanted him to relax, too.

Charles saw Willa's concerned look and knew she was on to him. So he started off with something more pleasant than his day's doings.

"How was your day, Prue? Uneventful, I pray."

"It was very good, Charles. Thanks for asking. Now, may I tell you what an ingenious wife you have, Congressman? She's simply the best decorator I have ever seen."

"I take it you like the place. Willa did it herself. With a few small suggestions from me, naturally."

Willa squiggled her nose at Prue and said, "He likes to think that." Then she stuck her tongue out at Charles and snuggled deeper into her seat.

"I do love her, Prue; God knows I do."

"I guess that's a good thing since you're married now. You two belong together, that's for certain; I knew it from the minute you two met. Now, enough of this soppy romantic stuff. Tell me about Dawes and his gang of thugs."

Willa really didn't want to talk politics, but that was the price of having the three of them together. Still, she had hoped they could steer clear of serious things for a while.

"Well, Prue, this is going to be a major battle. I don't know if I can outwit this foxy bastard and win, but I'm putting a few wheels in motion to try to surprise him."

"What wheels are spinning so far, Charles?"

"I spoke to the party bosses today and it seems they are going to announce Pullman is leaving in the next week. His cancer is apparently pretty far along. He's a good guy, but they are very happy I am prepared to go when all this shakes out."

Willa sat silent while the two of them talked. She didn't enjoy it, but remembered what Prue had said: "I think it's either in your blood or it's not." Willa didn't have it in her blood, but she struggled with it for Charles's sake.

Prue noticed the look on her face. "Willa, what are you thinking? I can see you disapprove."

Quietly Willa answered, "I do. I mean I'm afraid for you, Charlie, and I don't want you to get hurt."

Charles stood up, walked to the fireplace, and stirred the logs around. He finally broke the tense silence. "I know you don't like this, Willa, but you do understand this more than you think. Have you forgotten it was you who came to my hearing not all that long ago and then took Miss Frances and that issue and ran with it? Even wrote a book about it? So, you can never say you don't understand this. You know how politicians are, and letting Dawes win again will be a disaster for farmers and, in particular, for people who are our neighbors now."

Prue watched Willa. The couple had become intense. Willa's eyes spoke volumes. Prue knew her friend would have to overcome this to make a good politician's wife. Charles was a Lee, and it *was* in his blood, just as she was a Harding and had that same competitive blood coursing through her veins as well.

Willa wasn't a shrinking violet. Her husband and her best friend knew she wasn't going to just sit there and say nothing. "You're right, Charlie, but the fight that time almost killed you. Dawes is just like Richardson. They're serial crooks and those kind don't quit."

Charles stared at his wife. She didn't like politics, but that didn't mean she was ignorant about them.

"Okay, Willa, you're right, but we can't give into these scoundrels or we won't have a country left. They'll steal us blind, taking what they want and leaving the people with nothing. We have to fight. We can't give in to them."

Willa saw his passion, and she didn't like to get upset with Charles. He had to do what he felt right. And who could find fault with this man's desire for openness and truth? She smiled slightly so he would know she wasn't completely turned off by the politics.

"I know how you feel, Charles. It's just you got so messed up last time fighting for the watermen. You were lucky it turned out well. I worry this time it won't."

"Willa, I know this isn't your world. You live in a world of literature and beauty, but Prue and I live in the world of blood and guts. And if I— we—don't stand up for those who are not getting a fair fight, then who are we? I care about those folks. Those farmers deserve so much better than what's going to come at them. Buster and his friends are good people. They raise their families to be decent and honest and they work the land to give us food and support an industry. We can't let them down. We can't sit by as the government steals their land and their hopes, and takes their dreams away forever."

Prue could tell Willa was proud of her husband. He was her glory. And he was also Prue's good friend. She waded into the conversation with her two cents worth. "I still think your run is an excellent decision, Charles, and let the chips fall where they may. I also think you're right to announce as soon as the party allows. Throw that old man off his game! Then go to the shore and talk directly to those fighting these challenges to their way of life. They will support you. Listen to them, and then go get that bastard."

At that moment, Willa knew the game of politics was not for those not totally committed to it. And, while she didn't like it, she would support the love of her life and her best girlfriend. That was the best she could do for them. And she would return to what she loved: writing romance novels and building her new home. She wasn't disappointed. She felt free, actually. For her creative mind, Washington, D.C., was a trillion miles away, but it was the life her husband and friend lived and loved. And weren't the differences what had attracted them all to each other in the first place, and now made life so interesting?

Charles smiled and looked at Willa. "When I win this election . . . well, just imagine the book you and Tug can write about this. I see Pulitzer Prize all over the two of you."

"Dream on, Charlie. Now, please, let's not talk about this anymore. Let's get ready and go to The Willard. This will be such fun. Together again."

Chapter Forty-Five

Charles was sitting in his office unhappily looking at a list of potential assistants Prue had hunted up for him. He had been crushed when Prue had left him to go into politics herself, and now there had been the episode with Steve that didn't end well . . . so, back to the drawing board. It wasn't going to be easy to find a really good office manager who could also handle a man running a campaign.

Charles was interrupted by the fax machine delivering the day's pile. He stepped outside his office and signaled the temp at Steve's old desk that he would get it. Lo and behold, it was what he really was looking for: Tug's draft announcement of his run for the Senate. As always, succinct and to the point.

FOR IMMEDIATE RELEASE

Contact: Tug Alston
154 Water Way
Somerville, MD

The Honorable Charles Lee announces he will make a bid for the United States Senate seat from the proud state of Maryland. He will be replacing Senator Seth Pullman who had to leave the race suddenly due to health issues. Lee has served with honor in the United States House of Representatives for two terms. He sits on several congressional committees and is presently involved in forming new initiatives for Maryland crabbers and oystermen and also addressing challenging farm issues of the state. Congressman Lee is married to renowned writer Willa Carpenter and they reside part time in Washington, D.C., and part time on James Island, Maryland, in Tuckerton.

***What do you think, Charles? Just enough, or not?

Tug

Charles sat there, reading it several times, mostly trying to believe he was actually doing this. Then he called Tug.

"Well, that didn't take you very long, Charlie. Are we good?"

"Tug, we are good. It's enough. In fact, just right. I am stunned seeing it in print—and realizing I really am fool enough to take this on."

Tug responded quickly, "I remember that feeling when I went for it with Max and ole Dickie. It takes guts to take on the establishment, but you know you will feel really good when this is out and your opponent begins to fight back. Really, you will."

Charles swallowed hard. "Do you think I'm battle ready?"

"Don't know why not. You've been here before and came through like a champ. By the way, I spoke to Buster and he's working with the Shore Farm Bureau, and I'm working with the local co-op stores and regional Farm Bureau representatives. We should have it all put together for when you come over here. Do you know when?"

"Right after the announcement hits the papers, in particular, the shore papers. What's the time frame on that?"

Tug scratched his head and answered, "Depends on Max, but I think it will be soon. Maybe tomorrow, unless you start throwing up and chickening out."

"Not going to happen. I just want to be prepared for Senator Dawes to come to my office locked and loaded."

"You're making the right decision, Charlie. The people over here on the Eastern Shore have your back. Now it's up to you to get the folks on the Western Shore to love you enough to outweigh the vote from some of the more liberal counties to the north. Are you working on that?"

"Yes. I've been working with them since the crab situation, and a lot of them see eye to eye with me. They'll get out the votes, and then we just have to pray."

Tug laughed. "I always say to Lindy, 'Yes, Virginia, there is a Western Shore.'"

"Know that expression well. Remember those great billboards for the good old Roanoke Hotel? Such a landmark in Virginia."

They both chuckled, then Tug said, "Well, Lindy never fails to answer, 'There may be a Western Shore, but it can't hold a candle to the Eastern Shore.'"

"She has something there, but they are two very different areas now. Wasn't always that way, but they are today."

Tug sat back in his chair, remembering how Dickie had used to talk about the other side of the shore. Dickie had loved it, but had also seen most of the farms over there sold off and the old way of life slowly disappearing. He would become rather philosophical and sad thinking about the big plantation homes and beautiful farmland. "'Yes, sirree, Tug,' he would say to me, 'that place over yonder is surely gone with the wind. That's why we're fighting so hard over here to hold on to our history and traditions.'"

Charles said, "Well, we'll do ole Dickie Short proud and try our best to keep traditions going on for a very long time. We will help those farmers out by keeping their land far away from the hands of Buddy Dawes and his friends."

Chapter Forty-Six

When Buddy emerged from the lavish bathroom inside his office, his new aide, Mark Daniels, had the dubious joy of handing his boss the morning newspaper. There was always something that got him upset, but not like it was going to do today. Mark just wanted to complete his task and get out of Dodge fast. The news was on the front page, so no one could miss it. Boom!

In his usual pleasant voice, Senator Dawes took the paper and said, "Good morning, Mark. Isn't it a lovely day?"

"Why, yes, Senator, it is. I thought I would get you some of the coffee that's being freshly brewed."

"Excellent, Mark. You seem quite on top of your game this fine day."

"Thank you, Senator," Mark said, beating a hasty retreat before the bomb dropped. He didn't make it far.

The booming voice of Senator Dawes, sounding like a gorilla gone crazy, shouted, "Mark? Mark Daniels? Come back here now!"

Mark was trapped. He couldn't deliberately keep walking. He scurried back into the lion's den.

"Yes, sir. What's wrong?" He knew damned well what was wrong.

"Did you see this headline?"

"No, I did not, sir," Mark lied. He just wasn't going there.

"I can't believe that young shit has the audacity to think he can . . ."

Buddy was turning red when Mark removed the paper from the senator's shaking hands. He faked reading it as if for the first time; good aides always did read things first, so they knew what was going on.

"Get that young bastard on the phone, Mark. I want to see him in my office right now!"

Mark looked terrified. "I'll try, sir, but it's still early, and he might not be in yet."

Buddy got so close to Mark that he could smell the toothpaste on his breath. "I didn't ask you what Lee's schedule was this morning, or what time he would come in. I told you to get him on the phone and tell him I want to see him right away."

Mark felt his stomach turn as he walked through the door to his office to make the call. He prayed Charles Lee would have come in by now, but he knew what a busy congressman he was. *Please, dear God!*

By the third ring of Charles's office line, Mark could feel his meager breakfast crawling back up his throat. *Answer this phone, someone, damn it.*

On the fifth ring, Charles picked up. "Hello?"

Surprised that Lee had answered himself, Mark stammered out his boss's demand.

"Congressman Lee? Mark Daniels of Senator Dawes's office here."

"Oh, good morning, Mark. What can I do for you?" The congressman sounded surprised, but it must have been an act.

"Sir, Senator Dawes would like to see you in his office as soon as you can make it."

Charles smiled. The arrow had hit its target. Now he was going to push it a little more. "Tell the good senator I'll be in my office for another hour. If he can make it over here before the hour is up, I will have time to speak to him. Tell him those exact words, Mark. Thank you." Click.

I'm going to throw up. How can I go back into that office and tell him those exact words? He'll kill me!

Buddy had heard Mark talking to Charles and walked into the outer office. Seething still, he asked, "What did the little shit say?"

Mark was visibly shaking now. "He said he would be in his office for the next hour, sir, and that, if you could get over there, he would speak with you."

Buddy's eyes bulged. He looked as if he might pounce on and devour him. Instead, he turned and said, in the scariest voice his aide had ever heard, "Thank you, Mark. That's all for the day."

What did he mean? Could he go home? He didn't dare say a word more, for fear for his life.

Buddy stopped, turned around, and said, "I mean it, Mark. You go home now. You look as though you've seen a ghost. I'll be okay, and, when this is all over, you will have seen how the big dogs play this game."

"Yes, sir. Please take care of yourself, sir. I will see you tomorrow." Mark picked up his belongings, headed out, closed the office door, and sat down on a chair in the hallway. His head was spinning and he felt as if he were going to die right there.

He had been so happy when he had gotten this job. Such prestige in working for a leading senator. His family was so proud. Plus, he, too, had loans to pay back from his expensive college education. He had never missed a payment, and Senator Dawes had offered him a tidy salary to start. He had always admired the senator, but now he had seen a side of him never before exposed. He was a force to be reckoned with, and Mark knew that, whatever this was all about, it wasn't going to end well.

He had seen Congressman Lee on the floor of the House during hearings, including when that old woman from James Island had been fighting for her people. Charles Lee was incredible, and he wanted to be just like him one day. Maybe he could approach him for a job? Anything, just to get out of the path of Senator Dawes. now clearly losing control of himself.

Mark now remembered overhearing other phone conversations when Dawes had lost his temper. Maybe he was into something that wasn't on the up-and-up? Mark did not want to lose his chances in this town for any man who was this corrupt.

Charles had known Buddy would come. The table was set for quite a brawl, but, before serving that up, he first wanted to speak to Buster Talbot and get some idea of what he was hearing back from the farmers.

"How ya doin', Congressman?"

"Well, I should be able to answer that question completely in about an hour. Senator Dawes is on his way over."

"It was all over the TV this morning that Pullman has left the campaign and that you qill be running in his place. Well, I 'spect everyone will ave heard it by now. Alston did his usual good job."

"He sure got it out fast."

"People like the kid and he is respected."

"Look, Buster, why I'm calling—"

"Yeah, I know. You want meetings set up. I do have most of them set up but need a day or two more to finish."

"Thanks so much, Buster, but that's actually not why I am calling. I want to know if you have any idea how the farmers feel about growing cannabis? I need to have that information in my quiver before the good senator walks in here and scalps me."

"Well, I tell ya, I've spoken to right many of them and some don't mind a bit, but the most of them are bothered a lot by it. They know it will mean a lot of money for them, but us folks are family people, and we know what it will bring to our farmland and culture. You and I both know it won't be just for medicinal uses; the legislature wants it to become legal for any use and that just isn't what we want for our young ones."

"Well said, Buster. I needed to have a feel for this so I can do battle for all of us over there."

"The government has been so corrupted, Congressman, and they are always just looking for the money. They have spent us into a thousand years of debt and so they need a way to pay down a lot of it."

Charles shook his head. "I don't know what lies ahead, but we must do what we can that's right in front of us."

"We trust you, Congressman. Go to it. When will you be over?"

"I would think day after tomorrow. Can you set it all up by then?"

"Looks like I'll have to, won't I?"

"I'll let you know what comes of World War III."

"Good luck."

Charles hadn't finished clicking off the phone off when he heard the outside door fly open and watched Buddy storm through his.

Removing his coat and tossing it on a sofa, Buddy said, "I see you don't have anyone left out there to announce me, so thought I would just come on in."

Charles wondered why no one was in his office, but that didn't matter right now. What did matter was about to hit the fan. He wasn't going to draw first blood. He would wait. He knew that, within mere moments, everything would be out on the table.

"What the hell do you think you're doing running against me for my Senate seat? Do you have any idea how powerful I am? I will crush you like a bug and send you back to ole Virginny, son."

Charles stood up, then walked calmly around the man standing there. He was giving him fair warning this wasn't going to be easy. He eyed him for a few moments before firing back.

"Crush me, Buddy? Ole Virginny? I'm running in Maryland; that's my home now."

"So you think. You are a Virginian all the way. I knew your Daddy and he would throw up thinking of you a Marylander."

"My *Daddy*"—Charles emphasized the word—"would be proud of his son for taking you on and saving a state from the likes of the corruption you're about to dump on it."

Buddy took a step back and looked at Charles. "What corruption? I'm afraid you're reading too many of your wife's novels. Business in D.C. can look like corruption at times, but it's not. You haven't been here long enough to understand how to make deals, son."

Charles was now so mad he didn't care. "Stop calling me 'son.' And leave my wife out of it. You know damned well what I am talking about. Try to deny you aren't buying your way into the Maryland legislature and using your federal power to do it. I know what you want to do to those farms, Buddy. Well, let me tell you something: those farmers aren't going to sell to you or the state. They will fight for their farms, and most will not grow cannabis either. You may try to sell them on all the good it will do, but we all know how far you want to go with this."

"Well now. The boy has grown into a man and thinks he has discovered the reasons for everything and wants to ride in on his white horse and save the day. Let me tell you, Charles Lee, the state will buy some of those farms, and some of the farmers will grow the weed and some will fight, but we will win in the end, just like the developers won to build housing on that land and develop shopping centers and business complexes. The land is changing and so are the needs for it. The days of chicken farming must come to an end to save the Bay, and what are the farmers going to do then? Grow corn and soybeans for something that isn't there anymore and no place to ship it?"

Charles wanted to put his fist right through Buddy's face, but he backed off and got control of himself. "How can you sleep at night? How can you face those people on the shore? Do you know how long that culture has been around?"

"I've given them more than any other legislator in their history. They have made money from some of my legislation, but now the time of the farmer, as they knew it, is over. Times are changing and they have to change with them."

"Buddy, do you know how hard they are working at finding alternate fertilizers, ways of growing crops to save land, new concepts of farming to meet environmental needs and take care of the waters? You look at them as if they have no sense of the land they love. Your view of what they have toiled over to keep in their families for generations and serve food to the population is nothing more than a big, fat retirement fund for you! It's sickening, and you have been so disingenuous with these good people."

Buddy sneered at Charles. "So pious, aren't you? You think everything you're doing is solely for them? Please spare me the Pollyanna sentiments. You want to take the crown off of my head and put it on your own. You want to live out your days on that island as their shepherd of the waters and land. Get real. You're just as deceptive as I am, using your position to make things go your way. Well, I say run against me, boy, and let's see how it works out for you. I think, at the end of the day, you'll come crawling to me for the scraps."

"You'd like to believe that wouldn't you? But I won't back away, Buddy. Let the games begin."

Chapter Forty-Seven

Charles was proud he had faced off with Dawes and was still standing. He called Willa and asked the girls to lunch. Yitzi's, of course.

As usual Yitzi's was packed, but, despite the wait for everyone else, Yitzi himself managed to get an out-of-the-way table for the three of them.

Since they all knew what they wanted to eat, they were able to place their orders quickly and begin to talk.

Prue couldn't wait to hear all about Charles's encounter with the powerful Buddy Dawes. "How did it go? We want to hear every gory detail."

Charles thought he caught a slight look on Willa's face, but, not sure what it was, he went ahead. "It was rough. He stormed into my office ready to eat me alive. Have to say I was a bit nervous . . . knew it was coming . . . but the mission gave me strength."

"Well, Charles, go on," urged Prue.

As Charles began to recount the shouting match, Willa excused herself to the ladies' room.

"Did I say something wrong, Prue?"

"I don't think so, Charles. Willa did seem upset, but I don't know why."

"She's mad, and mad enough to get up and leave the table."

"Well, you know Willa. If she's pissed about something, she'll let us know in no uncertain terms."

"I'm not so sure, Prue. She keeps her own counsel about a lot of things. I think she learned to do that growing up without parents. Even though she was raised by her aunt, there are many things she doesn't share with her either. She gets into moods sometimes. I love her more than life, but have to say, I don't always understand her."

"Then don't try, Charles. Willa is a very complicated lady. She has many dimensions, and she thinks things through more than anyone else I know. That's why I lean on her many times for answers. So let her do that with whatever it is that's bothering her."

Charles became quiet when he saw Willa returning from the bathroom. He watched her for a clue, and his face told the story: he was in love with her, but at a loss for words at the moment. Finally, he whispered to Prue, "Maybe she's sorry she married me."

Prue sat straight up in her chair and grabbed his arm. "No way on that one! She is so in love that she's lost. Give her time to work this out."

Willa arrived back at the table just as the server brought their food. Perfect timing. They ate and did not talk about Buddy or politics.

Prue finished her lunch rather quickly and said, "I hate to break this up, but I have to go. I'm taking off the afternoon to meet with a lot of the staffers who are going to be working on my campaign. It's time to start sorting through things. Want to join me, Charles? Willa?"

Charles jumped at the opportunity to see how Prue would fashion her campaign, a campaign of which he was in full support. He had already contacted his powerful Virginia friends, and, surprisingly, they were all in for donating and helping her, and him, too, even now that he was running for the Maryland Senate seat. He was a Lee and that bought great allegiance, even when it might not help them at the moment. They knew he would be there if they needed him. And Charles knew Buddy would be putting together some real heavy-duty players in the campaign world, too.

Willa's body language was unmistakeable, she was angry. "I'm going home to write, Charles."

Charles looked at her and saw fire flying from her eyes. Prue caught her tone, and, knowing her girlfriend so well, got up and said, "See you both later. Charles, if you want to join us, we'll be at the Ohio congressional offices."

"Okay, Prue. Thanks. I'll join you later."

After Prue left, Willa looked at Charles. "I'm sorry, love. I can't do this anymore. I'm a writer, not a politician's wife. I'm going home."

"Okay, I can understand you don't have the stomach for this, but it's the way it is. I don't blame you, Willa. I thought you understood what I did and who I was, but I love you and don't want to lose you. Please don't leave me now."

Willa looked into his eyes and said, "I don't think you understood me, Charlie. I'm going *home*. Home to the island. I will leave tomorrow morning. I need to get on the water and be surrounded by the water and see the sunsets over the Bay. I need to be with Miss Frances and in my bed . . . our bed. When you're finished with all this, then come home and back to me."

"Willa, I am going to be in this for months, right to November and the election. I will be on and off the shore and in Virginia with Vernie, and you, I hope. I will be all over."

"Does that mean I won't see you at home, or be with you in our bed?"

"No, darling, that's not what it means. It means I'll be very busy. I'll come when I can, but you have to understand. I thought you did."

"What I understand is that I love you more than life and need you just as much. I don't care about Senator Dawes, or any of this really. I need to think this all through, Charles. I'll see you at dinner, but I leave tomorrow. I will make all the arrangements for my flight over."

Charles was now angry. He slammed his fist on the table and shouted—louder than he liked in a public place—"You will not make your arrangements, Willa. I will take you home. I'm going over to the shore anyway. I have meetings to attend the day after tomorrow. From there, you can take my car and drive on down to Somerville and I will make sure there is boat ready to take you over to the island. Do you understand me?"

Willa had never seen Charles like this. She had pushed him too far. She knew she was running away, but now he wouldn't even let her do that by herself. She grew angrier than she imagined she could get with him.

"I don't want to fight, and particularly in public, Charles. No more now. I need some space from you. We're both angry and need time to think—"

"Time to think?" he cut her off. "There is no *need* to think. You're my wife and I love you so damned much, Willa." He felt the tears start to form, but he held them back.

Willa's eyes weren't much drier. "I love you, too, Charles. This will pass, I'm sure. Just let me go and be by myself. As a matter of fact, I think I'll go this afternoon. You and Prue can talk all night about what it is you're both doing. You need to do this and I need to be on the island. Please, let me go. Please?"

His heart was breaking watching her plead with him. But, as much as he wanted to, he couldn't hold her; it didn't seem the right thing to do just now. Instead, he took her hand and held it tightly. "I won't keep you here if you want to leave. Go . . . think. Just don't ever leave me, Willa. You are my life."

Willa smiled gently. Her temper cooled some. "I love you too much to ever think of doing that. You need to live here, in this world, now. But, when we're together again, you must promise to leave this world behind. That's how it has to be right now. Can you do that, Charles?"

"It seems you should be the one who runs my campaign. You're pretty good at negotiating, you know. I understand not all women are cut out for this, but I make you this promise, Willa: when I come to you, we will shut the world out and we will be us and our friends or anything else won't stand between us."

Right there in the middle of Yitzi's, surrounded by noise and clatter, Charles kissed his wife, ignoring all onlookers. He wanted her to know exactly how he felt.

Chapter Forty-Eight

Buddy wasn't going to waste any time. He wanted to get a team together to begin the battle. Charles Lee wasn't going to waltz in and take it from him after his years of holding it and the chairmanship of several powerful committees. That was *not* going to happen.

Roy Davis was his first call and he found the conversation most unsettling. Charles had already moved the first chess piece.

The senator said, "I can't believe the ground that young upstart has already covered. Well, he isn't going to stop us. He just thinks he can."

"You know, Buddy, that may be a good strategy right there. Let him think you aren't doing anything when you are."

Buddy sat back, rubbed his chin, and smiled broadly. "You just might be right, Roy. Now, how do those farmers feel about growing cannabis? Give it to me straight. I have to know."

"Okay, but you might not like the answer, Senator. A few are all for it and see the financial gain to them, but most don't want it on their farms. These folks are God-fearing and family people, you know."

"Hmm, well, they'll like it or they'll sell their land to me. But, of course, they won't know that when they sell. That shoe won't drop for quite a while. Do they like the idea of growing their fruits for wine? That'll bring them more money in the long run."

"They were okay with that, especially when I told them a corporation was interested in building many wineries around the shore. They liked that idea a lot."

"How about the damned chickens? Did they talk about their beloved chickens?"

"Buddy, that's a really sore subject. Most of the farmers have some involvement with the chicken industry, and they are very wary of what the state is doing in regard to poultry. You know as well as I do, they don't just raise them, but they grow the crops—soybeans, corn—that support that industry, and they know the powers that be aren't too happy about fertilizer

259

from chicken droppings and complications that causes in the Bay. They have made huge improvements—"

Buddy snapped his chair back to his desk and cut Roy off. "I know what they do, damn it, Roy. I've been over there a million times in past years, and, as you know, I grew up on that shore. But the time has come for a new day and new things out there. I got a heap of folks, with deep pockets, beating on me to end the reign of the chicken."

"Well, I don't think that will happen. Not as long as these farmers have breath in them."

"Well, we'll see who wins this war. I can tell you it won't be Charles Lee. Besides, that kid is an interloper. He's from Virginia, and now he thinks that, simply by buying a home over there and marrying that fancy girl writer, he can walk in and do this to me."

"They do love him, Buddy. He's a folk hero to them, and so is that writer friend of his, Alston."

"I know that, but they are both young hot dogs who can't outwit this old fox. They'll see how it is in D.C. We play by different rules than they do over there, even than those that govern the congressman and his friends."

"Maybe, but they're smart young men. They bested Rennie, you know, and the people are grateful to Charles."

"The people will be grateful to me, Roy, when I put money in their pockets. And, if they don't come along with the plan, they will end up very sorry."

"I'm with you, Senator, and I can get up a team pretty quick. Where do you want us to begin?"

"Get a campaign going, man, and don't be nice about it. Spread some money around in the right pockets. Catch my drift?"

"Got it, Senator. Just don't forget who did this for you."

"Just get going, Roy," Dawes snapped. "And stay in touch."

Buddy called Rennie the minute Roy cleared his office. He knew he would be just the man to help him teach Charles Lee a thing or two about interfering with his plans. Buddy needed his advice, but, to date, Richardson had stayed mum.

"Ah, glad you're home, Rennie. Buddy here. I need some advice."

"Thought you would surface after the news of the day."

"You saw it? They must have run that announcement everywhere, in every state. Bastards!"

"Now what's got your dander up this fine Virginia day?"

"Sorry to interrupt your fine day, Rennie," Buddy responded sarcastically. "It's that little piece of crap who has me all spun up. I need you to help out an old friend."

"Depends on what that old friend wants."

"Now, Rennie, don't sound so dubious about my intentions."

"Can you give me a good reason not to, Buddy? You seem to always have yourself in some scheme. Is this the one that's supposed to pay off for us?"

As insulted as Buddy was at Rennie's implication, he tried to remember this wasn't personal. Or so he hoped. "This is business, Rennie. I think you'll like it, too. I want to stop that little bastard from getting in the way of something I've . . . we've been working on with legislators in Maryland for a long time. Shall I go on?"

"Still listening."

"God, man, you don't make this easy. I want you to help me crush Charles Lee."

There wasn't a sound on the other end.

"Did you hear me, Rennie?"

"You told me this is all respectable, nothing underhanded. What happened?"

"Oh, I thought you hung up. No, it's all legit, trust me. However you know you have to spread some green around to get people's attention. We're still going to redirect the farm industry in Maryland away from chickens to growing medical marijuana and fruits of all kinds for new wineries. This will be great for the folks."

Rennie chuckled softly. "And, of course, *we've* been doing this all on the up-and-up—no bribes, no money exchanging hands—just an altruistic vision for the future, right?"

"You know, Rennie, you can be a real asshole when you put your mind to it. I've been working on this for several years with men and women who want to change the state in ways they never thought they could, all while helping preserve the Bay and the waters surrounding that shore. We'll be bringing a whole new image to the state, instead of that infernal chicken."

"You know how Lee feels about those people. Who, I see, are *his* people now."

Dawes snapped back, "If he wins, damn it, he will destroy everything for us."

"Well, he might just win at that. Lees aren't losers, you know, no matter where they live. And I'm not so sure I want to get all riled up about this anymore. Even though I returned here with a dark cloud over my head, I am still a Virginian and that still holds sway. I'm tired of it all. If we get caught, this time I'll be thrown out of the state and die a disgraced man."

"You're telling me you're out? You can't do that."

"I can, and I am, sir. I am over and out. I thought it was a good idea in the beginning—still do to some extent—but I'm too old for all this intrigue. Besides, I still have nightmares of that mean, cussed woman from that island where Lee now lives part time."

"I don't believe what I'm hearing."

"I don't want any more battles, and especially with the Lee family. I was his Daddy's good friend, and he would come back and haunt me if I hurt his son."

"Well, you old sonofabitch, you're missing out on a huge opportunity."

Rennie was tired of the conversation. Instead of saying good-bye, all he said was, "Don't say I didn't warn you."

The call was over, leaving Buddy fuming and mumbling, "Leave him to his brandy and cigars and leave me to do my business."

Chapter Forty-Nine

Prue went back to a borrowed friend's apartment since Charles and Willa were both leaving for the shore, Charles for his meetings and Willa for the peace and quiet of the island. She still felt bad about Willa's mood and opinions, but Willa had always been the creative dreamer and she, the realist. Even though they had blowout, she knew the couple would make amends sooner or later. They were in love, and everyone knows that love conquers all.

As Willa arrived on the island, she left her bags at the dock in order to first take care of the most important thing. She walked down the now familiar path that led to someone she needed and loved. Thankfully, Miss Frances was home.

"Well, I'll be. What ye doin' here? Thought you were staying in Washington for a much longer time." Then Frances caught the look on Willa's face and knew something was eating at her. "What is it, girl?"

Willa followed the island woman back to her kitchen. "Everything is okay, well sort of, I guess. I just needed to come back home."

"Where's Charles?"

"He's at meetings over on the shore."

"Excuse me for puttin' my nose where it don't belong, but isn't he comin' back here?"

Willa smiled halfheartedly. "No. No, he's not, Miss Frances. We had a bit of a fight and I drove over with him—we didn't say much to one another. We had a driver bring us because he had to come over anyway—but I parted with them and had a ride waiting for me to drive me on to Somerville to catch the boat."

Frances sat down across from Willa. "It'll pass, sweetheart. All couples have fights."

"Not about the one thing the other does for a living and is passionate about."

Frances slid into a chair quietly and said, "Oh, I see. Hey, I read the announcement, and everyone is delirious about Charles running for the Senate seat that that old Dawes has."

"People really don't like Buddy Dawes, do they? Then why did they elect him?"

"This part of the state didn't, and that doesn't really matter to anyone in the politic game. The counties across the Bay—they're who determine the outcome of our elections most times."

Willa said, "You know, that's what's killing this country. A few counties here and there, and a few states, too, determine it for everyone, leaving the majority of folks mad as hell."

Frances said, "I think Charles has a real chance, though. Watermen and farmers are all riled up, and they have family and relations on the other side. And then there are those who just don't want a major shift in the future of this state. From the beginning it was fishing, agriculture, tobacco, timber and land uses the state was known for and now they want to change everything. I don't know what's to come of all this."

Willa smiled sweetly at her dear friend. "I don't understand anything anymore, but I do know women still love romance, so I'm in a good situation. Maybe one I ought to pay more attention to myself."

Now it was Frances who began to smile. "We sure do love to read that sort of story. Takes us all away from the reality of this here life and makes us think about those we love. You're a relationship and connection writer, not just love between a man and a woman."

"Miss Frances, can I stay here with you and Jimmy for a couple of days? When we talked the other day, you said Clyde was just about finished with the outside—which is amazing and wonderful!—but I'd really rather not sleep there until that's done."

"Sure ye can, but you are going to walk on over there to see it, aren't ye?"

"Well, of course!" Getting to her feet, Willa leaned down and kissed Frances on the cheek. "Thank you so much! I needed to talk with you. You are the closest person I have to a mother now. I love you. Can I take the golf cart and pick up my bags while I'm at it?"

"Hold on there, girl, I'll come with ye. I didn't go over to the house today, so I want to see your face when you see what he's done."

"Come on then, Miss Frances. Time waits for no one."

Charles was knee-deep in meetings the rest of the day after Willa left him for Somerville. He was still feeling that sick feeling you get after you have words with your partner, but they had, at least, kissed, no matter how tepid it was, before her departure. His body was with the people, but his soul was with Willa.

Tug introduced him to a crowd of the folks from the interior of the shore. Buster had arranged it all, but wasn't going to meet with them. He was comfortable with Tug doing it because the people loved Tug Alston, too. He had earned his stripes fighting the banks and developers over the land earlier, and he had won the battle. When Tug traveled around the shore discussing his book, people still talked about the beloved old waterman, Dickie Short. That was always special. He knew they were going to love his new book on local waterfowl, too.

"I think it's going very well, don't you, Charlie?"

"I sure do, Tug, and I can't thank you or Buster enough for all you're doing on such short notice. However, I have to say, it's really not this side of the shore I'm worried about; it's across the Bay on the Western Shore. That's going to be entirely different."

"Yes, some counties over there will be tough, but the southern part of the state is still filled with old-timey farmers, many of whose forefathers came from all over Europe to farm these lands. They are all linked together, Charles, so they'll be interested in hearing what you have to say. If the Eastern Shore suffers, they know they will, too."

"Good point, Tug. Are we about done for the day?"

"To be honest, Charles, I think we are done for now. Period."

"What?"

Tug answered, "We've been to this part of the shore and they have responded well. I'm glad to see it. Some of these folks can be difficult on some issues. But, if I were you, I would go back and work on your campaign and get that going strong. That's what will count in the next couple of months. I'm certain our friend Buddy is doing that while we're here. He will come at you with every arrow in his quiver, Charlie. You have threatened him, and that's when the Washington inner circle closes ranks."

"I think you're right, Tug. For one thing, I have to find a new assistant, fast. Prue said she would help on that score. She feels terrible after the one she recommended turned into a little shit. But, right now, I think I'm going to head home—the island home. I'll have my car and driver take me on from here. You go on. I still have a few people here I want to speake to who had some questions and I will call ahead and get a bost to take me the rest of the way. Thinking on some things, I want—no, need—to go over there."

"Sure. I understand, Charlie. When women get all put out, men are a mess. You don't need to say another word. And, if you can't get that boat across and need to wait for the morning ferry, you're always welcome at our house, you know. Or you could sleep in the shanty." With that remark, both men laughed out loud.

"I don't think I'm quite ready for that, Tug. Being on the island is as close to the water as I want to get. Except for being on *The Willa Lee*, of course. She's out and docked for the summer, as you know, but she's over there."

"Call me on the cell if you need anything on our way down. Other than that, safe travels and have a good weekend. Give Willa our love."

"Thanks so much for all you're doing."

"That's what friends are for, Charlie. Now I better get back to Lindy. I am trying to stay close to her until I'm sure she's over the miscarriage."

"I completely understand. Give her our love, and thanks again."

Tug waved good-bye, got in his big Jeep Cherokee, and sped off.

Chapter Fifty

Tug was exhausted and glad to be home with Lindy. Though she said nothing about the baby she lost, he didn't like being gone from her. She had had some very difficult days following the loss, and he wanted her to understand that this wasn't the end of things. There would be other babies later on. Besides, he truly liked being with her. They were good together, even though his father thought differently. That hurt him deeply, but he couldn't change the man. For a while, he thought they had patched some things up, but now, with his parents' separation, everything was falling apart again. Max was more a father figure than the almighty Ted Alston. Mikey had always been Ted Alston's star, but he couldn't and wouldn't blame his kid brother. He loved him too much to let his father ruin that relationship, too. Harvard was the only thing Tug had done right, and even that hadn't been good enough because he wasn't an athlete. He was the nerd in the family.

Lindy rushed to him and gave him a tight hug. "Hey, sexy husband, what took you so long?"

"Saying good-bye to Charlie and driving home. It was a long day."

"You can say that again. How did it go?"

"Great. Charlie sure is a born politician, and I mean that in a good way. But he couldn't wait to get to the island and be with Willa."

"I thought she was in D.C., but Aunt Rita said she saw her going over to the island earlier today. Rita said she looked down in the mouth. Trouble in paradise?"

"Now, Lindy, leave it be. You know how stories get going in this town. And I don't want any about Willa or Charlie coming from either of us."

"I would never say anything. I love them both and Willa has become a good friend. I am honored she likes me, being a famous writer and all."

"It's interesting how humble both of them are. It's neat to be around them. Charlie is from an illustrious family and Willa is a best-selling novelist. Yet they are both so down-to-earth."

"My guess is he's going to be our next senator. Now doesn't that beat all?"

Though Lindy was following the news as everyone was, Tug had purposely not involved her in all the gory details of what was going on. He wanted to keep any and all drama just between Charles and him.

Lindy spoke again. "Tug? You haven't talked to your father in a while. Don't you think you should?"

He took her in his arms and hugged her. "Always the matchmaker, but this is one of those things that can't be worked through, Lindy. However, if it will make you feel better, and you'll stop asking me to, I'll head upstairs and call him."

"Supper is in an hour, so get going."

"Yes, ma'am."

"And don't forget to tell him I love him. Maybe he'll come around one day if I tell him that enough."

As Tug climbed their narrow stairs, he was thinking of what exactly he would say to his father. He really hadn't spoken to him in quite a while, and it was always an uncomfortable conversation at best.

He felt really tired all of a sudden, and looking at his desk, piled high with papers, didn't help any. Charlie was taking a lot of his time, but he was a friend. *Good thing I really like that man. I need to get done with my own work.*

He reluctantly picked up his cell and dialed Boston. After four rings, Tug was about to hang up, but then the gruff voice he knew so well answered, "Hello?"

Tug's stomach was already churning, but he answered the man he loved to hate. "Dad? It's Tug. We haven't talked in a long time, so thought maybe it was time."

"Hi, Tug. I'm surprised to hear from you."

Always the first punch. "Well, I have been really busy. I am helping a friend out with his political campaign and that has taken up my days and nights."

"Well, I guess that's as good an excuse as any not to call your old man."

Why does he do this? Bet if I were Mikey, the entire tone would be different. Tug kept his thoughts to himself and tried to stay on neutral ground. "How are you now that you're not racing to the *Globe* anymore?"

"Pretty bored and pretty boring. It's not just the retirement thing, it's . . . well, you know what it is."

There it is, out on the table—the hard, cold truth of his constant self-pity. Makes me sick after how he went on about me getting away from home and learning to be alone. "I know it's tough, Dad, but are you sure this is the end between you and Mom? Maybe the two of you could make amends, or something."

"No, we can't, Tug. She made it perfectly clear she was done, and now she's moved all her stuff out to the Cape. That looks pretty final to me. She's made her decision and thrown away a hell of a lot of good years."

He never sees his fault in anything. Took us years to just talk and now here we are again with nothing but insincere pleasantries to exchange. He only cares about himself. "Well, I was hoping, that's all, Dad."

"Hmm."

That was his father's entire response. Not what Tug had been hoping for, but, with Ted Alston, you never knew what you were going to get.

"Mom was down and Max came with her. They surprised me for my birthday. And Mikey came down to see his big brother. He's doing great, selling farm equipment. Don't see him as much as I would like to, but, hey, that's life. It was great to see them all. Missed seeing you, though," he added, just because he wanted to be the nice guy.

At the mere mention of Mikey's name, Tug could hear his father's entire disposition change. It was as if Tug had said his dad's all-time hero, Jim Lonborg of Red Sox fame, had come down to see him. As the sports editor of the *Boston Globe*, he and Lonborg had gotten pretty close. His dad always said that Jim Lonborg was the best player ever because he was a regular guy, not all puffed up with himself like today's players who made way too much money for his liking. Lonborg was a stand-up guy who had left the game, gone back home, become a dentist, and enjoyed his family. A stand up guy, and one who had gone on to do something meaningful with his life and give back to the country he loved so much.

"I'm glad to hear Mikey is doing so well. I don't hear near enough from him either. I don't know what's wrong with my boys."

"Maybe you should come down and visit us." Tug knew that would draw fire, but, instead, his father didn't take the bait as he would have in the old days. Instead, he just grunted softly. There was no use in going any further with the conversation. He knew his dad was uncomfortable talking about . . . well, anything really.

"Well, Dad, I wish you were happier and enjoying this time off now. Maybe you could do some fishing. I'm sure Uncle Max would love to join you, and the two of you could talk about the old times in Harvard Yard."

"I don't think so, Tug. Max is spending a lot of time with your mother now. He always loved her, but I was the one who got the Beautiful Miss Kay. Now the field is wide open for him."

Tug got angry. "You know, Dad, maybe if you had tried harder to make her a bigger part of your life instead of leaving her behind for the sports arenas you constantly went off to, maybe she would have been able to stand your self-pity and constant preening."

As always, especially with Tug, Ted's temper flared quickly. "Maybe if you were to mind your own damned business, Tug, you would have gotten farther at the paper instead of sitting all day writing worthless words."

That was the end for Tug. He was done. His dad had finally come right out, in his bitterness, and told the truth. He resented his son's happiness and choice of work. Tug was a total failure in his eyes. He really never had broken down that barrier as he had thought. His father had returned to being the SOB he'd always been.

"I have to go now, Dad. Sorry I've been such a disappointment to you. I don't feel that way, though. I am changing lives, and those 'worthless words' are my way of expressing my thoughts and hopes. Everyone has them, but yours are all gone now. Good-bye, Dad."

With Tug's words ringing in his ears, Ted Alston slammed the phone down. He hated his son for what he had said to him, but, more than anything, he hated himself for what his life had become.

Tug sat in his chair stone-still. He was shocked that he had said what he had, but he didn't regret one word. To Tug, words—written and spoken—meant things. His father had become a mean old man, a further extension of what he had been anyway, but had tried to keep hidden from all around him, except for the most important ones: his family. Now that he had time on his hands, he had just given up and Tug guessed he was firing off at everyone now, including the ones he was supposed to love the most.

Lindy heard Tug's side of the fight as she was coming up the stairs to tell him dinner was ready. She stood frozen outside his office door. Finally, she slipped in quietly and stood behind him, rubbing his shoulders. When the call was over, she leaned down and whispered, "I'm so sorry, darling. He's just lost, I think. I'm glad your mother left and that she came to see us. She just couldn't spend her last years with him."

Staring out the window to the Bay, he said, "I am, too, Lindy. She's so happy now. Do you think Max and she . . .?"

"Wouldn't that be something if, after all these years, they fell in love?"

"Funny thing is, Lindy, Max apparently has been in love with her his whole life."

"Get out of here. How do you know that?"

"Dad just told me as much. And, actually, now that I think of it, Max implied that to me before he left."

"He did? Tug, you've been holding back on me."

Tug grabbed her hand and pulled her down on his lap. "Not really. I've just been a bit busy since Max and Mom left, and, of course, Charlie has turned my life upside down."

"Well, Mr. Upside Down, dinner is ready if you're interested."

"Wouldn't miss it for the world."

Chapter Fifty-One

Willa and Frances's visit to the island home found Clyde finishing up the outside walls. She was very grateful for how quickly and carefully he was working. Seeing the outside walls up in the back of the house, she suddenly wanted to stay in her own home, so she drove Miss Frances back to her home, let the gold cart and then, needing some things to make dinner, headed over to Bradshaw's store.

She loved this small island, where it was so easy to walk to everything you needed. And, if the weather wasn't so good or you had a lot to haul, you just hopped on your golf cart. She had bought one for them not long ago. Of course, it had to be delivered by boat; that was how things went when you live on an island.

Denny was almost done for the day and Nellie was helping him put things right before the next day's business when Willa walked through the door.

"Hope I'm not too late to pick up a few things. Time got away. Sorry!"

"Come on in, Willa. Denny and I are just prepping to leave; besides, I haven't spoken with you in ages. I know you're busy with your writing and the house—I hear from Mom, of course!—and I am busier than a gopher making a new hole with another report I'm working on for the state."

"Your mother is a godsend. I left for D.C., though I didn't stay as long as I expected. Still, she kept a close eye on the house and Clyde. She's one in a million."

"Yes, everyone loves Miss Frances. I'm afraid I could never fill my mother's shoes. She is a different kind of woman, and, when she goes, there won't be anyone to replace her."

"Your whole family is like that. Miss Millie is astonishing in her commitment to making those cakes every day. Up before the sun rises and then baking for hours to get them to the boat to go over before noon. She's something."

"I love my aunt. She's a role model, just like Mama. Their kind of women are in short supply today. Good common sense leads the way for them. And most people don't have much common sense today. They are just plain ignorant of what they should know—and they get paid so much money for it! Well, to change the subject, why didn't you stay in D.C.? You know Mom is more than capable of keeping things under control."

"Oh, it's not that, Nellie. To be honest, Charles and I needed some space."

"Care to talk about it? You know my lips are sealed when it comes to you, Willa."

"Just one of those things, I guess, but, when I think about it, I don't know if we can sort this out. I just don't like the game of politics and now Charles will be up to his ears in it. To my way of thinking, it isn't an honorable way to make a living. And they all stay too long in their positions. It jades them as people and turns them into something they were not when they went there."

Nellie looked at her friend and then started laughing. "Willa, you knew all about that before you married Charles. You write this stuff! Only you call it fiction—and it always has a happy ending."

Willa cracked a smile and said, "Got me on that one. Perhaps Willa Carpenter ought to write a good political romance mystery?"

"Hmm, a mystery, eh? Could be really great. You know all the ingredients you need to bake that cake."

"We can't seem to get away from the cakes, can we?"

"Speaking of cakes, how is that wonderful sister-in-law of yours?"

"Vernie is all right, but I think she is rethinking the idea she could do what Miss Millie does. She is a perfect wife for her husband and he adores her. He doesn't have to work—family money and all—so he spends his time with his horses."

"Horses? I didn't know that. What does he do with horses?"

"He rides some of them, but, mostly, he boards other people's horses and makes a lot of money from it. He has a good deal of help who live on their property."

"I would love to see that horse farm. I love those animals; in fact, I think they are the prettiest of God's creatures."

This time it was Willa who laughed. "I would have thought you would think that title went to your beloved Chesapeake crabs."

"Well, now that you say it . . ."

Denny was enjoying hearing the two friends talk. He really liked Willa, though he didn't have a clue about her way of life or about writing books. Then again, he had fallen in love with a very bright young gal who was no slouch in the education department. She worked on some of the state's most important Bay-related research projects. Yep, he was way over his head and still wondering how she had fallen in love with him, a shy waterman. However, they were both islanders, and that is something that's a bond for life.

"Okay, you two girls, could you break from your gabbing a minute and grab your stuff, Willa? And I need you, hon, to help me with wrapping up this food."

Nellie leaned over to Willa and whispered, "I like to let him think he knows all about the market business, but it's crabs he's in love with."

"Does he miss being out there every day?"

Nellie looked away for a moment. "Yes, he does. He still does go sometimes, you know. And I always worry when he's out on that water. There's so much danger. People who love eating crabs have no idea how mean that Bay can get."

"I know, Nellie. I don't think people think about much of anything when they eat their food. Whether it's watermen or farmers, they all take great risks."

"You're right, Willa. Now come on before Denny begins to get impatient with us. Get what you need and I'll walk you back home. I want to see what's going on with your house."

"I would love that, Nellie. You're a great friend, you know. Funny that, now I'm living on this small island, I see you less than I did when we were working on that project in D.C. Come on, let's make Denny happy and get out of here. I would love your company on the way."

Nellie felt a chill at Willa's comment about the couple needing space. She knew they would work through whatever it was. They could never break up. They has mission together and the people needed Charles to be their senator, and they loved the idea he would be living on the island with them. He was a fair man who loved the people he served. He would make a great senator—as long as he didn't stay too long in that city across the Bay. If you stayed too long, a silent cancer called corruption apparently stole its way into your soul.

"You're a good friend, too, Willa. I'm so glad our paths crossed in life. Everything will work out. Give yourself time time to get settled in and used to one another's ways."

Willa stared into space but deliberately didn't answer her friend. Nellie was wise beyond her years, just like her mother. They had been family to her when she had needed family. She still desperately missed her parents, and the Evanses continued to help make up for that special loss and the emptiness inside her.

Chapter Fifty-Two

Charles called ahead and arranged for Cap'n Tuck to have his boat at the dock as he would be arriving shortly. As luck would have it, Tuck was already in Somerville and hadn't left for the island yet because he'd gone back to Virgil's to fill up a thermos before heading over to the marina.

When Charles got there, both men were ready to roll. Charles was eager to get back to the island to clear the air with Willa. He had been wrong to expect her to embrace his political life right away, and then to throw a campaign on top of that had been brutal for her. But he hadn't expected this to happen. She had her own life and career, but he couldn't lose her. They would have to come to some agreement.

"You look tired, Congressman, or should I say Soon-to-Be Senator? I can't believe I am ferrying such an important man across the Bay."

"I'm the same man, Tuck. Just an exhausted one right now. I'm in need of the island's magic to bring me back to my center and give me some peace for a little while."

"It sure can do that, Congressman."

"Please call me Charles. I like that better."

"Okay then. It's going to be different when you are a senator, though. Will be hard to call you by your first name."

"Why is that?" asked Charles. "What's the difference? If you call me Charles now, why not then?"

"Don't know. Just will be. Some things are just that way. I can't imagine me calling Senator Dawes, Buddy. Although I think a lot of his childhood chums do. Seems disrespectful."

"What's his real name anyway?"

Tuck scratched his head and then said, "Lawrence. I remember that because, way back, someone called him Larry, and he got all bent out of shape and stated clearly his name was Buddy. So I figured his name must be Lawrence."

Charles smiled at the man's logic; it worked, so why try to fix it?

276

"The waters are a bit rough today."

"Often are this time of the year. You okay?"

"Yes, I'm fine. Just noticing."

"Will you be staying awhile?"

"Not really. I was on the shore and have just learned I still have meetings to get to, but wanted to come over and be with my wife for at least an overnight or so."

"Miss Willa came back earlier. She seemed so happy to be back."

"I'm sure she was. The island is a tonic for her, and she wants to get back to her writing."

"A lot of women love her books. They're all romance stuff. I don't read much, and, if I did, I don't think I would read that."

"I think you have a lot of guy company, Tuck."

Cap'n Tuck's boat entered the thoroughfare and they were nearly home. Charles loved coming to the island this way, rather than by seaplane. He could see the seabirds getting ready for night, and the sounds the geese settling in the marsh near the island was a comforting sound.

Cap'n Tuck turned to look at Charles. "Always good coming back to the island. My soul misses it when I am away."

"I'm beginning to understand that statement completely."

Tuck swung the boat around and brought her in to the dock in one perfect motion. He had obviously been doing this all his life.

"Thanks, Tuck. Enjoyed it."

"You let me know when you want to go back, Congr . . . I mean Charles."

"See? You can do it. Thanks, and I'll call your cell when it's time for me to say good-bye again."

Charles grabbed a rail and left the boat. A five-minute walk and he would be home. Because this visit was on the spur of the moment, he had no bag or anything. He had clothes at the house. He felt so entirely free out here.

Nellie said good-bye to Willa and walked back to the store to see if Denny had already gone back home. Nothing on the island was really very far away. The best way she could describe to her mainland friends what life here was like was that it was the closest thing to freedom she could think of. It was then she saw a man walking toward Willa's house. She paused, then realized who it was. She smiled. Willa would be surprised. She didn't call out to him. Just let it be.

Charles couldn't believe his eyes. As he walked around to the back of the house, he saw Clyde had taken off that entire side and the new design was all framed in. The porch was in the process of being both torn down and expanded. It was simply astounding what Clyde had gotten done.

Charles walked back to the front and up a wide plank leading to the front door. Then he stepped in. They never locked their doors until bedtime. He heard Willa in the back, and headed that way immediately, but she must have heard something because she turned around.

Her heart almost leaped out of her chest. She yelled, "Charlie, what are—" She didn't get a chance to finish. He dropped his briefcase and rushed over.

Neither seemed to want to let go. Everything standing between thempreviously melted away in that embrace. They would go on without saying anything more about the world of politics.

The sun hadn't made its appearance yet when Charles began perking his morning coffee. Willa was still asleep. He loved this part of island life the best, being up early and listening to the fishing boats leaving to get oysters. Summer was crab time; winter it was oysters. There was such a sense of rhythm to these fishing communities, much as there was in farmers' lives. Everything began before dawn and went all day.

These people, Charles realized, worked their whole lives to bring food to their own tables, and tables all over the state, and then beyond in many cases. And, yet, the government didn't seem to care. They looked down on these people who go out every day to do what they had been doing for generations. Now it would be one of their own Marylanders who was about to sell them and their farmers out.

Charles was deep in thought about the old waterman, Dickie Short, whom Tug revered more than anyone else who had passed through his life. He pondered on how that old man had taken on an empire of developers and bankers and brought them to understand the folly of overbuilding in certain areas. Then his mind wandered to Miss Frances, who had overcome her nerves and gone before his committee to plead her case for her people on the water. Yes, it can be done, he knew. Maybe it took those in the line of fire to do it, though.

Willa was stretching as she slowly walked into the kitchen. She saw Charles sipping his coffee and looking out the window. She could tell his mind was a million miles away. Not wanting to startle him, she whispered, "Good morning, my love."

Brought back to the present, he turned to look at her and smiled. "Come here, you beautiful and sexy woman. I need a hug."

"With pleasure, husband." She slipped perfectly into his arms and snuggled closely for a moment.

"If I didn't know better, I would think you've been up and writing a love scene. You're purring like a kitten."

"Why do you say that?"

"Woman, you make my knees shake. Want to go back to bed and repeat our evening?"

"No, I don't. Clyde will be here shortly and I don't think he wants to catch us like that."

Charles chuckled softly and added, "Guess it wouldn't be good for that to get out. People don't want too much information about their neighbors—or candidates—you know."

Willa tapped him on the arm. "Well, maybe not good for you, but my readers would love to know if I actually practice what I write."

"Willa," he asked, "you would never write anything about us, would you?"

With a devilish smile, she stuck her tongue out at him and said, "Hey, a girl has to sell books, doesn't she?"

He grabbed her again as she turned to walk away and took her once more into his arms. This time he became passionate. "Now write that."

"Not on your life. There are boundaries, you know, even for twisted writers."

Walking away to brew her morning tea, she said, "What shall we do today?"

Charles really didn't want to tell her; they were doing so well.

"Charles, I asked you a question. Do you have to leave today? You just got here."

"Willa, I have to meet Tug and go to a few more meetings. I didn't know about them when I first made my plans, but he texted me just before

I got on Tuck's boat yesterday. We thought we were done, but apparently not. Buster set them up. I'm sorry, love."

Willa looked at the teakettle and just kept pouring the hot water. She stomped her feet. "I'm so disappointed."

"I know, but I have an idea. Let's get dressed, and, after we speak with Clyde, why don't you come with me? You could write your impressions while Tug takes notes. It would be so helpful."

Willa looked at him as if he were teasing.

"It would be fantastic, Willa. Come on. Say yes and come with us."

"That means you would come back home with me, right?"

"Is that the bargaining chip? If so, then I will, but only for a day. Then I really do have to get back."

"Okay, I'll agree to it. Now take a shower, and then we'll go face your adoring fans."

"You're going to love Buster."

Willa sat down at the table, smiling and wondering how anyone could love a man named Buster.

Chapter Fifty-Three

By the time Willa and Charles reached Somerville, the sun had made its appearance and was now doing its duty and shining brightly. However, they didn't see Tug's Jeep. "Hmm," remarked Charles. "Strange. Tug's always on time. I texted him just as we left the island."

"Well, you'd better call and find out."

Tug's cell rang only once before he picked up. "Hi, Charlie. I know you're waiting and I'm so sorry. I hate to say this, but I can't go today."

"What?" Charles didn't want to sound displeased, yet he needed to get to these meetings. "What's wrong?"

Willa immediately looked up at her husband. His voice told her he wasn't at all happy.

"Lindy's had an accident, and I can't go off and leave her. But don't worry, my friend. I will bring my vehicle over and you can take that."

Charles eyes widened. "I don't know how to drive that tank of yours, and I also don't know where we're going."

"Oh, okay, Charlie, I'll bring a map. You'll be fine. It's not a truck, after all—just a big SUV. You can do this. You have a big car over in D.C., don't you?"

"Not that big, and, besides, congressmen have drivers."

"Wow. Well, you'll do fine. But I can't leave Lindy for the day. I'll be right over."

Charles, dazed, stood there holding his phone.

Willa looked at him and asked, "What in heaven's name is going on? Is Lindy okay?"

"I don't know. Tug said she had an accident, so he can't go to our meetings, but he's lending me his vehicle."

"Okay. So I don't know what you're all upset about."

Charles looked at her with astonishment. He knew his next statement wasn't going to come out right. "Do you know how to read a map?"

"What? Of course I know how to read a map. I used to read them all the time when my parents and I took off for Maine every summer. Why would you say a thing like that?"

"Well, not everyone can these days. They use their GPS systems."

"Well, I'm not everyone, so don't sweat that. Just tell me where we are to find this Buster man and I'll get you there."

"This is turning into quite an adventure."

"You can say that again."

Just then, Tug roared into the marina parking lot.

"My God, Tug, aren't you afraid of being arrested?"

"Good morning to you, too, Charlie."

"Well, you know what I mean. You were flying."

Tug looked distracted. "Lindy fell through some planks out at the shanty, and I took her to the hospital for x-rays. I'm getting a ride over there, so don't worry about it."

"Hi, Tug," Willa said. "Should I call Aunt Rita, Miss Frances's sister? She could go over and see what's going on."

"She bakes cakes; what's she going to know?"

"These women know a lot, and I think Miss Frances told me her sister was a nurse before she started baking the island cakes."

"Yes, you're right. If you would, that would be great. Lindy's mother keeps calling, but all that is doing is upsetting her more. Lindy finally told her to come over instead of calling every two minutes."

"Well, you can understand her being upset, Tug."

"Yes, I guess I can. If that were my mother, she would already be here."

Willa laughed a little as Miss Rita answered her phone. Willa told her what was going on, and Rita was halfway out the door before they hung up.

"Situation under control. Miss Rita will be there in mere moments."

"Thanks, Willa. Now you two had better get going."

Charles still felt odd about taking Tug's vehicle, but reluctantly accepted the keys and said good-bye.

As they pulled away, Willa said, "Now, where are we headed?"

"Over to Easton to meet up with Buster Talbot."

Willa took the map Tug handed her and a magic marker and traced the course. "This is pretty easy. Up to Salisbury, hit Route 50, and then all the way on that, pretty much to Easton."

"I know it's easy, but I wanted you to get the lay of the land over here. If you use the navigation system, you never really know where you are. You get voice commands, but you could be in Alaska for all you know."

"Never thought of that, but you're right."

Charles smiled at her and said, "I know."

Willa swatted him with the map and grunted. "You aren't always right, you know."

"Really? When haven't I been?"

"I'm thinking, smart ass, but I'm sure you've made mistakes."

"I hope one of them won't be running against Buddy Dawes."

"It isn't. Think of something else. Oh, I have one. You hired Steve Allen."

"Bingo. You get lunch today. Prue's fault actually."

"I see. We are into blaming little girls, are we?"

"Please don't say that out loud, or I'll be accused of being sexist."

Willa broke out laughing. "You, a sexist? I think not. However, Dawes could easily fit that title, from the D.C. gossip columns I read."

Charles turned to her and said, "You read those things? Well, maybe in his case, it's true." He smiled.

"He's apparently quite the ladies' man. Bet his wife loves that."

"I can only imagine. But what did you expect from that man? Anyway, if you would like to hear a story, I have a good one from Tug about that old waterman."

"I'm not sure, but go ahead."

"He told me Dickie Short took him to something over around where we're going today called the National Outdoor Show. There they watched a rather bizarre ritual these folks have: skinning muskrats."

"What?!"

"They eat them in stews and sell the skins for extra income."

"I feel sick, Charlie. I can't imagine eating one, let alone skinning one."

"Well, don't you think they have to pluck their chickens? And what about cowhide?"

Willa slid down in her seat and mumbled, "I'm going to become a vegan."

"Guess you'll have to give up going to The Willard for their outstanding steaks then."

"I'll have to think on this a little, Charlie. Tug really witnessed this?"

"Yes, he did. And he said that, after he threw up, he went back in and watched the whole thing again, and then again. He said you get used to it."

"I don't think I could ever get used to that."

"Every culture has their peculiar ways and foods, Willa, and this is something the folks in the marsh love. It's a delicacy to them."

"Wow. Can we stop at the next McDonald's so I can get a drink?"

Charles looked over at her and chuckled. "Of course, dear."

"Why don't you tell me about this Buster person?"

"At first sight, I thought he was a maniac, but then we began to talk, and he is one hell of a man. Owns several farms that his brother and sons mostly work now, but he stays near them. They went to college and learned some 'fancy things,' as he calls them."

"What fancy things?"

"Farming is changing in many ways, Willa. They are experimenting with new fertilizer techniques to wean the system from using chicken manure. That's what they've used for years, but some claim its runoff has hurt the Bay. I believe it may have contributed a little to it, but there is so much other waste being dumped into the Bay, too—and some of it by other states sending it down the Susquehanna."

"This is certainly a complicated issue, isn't it?"

"Yes, it is, but nothing will be solved by growing massive amounts of marijuana. The farmers don't want to do that anyway. It's against their family values and it's just not what they do. They want to raise corn, soybeans, sorghum, beans, and a few other things that fire the engine of the chicken industry."

Willa turned to him in astonishment. "How did you learn this?"

"Buster. He's my expert."

"I am impressed. It's not just taking a tractor out and moving some dirt around and planting seeds, is it?"

Charles smiled. "No, not at all. I can't learn enough from Buster. The farms stretch all through here and over to the Western Shore, too. St. Mary's County was founded by farmers, and has some of the lushest farmland anywhere around, so I hear."

"What's happening over there? Are farmers there having problems with the government, too?"

"Yes. In fact, all the nation's basic industries are under siege right now, which is why we need some resolute leaders to stop a lot of the over-regulation that is killing farmers, watermen, timbermen, and just about anything else of that kind you can think of."

Charles could see Willa was taking all this in, and that her head was spinning. "More than you thought, huh? Well, I love these people, and now we live with them, and I will be damned if someone is going to take not only their past but also their future dreams, and crush them for their own profit."

Willa leaned over and put her hand on his arm. "You sound like Miss Frances. You also have what gave her the courage to fight for the island, the crabs, and her people."

"They are our neighbors now, Willa, and the fight goes on until we can stop those who would destroy it."

"Turn left at the next light."

Charlie squeezed her hand and said, "I know. Buster is meeting us right in town. You're going to love this man, Willa."

Not too sure, she answered, "We'll see."

For the next few hours, Buster took Willa and Charles to four different meetings in four different small towns. The greeting was the same in all the big metal buildings, filled with farmers who wanted to meet Charles Lee. They held up signs that said, "I AM VOTING FOR LEE, HOW ABOUT YOU?" It was simply overwhelming.

Willa always sat in the back of the room, taking notes, but also doing sketches of some of their faces—another one of her many talents. When they were ready to leave each meeting, she showed the sketches to the farmers she had drawn, then gave them the pictures and said, "It was our privilege to meet you."

Charles was amazed at her. She had so much creativity and, whether she knew it or not, made a pretty good politician herself. Imagine thinking of giving them something they would never forget. Yep, she was fabulous.

They were nearly exhausted by the time the fourth stop was over. Each had been the same: filled buildings . . . farmers wanting to reach out and touch her Charles . . . Willa sketching away . . . everyone talking to Charles and Buster, giving them more and more energy to move forward and not look back.

"Well, Charles," Buster said as they climbed into the vehicle and headed back to Easton, "you knocked them over. I have never seen farmers so animated and ready to help."

"I couldn't have done it without you, Buster. I can't thank you enough. I will carry this back to Washington and then build on it. I hope you'll be an official on my campaign committee."

Buster blushed. "Gee, Congressman, I don't know much about politicking. I know farming and that's about it. I can help you with that."

"That's enough, Buster. This whole campaign is going to hinge on farmers and watermen and the culture here and all your dreams for your families and the future."

Buster looked at him for a minute and then said, "Well, I guess I'm in then. But I don't want to go to that miserable city much iffen you and I can agree to that."

"Don't blame you a bit, Buster. And thanks. It means a lot to have a man like you standing beside me."

After they dropped Buster off, Charles was visibly relieved and much more relaxed driving back to Somerville. "It was a good day indeed. What did you think, Willa?"

"You're going to be a great, Charlie. Are you prepared for all this?"

Just as Charles was about to answer, his phone rang.

Tug started talking the minute Charlie picked up. "How did it go for you today? I mean, did you nail it with the people?"

"Ah, Tug. How is Lindy? Did she break anything?"

"Yes, she did. Broke her foot in several places, but they put a cast on it."

"Ouch!" Charles said. "That sounds painful."

"Yes, it is, but they have her pretty doped up right now."

"Stay calm, Tug. We are on our way right now; we aren't far out."

"Charlie, be careful and take your time. We're at home and won't be going anywhere else for a while."

"I will, Tug. Hold the fort down until we get back to your house." After he finished, he turned and looked at Willa and said, "Funny isn't it, how uncertain life is. One minute you're on top of the world and the next, it turns upside down."

Suddenly, he remembered their original plan. "Oh, Willa, please text Cap'n Tuck and tell him we're delayed and will let him know when we'll be going over to the island. We can't leave Tug and Lindy until we know they will be all right."

Chapter Fifty-Four

When Charlie and Willa reached Tug and Lindy's house, Tug was waiting outside with a beer in his hand. He smiled when they pulled up.

Charles said, "Boy, looks like you're handling the stress just fine, Tug."

Willa smiled and went inside the house to find Lindy on their big sofa, totally conked out from the drugs. She stirred a bit, then said, "Is that you, Willa? You shouldn't be here; you should be on your way back to the island."

"Charlie and I had to return your Jeep didn't we? Besides we couldn't leave without checking on you."

"Would you help me sit up?"

"Just go back to sleep, Lindy. I'll call you later."

"No, I want to tell you something. Now."

Willa pulled Lindy up a little and put more pillows behind her, then sat down on an ottoman and said, "Okay, tell me what's going on."

In a half-groggy voice, Lindy smiled and said, "I got some of my drawings accepted by a customer up in Salisbury, and she said she wanted me to do some more for other rooms."

"Lindy, this is great! All your schooling is beginning to pay off."

"Yes, it is, Willa, and, when Clyde is done with your house, he said he wants me to work with him with his other customers who want to build."

"Wow, a real businesswoman. Will you still work at Virgil's, too?"

Lindy laughed. "Maybe a little. I love those guys who come in there, and they all knew Dickie, so it's another way of staying close to him and the whole water community here."

"Yes, it is. I am so proud of you, Lindy. Now we just need to get you on your feet again."

"She is going to do no such thing, not for a while, at least."

Willa turned quickly to see Tug and Charlie walking into the living room.

"Well, I didn't mean tomorrow." Willa laughed. But isn't this great news for Lindy?"

Charles's brow furrowed. "What's great news?"

Proudly Tug said, "My wife is going to be more famous than her husband. Some of her house drawings were bought, and she is going into business with Clyde, designing and doing interiors for his clients."

Charlie looked at Lindy with a big grin. "You can come to Washington and do my office when I win. That would really set you up over there."

Willa frowned slightly at her husband and said, "Slow down there, man. Let's get you elected first."

Tug broke in to say, "From what Charlie just told me, he is on his way for sure. If he can get these farmers and other folks working for him and campaigning over here, he stands a damned good chance."

Willa cheered and then looked at Lindy, who had gone back to sleep again. "I think we should leave quietly now, Tug."

Charlie shook his friend's hand. "Thanks so much for the use of your Jeep. I like it and the way it handled so nicely on the road."

"Bet you wouldn't give up your big monster and its driver, though! Now, let me drive you two down to the marina. Lindy looks like she's out for the long haul now, so she won't even know I'm gone."

Charles responded, "What a day it's been. Ready to go, Willa? I think we both want to get back to the island."

"Thanks again, Tug," Willa said, then kissed him lightly on the cheek.

Chapter Fifty-Five

Charles had been back in D.C. for two months now, and life was hectic, but falling into place for a change. Willa stayed on the island and loved it. She missed Charles terribly, but this was where she needed to be. She couldn't stand the mess in D.C. under the best of circumstances, and now Charles was up to his ears in a campaign that was drawing to a close. The campaign was anything but nice, but were they ever? It was all so nasty, even if Charles did try to keep above the fray.

Willa and Lindy talked often, and, when Lindy finally was able to get over to the island, she just couldn't get over how beautiful the Lees' house had turned out. Willa wanted to have a big party there—hopefully to celebrate an election win.

With that election only a few weeks away, Charles wasn't sleeping much. Something was upsetting him.

Tug answered the phone groggily. "Morning, Charlie. You're up early, aren't you?"

"These days no one sleeps much."

"How's it going?"

"Okay, I think. I'm going out to two of our toughest counties today."

"Know them well. Their legislators were hard on Dickie and me, too. Anything I can do?"

"Yes, there is, actually. Oh, before I get going here, how are you doing with your new book? Can you spare any time?"

"Happy to say I finished that darned coffee-table book two days ago, so I am all yours. What's up?"

"I need you to plant some press in the *Baltimore Sun*. Do you think your friend Max can help us out again?"

"I sure do. I have needed to call him anyway. I haven't kept up much with him or my mother, for that matter. Mikey tells me she's missing all of us and wants to come back soon. She would be a big help to Lindy, who's still hobbling around some, so this is a good excuse. I don't even know if she and Max are a 'thing' anymore. Just too much going on."

"Whoa, man! Take it easy on yourself. Slow down. Sorry to hear Lindy is still gimping around."

"She gets on pretty good, but she's mostly still living downstairs. She just can't be going up and down those narrow wooden too many times a day. She is happy, though, to be back in her own bed. Makes me happy, too." Tug's grin could be heard through the phone.

As much as I hate to do this, I have to keep this call to mostly business. "My new assistant, Mark Daniels, will be sending you a fax shortly."

"How's he working out for you? Couldn't be half the disaster the last one was."

"You can say that again. Steve was such a disappointment. Funny that Mark worked for Buddy, too, but he couldn't stand being around the man. He told me Dawes was plenty pissed when he left him to come and work for me. And Mark also told me Buddy had a real blowout with Rennie, your old pal. Apparently the saying that rats run from a sinking ship is correct."

"Well, that's a real shocker. Maybe Rennie is rich enough and doesn't want the threat of going to jail at his age? Hope springs eternal. When should I expect to see copy?"

"Will the next five minutes be too soon?"

"Great. After I read what you send, I'll edit it and then talk to Max. I assume that's what you want me to do, right?"

"You know my every thought, Tug. Yes, that's what I would like if you can do it. By the way, I'm going home tonight for the weekend. Want to see you and Lindy on the way there."

"We'll leave the light on."

"I sure miss my Willa and can't wait to be home. It's been too long, even if we talk every night. And I'm very anxious to see the house. I haven't seen it totslly done. I've heard enough about it, but she's told me she's very lonely there without me."

"Got to keep the ladies happy, Charlie."

"You can say that again. Okay, let me tell Mark to get it over to you and thanks so much. Let me know what Max says."

"Go on now and good luck in those nasty little counties today."

Tug didn't waste any time dialing Max. He was excited to do this for Charles. Between having completed his new book on the waterfowl of the Chesapeake and helping Charlie try to become the new senator from Maryland, Tug felt quite pleased with his life.

Max finally answered. "Hey there, Tug. What's up?"

"I'm waiting on a fax to come in from Charlie, and then I want to shoot it up to you to look at after I go over it and edit anything that needs to be changed. And, if you meant what you said about helping some more, can you please get it into the paper as soon as possible?"

"I meant what I said and will help you and Charles any way I can."

"That's great." Tug paused awkwardly. He didn't know if he should ask about his mom.

Max heard the hesitation with Tug and knew what it was about. "Your mother is so excited to see you all again. She really loved the last trip, and Somerville, so I guess another trip south is in the offing fairly soon."

Max had come through again and read his mind. The man was uncanny, but he always had been. It's what made him such a good editor of such a prominent paper. "Well, I guess you answered that question."

"What question was that?"

"You know, you sly ole dog. About you and Mom. You two are still seeing one another, huh?"

"You and Mikey, so nosey. But, yes, we are still *seeing* one another. It's nice. Comfortable."

"I think that's great, Max. I just want her happy. You too, of course, Have you heard from Dad?"

"One time. He called to tell me I was a prick, and then said he was divorcing your mother."

Tug chuckled quietly. "And who's the prick?"

"Well, I guess I would have done the same thing in his place. Kay is a fabulous lady and deserves to be happy for once in her life. Ted was pretty rough on her."

"That's putting it mildly. Is she upset about a divorce?"

"I don't think so. She knew it was coming. She knew Ted would never stand for her being away so long. By the way, she's done wonders with the house on the Cape. Looks fabulous, but she said she could use some expert opinion. Maybe Lindy?"

"That would be great. I know Lindy would love to do it for her and she is really good at that sort of thing. Mom is a talented woman too, and she has always loved that house. She never really liked living in the city. The beach is her thing."

"And I'm finding it's mine, too. She has me taking long walks in the fresh air and I'm loving it. I can now understand completely why you love being where you are. But I don't think your father is ever going to understand why both his sons are down there."

"I don't care what my father thinks and neither does Mikey. He is like a pig in you-know-what what selling farm equipment and being around farms and farmers."

"And you a big-time author. How's the new one going?"

"Done and at the publishers. I can't believe some of the photos I was able to take. It's conducive to it down here. The sunsets are like paradise and the natural life is abundant . . . so what's not to love?"

"I'm so happy for you. Send that piece on to me and let me know the timetable for anything else. Will there be a lot of them coming?"

"I suspect so. The election is getting close."

"How's it looking?"

"Farmers, watermen, and business folks on the shore will all turn out for Charlie. They trust him and that crosses any party lines, so that's great. It's just a couple of troublesome counties, but miracles do still happen."

"Well, I keep reading about his accusations of Senator Dawes. It's pretty nasty, but, if he's right about all that, Dawes could well end up in jail."

"I think that's what Charlie's hoping for. Would make it a whole bunch easier. Seems he was taking a lot of money from a lot of people when he shouldn't have."

Max said, "These political types all get caught up in the money."

"Yes, it's all about the money, we know that. Such a shame we can't do business without all the corruption."

"Son, that's a conversation for another time and place. Not going to happen for a long time. Won't happen until a generation decides to stop it and make real changes—changes that are good for everyone, not just themselves."

"That should be another book. But I'm not sure I have enough life left to see that one to the finish line!"

"I will do what you need me to do, Tug, for the future Senator Lee."

"Thanks, Max, and tell Mom she'll get a call very soon."

"You better."

Chapter Fifty-Six

Charles made sure all the faxes were in order and then had Mark send them out to Tug. He knew Max would say yes. He was an old newsman and they loved a good election brawl.

Mark stopped by Charles's inner office before he left for the counties. "Have a good trip to Anne Arundel and Prince George's, Congressman. Is there anything else I should be looking out for?"

"Nope. That's all for now. And I won't be coming back after I visit in the counties. I have several meetings, and then my driver is going to take me over to the shore. I've arranged for a boat to get me back home."

"Just curious, Congressman. Do you ever mind going through so much to get out to the island?"

"Not at all. My heart is there and so is my wife. How's it going here with you, Mark?"

"Just great. I really like your style, Congressman. So different. I know the past couple of months have been tough for you, but it will be over soon. You're going to win, you know."

"I wish I was as positive as you are. Why do you think that?"

"Because you're the man who should be senator. And, from what I'm hearing through the grapevine, Buddy Dawes will soon be asked to appear before the Senate ethics committee. He's on his way out, even if kicking and screaming, because you have exposed his schemes. And everyone is happy about that. Taxpayers are sick and tired of all this rotten behavior in Congress."

Charles stood up and walked around to sit on the front of his desk. He let out a long sigh and then said, "I know it's been tough on Buddy, but he did this to himself. He's no spring chicken and there are moments I almost feel sorry for him. A whole lifetime devoted to his state and people, and to end up like this? Such a disgrace. Doesn't anyone around here understand how to do business like regular people? Do they have to do it underhandedly? I just don't get it. Sometimes I wonder how corrupt it was when the country started. From our forefathers' writings, we can tell they were on the moral high ground. I think they would die if they came back today."

Mark, while fairly young, already had a lot of experience in D.C. "They were men with a vision. There's very little of that today. You have a vision, Congressman, and now you have to take that to the Senate."

"Thanks, Mark. And, yes, I need to remember the good vision. And then, when I'm done, go back home."

"That is a noble goal, Congressman. So, you see, you *have* to win this election. Then you can accomplish the things you know are good for your state and country."

"You are way ahead of yourself in wisdom, Mark. I'm a lucky man to have you. Yes, I want to set things right for the people I have come to love. They deserve no less."

Handing Charles his raincoat, Mark smiled and said, "Then you know what you have to do. Go knock 'em dead."

"Thanks, Mark. I'll be back on Monday."

Charles was a bit nervous about this particular meeting. Buster had met him and given him the scoop on these people. They weren't farmers for the most part, and they weren't sure about this young man, Charles Lee. This county's polls looked pretty bad for Charles, but he could never give up without a fight.

The congressman took the podium after his introduction by a local politician—who obviously wasn't too gung ho about Charles. However, he had to overlook that, and, after his opening remarks, he pressed on. Oddly, he realized he wasn't getting that sinking feeling he usually did when his ship was going down.

Hands began to go up with questions. Good ones. Charles had all the answers, which made him feel awfully terrific. One after the other, and the time flew. Soon it was time to leave. He thanked them all and, surprisingly, got a rousing round of applause. One down.

At the next stop, more farmers showed up and even Buster was stunned. He had thought this one would be tougher than the last, but, after the response Charles had just received, he was believing in miracles.

"Well, we'll see how this one goes, eh, Congressman?"

"They don't look like they're going to tar and feather me."

Buster laughed softly and said, "We'll see about that. This county is known to be in opposition to a whole bunch of your thoughts on things."

Charles once again took to the podium after being introduced and then decided to change it up a bit. He stepped down to be with the people, not above them. He needed to engage with these prospective voters.

The questions started again, but this time they were negative and tough. However, at every turn, he was able to answer them adequately. Then came the big one.

"Congressman, why are you so against growing marijuana on the shore and elsewhere in the state? Look at the money it would bring in."

"Well, I've been waiting for this question. First, I don't think our farmers should be forced to give up growing other crops that are needed. Second, Senator Dawes wants no limits or restrictions on growing cannabis. That's not good. I don't believe our state's families want that, and I don't think Maryland should become known as the home of marijuana. No matter *how* much tax can be collected. If any of it is to be grown, it must be regulated and regulated carefully. No one person or persons should make deals that others don't know about to make huge gains for themselves on the backs of young people and their health and welfare."

"Do you think that's your business?"

"Yes, I think responsible government must do its best to protect our people if it's in their power to do so, while allowing freedom to raise the crops our farmers choose. It's not just the cannabis situation that's concerning, you know, but the endangerment of chicken breeding here as well. Some want to stop that permanently. But, from what I have seen and heard, chicken farmers are working hard to find new fertilizer alternatives and new modes of farming, different from what their parents and grandparents had. Young farmers today have an extraordinary education in agriculture, and that gives them new ideas. Right now, they are already experimenting on amazing, wondrous things to provide produce and to feed the world in many different ways in the future."

Dead silence. Then someone in the back began to clap until the whole room erupted in applause.

A different man stood. "Your answers are good, Congressman, but do you think you can do it? Do you think we can have our cake and eat it, too?"

Charles breathed deeply and then walked down the aisle to where the man stood. He stuck out his hand, and the man didn't know what else to do but shake hands with him. A sign of goodwill was there for all to see. A bold move, and the right one.

"I do believe I can do it. All it takes is leadership, and, as you know, I won a battle before over fishing regulations and a way of life, and I think I can do it again for farmers. Farmers, like watermen, and other people all over the state, just need to have someone they can trust. Someone willing to get down with them and fight in the trenches."

At this point Charles had the attention of every single person in the overflowing room. Buster would say later this was the transformative moment of the election.

Charles went on, "If you can't work alongside your elected officials to try to get the job done, then what good are we anyway? If we can't all reach agreement, or at least try to help one another, then we are lost. Freedom is lost and, with it, our dreams. No, we are all good people who want fairness and a right to speak on anything, even if we know there will be dissension with many. That is what we should expect from all who lead us. We are your servants and we should never forget that or take advantage of you in any way. Maryland has led the way in agriculture for years, and, if we don't pay attention, it will slip away from us forever, never to return. Then our dreams of passing our land and our boats and our businesses down to the next generation will be over forever." He paused and then said forcefully, "I say this cannot be. I say the dream must live on for all who treasure and hold dear our next generations. I will not let you down, I will keep my promises, and I *will* keep our dreams safe."

Buster Talbot's tough exterior melted as tears filled his eyes. The crowd cheered and came to their feet for a long ovation. Charles blushed, but then shook the hand of every man and woman who had come to the meeting.

When it was finally over, Buster stopped at Charles's car and hugged the young congressman.

"I'm proud to be on your side, Congressman. You were amazing in there. They love you now. They will never forget what you said, and they will turn out in droves to vote for you."

Charles was drained. He hugged Buster back and said, "I need to go home to the island. I need to decompress. I only wish Willa had been here with me. I don't know where all that came from, but I meant every word. It was as if my entire soul was pouring itself out."

Charles's driver got into the car as the two campaigners said one last good-bye.

Then Buster handed him something. A tape recorder.

"Why, I'll be, Buster Talbot."

"Don't lose it. You can send that speech to your fancy friends and get all those words in the paper. You will win in a landslide. But, for now, you can play it for that special gal you love. Have a safe trip."

Charles didn't know what to say. Anything he would have said would just have embarrassed Buster, so he took the recorder and its tape and got into the car. He loved the big, old farmer. As a matter of fact, he loved them all.

Chapter Fifty-Seven

Crossing the Bay Bridge back to the Eastern Shore, Charles finally had time to reflect on the meetings. They had gone better than he ever could have imagined. As the car drove up and up onto the bridge, he looked out at the Bay and felt something he hadn't before. This, he realized, was where his heart sang. He had never truly understood that when Willa had said it to him, but now he did. This place was his anchor, even more than Virginia had been. And he had never thought anywhere could take Virginia's place in his heart.

He had so much to tell Willa. He wanted to play the tape Buster made for him. What a man Buster was, and how wonderful that life gave us people who really taught us—if we just listened. He was excited to see his house and all that Clyde had accomplished. It was done now, and he knew Willa would be decorating it, the thing she loved so much to do, almost as much as writing.

"A good day today was it, Congressman?"

"Yes, it was, Jack. By the way, I keep meaning to tell you what a good driver you are. Hard to find in Washington these days, and I appreciate it. Anyway, yes, it was a very good day. It's been a tough campaign, but now I just want to relax, see my wife, see what's been done to my house, and leave everything else up to the people."

"Well, sit back and unwind. We'll be there before you know it. The only hang-up is the Salisbury traffic at this time of the day."

"I know what you mean. It's gotten dreadful and will just get worse with all the development on the shore. I don't know how the land will ever survive."

"It's awful, isn't it, Congressman? I swear the banks and the developers are in cahoots."

As Jack talked on about the overdevelopment situation, Charles was reminded of Tug's adventures with that old waterman and how they had fought to limit what was going on. How the soil's upheaval and subsequent erosion was causing great changes to the Bay's runoff. He wished he'd met Dickie Short. He must have been one incredible character whom everyone knew—and most loved.

"I know this may be rude because you can't join me, but I think I'll help myself to a stiff drink from the car bar." Charles saw Jack looking at him in the rearview mirror, a big grin on his face.

Jack stopped going on about the housing boom and said, "Buster told me how grand you were today. You must feel so good those meetings are over."

"Yes I am. I have to say all of a sudden, I seemed to break loose and give them my true thoughts on what politicians should be and how we should be working for them and not ourselves. But the question is, will they vote and will they vote for me?"

"Well, I don't know much about these things, but I know you'll do what's needed. And I certainly expect you to become a senator. Come to think of it, I've never been a driver for a senator before."

"We will see how all this plays out. I can't believe how fast the time is going and how close we are to the election . . . 'and miles to go before I sleep.'"

Jack arrived at the marina in Somerville right on time, even with the traffic through Salisbury. Cap'n Tuck wasn't there yet, but Charles could see his boat off in the distance chugging along to get him. While he had a few minutes, he called Tug.

"Hey, Charlie! What's going on? How did it go today?"

"If I must say so myself, I won them over. Or, at least, they looked like I did. Even got a standing O."

"Well, look at you, Charlie Lee. I did get the press items up to Max, and he said he was glad to do what he could to help you. He's amazed at the number of friends he still has at the paper and how many will help us."

"Good to hear that, Tug. How is Lindy doing?"

"She's doing okay. You know her—tough and determined. Are you waiting to go over?"

"Yeah. I see Tuck's boat way out, but this gives me time to talk to you and make a few other calls."

"Like one to Willa? She misses you a lot. Lindy has gone over to the island several times recently, and she said your house is not to be believed, it's so beautiful. By the way, I really want to thank you, Charlie: now *she* wants to do something—like maybe moving over to Tuckerton."

Charles laughed. "Well, it would be great to have you both out there."

"No way. We might eventually build over here, but we won't give up this old relic yet. She has her mind set, though, on a new house over a bit from us. One that will be right on the water and look out to the sland. Do you need anything else right now or are you set for a while? We're getting close nad if you need something, let me know soon."

"I know there will be stuff in the next few weeks, so I'll keep you in the loop. Thanks so much for what you have already done."

"My pleasure to serve you—*Senator.*"

"Good grief, Tug. Get off the phone, man, before you make a complete fool of yourself."

Charles was still laughing when his phone rang again. He didn't look at the caller ID, assuming Tug was simply calling him back. He was wrong.

"Please hold for Senator Dawes." In mere moments, the bane of his existence was on the line.

In his most condescending voice, the man on the other end said, "Why, I hear you were outstanding at the meeting in Prince George's County today. Now, you know I own that county and its votes, so don't be thinking you can do anything there. You'll have to rely on your ragtag group on that blasted shore to help you take me out, and you know that isn't going to happen."

"And hello to you too, Buddy. I have to say, your communications tree is pretty fast. Yes, the meeting went well. Much better than I expected. But do you really think you can keep all your illegal dealings hidden from the people?"

"You know something, son? You have no proof of anything. My name isn't on anything and a whole lot of folks owe me. So, how do you think you're going to overcome that?"

"By telling the truth, Buddy. You'd be amazed how many folks rally to the truth. You've been in the slime pit so long, you don't know what is going on, and you don't even understand anything about your own people. They read newspapers, you know."

"Maybe *you* don't know what's going on, Charles. I thought you were smart, but you still don't know how this game is played. You thought you could do to me what you did to Rennie, but, when this is over, you won't be able to go home to either Virginia or that island."

"You know, Buddy, I would love to stay on the phone and talk awhile longer about your overinflated ego, but my ride is here and I'm off to *that island*." Charles hung up on the great Senator Buddy Dawes.

Cap'n Tuck was throwing the ropes out to moor the boat so Charles could get on. "Hey, Congressman, I'm so sorry I'm late, but one of the men come down to the dock and asked me to haul this here generator for him. It needs fixin', and, if you can wait a few minutes more, Harry Benson is comin' to get 'er."

"No problem, Tuck." Charles turned to his driver and said, "Thanks for the lift, Jack, but it's time for you to head out now."

"If you say so, Congressman. How are you getting back?"

"I'll call when I need you."

"When you get it all figured out, I'll be waiting."

"Thanks, Jack. Safe travels back."

The truth was, Jack had a small second house on the shore near the Bay Bridge. An old family home he'd inherited, it was most convenient. Jack wasn't married, so, instead of going back to his tiny apartment in Washington, he would just bunk there for the weekend and wait for Charles to make his plans. He was thrilled with this trip because fishing was his favorite thing to do and the rockfish were running real good. He couldn't wait to get on the water.

Charles arrived at Tuckerton a little later than he had planned, but Willa was still waiting at the dock for him. Every time he saw her, she seemed more beautiful. His heart never ceased to tell him how he felt about her.

"Hey, there, beautiful. Waiting for the perfect man?"

Willa tilted her head back and her long hair blew in the wind. Laughing, she answered, "Yes, I am. Have you seen him?"

Charles always enjoyed the easiness of their relationship, the little jokes she played on him and how he always fell for the bait, even if he knew what she was up to. She was the yin to his yang. The best part was, she felt the same way.

"Charles, did you have a good drive over?"

"Jack's the best. I didn't even mind crossing that darned bridge."

"You'll get over it in time. Gets better with age."

"I hope so. When I have to drive it myself, I freeze up, so I was glad I had Jack this time."

"Spoiled baby. Come on and let me show you all of Clyde's handiwork."

"I can't wait. I'm all yours."

She was about to pat him on his rear, but then heard a man's voice calling. It was Jimmy, Frances's husband, on his way back home from a day of fishing. "Hey, Charles. How ye comin'? Gonna stay awhile?"

Charles waved back and shouted, "For a day or two, but then I have to get back. How are things out on the Bay?"

"The crabs are still running real good, but they'll be going soon with the colder weather comin' on. Hi, Miss Willa. You two be sure to come around before Charles goes back."

"We sure will, Jimmy. Say hi to Miss Frances. Is she okay?"

"Sure is. She's up to her ears in church work and running the island."

Charles laughed. He loved them both. And he and Willa would make a call on them sooner rather than later. Jimmy waved as he walked away.

"He's the best, isn't he, Charles?"

"Yes, he is. They all are. They're good people and good neighbors. Nice to come back home to. Not like the assholes in D.C. who think they run the world. What arrogance."

Willa kissed him gently on the cheek and giggled. "Forget about that now. You're home."

The words were hardly out of her mouth when Charles turned on the path and saw his house at the end of the lane. "Willa? What have you done? Is that our home?"

Beaming, she said, "Yes, it is. And just wait 'til you get inside."

"If the inside is like the outside, I have died and gone to heaven."

"Don't do that! But I love it, too. Clyde did amazing things with her."

"He followed your plans, though, didn't he?"

"Oh, yes, he was wonderful about that, and what a craftsman. But he suggested little things that I would never have thought of."

Willa went up the porch stairs and opened the front door but wouldn't let Charles in.

He didn't understand. "Hey, girl! Let me inside. I want to see it."

"Not before you lift me up and carry me across our threshold."

Charles turned and looked around to see if anyone was watching. He blushed when he saw a few older women staring. "Willa, this is silly. Come on."

"No, you don't, Charles Lee. It's not silly; it's good luck. Now pick me up."

He could see he wasn't going to win this argument so he dropped his coat on the porch floor, leaned down, and picked her up. She kissed him as she threw her arms around his neck. Then he slowly walked into the house with his wife in his arms. He kissed her back, and, as she slid from his arms, he held on to her. When they finally did break loose, they could hear a few hoots and hollers from the island folks. Charles turned beet red, but it didn't bother Willa at all.

"I will be the talk of this Island, Willa Lee, as he walked slowly around the house, stunned at how different it was, and how beautiful. He ran his hands along the moldings and the walls. The kitchen was enormous and now ran from front to back so they could see out the large panel of windows along one wall. Off the kitchen was a family room lined with bookshelves, and windows with views into the woods and marsh.

"Go, look at our bedroom."

Charles walked down a short hallway and into their bedroom—truly now a master bedroom. Clyde had removed the entire back wall of the house out some twenty feet for the family room and their bedroom. The master bath included a shower with glass doors leading into a very private walled garden. Water jets promised a luxurious experience both indoors and out.

Charles couldn't believe it. "This is a fairyland, Willa, but I thought you were going to put the bedroom upstairs."

"I decided not to and you'll see that I redid one of the smaller rooms up there to be my office. It looks out to the Bay."

"I think you were right to do that, but where do you think these things up? I mean the shower and garden are out of this world."

"Well, I imagine these places in my head when I write, so why not build them?"

Charles turned and left the bathroom and went back into their bedroom. He walked over to a huge bed and sank into a deep, down mattress covered with comfy linens. His eyes took it all in, including built-in closets and shelves. "Have you missed anything?"

Willa smiled. "I don't think so. It's neat, isn't it? And yet, from the outside, it isn't too daunting or changed too much. I don't want anyone to feel like this is a palace or anything. Just a beautiful home."

"You have succeeded there. How will I ever go back?"

"Maybe you won't have to so much when this election is over."

"If I win, there will be even more work to be done, so I can't promise that."

Willa stood up and slipped out of her dress. She ran her hands along her well-built, pleasing body, and Charles, seeing her like this, knew they were in for a long homecoming. He walked over and closed the door. The world outside was not welcome.

They both sank into the bed and shut the world out behind them. It was peaceful and quiet as they kissed, and, for the next few hours, they would reacquaint themselves, making love until the dawn. Charles was home, and, for as long as he was there, she wouldn't let go.

Chapter Fifty-Eight

Charles left paradise way too soon, and, as the last weeks flew by, the campaign got more and more savage. No one even had time for rubber chicken events anymore. It was a miracle any of them got to their campaign stops at all. The race was tightening, much to Charles's astonishment. How could people even think of voting for such a corrupt human being? The answers weren't all clear, but Charles found himself in the clash of his life with a titan of a politician.

One of his hurdles was that he was a new resident of Maryland, and, as always happens in such cases, had been labeled a carpetbagger. However, Charles had proven himself to a great many of the people. Only the "come heres" and transplants saw him as a meddler from elsewhere.

Willa decided to go back with him, so she could be seen with her husband, an important thing in campaigns. He thought she would make a tremendous asset, and he was right. The voters loved her, and he knew, deep down, if he won, Willa would have helped earn the extra mile that would get him across that finish line.

Charles also knew it was time to bring the hammer down on Buddy Dawes. Get the Justice Department involved to the extent they could. The senator was taking money for influence by those who wanted to see the state's farms be led down the path to becoming the tools of legalized marijuana, and not for medicinal purposes alone. Dawes was also in bed with those who wanted to take the chicken out of the state's economic equation so developers could come in and buy land for pennies on the dollar. At the same time, farmers who wanted to keep their way of farming— their way of life—and pass it down to their children were going to find it hard.

Buddy had a lot of corrupt friends, and they helped him spread money as if from a water tap left running in a drought. They all drank it up and didn't give one whit about farmers or watermen or anything except their bank accounts.

Now Charles was telling people that it was time to stop the politics as usual nonsense all the taxpayers had put up with for far too long.

He and Tug had both called in favors and articles about D.C. corruption would soon be appearing in the press. Buddy could keep on playing his game of making Charles Lee look like a kid, wet behind the ears, but that tactic wasn't going to work anymore when the papers came out. Buddy would come unhinged when he saw what was going into print, and, for all of it, Charles had proof.

Yes, this Sunday it would begin to rain fire down on Buddy and his pals, and Charles prayed the Hail Mary pass was enough. The election was now only ten days away. For the sake of the state and all good people, the time had come to end the run of the present senator from Maryland.

Tug was busier than ever with Charles's run for the Senate and really hated the time away from home, but it was imperative as the last days of the campaign were upon all of them.

Tug's mother was so excited about the campaign and her son's involvement in it. She had also told him she and Max were considering "living together," but not until the divorce was final. He and Lindy laughed about this because they knew that living together for Kay and Max would mean marriage. And Tug was warming to that idea. In the meantime, he and Max were working together regularly during these final days of the campaign.

Meanwhile, Lindy was busy doing more and more renderings for Clyde and had all but put away the sadness of months ago. Sometimes she did get impatient with Tug, though, because his evenings seem to be spent entirely on the phone with Charlie or Max.

Tug defended himself. "Lindy, come on. You know this is important. This isn't just a Senate campaign; we're fighting for an entire way of life here."

Lindy felt bad when he said it like that for he was right, of course. Still. "Okay, Tug. I'll go with you on this, but I swear if isn't over soon, I will . . . well, I just will!"

Tug started laughing, but the more he laughed, the madder she got. "Don't push me, Tug Alston."

"Or what? You'll go over to the island and spend a couple days in Willa's gorgeous home? Tough, isn't it?"

"Well, you just wait. After this election is over, I'm talking to Clyde about doing something for us this winter."

"Now hold on, Lin. What are you thinking?"

"You know what I am thinking. We discussed it, but guess your head was someplace else. I'm thinking of going forward with building that house over on the water looking out on the Bay. The lot I was has been for sale for a while and I don't want to lose it."

"Well, we can certainly think about it."

"No. No, Tug. Talking about it leads to doing nothing. I mean it."

"Well, I guess you're right. We are landlubbers, after all, plus living out on the island would just be too isolated. But what about this house? Why don't we just renovate this one that Dickie loved so much? I know it needs a lot, but we could."

"Well, maybe we can fix it up a little, but I really want to build a new one."

Tug thought a moment, then said, "You're right. We probably do need to make a decision. But after this election. Can it wait until then?"

"Oh, Tug, you mean it, don't you? I love you so much."

"Slow down, Lindy. I know what happens when women get all excited about something." He grinned. "And another thing: I will help you pay for this. You aren't going to spend all your money. I would like you to use a good chuck of that to get your own design company started."

Lindy ran to him, wrapped her arms around him, and kissed him. "That would be so neat, Tug. My own company. I could never have dared dream of anything like that. I love you so much."

"I love you, too, very much, Lindy Short Alston. You remember that."

As the last campaign days passed, the weather got colder and Election Day got closer. Max had pressed a lot of people for a lot of favors that had been outstanding for a long time. He smiled, thinking of those who had thought they were off the hook when he retired. *Think again, friends.*

He had done a lot for many people. Career promotions for some . . . big raises and a new city for others . . . plenty owed him a lot. Now the payback for all this generosity was a slew of front-page pieces every day until the election, starting yesterday. Now *that* was cashing in all your marbles; it doesn't get better than that. Buddy Dawes would get pummeled and that would keep on until the battle was won. Everyone would know what a crook Buddy Dawes was.

His paper had always prided itself on calling it as they saw it and staying focused—what real journalism can do if it wants to. Well, they had no choice this time. When the leaks began to the flow into the paper from an unnamed source, and they were corroborated, the paper had to print the bombshells. What Dawes was involved in would completely change the way the state did business. Maryland's backroom powers really didn't want to see such a paradigm shift and, especially, all at once. It wasn't going to play well at this time. Maybe never.

Charles was now out campaigning all the time. He wasn't going to waste any more time talking with his opponent. It was full throttle now, with no time for anything that wasn't very important. Buster was now a regular on his campaign stump, and the two men, one older, one much younger, had become very close. Tug was also never far away, but he and Max were doing their damage behind the scenes.

Willa found herself so involved in her writing and her entertaining for Chalres's campaign folks that she actually was enjoying being in D.C. She forgot how many small, lovely bistros there were and she saw old friends again. And she even got along better with the dreadful Kay, her publisher, who never failed to rile her up to the point of boiling, but she knew kay was good to do that. Kept her on track for a new novel and it helped Kay Winthrop make a whole lot more money.

The campaign was getting horrendous with the slanders and slurs coming from the Dawes campaign, Willa was glad to be by her husband's side.

Then, all of a sudden, something changed. Out of nowhere, like a stealth bomber, Buddy Dawes was handed a subpoena to appear before the Senate ethics committee. Now Charles—and everyone else—*knew* Buddy's days were numbered.

Charles was in his office, speaking with Max on the phone, trying to find out just who might have gotten wind of something. Max Pierson had a nose like a bloodhound, and, if anyone could find out that kind of information, he'd be the guy.

"I'll do my best, Charles, but my advice is to steer clear. The source really doesn't matter; all that matters is that it happened. Probably someone at Justice. They will never be made to look incompetent. When it comes to catching a big fish, you never know who your enemy is. There's a lot of money for that kind of information, and we all know the Senate is not going to take the hit for one of their own corrupt assholes. Unless—and I repeat—unless it could cast a wide net and catch many of them. Then the one who is the most expendable will fry before they all catch the infectious disease. Chances are this has come from a top dog in the Senate who wants him out with all this swirling around. They would rather lose the seat than get the rest of themselves into this kind of mess. There's always another day."

"But, Max—

"I mean it, Charles. You had better stay far away from anything to do with any of this, you hear me? No potshots; no nothing. Just remain the young congressman who wants to save the shore, the farmers, and the Bay. They'll love you. Let his own snakes bite him and clean out the nest."

Charles was taken back by the genuine concern and feelings this man had for him. Max had given him wise and safe advice. He wasn't used to that around the capital. That just didn't exist.

"Thank you, Max. I can see why Tug admires you so much."

"Go on now, Congressman. Go out and win that election, so I can get down there to congratulate you in person."

"I wouldn't miss it, Max. I really do appreciate all you've done for me. We never said anything that wasn't true. Dawes is going to pay for his sins. I just want to help the people."

"I know you do. So go do it."

Chapter Fifty-Nine

The excitement was building by the minute. Charles and Willa were at their Georgetown home. If it looks like they call it for Lee, he and Willa will head down to their headquarters and thank their workers and all the invited guests, who were, no doubt, enjoying the refreshments that were being offered up while they wait.

In Somerville, where the whole town was watching and praying, Tug and Lindy were hanging on every number coming over the TV. On the island, nearly everyone was waiting at the fire hall, watching the big-screen television—typically used for Saturday night movies—but, tonight, they were viewing what they hoped would be the election to the Senate of their good friend, Charles Lee.

Those island residents who were most like family to Charles and Willa—Miss Frances, Jimmy, Nellie, and Denny—were gathered at Miss Millie and Richard's home, also watching with great anticipation. And eating cake.

Everyone wanted Charles to win. He seemed to have ignited and united the entire shore, Eastern and Western, and the numbers were beginning to look solid, even in the questionable counties. But they all knew it wasn't over 'til it was over. Then the networks called the election for Charles!

Nellie and Denny went outside and began yelling the news to everyone not already at the church hall. Tonight, there would be a big party there in honor of their own Senator Charles and Willa Lee.

Miss Millie, naturally, was bringing some of her cakes, and, by the time the family got there, coffee was brewing and the smell was as heavenly as if the angels themselves had brewed it for Charles's celebration. Nellie dialed Willa's number and was surprised when the new senator's wife answered; she had been sure she would have to leave a message.

"Willa? Oh, Willa, what a night! Charles must be delirious. And you, girlfriend, a senator's wife. Listen! Listen, Willa." Nellie held her phone up to the crowd, which cheered wildly.

When Nellie came back on the phone, she said, "We're all at the church celebrating." However, she wasn't talking to Willa anymore, but to Charles. She was dumb struck at first and then said, "Congratulations . . . Senator."

The crowd heard her and they whooped it up even more.

Charles started laughing, then said, "So this is what everyone does for fun on a cold November night, huh? Guess you heard that they called it for me."

Miss Frances grabbed her daughter's phone. "First time we've had a senator from our island. How ye comin', Charles? We sure are happy for ye. We all know how busy ye are, so we'll let ye go. But we're all so proud of ye. Come home soon. Be safe."

Charles had tears in his eyes. "You know, Miss Frances, I don't think any of this would have been possible if I had not met you."

"Funny how that works, isn't it, Charles? Enjoy this moment. It doesn't last for long and then you'll have to really work. Come home soon."

"I will. I promise." He hung up and smiled across the room at Willa. She didn't even have to ask with whom he'd been talking. She knew how much he adored that island woman.

Charles couldn't get back for another week, but Willa had headed over to the island home without him as soon as all their thank yous were said. She was exhausted by the election and her nerves were shot. But she also had something else she was working on—a huge celebration party in their new home, planned for Charles's arrival.

Miss Millie's kitchen was churning out cakes for the event, and Willa had sent a lot of invitations to some pretty big folks flying over for the event. Willa chuckled a little to herself, wondering what these watermen and their families would think of all this fuss.

Vernie and Tom had come out a bit early to be part of this shindig and Vernie was in her element working with the "Cake Lady." They talked while they baked. In the meantime, Tom helped Willa at home, doing a ton of things for the party.

Max, Kay, and Mikey met at Tug's house before the event. They were all ecstatic and looking forward to going over by boat with many other folks. They were preparing to leave for the island when Kay asked Tug and Mikey if she could speak to them privately

"What's going on, Mom?" Tug asked. "You seem so serious, and this is anything but a serious day ahead."

"What's going on is this: your father and I are officially divorced. He didn't waste any time getting this done. I guess when you have the prominent friends he does, it doesn't take much to get anything you want."

Mikey noticed an odd look on his mother's face. *Was she sad, or was it more a look of regret for what could have been?* "Is this a good thing, Mom? You seem upset or something."

"What I am, dear boys, is relieved. I'm relieved this chapter of my life is over now."

Tug smiled. "Seems like a long chapter. Lasted a lot of years, Mom. Are you sure you're going to be all right?"

Kay wrinkled her nose in a funny way as she had used to do when they were little and she'd had to smooth something over after their father had upset them. All three of them started laughing and then they couldn't stop. It was their way of getting it all out. Tug looked at his kid brother, all grown-up now. "It's all okay, Mom. Mikey and I have known for a long time you haven't been happy. You are now."

Kay looked at the two most precious people in her life and said, "Go on. Ask. Ask if Max and I are going to marry. I know you both want to. Well, I'll beat you to it. He's asked and I've said yes, but not right away. I want to wait a few months and let the ink dry on the divorce papers. It's not that I would ever change my mind. As I said, that chapter is over. Max is a new one. A good and wonderful—"

Mikey interrupted his mother. "I don't get it. Why wait? Go ahead and start living your lives together. Tug and I have known for a long time that Uncle Max liked you more than you ever knew." It was so like Mikey to be the one in a hurry to experience a new adventure.

Kay smiled at them both. "That may be so, but Max and I are also thinking of making another great change, one we hope you two boys will approve of."

Tug and Mikey looked at one another and then Tug hesitantly asked, "What's that, Mom?"

"Well, if you must know everything, we are thinking of moving down here. You boys are here, Lindy is here, one day there will be another child or two, and maybe even a new daughter-in-law," she stated looking directly at Mikey.

Tug's smile showed his joy. "Are you kidding? We would love it! This is the best news you could give us, isn't it, Mikey?"

"Yes, it is. I might even get you on a tractor or combine before this is over."

Tug burst out laughing. "Maybe even get Max to go out crabbing on one of the workboats. I'd like to see that."

Kay chuckled. "I'm sure he would adore it. He loves you boys. Now, let's get on that boat and go over to the island. I can't wait to see Willa and Charles again."

Tug cleared his throat, stood up especially straight, and stated loudly and clearly, "You mean Senator and Mrs. Lee."

When Max came back in, he had no idea why they were all laughing so hard. Neither did Lindy, who walked down the stairs and said, "We better get going or they will wonder what happened to us. I'm sure all the guests are waiting down at the marina."

They left the house, all smiling and looking forward to the day. Kay was beaming as Max took her hand and squeezed it. He knew she had told the boys, but she didn't need to say anything to him. They were so in sync with one another, they didn't have to say a word. They just understood.

Tug took his mother's hand and said, "Now we have the perfect ending for this old house. I know Lindy will agree with this, too. Won't you and Max live here, at least for a while, until you can figure everything out?"

Kay and Max smiled at each other. Then she said, "We would love to, and we will even make a lot of the improvements you've been wanting. You two should go ahead and build that house you want out on the Bay shore." She laughed. "Oh, we are all going to have a wonderful time together."

On the way over to the island, Tug asked Max what he thought would happen to the former senator. Max's answer was blunt and quick: the minute the election was over, Buddy had become toast.

"He's in a heap of trouble. It's really a good thing he didn't win the election because he would have to resign anyway. He'll probably go to jail for a while, but I'm guessing to one of those country club jails for old politicians who stay too long in Washington and get themselves into too much trouble."

Tug looked out on the water. Lindy walked up next to him. "Hard to believe we have such a wonderful family. We're so lucky. I just wish . . ."

Tug wrapped his arms around her and whispered, "I know who you're thinking of, Lindy. Dickie's here, you know. He's smiling, sweetie. I don't think anyone ever truly leaves. Their energy and their love stay within us always."

Lindy sniffled and tucked herself in close to Tug. "I miss him so much, and I know you do, too. There will never be another one like him."

Tug couldn't help but laugh. "You can say that again."

As the boat pulled up to the dock, everyone stepped off onto the island, always so welcoming, like a mother with her children. Willa and Charles stood waving to them all. The day was cold but gorgeous. They all walked down to the little Tuckerton Methodist church to give thanks for Charles's new post in life.

The minister didn't take long. Everyone was there, including Buster Talbot—more dressed up than anyone had ever before seen him—a few big shots from Washington and some celebrity writing friends of Willa's. Prue had come, of course, to celebrate Charles's victory. Next year, she hoped they'd be celebrating her own.

Now it was time to party and the entire island population, other invited guests, and family walked over to Willa and Charles's house. What a shindig this was going to be.

Food of all kinds had been prepared. Crab cakes, oysters in all forms, salads, Jell-O molds, and so much else . . . well, it was hard to see it all. Everyone had been given a glass of bubbly ginger ale. His own glass held high, Jimmy made the toast, Miss Frances by his side, proud as she could be:

> *To Charles Lee, our dear friend and new senator:*
> *We salute you and thank you from the bottom of our hearts.*
> *You will do us proud.*

The party went on for hours before everyone finally left by boats they brought over, private sea planes, or went back to their homes there on the island. Tom and Vernie headed up the stairs to sleep. They would clean it all up the next day. Tug and Lindy and other family and friends were scattered all over the island to stay for the night. It was that kind of place: everyone was family and nothing was too good for family.

Charles and Willa quietly poured a glass of champagne and slipped outside to sit on their new, expanded porch. The wicker sofas felt soft and so comfortable after all the merry making. It was cold, but they pulled some down comforters around them. Willa snuggled up with her Charles.

"It was a good party, wasn't it?"

"Yes, it was. You sure know how to have a good time, Willa Carpenter Lee. These past weeks and months all seem like a dream, don't they?"

"One with a good ending, thankfully."

"You know, Willa, I think we can do this. I think our lives are just about perfect. I know I will have to go back and forth to Washington, but the island is where our hearts sing. It gives us perspective. I think about all the people I've met in this wonderful state of ours. The whole world should be like these people . . . farmers out on their land, working it, loving it . . . watermen out on the Bay, crabbing and bringing in oysters. Life has a rhythm here. It moves with the seasons, and the people are good, and they trusted me enough with what they hold so dear."

Willa smiled, looking up at her husband. "Yes, they did, Charles. You must never forget that. You know, this place reminds me of my childhood vacation times up in Maine. Those days were filled with the beauty of nature and the nights were safe. Until I met you, they were my most cherished memories."

Charles held her close and gently kissed her. As they sat quietly looking out on the water and listening to the sounds of the island settling in for the night, Charles was overwhelmed, but yet humbled by it all and what people had asked of him. He would take up their fight and preserve this land of magic and tradition.

"You know, Willa, the people have asked much, and, in return, I must give much. I must always do what's right and just. I won't forget how incredible this magical and wonderful place is and what it means to so many. We are safe here. Our lives continue going forward, and now, for at least a while longer, the dream will live on."

Acknowledgments

We all know a book starts with a kernel of an idea and then grows from there. Many people who crossed my path added to my knowledge of what farming is and where it's going. I learned of the hardships farmers are facing in light of so many changes to the law. Just as watermen of the Chesapeake have experienced their culture changing—including a great threat that it may not survive too much longer—farmers also are facing these same challenges to their culture and lives. We will always need farmers and fishermen, and it will be their grit that determines how their future unfolds.

My thanks to so many, including

- RF Productions, headed by Rich Fox, for the wonderful photo of me, your humble author. He continues to make me look good.

- my editor, Kathy Grow, for her incredible patience and her wisdom about where to cut and how to keep the integrity of the words I write.

- Miss Millie, fashioned after a wonderful woman who lives on an island in the Chesapeake, whose real name is Mary Ada Marshall. She truly is the cake baker extraordinaire. Visit her on Facebook to see her bake an authentic Smith Island Cake. Go to Facebook and type in Mary Ada Marshall, and you will see her "how-to" video. You'll really enjoy getting to know her.

- the Island Woman, Janice Marshall. Yes, she is related to Mary Ada Marshall, and her story continues to inspire. She is my joy and my trusted friend. Thank you so much for being who you are.

○ to each and every farmer who spent time with me, teaching me so much. This country was founded on fishing and farming, and today great changes are coming to both industries. The farmers are learning new ways to bring us our food and keep our land bountiful and safe for the environment. Always remember: without farmers, we don't eat. Thank you for all you do.

○ And, lastly, to a special farmer named Sonny, who might well have been my model for Buster. He has taught me more about the fishing and farming industries than I thought anyone possibly could. He patiently emphasized the most important lesson: respect for the waters and the land. From an immigrant farming family, he learned the special lessons of how to farm and how to get along with others. He is a man for all seasons and very appreciated by all who know him.

○ Sonny Baroniak (photographer)

As always, my thanks to you, my readers. You are my strength and make all the time spent learning so rewarding for me. Please visit me at my website and leave your comments. Thank you!
www.annagill.com

***For anyone wanting a recipe for Smith Island Cake, the state cake of Maryland, they can go to www.chesapeakebayfoundation.com and click onto "How to make a Smith Island Cake." There you will see Mary Ada Marshall from Smith Island making a cake for all to enjoy. Or you can contact the author at:
www.annagill.com